Praise for EMILIA

Christa Polkinhorn's new novel, EMILIA, is hard to put down and impossible to forget. This nuanced book about a tight-knit family in conflict unfolds in interweaving chapters, narrated by four characters: the painter Karla Bocelli, her stonemason-husband Andreas O'Reilly, their son Tonio, and their daughter Laura. It's a storytelling technique that lends texture and variety, and in scene after scene Polkinhorn offers a complex portrait of midlife marriage and parenting, adult temptation, childhood yearning, and young love. Yet while the author portrays these universal subjects with warmth, sensitivity, and an eye for the telling detail, she never lets the plot become sentimental or predictable. The action is set in picturesque small towns in Switzerland, Italy, and Peru with a charming side trip to Paris, allowing the author to create a feast for the senses, and though EMILIA is the third volume in Polkinhorn's Family Portrait trilogy, the book stands firmly on its own. EMILIA offers characters to root for and cherish, and I heartily recommend this luminous and ultimately hopeful novel."

– Susan Dormady Eisenberg, author of THE VOICE I JUST HEARD, www.susandormadyeisenberg.net.

"In the final book of her Family Portrait trilogy, author Christa Polkinhorn once again placed me in the Swiss countryside and with her wonderful descriptions quickly carried me back to locations from Europe to Peru. Karla and Andreas had become successful while raising their two children. Laura was training to work with stone like her father while her brother Tonio, blessed with his mother's talent for drawing and painting was studying fashion design. This was not his father's first choice for him but he was doing well in school. The family was well settled and then came the surprise. Karla found herself pregnant and in shock with emotions racing through her from joy to the unbelievable realization she would be forty-six when the baby came. Enter Emilia. Would the dainty little girl drive a wedge between her parents or become the glue that would bind their fracturing relationship? Christa has successfully tied her three books together to a final, satisfying conclusion. I believe those who have read AN UNCOMMON FAMILY and LOVE OF A STONEMASON will agree with me. EMILIA also works well as an enjoyable stand-alone novel."

– Elizabeth Egerton Wilder, author of THE SPRUCE GUM BOX and GRANITE HEARTS, www.virtual-zen.com/liz logic/.

EMILIA

Family Portrait, Book Three

ALSO BY CHRISTA POLKINHORN

NOVELS

An Uncommon Family
Family Portrait, Book One

Love of a Stonemason
Family Portrait, Book Two

The Italian Sister
The Wine Lover's Daughter, Book One

Finding Angelo
The Wine Lover's Daughter, Book Two

Fire in the Vineyard
The Wine Lover's Daughter, Book Three

POETRY

Path of Fire

EMILIA

Family Portrait, Book Three

Christa Polkinhorn

Bookworm Press

Bookworm Press
1223 Wilshire Blvd., #1054
Santa Monica, CA 90403

Cover design and author photo: Diane Busch
Cover image: iStock, eclipse_images

ISBN: 978-0-9600135-4-8

Printed in the United States of America

For Rico, Claudia, and Eveline

PART ONE: STORMY WEATHER

Chapter 1: Karla

The storm during the night had been loud and fierce, with thunder and lightning followed by a cloud burst. The rain had cleared the air and brought some relief from the muggy August heat in the south of Switzerland. Now, it was early morning and the sun was just about to rise. The mountains in the east stood dark against the sky, but the ridge was bathed in a halo of golden-white light.

Karla sat at the kitchen table, her hands around a cup of weak hot tea. She took an occasional sip while staring absentmindedly out the window. A few small branches from the chestnut tree lay scattered on the ground and a carpet of purple and pink blossoms of the azalea bushes covered the patio in front of their cottage.

Aside from that, there wasn't any visible damage from the storm. But the beauty of nature was the last thing on Karla's mind at the moment.

Please, God, this can't be true.

It was the second day in a row she had woken up sick to her stomach. The day before, she had attributed it to the rather rich dinner she and Andreas had enjoyed at their favorite restaurant in Locarno or to the summer flu going around. In the course of the day, the nauseous feeling had disappeared. Now, however, she felt sick again. This wasn't the flu or food poisoning.

Counting the days to her last cycle, she realized with dismay that she hadn't had a period since returning from Venice six weeks before, where she and Andreas had celebrated their twentieth wedding anniversary. There was no doubt, she was overdue. She was approaching menopause and her cycles were becoming irregular. That was natural. However, skipping a period combined with feeling sick to her stomach in the morning didn't bode well.

I can't be pregnant.

Karla stepped outside and glanced at the stone cottage next door, a second *rustico*, a former stable made of natural stones with a granite roof. She and her husband had bought it years before and converted it into two bedrooms for Laura and Tonio when the children got older and the main cottage wasn't large enough anymore. She didn't see any damage from the storm there either.

It was still pleasantly cool. Karla inhaled deeply, trying to calm her stomach, then held her breath. She wrinkled her nose at the overpowering scent of the honeysuckle nearby. It was another ominous sign. During her former pregnancies, she had had an acute sense of smell and she hadn't been able to tolerate any kind of heavy perfume.

But I'm not pregnant. I don't want to be pregnant.

Surely she was too old for another child. She was almost forty-five. If she was pregnant, she would become a mother again at the age of forty-six. Laura was nineteen and Tonio almost seventeen.

Having another baby would mean nine months of pregnancy and another sixteen years or so of raising a child. And the risk of complications and possible health problems for the child was much greater at her age. Karla sighed and shook her head. And the time it would take away from her painting.

Both Karla and Andreas had successful careers as artists, Karla as painter and Andreas as sculptor. They took part in exhibitions and were able to sell their work. To supplement their income, Andreas had his stonemason business and Karla worked at a friend's art gallery a few days a week.

It just can't be.

Karla went back inside and sat down. Her head ached and she felt sick again. She forced herself to breathe deeply and evenly and took little sips of tea.

Emilia

The sound of running water came from the bathroom. A little while later, her tall, muscular husband stepped into the kitchen, yawning and brushing his disheveled dark hair out of his face. Andreas poured water into the espresso machine and pressed the button. Seeing Karla sitting at the table with her cup of tea, he gave her a probing look. "Why are you up so early? You're feeling sick again?"

Karla wanted to deny it at first, but then nodded. "Andreas, I'm afraid."

"Why?" He placed a cup underneath the spout of the espresso maker and watched as the fragrant dark liquid filled the cup, then sat across from her. "What's the matter with you?" He touched her cheek; his hand felt warm against her face.

Karla's eyes misted over. "I think I might be pregnant." She leaned her head into her hands, then looked up again. She watched Andreas's face, the face she knew so well—his verdigris-green eyes, the slightly aquiline nose, his unshaven cheeks and square chin—as different emotions flashed across it: surprise, doubt, joy. Yes, joy.

Karla had known from the moment she suspected being pregnant that Andreas would love to have another child. She also knew he wouldn't understand why she herself was less than enthusiastic about it. For him it was a great adventure. He loved children, always had. He was the perfect father and had done more than his share of changing diapers and feeding and burping their babies.

"Are you sure?" Andreas put his hand on hers.

"No, of course not, but it just feels like it. This is like the morning sickness I've had before and I haven't had a period since Venice, so I'm off. I was probably off in Venice without knowing it, and you know we weren't very careful. Oh God, Andreas, I don't want to be pregnant."

Andreas laughed. He got up and sat next to her. "You're getting ahead of yourself. You don't even know if you're pregnant. Don't you have a doctor's appointment in a couple of weeks, anyway?"

"Yes, we were supposed to talk about a new kind of birth control. Oh God, how ironic. Andreas, if I am pregnant, we'd have to start all over again. We'll be in our sixties or seventies by the time the child is grown."

"Well, what's so bad about that? Lots of people have children in their forties."

"Yes, but . . ." Karla didn't know an answer to that. She put her head on her arms and moaned. "I don't want to have any more kids."

"Think how happy you were with Laura and Tonio." Andreas hugged her.

"That was twenty years ago. Of course I was happy. I love my children, but now . . . we're almost ready for grand-children. Besides, I want to focus on my painting more again and . . . oh, I don't know. I'm so confused."

"Honey, you're blowing this out of proportion. Besides, well, to be honest, I'd rather be a father once more than a grandfather. That sounds so old. But why don't you call your doctor and tell him you need to come in right away. Then, we at least know for sure, instead of guessing."

Karla nodded. "I'll get a pregnancy test at the pharmacy first." She didn't want to call the doctor yet, still hoping it was false alarm. She got up and pressed the button on their coffee machine.

"Perhaps you shouldn't drink coffee, just in case you—"

"Andreas, stop right now." Karla turned around and glared at him. "I'm going to have coffee. Don't start, please."

"Okay, okay." Andreas raised his arms in defeat and beamed.

Andreas's cheerfulness upset Karla even more. It was just unfair that she might have to carry the major burden of an unwanted pregnancy and her husband seemed so damn happy about it.

"What if the baby is born with Down syndrome?" She hated herself for trying to make him feel bad. She set the coffee cup on the table with too much force, almost spilling its content. She sat down and put her head on her arms.

"Please, calm down." Andreas gently brushed through her hair. "Come on, look at me." Karla raised her head and wiped the tears from her cheek. Andreas took her face between his hands and kissed her. "You're not alone. This is—or would be—*our* baby and I would do whatever I can to help. Besides, we're talking about a baby that we don't even know exists."

Karla took a sip of coffee and grimaced. "Yuck, this tastes awful. What's wrong with it? Oh God, I know I'm pregnant. If coffee doesn't taste good . . ."

The doctor confirmed what Karla by then knew was true. She was pregnant. "I hope congratulations are in order," her gynecologist said with a wide smile.

"Not exactly, but . . ." Karla sighed.

Andreas tried not to show too much exuberance, knowing Karla's ambivalent feelings. Karla was torn between joy and despair. They hadn't told the children yet. Andreas suggested they wait until they were home. Laura was at a sculpting workshop and Tonio was on vacation with a friend of his.

Chapter 2: Laura

Laura unpacked her clothes in her room at one of the two houses the Scuola di Scultura di Peccia owned. Through the window of the two-story building, she had a view of the chestnut and pine woods surrounding the small town. Peccia, situated in a tributary valley at the very end of the Maggia Valley in the canton Ticino, was home to a well-known sculpture school. The extensive marble quarries nearby provided the raw material for the beginning as well as the experienced artist.

The three-week-long sculpture workshop Laura was enrolled in was a present from her parents for her successful graduation from her apprenticeship as a stonemason. Laura had inherited Andreas's love of stone and sculptures, and taking a class at this school had been a dream of hers ever since she knew that her father had studied there for some time as a young man.

Laura glanced at her watch. She had a few hours until the reception for the new students started, time enough to look around the village. Next to the school, a creek led through the woods down to the river Torrente. As she crossed the bridge, she saw the sculpture of a human head in the middle of the creek. It was part of the famous sculpture path. Every year sculptures from different artists were placed at various spots throughout the village—on squares, in the narrow streets, and in the surrounding fields. Laura followed the path and marveled how well the works of art fit into the village and the landscape.

When she returned to the school, she passed by a small garden area. A young man stood next to an empty freshly dug-up flower bed. He began to walk along the garden patch, taking big steps as if he was measuring it. Every once in a while, he stopped and took notes or made a sketch on a small pad. Laura watched him for a while. When he felt her eyes on him, he looked up and smiled at her. He was a tall good-looking guy, with an athletic figure and broad shoulders, probably in his early to mid-twenties. His curly brown hair was held back by a yellow bandana, and he was dressed in black work pants and an army-fatigue undershirt.

Laura asked him if he knew his way around the school. "I just arrived and I'm looking for the picnic area. There's going to be a barbecue tonight for the new students."

"Yes, it's just behind this house." He pointed at one of the longish wooden buildings. "You can't miss it, you'll see the smoke once they begin. Are you one of the workshop participants?"

Laura nodded. "Yeah, I'm taking a marble-sculpting workshop."

"Hmm. You may be working with my uncle. He is one of the teachers."

"Do you also study here?" Laura asked.

"No, I work here. I'm a gardener and I do some landscaping." He pointed at the small field he had been examining. "They want a stone garden with a mixture of plants, flowers, perhaps a small pond, and a few of the sculptures the students make."

"Great," Laura said. "That would look beautiful here."

"Yeah, my uncle got me the job. I normally work at a garden shop, but I do some freelance landscaping on the side." The young man smiled at her. "But what do you do? Aside from taking a workshop, I mean."

"I just finished an apprenticeship as a stonemason. I love sculpting. I want to learn to work with marble."

"Well, you're at the right place here." He wiped a few pearls of sweat from his forehead. "It's a good school. Anyway, I might see you at the barbecue."

"See you later, then." Laura went on to check out the rest of the school and then walked back to the hotel.

When she opened the door to her room, a tall young woman with short blond hair and blue eyes was unpacking her suitcase. Inge was going to be Laura's roommate. She was from Denmark and had signed up for a clay workshop. After getting acquainted, they went outside, looking for the picnic area.

"It smells good." Laura inhaled the scent of smoke and barbecued meat as they walked toward the smoke rising from behind one of the buildings.

On a grassy spot next to a group of wooden studios, students, teachers, and the director of the school had gathered around to get acquainted and enjoy a meal of chicken, salads, and all kinds of appetizers.

The young gardener Laura had met earlier was standing next to an older man, most likely his uncle. When the young man saw them, he came over, holding a plate heaped with food. "It's really good. Have you tried the sangria yet? Can I get you ladies a cup?"

"Yes, please," Laura said. While she and Inge grabbed a plate and helped themselves to some chicken and salad, he filled two cups with a mixture of red wine and fruit. "Sorry, I didn't even introduce myself. I'm Stefano."

Inge saw a friend of hers and went to join her. Laura and Stefano sat at one of the wooden tables. There were twenty to thirty people of all ages and, it seemed, of several nationalities who had come to take classes. After they finished eating, Stefano wanted Laura to meet his uncle.

They made their way through the throng of people lined up at the barbecue. Stefano's uncle was a short, skinny man about the age of Laura's father, with curly black hair and a dark beard streaked with grey. Stefano introduced her. "Uncle Enrico, Laura might be in your class."

Stefano's uncle examined her with his lively dark eyes. "What's your last name, Laura?"

"O'Reilly."

"Laura O'Reilly. Yes, you're in my class. In fact, I wondered about your name when I saw it on the class roster. Are you related to an Andreas O'Reilly by any chance?"

Laura looked at him, surprised. "He's my father."

"*Mamma mia!*" Enrico laughed. "What a small world. Your father and I were in the same class right here. It must have been about twenty-five years ago."

"You know, Papa told me that he knew one of the teachers here. It must be you, then."

"Well, let's sit down somewhere. I'll be darned, I never dreamed I'd get O'Reilly's daughter as a student." Enrico gave a broad smile. "How is he? What's he doing? I read about him in an art magazine a couple of years ago, something about an exhibition in Germany."

"Yes, my father participated in a few sculpture exhibitions in Europe."

"We'll have to get together one of these days. Unfortunately, I've lost touch with a lot of my friends, since I lived abroad for many years."

"I'm sure he'll be excited to find out that I met an old friend of his," Laura said.

"Well, I look forward to seeing him again." Enrico finished his glass of beer and got up. "Unfortunately, I have to leave you guys. I still have some preparations to make for the class. I'll see you tomorrow, Laura." He shook hands with her and patted his nephew on the shoulder.

"What a coincidence." Laura shook her head. "I happened to walk by you this morning, we happened to talk, and we find out that your uncle and my father are friends."

Stefano gave a wide smile. "Perhaps it's destiny." He raised his glass and toasted her.

The following morning Laura and Inge got ready for their first class. The two girls had a quick breakfast and went their separate ways. When Laura passed the small garden area, Stefano was already at work, digging up the ground. He had taken off his shirt, exposing a suntanned taut body. Laura watched him for a while. He stood up straight when he noticed her and smiled.

"Off to your class?"

"Yes. You're already working hard."

Stefano leaned on his shovel. "It gets too hot later on. I'm already sweating." He ripped off his bandana, took a sip of his water bottle, and splashed some water on his face.

They chatted for a while. Laura looked at the sky, where dark clouds began to tower in the west. "We may have a thunderstorm."

"Yeah, that's why I want to get as much as possible done before it starts to rain. By the way, have you ever been to the Botta church in Mogno?"

"A long time ago with my parents once," Laura said.

Stefano shook his head. "Believe it or not, I've never seen it. It's shameful. Mario Botta, the architect, is one of the few people from the small canton of Ticino who is world-famous. I read he designed the Museum of Modern Art in San Francisco. Do you want to go with me? Perhaps after class tomorrow?"

"Yes, why not?"

"Great. We could have dinner at the grotto here, down by the river. I heard they serve the best polenta. My treat."

"Thanks, that would be nice." Laura was surprised at the sudden invitation. She hadn't thought of him as a possible date. But then, why not? He seemed nice enough. "I better hurry or I'll be late for my first class. I don't want to make a bad impression on your uncle, particularly since he knows my father. I better do well."

"Oh, don't worry. My uncle is easygoing. You won't have any problems. Anyway, good luck with your class."

The sculpture class turned out to be quite a challenge for Laura. Enrico may have been easygoing in private, but as an instructor he was serious and tough. He didn't cut Laura any slack because of their personal association.

Each of the students had a piece of marble to work on. After a short introduction on the nature of the stone and a film about a workshop in Carrara, Italy, which showed an elderly sculptor design, carve, and finish a marble sculpture, Enrico had them start on their individual projects. He asked them to begin with a small sculpture. They were to make a drawing, then go on to a scale model in clay, and from there to carving the actual stone.

The first day they spent mainly on drawing and sculpting the model. To Laura, that seemed an easy enough task. On the second day the work on the actual marble began. Enrico came by and gave some advice, but he mostly let the students work on their own.

Laura didn't feel comfortable with her block of marble anymore. She had worked mainly with harder stones such as granite, for which she had needed power tools and the help of her father. Now, working on the softer material, which for most students was easier, proved to be more difficult for her. She hit the chisels with too much force and broke off pieces she didn't intend to remove. After half an hour, her stone looked nothing like her model.

"What's this supposed to be?" Enrico squinted his eyes and looked at her work with a scowl.

"I'm sorry, I don't know what's the matter with me. For some reason, the stone and I don't get along." Laura was close to tears.

"Don't worry." Enrico gave her a gentle pat on the back. "At least you learned what not to do. You're murdering the marble. Be a little more gentle. This is painstaking work. You can't just hammer it to death. Forget about the model for right now." He took the clay sculpture away from her. "Look at what's left of the stone and let it guide you." He handed her the chisel. "Try again."

After a while, Laura did get the hang of it. The stone in front of her was longish and reminded her of a fish. She left most of the rock the way it was but focused on where she imagined the fins to be and began to carve a fine pattern of fish scales, which turned out pretty good.

"Okay, you're getting there." Enrico smiled encouragingly. "That's the wonderful thing about marble. It lends itself to detail work."

"I'm sorry I'm so dense today," Laura said. "I'm used to working with rougher stones and tools."

"That's why you're here to learn. And by the way, you're not the only one who wasn't quite with it today." Enrico raised his voice so that the other students could hear him. "Fortunately, nature provides enough raw material to allow for a lot of mishaps. If all of you did well right at the beginning, I soon wouldn't have a job anymore. So I'm always relieved to realize that I still have something to teach you." He called everybody together and went over each student's work, pointing out things done well and things he didn't like. "Tomorrow, we'll go over it again and I bet you'll feel more comfortable and you'll do much better."

After class, Laura went to her apartment to get ready for the evening with Stefano. She hadn't brought any dressy clothes with her, since she hadn't expected an invitation. After sorting through her stuff, she picked a pair of new jeans and a green-and-yellow patterned blouse, which accentuated her green eyes. She brushed her chin-length dark hair, put on some lipstick, and checked herself in the mirror. It would have to do; it was a casual date, after all. She grabbed her purse and left. At the entrance of the school area, she sat on the low wall, waiting for Stefano.

It was the first time in months she was going out with a man. After a devastating breakup with a guy who had dumped her for another girl, she had lost all courage to go on dates.

As a child Laura had been a real tomboy, self-confident to the point of cockiness. During puberty, however, she had become shy and insecure around boys. Like many young teenage girls, she had been unhappy with her looks. Although all of her adult friends felt that Laura was a very attractive girl who had inherited her father's sparkling green eyes, she was the opposite of the ideal teenage female beauty of the time. Laura was tall and strong, with a somewhat square body shape at a time when girls starved themselves to become thin. She had unruly wavy hair when the smooth, straight look was in.

Laura smiled as she remembered those painful days. She had become more self-confident and happy with herself. However, it didn't take much to threaten her still-fragile self-esteem, and being dumped for another girl brought up all her old insecurities.

"Hi there, how is your class coming along?" The dark voice startled Laura. She turned around. Stefano had made an effort to dress up a little. He was wearing clean jeans and a short-sleeve shirt that could've used some ironing but, on the positive side, showed his tanned muscular arms.

Laura shook her head. "Miserable. I basically butchered the beautiful stone. Fortunately, I wasn't the only one. I find marble difficult to work with." She gave Stefano a punishing look. "And by the way, your uncle isn't as easygoing as you made me believe. I was sweating buckets and he just looked at me, scowled, and shook his head."

Stefano laughed out loud. "I know. He's a very serious teacher. I stretched the truth a little. I didn't want you to get discouraged. Anyway, I'll make it up to you. Are you ready for a little outing, a church visit and dinner? You could pray there for a better day tomorrow." Stefano winked at her.

"Sounds good," Laura said.

"My car is parked over there." Stefano pointed his keys at a shiny metallic-blue Honda and deactivated the alarm.

"You own a car?" Laura had only seen his old pickup truck he used for work.

"I wish. No, it's my uncle's car. He lets me use it once in a while. I haven't been able to save enough money for my own wheels. Too many other more pressing needs."

"I understand. I just received my driver's license a few months ago. My parents let me use their car once in a while as well, but my father is a firm believer in public transportation. 'Take the bus or the train and do something to preserve the environment,'" Laura said, imitating Andreas's throaty voice.

After a ten-minute drive along a narrow mountain road, they arrived in Mogno, a small village of stone cottages surrounded by mountains.

"There it is," Laura said and pointed at a modern, round structure in the middle of a meadow. It was the new church San Giovanni Batista, designed by Mario Botta.

Stefano parked the car and they walked the short road up the hill. At the entrance to the village, a stone plaque described the history of the church. The old seventeenth-century building and part of the village had been destroyed by an avalanche in 1986 and the Ticinese architect was commissioned to build a new church.

"Amazing," Stefano whispered as they admired this gem of architectural ingenuity. The church was round, with a glass roof that let the sunrays enter the building in an alternating pattern of light and shadows. One side of the roof was higher than the other, making the church look like a cylinder with a slanted top. The walls were a checkerboard of white marble and black granite bricks. Inside, the most striking feature was the large arches of alternating dark and pale stones behind the altar.

"How this man managed to fit a modern building into a traditional mountain village is beyond me. And it doesn't even clash with the environment. Only a great artist can do that." Laura shaded her eyes as she admired the church.

They took a brief stroll through the sleepy village and then drove back to Peccia for dinner. The restaurant by the name of

Emilia

Pozzasc, a former grain mill which was transformed into a grotto, was situated along the river. Grottos were small rustic inns, usually made of granite and often built into a rock. They only opened for service from May to November and served a limited but excellent choice of specialties from the area, such as polenta and stew, salami, goat cheese, and the traditional Merlot del Ticino wine.

Laura and Stefano sat outside under a canopy of tree branches. It was still early and they were almost the only guests. Laura looked dreamily toward the woods. The soothing sound of the river flooded her with a sense of well-being. "It's lovely here."

Stefano nodded and smiled at her. His eyes had the soft brown color of chestnut kernels. She lowered her gaze, not wanting to stare at him. The breeze carried the smell of roasted meat, making her mouth water. "I'm hungry."

"So am I," Stefano said.

For the following half hour, life was simple: tender pieces of stew with a touch of garlic, polenta topped with parmesan cheese, all washed down with red wine. After dinner, they sipped espresso with a shot of grappa, a liquor made of grape pomace.

The sun had sunk behind the trees, sending shots of light through the leaves and branches, which bounced off the clear blue-green surface of the river. It was still light and would be until after nine o'clock.

"Let's go for a walk. I need to digest the food and wine," Stefano suggested after paying the bill.

"Good idea." Laura thanked him for dinner and Stefano lightly touched her arm. She felt the calluses on his fingers. *A laborer's hands.*

They walked along the river. The breeze rising from the water brushed through the tall grass and made a light raspy sound. After about ten minutes, they came to a bench at the side of the path. They sat down and watched the river flow by.

"Water can be so peaceful, and the next thing you know, it rages out of control." Laura turned to face Stefano, who was gazing at the river.

"Yeah, you're right," he said in an absentminded tone. Then he shook his head. "Sorry, I was just thinking of something I have to do tomorrow. I have to order the flowers for the garden patch."

"When did you decide to become a gardener?" Laura asked.

Stefano glanced at her quickly, then continued to look down at the water. "It was my mother," he said in a soft voice after a pause. "She had a green thumb and she got me hooked on plants and flowers." His voice assumed its normal upbeat tone, but Laura detected something forced in his gaiety. "She loved nature." He gave Laura another quick glance. "She died of cancer when I was ten."

"I'm sorry," Laura said.

"It's all right." Stefano swatted at something in front of his face, as if chasing away an insect. "She was amazing. Her garden was the talk of the village. She had this ability to grow anything she put her mind to. It wasn't one of those neatly organized gardens—you know, the ones with cleanly divided flower beds. Her garden was carefully arranged, but in such a way that it looked natural. There were all kinds of plants next to beautiful stones. You could find every conceivable color of flowers in her garden. She particularly liked irises, roses, nasturtiums, and poppies. There was something growing all year round—well, except in winter, of course. Even in winter, though, there were bushes of evergreen." Stefano stopped and gave Laura an embarrassed smile. "I get carried away talking about it."

"It sounds wonderful," Laura said. "So you inherited her talent."

"Well, I inherited her enthusiasm for gardens. I don't know about talent."

"Come on, don't be so modest."

"Anyway," he continued, "as a little boy, I helped her weed and plant. And since I wasn't much good at anything else, I decided to make the one thing I really cared about into a profession. Somehow, gardening for me is like a . . . how shall I put it . . . a way of communicating with my mother. When I garden, I feel connected to her. I guess it's kind of a way to keep in touch. Something like that."

"I understand." Laura watched him as he continued to look down at the water. He was good-looking in an unconventional way. His nose was slightly crooked. He had fleshy lips and a round chin. His brown hair curled just below the ears.

He glanced at her and Laura was struck again by the warm color of his eyes. "I hope I'm not boring you with my stories."

"No, not at all. But what do you mean by 'I wasn't good at anything else'?"

"Oh, well, I wasn't exactly a model student," Stefano continued. "I had a lot of trouble in school and I got into fights with other kids. This was after my mother died. It was a long and painful death and it almost wiped out my father. He couldn't get over the loss and he kind of withdrew from life, and from me as well. Exactly at a time I needed him the most.

"So I dealt with my grief on my own and I didn't do a good job of it. I was angry at her, at everybody else, at the whole world. I was doing poorly in school, I began to steal and do all kinds of stupid things. I'm sure I just tried to get someone's attention. Finally, my teachers and the authorities intervened and confronted my father. They told him I was on the way to becoming a full-blown juvenile delinquent and I would end up in jail, and what was he going do about it?

"I guess that knocked my father out of his lethargy. First, he beat the shit out of me—not a very sophisticated way to raise a child. But somehow it was almost a relief compared to his total neglect of me. Eventually, things began to improve. My father encouraged me to continue my mother's gardening. So our garden at home became a kind of memorial to my mother."

"How is your father today?"

"He's doing well. He got married again. At first, it was hard on me. I felt somehow that he betrayed my mother. But I got used to it and my stepmother is a very nice person. So it's okay. . . . Well, enough of that. We can't spend the whole evening talking about me. Tell me something about yourself." Stefano put his hand briefly on Laura's shoulder.

The sun had disappeared behind the trees and the evening was moving into dusk. With the heat of the day gone, the breeze rising from the river felt refreshing.

"Well, compared to yours, my childhood seems pretty uneventful. I guess my brother and I have been very lucky with our parents and life in general. But when I was little, I began to resent my younger brother. My father and I were very close, and when Tonio appeared on the scene, I became jealous. One day, I threatened him with a hammer. Fortunately, my father was nearby and prevented me from committing a murder. It was the only time he ever hit me or any of us children. He had been physically abused by his own father and said he never wanted to lay hands on his children. Anyway, that day he lost his temper and whacked me one on the butt. Then he felt guilty for weeks." Laura smiled.

"But talking about problems with authorities, I did get caught shoplifting one day when I was a teenager. That was pretty dramatic."

"Shoplifting? I guess we're two of a kind. I stole a bunch of stuff as a kid," Stefano said. "You don't strike me as juvenile-delinquent material, though."

"Well, this was the low point of my teenage years," Laura said. "I was hopelessly in love with a boy at school who showed no interest in me. I wasn't one of the 'hot girls.' I wanted to impress him. It was a bet. I claimed I would be able to take something out of the store without being caught. Of course, I didn't want to steal it. I would've brought it right back."

"So what happened?" Stefano asked.

"I saw this jacket, I tried it on, put my own jacket over it, checked if anybody was watching, then walked out the door." Laura chuckled. "I forgot the alarm. The jacket had one of those chips, and when I walked outside, there was this horrible sound. The next thing I knew, this fat, mean-looking security guard grabbed me."

"Oh no." Stefano laughed.

"Yeah, it was pretty dramatic. Fortunately, the manager of the store knew my family and he finally believed my story about the bet. My father, however, was in shock. That was the worst part of the whole thing. I couldn't stand it when my father was angry with me. And he was furious.

"I was grounded for the rest of the school year, including summer vacation. At first, it felt like prison. But there were advantages: no more pressure to look good, no more worries about boyfriends. During vacation, my parents did all kinds of fun things with us. My mother took me shopping, getting me some neat clothes. She also took me to her hair stylist, who gave me a cool new cut and added highlights. So for the first time in years I liked what I saw when I looked at myself in the mirror." Laura laughed. "Some of the guys even asked me out."

Laura stopped talking. She glanced at Stefano. "Come to think of it, those weeks in prison camp were some of the best times of my teenage years. Strange, isn't it? God, I'm sorry, I'm babbling on and on."

"That's an excellent story," Stefano said. "Your parents were great. They used punishment as a way to bolster your self-esteem. Very smart. But I really don't understand why you were so uptight about your looks. You're a very attractive girl."

Laura's face felt warm. She knew she was blushing. "Thanks."

It was quiet for a while, then Stefano cleared his throat. "Well, are you seeing anyone right now?"

Laura hesitated a moment. She felt Stefano liked her and wanted to go out with her again. Laura liked him, too, but she didn't know if she was ready to start dating again. "No, I don't. My last relationship was a real disaster, so I kind of pulled back from getting involved with anybody right away."

Stefano looked down at his hands. "I understand. I'm not ready for a deep commitment either. I am preparing to have my own landscaping business one day. That takes up a lot of my time and energy. But I enjoy your company, so perhaps we could do a few things together."

"Yes, maybe," Laura said.

Chapter 3: Andreas

Andreas poured the pot of cooked spaghetti into the colander and gave it a light shake to drain the water. A small rivulet of sweat was sliding down his forehead. He grabbed a towel and dried his face, then picked up one of the noodles and tried it. The pasta was a little overcooked and it could use a little more salt. Oh well, he thought, the tomato sauce would make up for it. Fortunately, Karla had cooked a large batch of tomato sauce from Lena's homegrown tomatoes and had frozen a bunch of individual portions.

Lena was their next-door neighbor and longtime friend. Together with her husband, Luigi, she cultivated and sold roses. She also had a large vegetable garden. Since their children were grown and had moved out, they didn't know what to do with all the vegetables during a good harvest. She sold some and gave the rest to Andreas and Karla, who, in turn, helped her in the garden once in a while.

The last few days Karla hadn't felt like eating much, let alone cooking. Andreas had never been a great cook, but he insisted on helping out. Part of it was that he felt a little guilty about the pregnancy and the fact that he was overjoyed while Karla seemed to suffer.

"What's for dinner?" Tonio curled his nose as he stepped inside.

Andreas gave him a measuring look. "New outfit?"

"Just the shirt," Tonio said. He was wearing a pair of green jeans and a flowered top. Tonio was a handsome young boy; too handsome for a boy, Andreas sometimes felt. He took after Karla with his slender body and finely chiseled face, the large dark eyes framed by long eyelashes, and the shiny black hair with natural reddish-blond highlights.

"Why are *you* cooking?" Tonio asked. The expression on his face showed how little confidence he had in his father's culinary arts. "Where is Mama?"

"She's not feeling well. She's lying down." Andreas scowled at him. "Yes, *I* am cooking. Any problem with that?"

Tonio exhaled. "I guess I don't have a choice."

"You can eat out if you don't like it," Andreas said in a terse voice. "Go and set the table and tell Mama that dinner is ready." It was only then that he noticed the strand of green in Tonio's hair. He shook his head. *Fashion geek.*

Tonio loved fashion. Almost all his pocket money went for clothes. Another feature he had inherited from his mother was her talent for design and painting. Tonio, however, didn't have the drive and patience to become a professional artist. Trying to find a profession in which he could use his love of drawing, colors, and clothes, he decided to try his hand as fashion designer. He was in his second year at a fashion school in Lugano, the largest and most cosmopolitan city in the canton Ticino.

Andreas watched his son's fascination with fashion with a mixture of amusement and concern. He and Tonio were opposites when it came to clothes. While Andreas tried anything to avoid having to dress up, Tonio welcomed all the opportunities to gussy up. Andreas admired Tonio's artistic abilities, but sometimes he wished his son showed more interest in what he considered manly pursuits, such as sports and hiking.

After the table was set, Karla came into the room. "Thanks for cooking." She gave Andreas a hug.

"Feeling better?" he asked, kissing her lightly on the head.

"Yeah," Karla said.

Her hair smelled of strawberry shampoo. She looked up at him and Andreas was struck once again by her beauty: her soft, tanned skin; the high cheekbones; her dark eyes; and the shiny black hair, which reached to her shoulders. Andreas was overcome by a surge of love and gratitude.

"Is there any Coca-Cola?" Tonio asked and tapped Andreas on the shoulder.

"Of course not, you know we don't have soft drinks. Why are you even asking?" Andreas said, irritated at the interruption.

"There is Gazosa in the fridge," Karla said.

"Gazosa *is* a soft drink." Tonio glared at his father.

Andreas rolled his eyes. "Go get it and shut up."

"Come on, stop fighting," Karla begged.

After everybody was seated, Karla passed the plate with the spaghetti around. Tonio served himself a small portion. He picked up one of the noodles with his fingers and tasted it. "The spaghetti is overcooked."

Andreas felt like slapping him.

Karla put her fork down. "Stop complaining, please."

"Well, it's true," Tonio said. "Last night, it was store-bought pizza, and now—"

"Tonio," Karla yelled. "If you don't like it, you can either go out or prepare your own meals."

Tonio, startled by the unexpected outburst, stared at her. "What's the matter with you?"

"What's the matter with me?" Karla slammed her fork down. "I've been cooking for you guys for years and I don't think you had any reason to complain about the quality of my meals. Just because I don't feel up to it for once, you start bitching."

"I'm sorry, Mama. I'm not complaining about *your* cooking. It's Papa's cooking that sucks."

Andreas, noticing that Karla was close to tears, slapped the table with his hand. "I've had it with your whining. Your mother is right. Why don't *you* cook once in a while? It's about time you start pulling your weight around here, young man. You're old enough, for Christ's sake."

"Really. What's the matter with you guys?" Tonio asked. "Are you both on the rag or what?"

Andreas's eyes narrowed. He shook his head, and all of a sudden, the whole situation struck him as funny. "Well, if one of us was 'on the rag,' as you put it, we probably wouldn't even have this conversation."

"What do you mean?" Tonio looked at Karla, who dabbed her eyes. "Why is Mama crying?"

Karla suppressed a sob and put her hand on Tonio's arm. "It's nothing. I'm sorry I snapped at you. I've been kind of emotional these last few days, and no, I don't have my period. In fact, I wish I did."

Tonio put his fork down and looked from Karla to Andreas and back.

Andreas grinned. "We have to tell you something. We wanted to wait until Laura gets home, but I think that's no longer possible. Well, here it is . . . or do you want to tell him?" Andreas looked at

Karla, who shook her head. "Mama and I, well . . . we're going to have another child. Mama is pregnant."

"What!" Tonio stared at them, his mouth wide-open. "That's . . . that's . . . impossible. I mean, that's great . . . is it?"

"Well, Tonio, that's about how I feel. One minute I think it's impossible and the next minute I'm excited and happy." Karla managed a weak smile.

"When did this happen? Oh, I get it. You guys screwed without protection." Tonio guffawed and slapped his thigh. He punched Andreas's arm. "And you gave me all these lectures about safe sex and little bugs crawling up a woman's—"

"Tonio. I expect a little more respect. This is no time for locker-room talk." Andreas tried to give him a stern look but failed.

Karla burst out laughing and wiped away her tears. "What did you tell him about little bugs crawling up a woman's whatever?"

"I said sperms, not bugs." Andreas snickered.

After helping to clear the table, Tonio opened the door to the patio and started to walk toward the cottage next door.

"What about the dishes?" Andreas called after him.

Tonio stopped and turned around. He slid his hands into his pockets. "I wanted to go out. I'm meeting a friend. I'm already a little late. I'll help with the dishes tomorrow."

"It's okay. I'll do the dishes," Karla said. "I haven't done much else today."

"Wait, wait." Andreas pointed his finger at Tonio. "Where are you going? It's a weekday. You have school tomorrow."

"I'm not going to be out late," Tonio said in an exasperated tone. "Please."

"I want to see you before you leave," Andreas said.

"All right, I'll be right back." Tonio rushed outside.

Andreas shook his head. "He's been copping an attitude lately. I don't like it."

"I think you're too hard on him. He is a good student. He doesn't stay out late. Give him some freedom." Karla turned on the faucet and squirted a few drops of detergent into the water.

"I think he has plenty of freedom." Andreas picked up a dish towel and began to dry the dishes. "We don't even know who his friends are, who he hangs out with."

"Andreas, he is almost seventeen. He has his own circle of buddies. He doesn't always have to share everything with us. You have to get used to this. I don't hear you complain about Laura. She has her own life."

"Laura is over eighteen. She's isn't a minor anymore. Besides, Laura is much more forthcoming about her life. She tells us who her friends are, who she goes out with. Tonio is so secretive. I don't know how to put it. He could have a girlfriend and we wouldn't know about it."

Karla unplugged the sink and dried her hands with a towel. "Andreas, Tonio is just different. Why can't you accept this? Stop nagging at him. No wonder he feels you don't approve of him."

"That's not true." Andreas stared at her. "Of course I approve of him. I'm happy he's doing well in school. I just wonder sometimes—" Andreas stopped as Tonio came back.

He had changed clothes and was wearing a pair of low-rise black pants and a shiny metallic red-and-black patterned shirt. A black leather jacket dangled from his finger. "See you guys."

"Hold on," Andreas said. He looked him up and down. "Going to a fashion show?"

Tonio rolled his eyes. "No, Papa. We're going to the movies."

"We? Who?"

"Mario and I and perhaps some of his friends."

"Who's Mario?"

"My friend from school. I told you about him before." Tonio sounded annoyed.

"No, you did not. In fact, I have no idea who your friends are," Andreas said.

"Okay, then I must have told Mama. Mario is the son of the owner of Antonini Men's Fashion in Lugano. We're in the same class. He has light brown hair, blue eyes, and I don't know his shoe size."

"No need to be impertinent. I'm still your father. I have a right to know who you hang out with. And I also have the right to ground you indefinitely. And I've had it with your attitude." Andreas tossed the towel on the kitchen table and glared at his son.

Tonio's shoulders slumped. "I'm sorry. I just . . . you always pick on me."

"I don't," Andreas said. "I care about you. I'm still responsible for you. And that's why I want to know who you are with. Is that so hard to understand? If you were a little more forthcoming, I wouldn't have to worm everything out of you. What do you have to hide?"

Tonio flinched and lowered his eyes. "Nothing," he said in a low voice.

Andreas stared at him. *He's always been a bad liar.* "Any girls?" It was a shot in the dark.

"Girls?" Tonio looked at him, surprised.

"Yeah, girls, you know? Those lovely creatures with boobs and—"

"Andreas, please. You're being ridiculous," Karla said.

Andreas lifted his hands. "I just want to know if Tonio perhaps has a girlfriend and doesn't want to tell us. You can tell us, for heaven's sake."

"I don't have a girlfriend," Tonio said, his facial color darkening. "But once I do, I'll let you know."

"Do you have protection?" Andreas asked.

"Jesus Christ," Tonio yelled. "Yes, I do have protection. I still have the damn rubbers you gave me. I haven't had to use them yet. Besides, you're the right one to talk about protection."

"Stop it, both of you," Karla said. "If this is one of those father-and-son talks, it sure sucks."

"Well, tell Papa. He started it." Tonio grabbed his jacket and glared at Andreas.

Andreas exhaled deeply. "I'm just concerned, that's all. Go and have fun, but I want you home before midnight. Okay?"

Tonio nodded. He gave his father a last angry look and left.

Andreas sighed. He felt Karla's eyes on him.

"You sure know how to communicate with your son. Congratulations." She hung up her apron and left the kitchen.

"Karla, please—" He shook his head and went after her. "I'm sorry. I don't know how to talk to him sometimes." He sat next to her on the sofa in the living room. "I'm afraid . . . I'm afraid I'm losing him."

"God, Andreas, don't be such a bully. You have to trust him a little. No wonder you push him away with your belligerent attitude."

Andreas propped his elbows on his knees and supported his face with his hands. "I know," he mumbled. "He's just grown so distant over the last year. Think about it. Do you know any of his friends? He never brings anyone home. He goes out all the time, dressed like some . . . fashion model."

Karla faced him. "Andreas, he's studying to become a fashion designer. He's learning about fashion and he's experimenting with it. I've seen some of the other students at the school. They all dress a little outlandish. It's normal."

Andreas shrugged. "I guess so, I'm just not used to it."

"Well, get used to it. We both encouraged him to apply to this school. He got in, he's doing really well. His grades are excellent. You should be proud of him instead of always complaining. And as far as his clothes are concerned, he dresses really well. He's young. Let him have fun with it." Karla got up and walked to the window. She turned around and grinned. "In fact, you could take some lessons from him. When was the last time you put on some decent clothes?"

"Please, Karla, don't even start. You know how much I hate to dress up."

"Yes, I know, and I don't constantly pester you about it. I take you the way you are. People are different. Tonio likes clothes, you don't."

"Okay, I got the point." Andreas brushed through his hair and looked down at his torn jeans. "I guess I do need some new pants."

"Yes, and you also need a new outfit and some shirts." Karla sat next to him. "So I can show you off next time we go out."

"Huh? Go out where?"

"Well, when was the last time you took me to a really nice restaurant? Or to the opera or the movies? Once the baby is here, we won't have much time for any of that." Karla put her hand on his thigh. "We need to spice up our life a little."

"Not spicy enough?" Andreas pulled Karla close. He kissed her and opened the top few buttons of her blouse. "Well, let's spice it up."

Karla sat up straight. "I got an idea."

Andreas pulled her next to him again and slid his hand inside her blouse. "So do I. Let's retire to the bedroom."

"Wait." She held his hand. "Why don't you ask Tonio to take you shopping?"

Andreas sat back and looked at her, perplexed. "What? Are you nuts? He's going to make me look like a gigolo or a dandy."

"No, he won't. He has good taste. Just think how proud he'd be if he felt you value his opinion. It would be the perfect way to get closer to him again. He'd probably take you to that fashion store, the one that belongs to his friend's father. You may even meet some of his friends. Don't you see? Show an interest in his work, in what he loves to do."

Andreas stared at the floor. "I'm . . . I guess I'm just old-fashioned." He nodded and looked up. "You're right. I'll try. Okay, that's settled. Now, could we please change the topic? What about spicing up our life?" He opened the remaining buttons on Karla's blouse, pulled her bra aside, and kissed her breasts. He gently squeezed her nipples. "Your boobs are still as gorgeous as they were twenty years ago."

"You think so?" Karla gave him an impish smile. "What about the rest of me?"

"Let me see." He lifted her skirt and pulled at the elastic band of her panties and stripped them down to her knees. "Perfect," he said and kissed her belly. He looked up. "Would you marry me again?"

"Well, let's see," Karla teased him. "Have to think about that." She closed her eyes as he slid his hand between her legs. "Yes, yes," she moaned. "I'll marry you again."

Chapter 4: Laura

Laura stood outside the sculpture school next to her suitcase, waiting for her father to pick her up. It was the end of her three-week-long workshop. Although she was looking for/ward to seeing her parents again and working on her own, she felt the time had passed too quickly. After the first few unsuccessful attempts to carve marble, she felt she was beginning to develop a new talent. She always thought that she was more cut out to do the larger, rougher work her father had taught her. Enrico, however, had been able to trigger an interest in some of the finer aspects of stonework and to her surprise, Laura began to enjoy it and marble and alabaster became her favorite materials.

Toward the end of the seminar, she had carved a few smaller elegant sculptures, for which even her tough teacher had praised her. Enrico had picked the two best ones for display at the traditional exhibition in Locarno, which was devoted to works of the students from the sculpture school.

"Your dad will be proud of you," Stefano said. He stood next to her, holding her tool bag.

"I hope so," Laura said. "Well, here he is. But why did he bring his pickup truck? He must think I carved some giant sculptures. I hope he won't be disappointed with the small things I made." Laura looked at the longish shape of white marble sprinkled with black, bluish, and grey quartz and silicate she held in her hands. The rest of her work was still in the studio.

"He better like it or he'll have to answer to me," said Enrico, who stepped outside and joined them. He smiled and watched Andreas climb the steep path from the street to the school. "Hey, man, there was a time you used to run up that hill. What happened?" Enrico called.

Andreas grinned. "Life happened. Getting older. What do you think?"

The two men embraced and slapped each other's backs.

"Well, life seems to have been good to you. You still have your hair," Enrico said.

Andreas brushed through his wildish dark mane, which showed a few strands of grey, and motioned at Enrico's head. "So do you."

They went on joking together, while Stefano and Laura watched them, amused.

"Hi, sweetie," Andreas said and hugged Laura. "What have you got here?" He carefully lifted Laura's sculpture and looked at it from all sides. "Hey, that's good. Great composition, and look at the fine detail work." He touched the carvings gently, then handed the stone back to Laura.

His words brought a warm flush to her face. Her father was honest and didn't just praise her to make her feel good, so he was obviously pleased with her work. "I was afraid you were expecting large sculptures because you brought your truck," she said.

Andreas shook his head. "No, Mama needed the car. She had a doctor's appointment."

"Oh? Something wrong?" Laura asked.

"No, nothing is wrong, just a checkup." Andreas said quickly, then cleared his throat. Laura felt he acted a little embarrassed.

"Well, let me introduce my nephew to you." Enrico touched Stefano's arm. Andreas and Stefano shook hands. "I think he enjoyed entertaining your daughter." He winked at Stefano. "No wonder, such an attractive young woman."

Andreas narrowed his eyes and gave Stefano a quick measuring look, then glanced at Laura. Laura noticed that Stefano was blushing. "We went out a few times," she said.

"Aha. You're a student, too?" Andreas asked.

"Oh no, I don't have that kind of talent," Stefano said. "I'm a gardener."

"Come on, don't be so modest. He's a landscape artist and a very talented one," Enrico said. "He does beautiful work and he'll have his own business eventually."

Stefano blushed again and seemed to squirm inwardly at the praise. "Thanks, Uncle Enrico, but my own business will have to wait awhile. There's still plenty to learn."

Andreas gave a quick smile. "Well, modesty is a rare virtue."

"Yeah, except it usually doesn't help you get ahead in this world," Enrico said. He turned to Andreas. "Have you been here lately? They've made some changes."

"Actually, I come here occasionally, but I didn't realize you taught here. I just recently saw your name in the new schedule and I wondered if it was you. Then Laura told me."

"This is only my second term. I've lived in Greece for many years. But let me show you my studio." Enrico pointed to one of the school bungalows.

"I'll get the rest of my stuff," Laura said.

As Enrico and Andreas walked toward the studios, Laura and Stefano carried Laura's bags and stonework to the car and stowed it in the back of the pickup. They sat on one of the stone slabs. Some of the other students who finished their workshops walked by and said goodbye.

"Gee, it went by so fast," Laura said.

"Yeah, I know," Stefano said. He was twisting his hands, then put them in his pockets. "Hey, would you want to go to a movie or something once in a while?"

Laura had noticed that Stefano wasn't exactly experienced in asking girls out. She kind of liked his shyness. It was a welcome change from her former pushy boyfriend. "Yeah, why not? Want to go to the upcoming sculpture show in Locarno?"

"Definitely," Stefano said.

They heard Enrico and Andreas walk down the path laughing and talking.

"Well, I better get back to work," Stefano said. They got up and gave each other a hug. Stefano hesitated for a second, then kissed Laura on the cheek, blushing once again.

Laura smiled and turned around as Andreas cleared his throat.

Stefano turned to Andreas. "It was good meeting you." They shook hands and Stefano walked up the hill, waving back once more.

"Well, I'll see you soon," Enrico said to Laura, then slapped Andreas on the back. "And I hope to see you as well. Let's not wait another twenty years."

"No, definitely not," Andreas said and invited Enrico to visit them the following weekend.

It was quiet in the car for a while as Andreas concentrated on driving down the narrow, curvy road. Once they arrived at the bottom of the valley, he turned to Laura. "Seems like a nice young man."

Laura suppressed a smile. She knew her father wanted to know more but didn't want to ask her outright. "Yeah, he is. We went out a few times, but so far we're just friends. Don't want to rush into anything serious. Not after my last experience."

"Sounds reasonable," Andreas said.

After a while, Laura glanced at her father. He seemed preoccupied. He had asked her about the workshop but didn't seem that interested, which surprised her. "So what's the matter with Mama? Why is she at the doctor's? Is something wrong with her?"

"No, she's okay . . . well, something unusual happened."

"What?"

Andreas took a deep breath. "We wanted to wait before telling you until you got home, but Tonio already knows, so I might as well tell you."

"Mama . . . eh, we . . ."

"What? What's going on?"

"We are going to have another baby. She is pregnant."

"What? Whoa, how is that possible?" Laura's heartbeat stuttered. She tried to figure out what this meant. "I'll have another sibling. A baby that could be my own child, age-wise. I think that's kind of fun . . . isn't it?"

"I think it's great," Andreas said. "A little scary—we're not the youngest parents anymore. Mama isn't exactly enthusiastic about it. It's going to be hard for her, but we'll manage."

"We'll help you guys, babysitting and so on," Laura said.

"Thanks. Yeah, your mother will need some help."

Laura's mind swirled. Although she liked the idea of having another younger brother or sister, she also wondered what it might mean for her parents. She shook her head. "And all these lectures you guys gave us about birth control and being careful and all that. What a riot."

Andreas gave a snort. "That's what Tonio said, too. You know the saying 'There is no fool like an old fool.' We were careless a few times and it happened."

"Oh well, then it was meant to happen, I guess," Laura said.

Andreas lifted his shoulder. "That's what I think." He glanced at her; there was a twinkle in his eyes.

Chapter 5: Andreas

Andreas cleared his throat and brushed his hand through his mop of hair. "I need some new clothes."

Tonio, who had just come home from a day at the fashion school, looked his father up and down. Andreas was wearing his regular torn dungarees and an old work shirt. "Yeah? That's a splendid idea."

"Stop being sarcastic," Andreas grumbled. "Anyway, you know how bad I am with such things. I thought that perhaps . . . you could help me pick out something?"

"Oh? Why don't you take Mama along?"

"I want to surprise her. And . . . you have such good taste." *Just don't make me look like a goddamn dandy.*

"Okay. Sure. What do you need?" Tonio asked.

"Well, a pair of jeans, a suit, and perhaps some shirts."

"Sounds good." Tonio took off his jacket and loosened his colorful tie.

"You know, you told me about the men's fashion store in Lugano. The one that belongs to your friend's father?"

"Yeah, we can go there. They have great stuff." Tonio's eyes lit up.

"Great. What about Saturday?"

On Saturday morning Andreas and Tonio drove to Lugano. They parked the car at one of the parking garages and walked to the old center of town. Most of the elegant shops were along Via Nassa, a few streets away from Lake Lugano. It was a sunny August morning, but a fresh wind from the lake whipped through the streets. Sweet scents from the flower shop they passed competed with the smell of roasted coffee beans from the cafeteria across the street.

Andreas was nervous. He had decided to let Tonio be in charge, but he was concerned he might not feel comfortable with the choices his son made. "Nothing flashy," he warned Tonio as they walked to the store.

"Don't worry," Tonio said in a placating tone and patted his father's arm.

Andreas's concerns were in vain. Tonio, knowing his father's rather conservative taste, was careful to pick something elegant but discreet. They decided on a grey-green suit that accentuated Andreas's green eyes and a beige suit with light-brown vertical stripes to counter Andreas's sturdy figure. While Andreas was trying on the suits, Tonio disappeared briefly and came back with a bunch of shirts, belts, and ties.

"It's the accessories that make a difference between a so-so suit and something really chic," he explained as he held up the shirts and ties to see how they went with the suits.

"Hold your horses," Andreas said as the clothes Tonio found acceptable started to pile up on the chair. "I may not have enough money with me."

"If you're short of cash, they can always put the suits away for you and we can pick them up later. Perhaps you should get yourself a credit card," Tonio suggested.

"And join all the other crazy people who are head over heel in debt? No thanks. I like your taste in fashion, but as far as finances are concerned, I still make my own decisions."

"All right, Mr. Stubborn," Tonio teased.

"I do appreciate you helping me with this, though," Andreas said. "I couldn't have done it by myself. I'm terrible when it comes to picking out clothes."

Tonio smiled at him, obviously pleased with his father's praise. "Oh, here is Mario." Tonio waved at a slim young man with longish light brown hair, dressed in an elegant steel-blue suit.

"Hello there," the young man exclaimed and gave Tonio a hug. "You're getting some new rags?"

"No, this time I am helping my dad pick out suits. He's not exactly, how shall I put it, an experienced shopper."

"You mean to say, I have terrible taste and know nothing about clothes?" Andreas added the last shirt he had tried on to the pile.

"That's not what I said."

"Yeah, but that's what you meant. It's okay. You're right."

"I'm pleased to meet you." Mario shook hands with Andreas. "What did you guys decide on?" he asked.

Tonio showed him the suits, shirts, and ties they had picked out.

"Good choice," Mario said. "You're going to look smashing."

"Yeah, Papa, when Mama sees you in these, she may not regret having married you after all," Tonio teased Andreas.

"You think so?" Andreas said, giving a slight smile.

"Well, I have to get back to work, I'm helping my dad today. Extra pocket money," Mario said. "It was very nice meeting you," he said to Andreas and gave Tonio a quick pat on the shoulder. "See you in school."

After they paid for their purchases, Andreas invited Tonio for lunch at a nearby pizzeria.

"Nice young man," he said while they were waiting for their order. "And probably quite lucky—he may inherit his father's fancy clothing store."

"Yes, that's true. Mario is great. He is a little older than the other students. He worked for a while at his father's fashion store before going back to school. He has a lot of experience in fashion and has been helping his father since he was a boy." Tonio's face was flushed with excitement. "He . . . he's really nice."

He lowered his eyes as Andreas gave him a probing look. He hadn't seen Tonio as enthusiastic as this in a long time.

"I'm glad you made friends at school. Perhaps you can get a job in his father's business as well."

"Yeah, perhaps. Or we can open our own fashion store together." Tonio's excitement was back. His flushed face showed the enthusiasm of the young for whom the future was still full of promises.

A feeling of love for his son flooded Andreas. He put his hand on Tonio's and squeezed it. "You'll do an excellent job, whatever you decide to do. I'm very proud of you."

Tonio's eyes misted over. "Thanks," he murmured.

At home, Andreas had to put up with a fashion show. Karla made him try on the new outfits and she and Tonio commented on how great he looked while Andreas rolled his eyes at their praise. All in all, he was pleased with the way the father-son outing had turned out. It seemed that he and Tonio were a little closer again. Deep down, however, something bothered him and he couldn't put his finger on it. Tonio was different from what he imagined a young guy his age ought to be.

"He's too damn sensitive. Too delicate. Sometimes I worry he's not made for this world. He needs to toughen up a little," he said to Karla later on.

Karla sighed. "Let him be. He's the way he is."

"What puzzles me, too, is that he doesn't date. He just hangs out with his male friends, with this Mario guy. Isn't that strange? I mean, he's almost seventeen."

"I don't know, Andreas. He's been so busy with school. There isn't much time for a social life. Besides, I don't mind. Keeps him out of trouble a little longer."

Andreas nodded. "Maybe. I guess he's just a late bloomer."

Chapter 6: Karla

Karla slammed her brush into a glass of water. The smell of acrylic paint made her nauseated. Being pregnant, she was trying to avoid paints that contain solvents, which could be toxic to the fetus. She had always been sensitive to scents during pregnancy, but feeling queasy from the smell of acrylic paint was new.

"Just another slap from destiny. I was obviously meant to focus on being a mother rather than being an artist," she muttered. She squinted her eyes and examined the canvas, where a new painting was beginning to take shape. It was one of a series she was preparing for an upcoming exhibition. She worked at it off and on whenever she felt well enough, but if her morning sickness and constant tiredness didn't improve, she might not be ready for it. She picked up the brush again, then tossed it on the table in anger. Tears rose in her eyes.

She went outside for a breath of fresh air. As she walked through the kitchen to the patio door, she glanced longingly at the espresso machine, but too much coffee was another taboo in her present state. She had had a miscarriage during her first pregnancy and didn't want to take any chances. "Six more months."

Karla stood on the patio, inhaling the brisk October air. It smelled of burning wood, roasted chestnuts, and some kind of herb. These were the aromas she could tolerate and still enjoyed. A vague smile teased her lips. She patted her belly, feeling guilty for her bad mood. "It's not your fault, little one."

"Talking to yourself?" She hadn't heard Andreas step out of his workshop. He stood next to her and put his arm around her.

Karla folded her arms in front of her chest, stiffening in his embrace. "No, I'm talking to my—I mean, *our* baby."

Andreas gave a quick smile. "Still blaming me, huh? I asked you if it was safe—"

"Yeah, yeah, I know. I just wish I wouldn't get sick from the smell of paint. I can't even work in peace."

"Perhaps you should keep the window open."

"Keep the window open? What kind of advice is that? Do I have to decide between feeling sick and freezing to death?"

"Aren't you being a little dramatic? Freezing to death? It's only about fifteen degrees and—"

"Shut up." Karla wasn't in the mood this morning for Andreas's down-to-earth reasoning. Although she knew her pregnancy wasn't all his fault, blaming him gave her a perverted sense of pleasure.

"Yes, ma'am." Andreas smiled. She knew what went through his mind. She would eventually accept her lot and look forward to being a mother again.

Karla sat on the bench underneath the chestnut tree, gazing at the colorful leaves, the radiant reds of the blood maple, the golden yellows of the birches. The last of the chestnuts had dropped overnight. Their prickly green shells had split open, exposing part of the shiny brown kernels. Karla remembered the fun times during fall when Laura and Tonio were little and they had walked for hours in the woods, gathering chestnuts. They had roasted the chestnuts from the noble trees in a special iron pot over the fireplace. From the nonedible horse chestnuts, they had made small figurines with matchsticks for arms and legs.

Karla smiled and a feeling of warmth and love flooded her. It would be okay, having another baby, hearing once again the voice of a small child. It had become awfully quiet with Laura and Tonio out all day and Andreas gone much of the time.

She got up and went inside, threw a cursory glance at the coffee machine and poured herself a glass of orange juice. She stopped by her easel, hesitated, then decided to check out the few baby clothes and toys they still had. Most of them they had given away, figuring they wouldn't need them anymore.

She went to the cottage next door, which housed the children's bedrooms. Underneath the first floor, there was a storage area for odds and ends. Karla pushed aside a few boxes of old dishes and clothes that they had prepared to give to the Salvation Army. She whisked away a few cobwebs and went to the back of the dim room, where the old suitcase with the baby stuff was. It smelled musty and the dust tickled her throat. She coughed as she wiped the dust off the top with an old rag. Sitting on an overturned empty bucket, she lifted the cover.

The first thing she found was Laura's old teddy bear. Its dirty yellowish face looked at her with one black button eye. Karla smiled and gently pressed on the bear's belly. It opened its mouth, showed his reddish velvet tongue, and gave a pitiful half growl, a weak protest for having been shut away for so long. Karla put the bear aside and pulled out a plastic bag with colorful bibs and a few tiny rompers. "Look at this," she said to herself and grabbed an envelope. It contained a few of Laura's and Tonio's drawings.

"They were good," she murmured as she paged through the childlike depiction of animals, fairy-tale characters, houses, trees, and stick figures. She put the drawings down and sighed. Tears gathered in her eyes and a sob escaped her. A mixture of sadness, joy, and gratitude flooded her. It would be okay, she thought. *Yes, it'll be okay.*

A shadow blocked part of the door. "What are you doing here?" Andreas asked.

"Come and look," she said, wiping the tears from her face. She pulled out a few more things. Andreas sat next to her and together they unpacked the suitcase, laughing and oohing and aahing over the small treasures.

After unpacking all of it and putting aside a few things they thought they could still use, Karla put the rest back into the suitcase. "I guess we need to buy a few things, most of this is dated."

Andreas put his arm around her and pulled her close. "Feeling better about it?"

Karla nodded. "Sorry for being a bitch sometimes. It's just . . ."

"I know."

Chapter 7: Tonio

Tonio and his friend Mario were on their way to the art museum at the Villa Malpensata, which was situated along Lake Lugano. There was an exhibition of expressionist paintings by, among others, Edvard Munch and Marc Chagall. They were two of Mario's favorite painters.

The museum opened at ten o'clock, and since they were early, they had coffee and rolls at one of the coffee shops on the promenade. Afterward, they took a walk along the lake.

It was Sunday and a pleasantly warm fall day. The yellow and brownish leaves on the chestnut trees and birches trembled lightly in the breeze from the lake. Quite a few had already tumbled to the ground and had been raked into small heaps at the edge of the sidewalk. Tonio playfully jumped over one of the piles of leaves, then turned to Mario.

"Guess what? My mother is pregnant. I'm going to have an eighteen-year-younger brother or sister. Is that crazy or what?"

"Wow. How did this happen?" Mario raised an eyebrow and gave Tonio an impish look.

"How do you think it happened?" Tonio said. "My parents did exactly what they have been warning me and my sister about for years: screw without a rubber."

"I figured that much." Mario laughed. "What I mean is, did they plan this?"

"Of course not."

"Oh, boy. And how do they feel about it?"

"My mother is kind of torn. One day she's all upset and the next day she says she's looking forward to it. My father, however, is excited, and I think that's what pisses my mother off even more. He walks around with this shit-eating grin on his face. It's a riot. I have never heard them argue as much as the last few weeks. But I think they're going to be all right."

Mario motioned at a bench along the lake. They sat down. He chuckled, then became serious. "Well, this is something I don't have to worry about."

Tonio shrugged. "I guess not."

They had never openly talked about the fact that Mario was gay, but it was a generally known fact among his friends.

"What about you?" Mario peered at Tonio and put his hand on his shoulder.

Tonio flinched but didn't pull back. "What do you mean?"

"Oh, come on, Tonio, how much longer are you going to hide the fact that you are like me?"

Tonio's stomach clenched. "What are you talking about?"

"You're gay, that's what. Why are you hiding it?"

44

"You're crazy." Tonio was angry and relieved at the same time. Now, it was out. The next moment, though, he was overcome with panic. "How could you possibly know this, anyway?"

Mario smiled. "When you're that way yourself, you recognize the signs."

"Leave me alone." Tonio's eyes filled with tears.

"Tonio, it's all right. It's not something we chose. There's nothing we can do to change it and there's nothing wrong with it."

Tonio's shoulders slumped and he kept staring at the lake. The greenish water glistened in the sunlight. Mario moved closer. Tonio faced him. Tears welled up in his eyes, blurring Mario's features.

Tonio had first noticed his attraction to boys when he was sitting on a boulder at the edge of the Maggia River. He watched a young man climb out of the water. The boy's bathing suit clung to his body and the bulge in his trunks was clearly visible. The drops of water on his tanned skin sparkled in the sun. He looked up and gave Tonio a bright smile. Tonio felt his penis grow hard and throb and all he could do to hide it was slide down from the rock and plunge into the cold water.

The incident confused and frightened him. What was wrong with him? He had noticed before that the bodies of young girls didn't attract him the way they attracted his friends. He participated in the pubescent sexual bantering and joking when the other guys talked about "hot chicks," but it was pretense on his part, an attempt to hide his otherness from them and from himself. However, until that day down at the river, it had never been that obvious to him that it was young men and boys he was interested in and wanted to have sex with, not girls.

He made every effort to feel attracted to girls. He even bought a bunch of porno magazines, which he looked at in secret, but nothing helped. He wanted so much to be "normal." He had laughed at the jokes about "fags" and "homos" his schoolmates made occasionally. He didn't want to be one of them.

Now, he could no longer hide his true nature. He kept staring at the lake. Mario put his arm around him. The heat of his friend's body enveloped him. No longer having the strength to resist, Tonio rested his head against Mario's chest and closed his eyes.

"Tonio," Mario whispered, "I love you."

Tonio wiped the tears from his face. "I . . . love you, too. I don't know what to do."

"It's going to be all right. Don't worry." Mario put his hand on Tonio's shoulder. "Come on, let's go and look at some paintings."

They walked to the museum and took a leisurely stroll through the collections. At first, Tonio's mind reeled from the unexpected development of the past hour. Every once in a while, Mario took his hand and squeezed it lightly. The reassuring gesture helped him relax, and in the quiet of the museum halls—it wasn't crowded that day—he was finally able to enjoy the pictures.

Later that evening, they made love at Mario's place. His energy spent, luxuriating in the warmth of his lover's embrace, Tonio felt for the first time in many months that he was being himself. A sense of peace descended upon him. Soon, however, the feeling of tranquility gave way to dread. "How am I going to tell my parents about this?"

Mario wrinkled his forehead. "Your family seems pretty open-minded. Don't you think they'll be okay with it?"

"I don't know. I think my mom won't mind as much, but I know it'll hurt my dad. He's the ultimate family man and he wants us to have normal relationships and kids and the whole bit."

Chapter 8: Andreas

Andreas glanced at his watch. It was close to noon on Monday at his workshop in Lugano, where he spent two days a week. His sculpting studio was in his home in the Maggia Valley. Since he had quite a few clients in Lugano, he rented part of a workspace from a stonemason friend of his. He did most of his work on gravestones there. The workspace was close to Tonio's fashion school and they often had lunch together on those two days.

The bells of a church nearby began to toll the midday hour. Andreas stepped outside and glanced at the sky, which was a clear blue except for the thin smirch of yellowish haze behind the mountain San Salvatore. He looked along the street, where Tonio usually came to pick him up. Tonio seemed to be late today.

Andreas locked the studio and began to walk along Via delle Scuole toward the school, which was situated at Via al Fiume. He figured he would meet Tonio halfway, but he arrived at the school without running into his son. A group of students came walking out, chatting and laughing. Next to the school building, somewhat away from the other people, he saw Tonio. He was standing close to a young man. Andreas recognized Tonio's friend, the son of the owner of the clothing store.

Andreas was just about to cross the street when the two seemed to say goodbye. Mario—Andreas remembered his name—hugged Tonio for quite a while and then kissed him on the mouth. Andreas's heart leapt. He watched as Tonio turned around and got ready to cross the street.

He had barely enough time to recover from the shock of seeing his son kiss another man. This wasn't a kiss between friends, that much was obvious.

"I'm sorry I'm late," Tonio said. "Our tech teacher never knows when to stop." Tonio rolled his eyes. "Have you been waiting for a long time?"

"No." Andreas's mouth felt dry. He looked across the street, but the man was gone. He clenched his jaw, trying to squelch the rising anger.

"Are we going to our usual place or want to try something new?" Tonio asked.

"What?" Andreas finally faced his son, swallowing again. "Oh, well, where do you feel like going?"

Tonio narrowed his eyes and stared at Andreas. "Anything wrong?"

Andreas shook his head. "Let's just go to our usual place." He started to walk toward the restaurant they sometimes ate at. His mind was twirling. After a few steps, he stopped and turned toward Tonio. "When do you have to be back at school?"

"Actually, I'm off this afternoon. Our clothing-design teacher is sick. We're supposed to work on our group projects, so I'm going to Mario's after lunch and —"

"Oh, yeah?" Andreas glared at Tonio, who looked at him, surprised, his large dark eyes worried.

"What's the matter, Papa? You're acting strange."

"Let's sit down somewhere and talk. I'm not really hungry." Andreas headed toward a small park next to a hotel and a spa. They found an empty bench and Andreas sat down and motioned to Tonio to sit next to him. Andreas stared at the lawn and the few trees without registering anything. He felt Tonio's eyes on him and finally faced him.

"That man who kissed you, was that Mario?" It wasn't really the question he wanted to ask, but he didn't know how to start.

Tonio nodded. He glanced at his father, the expression in his eyes changing from confusion to . . . was it guilt or fear? Tonio lowered his gaze, looking at his slim hands with long fingers. *Piano fingers* Karla called them.

The once-familiar features—the delicate face; the straight, shiny black hair; the slender body—they now seemed foreign to Andreas. There was nothing of him in Tonio's features, he was all Karla. *Why does he have to be so fucking handsome? No wonder fags are trying to seduce him.* He pushed the rising rage and desperation back down into his gut, took a deep breath.

"That wasn't a kiss between friends. What's going on, Tonio? What's this guy doing to you?"

Tonio averted his gaze for a moment, then turned his head and faced his father. The corner of his mouth trembled as if he was going to cry, but the expression in his eyes was one of determination. "He's not doing anything to me that I don't want. It's not his fault. We're . . . just different. Papa, I've wanted to tell you this for a while, but I was afraid. I knew you'd be disappointed and hurt, but I can't help it. Papa, I'm gay. Mario and I are in love with each other. It just happened. I'm sorry." His voice broke and tears gathered in his eyes, a few rolling down his cheeks. He wiped them away and a soft sob escaped him.

Andreas exhaled forcefully. His head was throbbing; he closed his eyes and rubbed his forehead. He propped his elbows on his knees and lowered his head into his hands. "I don't know what to say," he murmured. When he looked up again, Tonio was crying.

"I'm sorry, Papa."

Andreas shook his head. "It's just . . . well, a shock. I need some time to get used to this."

A few hotel and spa guests were walking by and glanced at them. "Come on," Andreas said, "let's walk for a while." He got up. "Better yet, let's go to my studio, Carlo isn't there yet."

They walked in silence down the street, turned the corner, and headed toward Andreas's workshop. The whole time, thoughts were tumbling through Andreas's mind; he felt his head was going to split. Now, it dawned on him why he had been worried about Tonio, why his love of fashion, his seeming lack of interest in girls, his other "feminine" traits had upset him at times. Deep down, he had been afraid of the very truth he was now faced with.

What did it all mean? What would it mean for Tonio? What would his life be like as a gay man? Was his condition permanent or just a temporary fluke of nature? *Why am I kidding myself? This is the way my son is.*

Andreas was so deep in thought that he would have walked past his workshop if Tonio hadn't stopped him. He unlocked the door and went inside, then let himself fall onto a chair. Tonio stood around for a few seconds, then sat on a bench next to him.

"Why didn't you tell us before? Maybe we could've done something about it," Andreas said in a low voice, as if talking to himself. Then he shook his head. "Don't mind me. I'm talking nonsense. Forgive me, I'm just . . ."

"I don't mean to hurt you, Papa, but—"

"Look, Tonio, you're my son, and whether you're gay or straight, I love you. But you have to understand, I'm worried about you, about the life you're going to lead. You won't be able to have a family. There may be other repercussions. You know how people are sometimes."

"I know, Papa, believe me, I've thought about that for a long time. It was difficult for me to accept this. But being with Mario is really great. I haven't been as happy as this in a long time. Since I accepted that I'm gay . . . it's been liberating. I know, it won't be easy, but it's better than hiding it and lying about it."

Andreas got up and sat on the bench next to Tonio. He put his arm around him. "You're being careful, aren't you? You know, about AIDS and all that."

Tonio smiled a little. "Papa, straight people get AIDS, too. Besides, Mario and I . . . we don't sleep around. We're committed to each other."

"Tonio, you're only seventeen. You may be committed now, but who knows how things are going to turn out."

"Please don't worry, Papa."

"I'll try not to." Andreas paused. "Have you told Mama?"

"No, I wanted to tell both of you at the same time, but there was never a good moment. And then Mama got pregnant and we all talked about that. I didn't want to cause any more upheavals."

"Oh shit," Andreas said. "Talk about upheavals. I'll be a father once again, Mama is upset about it, and my son turns out to be a . . . has a boyfriend. What did I do to deserve this?"

"I'm sorry," Tonio said.

"You don't need to apologize. It's me, I'm just confused." Andreas pulled out his handkerchief and wiped his eyes. He tapped Tonio on the shoulder. "Let's go and eat."

"Papa, can I bring Mario home one of these days? He wants to meet the family."

"What? It's that far already? Is he going to ask me for your hand in marriage?" Andreas tried to smile, but his mouth and cheeks felt frozen. "Sorry, don't mean to be sarcastic. Yes, of course you can bring him home. After all, I want to know who my children are dating." Andreas made another attempt at laughing, then shook his head. "I need a glass of wine or maybe something stronger."

Chapter 9: Laura

Laura checked her text messages on her mobile phone. There was a laconic one from Tonio: *Told Papa about you know. Was upset but I think will be ok.*

Laura smiled. Tonio had told her weeks ago about being gay. She had promised not to say anything to their parents, because he wanted to break the news himself. Laura knew Mario and had suspected that the two were more than friends. It was a surprise when Tonio told her, but Laura wasn't shocked. She just wondered why he had told their father and not their mother. She didn't seem to know anything, or she would have mentioned it.

However, Tonio's sexual orientation wasn't the most important thing on Laura's mind. She checked her cell phone in hopes of finding a message from Stefano. It had been over two weeks since she had seen him last. They had talked on the phone a couple of times and he had promised to call her. They were planning to go to the sculpture exhibition in Locarno together, which started in two days.

Since the sculpture workshop at Peccia, Laura and Stefano had gone to the movies a few times. Stefano, however, had been extremely busy with work and had to put in a lot of overtime. He apologized and seemed to regret not having more time for her, but Laura began to wonder if he was using work as an excuse not to get together more. Was he really interested in her or was he perhaps seeing someone else?

Laura missed him. At first, she had decided to go slowly and not rush into a new relationship, but now that he didn't call, she was disappointed. She browsed through all the messages, then put the phone down. "Jerk," she muttered.

"What's the matter?" her mother asked, as she stepped into the living room.

"Why doesn't he call or leave a message?" Laura said.

"Stefano?" Her mother must have noticed how preoccupied she was.

"Yeah. He was supposed to call and we had plans to go to the exhibition in Locarno." Laura wrinkled her forehead. "He probably changed his mind."

"Well, you know how busy he's been lately. Perhaps he just forgot the date. Why don't you call him?"

"I'm not going to beg him. He knows that I really wanted to go. After all, two of my sculptures are in the exhibition. How can he forget?"

"Laura, for you that may be the most important thing right now, but Stefano may have his mind full of other things. Don't take it personal."

"I don't know, Mama." Laura sighed, glanced at the cell phone again, then put it down.

Her mother sat next to her. "You like him a lot, don't you?"

"Yeah, well . . . he may just be another loser. Or maybe I'm the loser."

"Laura, have a little more self-confidence. You're a lovely girl and a wonderful person." Her mother hugged her and Laura put her head on her shoulder.

"Papa is coming," her mother said.

They heard Andreas's Fiat drive up the hill and park. Laura checked her messages again, although she knew there were no new ones. When she looked up, her father stepped into the room and Laura detected right away that he was in a strange mood. He mumbled a "*ciao*," dropped a bunch of papers onto the living-room table, and brushed through his hair. A deep furrow lined his forehead. Laura remembered Tonio's message.

"Something wrong?" her mother asked.

"Yeah, you can say that." He let himself fall onto the sofa. "Tonio," he added. He stared his hands.

"What's the matter?" Her mother sounded worried.

"I had a long talk with him," her father said. "He told me he had a boyfriend . . . that he's gay." His voice faltered. He put his head in his hands and rubbed his forehead. When he looked up again, Laura realized for the first time that her father had aged. The wrinkles in his forehead and around his eyes had deepened and the strands of grey in his dark hair seemed more visible.

There was a prolonged silence. Laura and her mother looked at each other. Karla took a deep breath. "Somehow, I had a feeling . . ." She sighed. "Well, I'm glad he told you. He must feel so relieved."

Laura felt sorry for her parents, particularly for her father, who looked pale and miserable. "I know Mario a little, he seems really nice," she said, trying to calm their fears.

Her statement had the opposite effect on her father. He stared at her. "Did you know about this?"

"Yeah, he told me a few weeks ago."

His face turned red. "Why the hell didn't you tell us? Why did he tell you and not us? After all, we're his parents. What else did you guys keep from us?"

"Papa, he wanted to tell you himself. I promised not to say anything. I'm not going to rat on my brother."

"Why didn't he say anything earlier?" Her father slammed his fist on the table.

"Jesus, Papa, perhaps he was afraid you would react this way. Blow up at him like you did now."

"I didn't blow up at him," her father said. "I'm angry because we're the last ones to find out. You've known this for weeks. Tonio only told me because I caught him making out with this guy."

"Making out?" Laura had to suppress a smile. Her father tended to exaggerate, particularly when he was upset.

"Well, kissing him." He got up, walked to the window, and stared outside.

"Tonio wanted to tell you, but he wanted to wait for a good moment," Laura said. "And perhaps he was afraid of your reaction? I don't blame him." Laura got up. She was getting upset as well. She had expected her father to show a little more understanding and compassion.

"Can we all calm down?" her mother said. "Where is Tonio now? Why didn't he come home with you?"

"He's over at his . . . friend's place. They're doing homework, supposedly," he said with a sneer.

"Come on, Andreas, stop acting like a jerk," Karla said. "Tonio needs us now. He needs to know we love him, no matter what."

"Yeah, yeah, I know. It's just . . . well, anyway. He wants to bring this guy home. I told him it was okay with us." He continued to stare out the window.

"Good, we'll all feel a lot better once we get to know him."

The phone rang. Karla picked it up. "Hello, Enrico." She lifted an eyebrow and smiled at Laura. "Yes, she's here." She handed the phone to Laura, who had to control herself not to rip it out of her mother's hand. She left the living room and went outside.

"Enrico? How are you?"

The voice at the other end sounded subdued. "Well, not that good." There was a sigh. "Stefano had an accident."

Laura's stomach clenched. "What happened?"

"He fell from the roof at home. He was trying to fix a leaky tile. He broke his leg. That wouldn't be so bad, but he hit his head in an unfortunate way. He's been in a coma the last two days."

"Oh my god." Laura's heart raced and she felt she was going to hyperventilate.

"Yeah, we hope for the best of course, but I just wanted to let you know. I know you two wanted to get together."

"Oh no. I wondered why I haven't heard from him. Can . . . can I visit him?"

"He's in intensive care, but I can let the nurse know that you're coming. They'll let you see him. When do you want to go?"

"Right now." Laura checked her watch. "Or is it too late?"

"No, I don't think so. Visiting hours are until eight. His parents may be there, but I'll give the hospital a call."

"Thanks, Enrico." Laura pressed the disconnect button. Her mind swirled. She took deep breaths, trying to calm her fluttering stomach. "Poor Stefano." Now she felt guilty for having been angry at him for not calling. She rushed into the living room, where her mother and father were still discussing the newest family upset.

"Can I have the car?" Laura asked.

Her parents stared at her. "What's the matter? You're all white," her mother said.

Laura told them about the accident. "He's in a coma." Her voice broke.

"Jesus Christ, another disaster. What's going on here?" Her father got up and pulled out the car keys from his pocket. He looked at them, then took Laura by the arm. "Come on, I'll drive you, you're too upset. Which hospital?"

"Want me to come along, too?" her mother asked.

"No, it's okay, Mama."

Her mother gave her a hug. "Try not to worry. He's going to be okay."

Laura nodded and rushed after her father. As they climbed into the old Fiat, Laura's mind swirled. "Put your seat belt on," she heard her father say. She snapped the belt into the buckle. Feeling his eyes on her, she turned to him. He put his hand on her shoulder. "You seemed to like this man quite a lot, huh?"

Laura nodded. "I guess more than I realized."

"Well, let's just hope he's going to be all right." He started the car.

The drive to the hospital in Locarno took only half an hour. They parked the car and went inside. The nurse at the critical-care unit asked for their names. "I only have your name here," she said to Laura, then glanced at Andreas.

"I'm her father, I just drove her here. I don't need to go in."

"That's fine." The nurse led them to the room. She pointed at a chair outside. Her father squeezed Laura's shoulder and sat down.

Laura stepped into the small intensive-care room. An older man who resembled Enrico sat on a chair next to a bed where Stefano was lying. Laura was shocked when she saw how pale Stefano was. His head was bandaged, one leg in a cast was propped up on the bed, and tubes were attached to his nose and body. The man got up and gave a weak smile. "You must be Laura," he said. "Enrico told me. I'm Stefano's father."

They shook hands and the man pointed at a chair. Laura sat down. "How is he?"

His father sighed. "The doctors are optimistic," he said. "There doesn't seem to be permanent injuries to the brain, but of course there are no guarantees."

"I had such a shock," Laura said.

"Yes." His father nodded. The two talked for a while. Laura kept glancing at Stefano, who continued to breathe into the tube with a hissing sound. He seemed unfamiliar to her now, and Laura realized she barely knew him. Yet, seeing him so helpless, she wanted to hug and hold him. She got up and stepped next to the bed, then carefully touched his forehead. There was a slight flutter of his eyelids. She glanced at his father, who nodded.

"Yeah, his eyes move a lot. I always think he's going to wake up any moment." His father sighed.

"Well, I'm going to pray for him." Laura was surprised at her own words. She didn't consider herself very religious and couldn't remember the last time she prayed. But the words didn't feel phony to her. "I guess I better go."

Stefano's father got up as well and accompanied her outside. Andreas was waiting by the window. The two men shook hands and introduced themselves.

"We'll let you know when there is any change," Stefano's father said and lightly touched Laura's arm.

On the way home, Laura and her father were quiet. Just before driving up the hill to their home, he glanced at her. "Strange how fast things change. I was upset about Tonio, and now, having a gay but healthy son feels like a blessing."

Laura nodded and blinked. Tears welled up in her eyes. Her father parked the car, then touched Laura's cheek. "He'll be fine."

An hour later, Laura got a phone call from Stefano's father. Stefano had woken up. He was still weak but lucid and the doctor felt he was going to make a full recovery.

"He came to about fifteen minutes after you left," his father said. "Your visit must have done it." His voice sounded overjoyed. "He was disappointed that he didn't get to see you."

"I'll visit him tomorrow," Laura said, her heart beating fast.

"Good, by then he'll be out of intensive care," his father said.

Laura hung up the phone and shouted, "Yes." She was so relieved to hear that Stefano was going to be okay.

"Good news?" Tonio asked, as Laura came rushing out of her bedroom.

"Yes, thank God." Laura hugged Tonio and squeezed him so tight that he made a face.

"Ouch." He pushed her back a little. "Darn heavyweight," he mumbled. Laura, however, was so happy she didn't even react to Tonio's taunting. milk."

Chapter 10: Tonio

"Are you sure you feel good enough to cook for a whole group?" Tonio asked his mother. He helped her unpack the groceries. They had invited Mario and Stefano for dinner. Stefano had been released from the hospital a few days before. He was still wearing a cast on his leg but otherwise he had made a speedy recovery.

"I'm fine," Karla said. "I haven't been sick in a while. I prepared stuff ahead of time. I just need to heat up the lasagna, so there isn't that much to do. And Laura is coming to help."

"I can help as well," Tonio said.

"We'll be fine. You have to entertain the guests while we're in the kitchen."

Tonio nodded. "Yeah, I just hope Papa isn't going to act strange around Mario."

"Oh, he won't. You know him. He needs to blow up once in a while, but he'll behave." His mother gave him a reassuring smile, then put lettuce, olives, and tomatoes on the table and began to slice the tomatoes.

"Yeah, I know." Tonio sighed. "Anyway, I warned Mario not to take him seriously when he starts giving him the evil eye." It was Tonio's name for the way his father checked out people he didn't know or didn't trust yet. He would give them a measuring look, his eyes scrunched slightly, a vertical line forming between his eyebrows.

His mother chuckled. "Don't worry. Can you hand me the salad bowl, please?" She began to toss lettuce, tomatoes, olives, and artichoke hearts. "I just heard a car."

"Yeah, it's Laura," Tonio said as he glanced out the window. The woods nearby had donned their fall foliage. The tree in the courtyard was full of chestnuts, and in the small flower bed in the corner, orange chrysanthemums and yellow marigolds bloomed. Tonio watched as Laura helped Stefano out of the car. She handed him the crutches and the two made their way slowly toward the door. "Gee, she sure picked a gorgeous hunk," Tonio murmured. "They go well together. If they ever have any children, they'll be heavyweight champions."

"Tonio, behave yourself," his mother said. "They're both well-built and attractive."

"Oh, I agree. That's what I meant. Especially him." Tonio grinned. His mother looked at him and shook her head, but her eyes showed a humorous spark. *At least she isn't all bent out of shape about me.*

"And here is Mario." Tonio went outside to greet the guests. Mario got out of his old silver Lancia and handed Tonio a bottle of wine.

"Wow, that's an expensive one." Tonio read the label on the bottle of Brunello wine from Tuscany.

"Only the best for you guys," Mario said and hugged Tonio.

After saying hello, the three men retired to the living room. Stefano limped to the sofa and Tonio put an additional pillow on it, so Stefano could prop up his leg. Laura came in with a plate of appetizers—dried beef, salami, cheese, and bread. After pouring them all a glass of wine, she sat next to Stefano, who put his arm around her. Tonio sat on the floor in front of Mario's chair and leaned his back against Mario's legs.

"Hey, *uomo*, man, what happened to you?" Mario pointed at Stefano's cast.

"It's a long story," Stefano said, and proceeded to tell them about his accident.

Soon, an amiable conversation developed. After a while, Laura got up to help her mother with the meal. Tonio was watching her set the table in the dining nook when he heard his father's dark voice in the kitchen. His heartbeat sped up a little. He turned around as he felt Mario's hand on his shoulder. The two gave each other a quick smile.

When his father stood at the door to the living room, Tonio realized once again what an imposing figure he cut. He stood tall and his athletic body almost filled out the doorway. Tonio had never been afraid of him, knowing him to be a kind person. His occasional angry outbursts blew over, usually within minutes. Yet he had always been someone who instilled respect. He had punished his children only rarely, and never physically. He was fair, but there were certain rules they weren't allowed to break, and if they did, they knew the consequences. Most of the time, however, he was easygoing and loving.

However, that was before he found out his son loved boys. And Tonio couldn't help but feel that he had broken one of those unwritten rules: boys were supposed to date girls and vice versa.

That's why now, when his father's verdigris-green eyes lingered on him and Mario, he felt a lump in his throat. Andreas turned to Stefano and greeted him, asking how his leg was. Then he turned back and faced Mario, who had gotten up in the meantime. Mario stretched out his hand and gave one of his cheerful, charming smiles. Tonio scrambled up from the floor and stood next to him, his legs feeling weak.

There was a hint of something in his father's eyes that made Tonio uneasy. Andreas's face, however, stretched into a smile. "Great to meet you again," he said and shook hands with Mario.

At that moment, Laura came in, carrying the salad bowl, and Karla called from the kitchen that dinner was just about ready and told them to start with the salad.

"All right, guys, let's sit down," Andreas said and waved them at the table. He picked up one of Stefano's crutches, which had fallen to the floor, and handed it to him. Then he turned to Tonio, grabbed him by the arm, and gave him a friendly squeeze. Tonio was so relieved that his eyes welled up. He blinked and cleared his throat.

When everybody was seated at the table, Andreas took the bottle of wine Mario had brought. He looked at the label, then at Mario. "That's quite a vintage."

Mario smiled, blushing a little. "To be honest, I got it from my father's cellar. He has a whole collection. His Italian vendors sometimes give him stuff."

"What does your father do?" Stefano asked him.

"He owns a fashion store in Lugano," Mario said. "Men's fashion."

"Are you going to take over once your dad retires?" Laura asked.

"That will take a while. I don't think my father will be ready to kick back anytime soon. He's a workaholic." Mario smiled. "But he owns a second, smaller store, just kind of a boutique. He wants me to run that store once I'm done with school. I'm looking for a partner, hint, hint." He poked Tonio in the ribs.

Tonio glanced at Mario, then at his parents.

"That would be great," his mother said as she passed the plate of spinach lasagna around.

"Quite a challenge," his father added. "But working for yourself has a lot of advantages."

"Well, Mario, I have similar plans," Stefano said. He had been quietly listening to the conversation. "I'm thinking about opening my own landscaping business. It's risky, especially when the economy isn't that great. But it beats working in a garden store. Boring, you never get to do your own thing."

"Yeah, you're right," Mario said. "I like to work for my father. He's pretty good about letting me make my own decisions. He doesn't hover over me all the time. But, still, I've been dreaming of having my own store."

"I'm trying to get Laura to join me," Stefano continued. "I could do the landscaping and she could create some sculptures to go with it. You know, there are still plenty of rich people who like that kind of thing."

"Oh, yeah?" Laura raised an eyebrow. "You haven't even asked me yet."

"Well, yes, I guess I'm getting ahead of myself. But wouldn't that be something for you?" Stefano put his hand on her shoulder.

"Hmm. Sounds intriguing." Laura glanced at him and took a sip of wine.

Andreas laughed out loud. "It looks like we're starting some extended family businesses."

Tonio's heart rate increased a bit. *Does that mean he considers Mario part of the family?*

Everybody laughed and the young people began to make plans. "If you start your own business, I can design some advertisement for it," Tonio told Stefano. Out of the corner of his eyes, he saw his mother and father smile at each other.

Chapter 11: Karla

"That was nice, wasn't it?" Karla said as Andreas stepped into the bedroom. She stood in front of the mirror, brushing her hair. Andreas had finished up in the kitchen so Karla could relax. The preparation and the dinner party with Tonio's and Laura's dates had tired her, but she felt content. She had to admit, she too had been nervous about Andreas's possible reaction to Tonio's boyfriend, but he had been on his best behavior.

"Laura said she might spend the night at Stefano's," she told Andreas. "I think that's a good idea. I don't like it when she drives around on her own late at night."

"Hmpf," Andreas mumbled, taking off his sweater and pants. "I guess so," he added. "She's taking him to the doctor tomorrow morning to have his cast removed. Looks like something is developing between the two. They've been together quite a lot ever since he was released from the hospital."

"Yes. I really hope it works out. She deserves a successful relationship after the disappointment with her last boyfriend." Karla put her brush down and opened the window a little. October had been sunny and warm during the day, but the evenings and nights were getting colder.

"I like Stefano. He is hardworking and steady," Andreas said.

"What about Mario?" Karla asked.

Andreas shrugged. "He seems okay. At least he's not some flaming homosexual."

"That's not much of a compliment. I think he's very nice."

"Yeah, maybe."

"You still haven't accepted the whole situation, have you?" Karla stood sideways and looked at her round belly in the mirror and patted it.

Andreas sighed. "I'm torn. Tonio obviously seems to like the guy. But I still hate the fact that it has to be a man, for Christ's sake." Andreas grabbed the down comforter on the bed and pulled it back. He stared at it for a while, then looked at Karla. "How do you feel about it?"

Karla took a deep breath and sat on the bed. "I've accepted it pretty much. I can see how much Tonio loves Mario. He's changed ever since he told us. He's become more relaxed, more open, more joyful. It's probably because he can finally be himself without having to hide and lie."

Another mumbling sound. Andreas plopped down on his side of the bed. "Yeah, I guess so."

"You know, Andreas, the only thing that bothers Tonio is your attitude. He wants so much for you to approve of him and Mario, to accept them."

"Look, I'm trying . . . . By the way, where are Tonio and Mario now? I didn't see Mario leave."

"They're probably still in the cottage next door, in Tonio's room."

"Is he going to spend the night, too?" Andreas wrinkled his forehead.

"Well, it probably would be better if he did. He drank some wine. They both have school tomorrow, so they could drive together in the morning."

"What the fuh . . . what is this anyway? A whorehouse?" Andreas scowled.

"Andreas, please." Karla glared at him, then turned her head toward the window. She heard voices outside talking and giggling. A car started and drove away.

"That was probably Mario leaving," Karla said. She got up and glanced outside. "Yes, and Tonio just went back inside." She turned around. "Happy now?" She got into bed and pulled the cover close. "I didn't realize you were such a homophobe."

"I'm not." Andreas sounded more subdued.

Karla glared at Andreas. "Oh, yeah? You didn't bat an eye when I mentioned Laura and Stefano spending the night together. Is Stefano's place a whorehouse now, too?"

"It's hardly the same, is it?"

"It's two people loving each other. What's the difference if it's a man and a woman or two men? You know, all Tonio wants is to be accepted the way he is. He's not a murderer, he hasn't committed any crimes. He loves someone. Why can't you give him a chance?" Karla lay down, pulled up the cover, and turned her back to him. She heard him sigh. He turned off the light and stretched out next to her. She felt his hand on her arm and stiffened.

"Look, Karla, I'm sorry. I love Tonio, no matter what. In time, I may see his relationship with Mario the same way you do. Right now, I'm just worried about him. I'm worried sick about his life, what's going to happen to him. And . . ." His voice broke.

Karla's anger dissipated. She turned around and searched for his face in the dark. She was shocked when she felt the tears. "I'm sorry, Andreas."

"It's okay," he mumbled.

She heard him rip a tissue out of the box and blow his nose, then felt his arm on her shoulder.

"You're tired?" he whispered.

"A little," she said. "But not too tired." She touched his chest and reached her hand underneath his pajama top, rubbing his skin. "Let's leave our almost-grown children to live their own lives. We have to concentrate on the next one." She took his hand and guided it to her belly. He pulled her close and kissed her. There was still a touch of moisture on his cheeks."

Chapter 12: Laura

It was dark when Laura drove Stefano home. She had been to Stefano's place a couple of times since he had been released from the hospital but had never stayed overnight. She was a little hesitant at first, not sure if spending the night might lead to more than sleeping, and not sure she was ready for more. But part of her was looking forward to getting closer to him, whatever that meant in this case.

When she started the car, Stefano bent over and kissed her on the cheek. "Thanks for the invitation. Your family is great."

"Yeah, it was fun," Laura said. "I'm so happy Mario got invited, too. I guess my father is slowly coping with the situation."

"About Tonio being gay?"

"Yeah, he still has a hard time accepting it."

"You know, my father would have a hard time as well," Stefano said. "Their generation is just not that comfortable with it."

"My mom is much more relaxed."

"I like Tonio and Mario seems to be a very responsible guy," Stefano said. "They don't strike me as the typical homosexuals, you know, the ones that really show it."

Laura glanced at him. "You seem to imply that as long as you can't tell it's okay."

"Oh no, I didn't mean it that way," Stefano protested. He was quiet for a while. "Well, I guess you're right. Why shouldn't they show it?"

"I think we all have certain prejudices," Laura said.

"Well, anyway, it was a fun evening. Your mother sure is a wonderful cook."

Laura smiled. "Yes, cooking is one of her favorite things, aside from painting."

"I saw some of her paintings in the house. Great stuff, particularly those colorful ones. I'd like to see more."

"She has an exhibition coming up in a gallery in Lugano. And there are always some paintings in her usual gallery in Locarno. I can take you there."

"Great. God, I'll be so glad when this cast is off and I can live a normal life again. Are you sure you're all right taking me to the doctor tomorrow? What about work?"

"My dad gave me the morning off, so it's no problem."

Stefano grinned. "That's one of the advantages of working for your father, I guess."

"Well, I don't know. He usually doesn't cut me any slack. He made that clear when he hired me. 'Now, Laura,' he said. 'I'm going to treat you like I would any employee,'" Laura said, imitating her father's throaty voice. "The funny thing is he doesn't have any other employees, so I didn't know what that meant. He's great, though, he treats me more like a partner than an employee."

After Laura had finished her apprenticeship at an outfit in the German part of the country, she wanted to move back to the Ticino. This was just at the time her father needed someone to help him with his stonemason business since he worked in two places now. He invited her to work for him for a couple of years, but told her she would eventually need to spread her wings and gain experience elsewhere. For the time being, however, Laura was happy with the arrangement. She had always been close to her father, and had worked with him even as a child. Besides, she got to work on many different projects. He gave her as much responsibility as she was willing to take on.

"We're a pretty good team," Laura added.

"Well, talking about a team. I was serious when I suggested my landscaping business," Stefano said. "I mean, I'm not trying to steal you away from your father and it probably wouldn't be for a while. I might start it part-time, do some landscaping and have you create a few sculptures."

"It sounds interesting," Laura said. "Sure, I'd love to do it. Do you have anything specific in mind?"

"I have a few leads," Stefano said. "It may take a while for them to materialize."

Laura drove the car up the driveway to Stefano's place. He lived in a guest house behind his father and stepmother's home in the town of Maggia. As he had told Laura, his parents let him live there rent-free so he could put money aside for his landscaping venture. In turn, they got a cheap and reliable handyman.

After parking the car, Laura got out and handed Stefano the crutches. By now he was pretty good at using them. He was no longer a danger to people around him, as he had been at first. He had almost caused another accident when an older lady stumbled over one of the crutches, which he had held too far away from him. Fortunately, Laura had been able to catch the woman before she fell. Aside from a few angry glances from the lady and a lecture on how to behave on the street, there had been no further repercussions. "I've always been a klutz," Stefano had said. "And these stupid sticks don't exactly help."

Inside the house, Stefano sat on the sofa, lifted the leg with the cast, and stretched it out on the pillow. He rubbed his thigh and grimaced.

"Does it hurt?" Laura asked.

"Yeah, a little. Not the part under the cast but the thigh muscles. They have to do a lot of work, lifting and moving the cast," he said.

"Shall I make us some tea or something?" she asked.

"That would be great. I have some of this new kind of tea—well, new for me. I can't remember what it's called, rowbush or something."

Laura smiled. "You mean, *rooibos*?"

"Yeah, I guess so. It's pretty good. It's in the cabinet to the right of the sink, and the teapot is in the sink. Oh, sorry, there are some dirty dishes there."

"Don't worry, I'll take care of it. You just relax." Laura went into the kitchen.

"Sounds good. It's nice to have a woman in the house," Stefano said.

"Hey, don't get used to it. Once you're on your legs again—I mean, on both legs—it's going to be the other way round. You're going to serve me," Laura said jokingly.

"Gee, these modern girls. Well, I might as well enjoy it while it lasts."

Laura turned on the electric water pot and washed the few dishes. She found the tea and some cookies, poured the boiling water over the tea, and carried the dishes into the living room. While waiting for the tea to steep, she looked through the window at the main house and the large flower bed in front of it. The garden was beautiful, even with most of the summer blooms gone. There was an assortment of different flowers and shrubs—chrysanthemums, sneezeweed, goldenrod, and stonecrop—next to a few small trees.

"Beautiful garden," she said, as she turned around and poured the tea.

"Oh, that's nothing right now. I haven't had time to keep it up." Stefano waved his hand in a dismissive gesture.

"Still beautiful. It must be gorgeous in summer and spring," Laura said.

"Yeah, it looks pretty colorful then." He took a sip of tea. "You know those large canvasses your mother painted, the colorful ones? Now, I know one reason I loved them so much. Reminded me of my garden," Stefano said.

"That's interesting, isn't it?" Laura said.

"Yes, now all that's missing is a beautiful stone sculpture," Stefano said and winked at her. He stretched out his hand and tried to put the teacup on the coffee table.

Laura took the cup and set it down. "You're serious about that, aren't you?"

"Absolutely." Stefano moved his casted leg off the sofa and groaned as he stretched it out in front of him.

Laura touched his thigh and began to massage it lightly. "Boy, your muscles *are* tense, all knotty."

"Yeah," he moaned, leaning his head against the backrest. "Don't stop. This feels so good."

Laura watched his face while she continued to knead his muscles. Relaxed and with his eyes closed, a curl of his brown hair falling onto his forehead, he looked boyish and innocent. A feeling of warmth spread through her chest. After a few seconds, he opened his eyes and put his arm around her. He pulled her close and hugged her tight. She closed her eyes, and when she opened them again, his face was next to hers. They kissed, and his kiss was anything but boyish. It was a man's kiss, tender, hard, and passionate. Laura, flooded by desire, wrapped her arms around him. Feeling an intense pressure and pain in her leg, she yelped. Stefano almost crushed her with his cast. At the same time, he moaned in pain and held his leg. They both sat up and burst out laughing, rubbing their legs.

"Darn it," Stefano said. "So much for passion. I think we'll have to wait with this until this stupid piece of cement comes off. Sorry about hurting you."

"It's okay. I forgot about the cast." Laura brushed her disheveled hair out of her face.

They sat on the sofa, their arms around each other. Stefano touched Laura's cheek. "I really want to make love to you, but—"

"It's okay, Stefano. We can wait." Although Laura was somewhat unsettled by the abrupt end of their first attempt at lovemaking, she was also a little relieved. She was aroused, but her mind still sent out a few warning signs. She felt she had rushed into her last relationship and had been hurt and disappointed. She took a deep breath. "We better get some sleep. It's already past one."

"Yeah, you're right," Stefano sighed. "It's going to take old gimp here a while to get ready in the morning."

"Where do I sleep?" Laura looked around the living room.

"Well, I'd love for us to sleep together in the same bed, but I'm afraid I might inadvertently turn around and seriously injure you with my lethal weapon." He grinned. "I mean, of course, the cast, not my other weapon."

Laura shook her head and laughed. "I can sleep on the couch here. It's okay."

"Oh no, you can sleep in my bed. I'll sleep on the couch."

"No way, you're the injured one. I want you to be as comfortable as possible. I don't mind at all sleeping here."

After some back and forth as to who would sleep where, Laura was lying on the sofa with a pillow and a warm down comforter. At that moment, the full moon peeked into the living room. Laura got up and stood by the window, watching the trees, bushes, and plants gleam in the muted silvery light. She took a deep breath and went back to the sofa. Trying to find sleep, she remembered a story her mother had told her, how at first she had been afraid to get too deeply involved with Laura's father. Karla had lost her mother as a child, had grown up a semi-orphan with a father far away, and those losses had haunted her far into adulthood. And now, they were still together, they had weathered all kinds of storms, and they still loved each other. "Sometimes you just have to take a chance," Laura murmured.

Chapter 13: Andreas

Andreas watched as Laura added the finishing touches to a clay sculpture. It was her first work for a landscaping project Stefano had secured. A wealthy man and his wife had bought and renovated an old villa above Ascona, a resort town in the canton Ticino, and wanted their property landscaped. The owner happened to be a patron of the arts and had agreed to buy a couple of sculptures as well.

The past two weeks Laura had been up until late at night, designing and modeling. Andreas knew she was nervous; this was her first paid independent job and she wanted to make a good impression. He had kept her company, in case she needed help or advice.

"Time for a break," he said, as she put down her carving tool and sat back. She wrinkled her forehead and narrowed her eyes, studying the finished sculpture. Andreas smiled as he recognized his own features in her. Karla kept remarking that they had the same expression on their faces whenever they looked at something carefully or critically.

Watching his daughter so focused on her art made him feel warm inside. She had made a leap in her development as an artist ever since she had taken Enrico's workshop in Peccia. As a young girl, she had loved to work with granite and gneiss and her sculptures had been rough and unformed but had shown promise because of their expressive quality.

After her workshop, she had become more interested in working with softer stone and more pliable materials. The forms of her sculptures had become softer, too, more rounded and curved rather than angular—more feminine, Andreas felt.

The sculpture she had just finished was a clay model of a mermaid-like form, a woman's body with a fish head. She had reversed the traditional picture of a mermaid. It was an intriguing and interesting image. Once it was dry, she would have it cast in bronze.

"Interesting motif. It will look great in bronze," Andreas said, pointing at the sculpture, and sat next to her.

"Thanks." Laura smiled and her cheeks showed a healthy flush. "You think it will do?"

"Honey, it will more than do." Andreas put his arm around her and hugged her. He loved to see her happy. And she was clearly happy with her new boyfriend and her new work. Although she still officially worked for him, Andreas encouraged her to do more of her own work. She could use all his tools and his workspace.

"I know you once said you wanted to take over the tombstone business," he had told her the other day. "I would love it if you did. But I don't want to force you. I'd much rather you did your own thing. I want you to branch out and to explore other opportunities as well. And if you decide you want to do something else, I have no problems with it. I'm not married to my business."

Looking at her work, Andreas immediately saw the progress she had made from her early attempts at sculpting to a more mature artistry. She was only nineteen and had plenty of time to develop her craft, but the signs of the future artist were visible in the composition and the way she merged material with form.

Andreas was proud of her. Laura had not been an easy child, being stubborn and a real tomboy. But she had developed into a sensitive and loving young woman. Although Andreas always believed he loved both his children the same, it had been obvious from the moment Laura was born that a special bond existed between the two. Laura had been a daddy's girl. Tonio, on the other hand, had been closer to Karla. Even as a toddler, Laura had been a fixture in her father's workspace, whereas Tonio had scribbled and painted next to his mother in her studio.

Tonio. Andreas sighed. The thought of his son's sexual orientation still weighed heavily on his mind. He wanted to accept Tonio the way he was and there were days he thought he had. Then anger and despair erupted and clouded his better judgment again.

Chapter 14: Tonio

It went so fast that Tonio didn't realize what had happened. He heard a thudding sound, then Mario almost lost his balance. He held on to the wall of the building they were passing to steady himself. Tonio turned around and watched as two tall, burly guys were about to turn the corner. One of them, the fatter one, made an obscene gesture and mouthed the word *finocchi*, "faggots."

"Are you hurt?" Tonio asked.

Mario was rubbing his arm but shook his head. "No big deal." He turned around, but the guys had already disappeared.

"Who are they?" Tonio asked.

Mario shook his head. "No idea."

"They just slugged you. They said 'faggots.' They must know us."

"No, they may have just seen us somewhere together or heard about us. People gossip, you know. Lots of people know I'm gay. Some don't like it."

"So they just hit you without any reason?"

"Yep, it happens sometimes." Mario kept on rubbing his arm.

"You don't care?" Tonio was getting irritated about Mario's nonchalant attitude. "You just let them slug you?"

Mario put his hand on Tonio's shoulder. "Tonio, you're a sweet guy but very naive. You better get used to a few slurs or a push once in a while. Be grateful that you don't get clobbered and beaten up by some thugs."

Tonio stopped and shook his head. "I guess that's one of the reasons my father worries about me."

They arrived at a coffee shop frequented by young homosexuals. The owner was gay and many of his friends hung out there, reading, writing, doing homework, chatting, as well as looking for possible mates. It was a low-key place with none of the glamour of some of the gay bars. Tonio and Mario came here sometimes after class to meet some of their other friends or simply to relax with a cup of coffee. Right then, the place was almost empty.

Fred, the owner, came up to them, put a plate of brownies on the table, and sat next to them. "Fresh, on the house," he said. He slapped Mario on the back and briefly touched Tonio's shoulder. "How are things?"

"Good. Can't complain. And you?" Mario said.

"Okay," Fred said. "We had some trouble here the other day. Some idiots came in and started insulting my guests. Called the police, but they were gone before the officer arrived."

Tonio stared at him. "I bet these were the assholes who hit Mario."

Fred, an elegant young man with green and purple strands in his blond hair, raised an eyebrow and glanced at Mario.

"One of them just punched me when they walked by," Mario said.

"Be careful," Fred said. "They can be nasty when they're drunk."

"I don't get it. He behaves as if nothing happened." Heat flooded Tonio's face and he stared at Mario.

Mario gave a quick smile. "Tonio, nothing really happened. I may have a bruise on my gorgeous body, that's all. I hope you don't mind." He leered at Tonio, jokingly.

This did nothing to calm Tonio's increasing anger. "What the hell? He could've killed you. How do you know what he's going to do next time you run into him?"

Mario scrunched his forehead. "Do you really think it would have been better if I had reacted, even punched him back? Man, you're more naive than I thought. Don't you realize he was just waiting for me to react so he'd have a reason to really beat me up? Tonio, you better wise up and learn some basic stuff pretty fast, or I'll have to visit you at the hospital, or worse, pick up your body at the morgue."

Fred chuckled. "Calm down, guys. Mario is right. Most of the time, guys like that are angry at something else. They look for a scapegoat and we are welcome targets. In general, people are more tolerant of us, but we're still outsiders."

"I just can't accept that it's okay for someone to hit us although we haven't done anything wrong. Does that mean we don't have the right to fight back?"

Fred and Mario looked at each other, then at Tonio. Tonio felt like a kid being placated by two adults. He was angry and sad at the same time. He blinked, trying to squeeze back the tears that had gathered in the corners of his eyes. As had often been the case over the past few weeks, he became painfully aware that, by admitting who he was, he freed himself from hypocrisy but also became more vulnerable.

Fred touched his shoulder and gave him a gentle squeeze. "Tonio, we are fighting back. But not by beating up a bunch of ignorant fools. We fight where it matters. We fight for our rights on a higher level. And we have achieved quite a lot. We are trying to raise people's awareness, so they see us as human beings who love and have the right to be loved. We fight against discrimination. It's a long fight and there will be setbacks, but this is a fight worth some sacrifices. You don't want to waste your energy battling a bunch of lowlifes. These people hate anybody who is different—blacks, Jews, gays or lesbians. They are usually a lost cause and the best thing you can do is avoid them."

Tonio took a deep breath. "I guess you're right. I just get furious sometimes, it's just not fair."

"True," Mario said. "Then again, who said life was fair? Look around you. Watch the news. We are not the only ones who sometimes have a hard time."

Chapter 15: Karla

"He doesn't seem to understand that I want to continue working here," Karla said to her friend Silvia, who owned one of the art galleries in the old part of Locarno. They were sitting at a table in a small room in the back of the place.

For the past years, Karla had been working part-time at the gallery where her paintings were exhibited on a regular basis. Silvia, a woman in her sixties, was semiretired and Karla helped her run the place.

"I can take the baby with me when Andreas doesn't have time to watch her. I'm sure it'll work out. I don't see why he gets so bent out of shape about it."

"Her?" Silvia raised an eyebrow. "You know it's a girl?"

Karla nodded. "Yeah, I had an ultrasound." She put her hand on her belly and smiled.

"He has always been very supportive of your career as a painter. I'm sure he doesn't expect you to only be a mother." Silvia brushed back a strand of grey hair, which had escaped her loosely tied bun. She got up, poured some tea, and put two cups on the table.

"He *is* supportive of my painting. He wants me to stay home so I have enough time to paint, besides taking care of the baby. He feels I'm wasting my time working here. What he doesn't understand is that I need the contact with other people, having friends outside of the house. Besides, I can paint here as well."

Karla had been painting in a room adjacent to the main gallery during the days she worked there.

"I just can't imagine staying home all day," she said with a sigh. "I'd feel isolated. It was okay when Laura and Tonio were little. But I've changed. And we can certainly use the extra money, particularly now with another child on the way."

"Well, I wouldn't worry too much," Silvia said. "Wait until the baby is here and things will work out. I don't mind if you take some time off or cut back on your hours. I'm flexible."

"I know, but it just irks me that he's so stubborn. He's been in a strange mood anyway lately."

"What's wrong?" Silvia asked.

"I think he's still upset about Tonio. He doesn't admit it, but I can feel it."

Silvia smiled. "He's worried about him. Just give him time."

"He can be such a grumpy old man sometimes." Karla sighed and looked outside, where it was snowing lightly. It was December, three weeks before Christmas. The temperatures had been below freezing for the past couple of days.

"Speaking of the devil," she muttered. The door made a screeching sound when it opened.

Andreas stomped his boots on the stairs and entered. He clapped his gloved hands and a white cloud rose in front of his face. "*Porca miseria*. It's cold, damn it," he said. He smiled at Silvia, then turned to Karla and gave her a cautious look. "Hello."

Karla glanced at him but didn't say anything. They had had an argument that morning, which had ended with Andreas slamming the door and leaving. She was still irritated at his childish behavior.

Andreas stepped next to her and pointed at the check on the table in front of her. "Sold a painting?"

Karla nodded, grabbed the check, and put it in her purse.

"Sorry about this morning," he murmured.

"Yeah, well . . ." She crossed her arms in front of her chest. She wasn't ready to absolve him yet.

"We had an . . . a discussion about Karla working here after the baby is born," Andreas said to Silvia.

"A discussion?" Karla glowered at him. "You yelled at me and slammed the door. I don't call that a *discussion*."

"I did apologize."

Silvia stepped next to them. "Why don't we talk about this in peace?" She turned to Andreas. "Want some coffee?"

Andreas nodded. "Yeah, I could go for some."

"It'll make him even crankier," Karla said with a sneer.

"Come on, honey, don't be like that."

"Okay, you two, calm down." Silvia turned on the coffee machine and let the fragrant dark liquid pour into a small cup. She put it in front of Andreas and poured Karla another cup of tea.

Karla sighed and looked longingly at the cup of coffee. Andreas pushed it toward her. "Have some. One sip won't hurt the baby." He obviously was trying to restore peace.

Karla shook her head. "No, I had my cup in the morning. Tea is okay. But thanks anyway." Since she was past the danger of a miscarriage, she allowed herself a cup of coffee in the morning.

"All right," Silvia said. "Why don't we just wait until the baby is here? Karla, you definitely need to take the first couple of months off. And then let's see how it goes."

"I just don't want her to overdo it and neglect her painting," Andreas said.

"Yeah, and you're probably trying to get out of changing diapers," Karla said, then felt sorry because she knew it was unfair.

"Jesus, you're unfair," Andreas echoed her feelings. "Have I ever complained about changing diapers?" Andreas's facial color deepened. He was about to blow up again.

"Sorry, I didn't mean that," Karla said ruefully. "I just don't want to stay home all day."

"Nobody is talking about staying home all day. I'll help out. Laura offered to babysit once in a while," Andreas said. "Lena said she'd help."

"I think you're putting the cart before the horse," Silvia said. "We don't need to make a decision now. Let's wait and see."

"Okay, let's wait, then," Karla said. She was tired of the constant arguments.

"Fine with me." Andreas got up. He looked at Karla. "I'm going to the store. Want me to get something?"

"No, I'm good," Karla said.

Andreas bent down to kiss her and she let him. He squeezed her shoulder and gave a quick smile. Karla sighed. *Why do we even argue?* "Love you," she said quietly.

"Love you, too." He smiled more widely, gave Silvia a hug, and walked toward the door in his leisurely gait.

After he was gone, Silvia and Karla looked at each other. "He's a great guy. You're lucky," Silvia said. Her face saddened. Richard, her husband, had died two years before and Silvia still longed for him.

"Yeah, I know." Karla got up and hugged her friend.

Chapter 16: Andreas

Andreas and Karla were just about to fall asleep when the phone rang. Andreas sat up and checked the time on the alarm clock—eleven o'clock. He reached for the phone and looked at the display, surprised. It showed Laura's cell-phone number.

Laura was staying overnight with a girlfriend of hers in Lugano and Tonio was with Mario at the movies in the same city. Tonio should be on his way home.

"Papa, there was an accident." Laura's voice sounded shaky.

Andreas's heart clenched. "What happened?"

"Tonio. He's in the hospital. Someone . . . there was a fight."

"What?" Andreas jumped out of bed.

Karla sat up and stared at him with large eyes. "What's the matter?"

Andreas's breath came in spurts. "Where? Where is he?"

"At the Ospedale Civico in Lugano, the one at Via Tesserete. I'm already here. Papa, he's going to be okay. He looks pretty bad, black eye and bruises and possibly a couple of broken ribs, but—"

"Where? Which room?"

"I'll wait for you outside the hospital."

"How did *you* find out?" Andreas asked. "Why didn't they call us?"

"Mario had my cell-phone number and called me. He's hurt, too, but not too badly. I guess a passerby witnessed the fight and called the police."

"We'll be there right away." Andreas put the phone down and pulled on his pants and a pullover.

"What's the matter?" Karla shrieked. She was already up, standing next to the bed and holding on to the headboard.

Andreas tried to talk in a calm voice, not wanting to upset Karla even more. "Tonio had an accident. He's going to be okay, though, Laura said. Something about a fight."

"A fight?" Karla ripped off her pajamas and grabbed her sweatpants and jacket.

"I don't know anything more. He's in the hospital in Lugano. Come on." He led Karla, who was six months pregnant, by the arm.

The drive to Lugano seemed to take forever, in spite of the fact that Andreas drove far above the speed limit and ran a few stoplights when there was no traffic. His mind was spinning. *A fight?* Tonio wasn't the kind of boy who got into fights.

The car came to a screeching halt at the hospital. They parked outside and rushed to the door. Laura was waiting for them. She was pale but looked fairly calm.

"What's the matter, Laura?" Karla was almost in tears.

"Where is he?" Andreas asked.

"Calm down," Laura said. She took Karla's arm and the three of them went to the elevator.

Inside, Andreas silently cursed the elevator's slow performance. It halted on several floors, although only a few nurses got off and on at this late hour. Andreas glowered at them, wishing them to hell for holding them up. He took a deep breath, trying to calm his frazzled nerves. When they finally arrived at their floor, he almost knocked down the nurse who stepped out of the elevator in front of him. "*Scusa*," he mumbled and charged down the hall.

"Room 512," Laura called and walked after him, holding Karla's hand.

Andreas ripped the door open and stepped inside. The picture he saw there almost made him gag. Tonio was sitting on the bed. His face was bruised, one eye partially shut, and he had a deep cut on his forehead. Andreas sat next to him and carefully touched his face.

When Karla saw him, she burst into tears. "Oh, my poor baby." She sat on the other side of Tonio and wrapped her arms around him.

"Careful, Mama. I have two cracked ribs." Tonio gave a weak smile, although a tear was sliding down his bruised cheek.

"Who did this?" Andreas's voice sounded hoarse.

"Three assholes," a voice said. Andreas looked up. Mario and a man in a white coat with x-rays in his hands, obviously a doctor, stepped into the room. Mario had some bruises on his face as well, but didn't seem to be that badly hurt.

Rage cursed through Andreas. *Why Tonio?* He got up and glared at Mario. "I want to know what happened." His voice cracked.

"We were on the way to the train station. When we entered the underpass, we saw the three guys who had insulted us once before. They were sitting in the underpass, drinking. When they saw us, they got up and started yelling at us. And the next thing we knew, they were beating up on us. We tried to run, but there was no way." Mario exhaled and grimaced. "They just clobbered us. Fortunately, two passengers came walking down the underpass and the jerks took off. One of the passengers had a cell phone and called the ambulance."

"Do you know the guys?" Andreas asked.

The doctor came forward with the x-rays. "Mr. and Mrs. O'Reilly?"

"Yes," Andreas and Karla both said.

"What's the matter?" Andreas yelled at him, then lowered his voice. "Sorry."

"I understand you're upset, but I have good news. Aside from two cracked ribs, your son doesn't seem to have any internal injuries. I'd like to keep him overnight, just to make sure. But I'm convinced he'll make a full recovery. The ribs will take several weeks to fully heal, so he'll be quite sore for a while, but we can give him something for the pain." The doctor shook hands with Andreas and Karla. He turned to Tonio. "How are you feeling?"

Tonio nodded. "Okay, I guess . . . under the circumstances," he said in a low voice. "At least I'm still alive."

The doctor faced Andreas and Karla. "His friend told me what happened. I called the police and I hope they catch the culprits."

Andreas turned to Tonio. "Why did they attack *you*?"

Tonio shrugged, then held his arm and grimaced in pain. "They don't like gays."

Andreas pointed his finger at Mario. "I want to talk to you. Outside." Mario took a step back and nodded hesitantly. Andreas realized he must present a threatening picture.

"Papa," Tonio begged. "Don't take it out on Mario. It's not his fault. Without his help, it would have been worse."

"I'm not taking it out on Mario. I just want to talk to him." Andreas sat on the bed. He gently touched Tonio's bruised face and kissed him on the forehead. "The guys who did this to you are going to get it. Get into bed and try to relax." Andreas stood up and glanced at Karla and Laura. "I'll be back."

"Where are you going?" Laura asked.

Karla got up and took his arm. "You're not going to do anything stupid, are you?"

Andreas shook her hand off. "Don't worry." He motioned to Mario to follow him and they both left the room. Outside in the hallway, he turned to Mario. "Do you know the guys? Do you know any of them? Names? Where they live?"

"Shhh," a voice said down the hallway. "This is a hospital. Please keep your voices down." A nurse gave them a stern look.

"Let's go outside." Andreas took Mario by the arm and pulled him toward the elevator.

"Mr. O'Reilly." Mario made a weak attempt to stop Andreas, but Andreas ignored him. They took the elevator to the ground floor. The light was dimmed downstairs. The hospital was closed except for emergencies.

Outside, Andreas took a deep breath and faced Mario again. "Do you know them?"

Mario shook his head. "I don't know them personally. One of them has been causing trouble in the coffee shop we go to sometimes. He comes in and shouts insults, then leaves."

"Do you know where he lives? They're not getting away with this. If the police don't take care of them, I will." Getting impatient again, Andreas grabbed Mario by the shoulder.

Mario flinched. "Ouch." He held his shoulder. "I—" Mario's voice broke, his face turned even paler, and his shoulders slumped. He began to tremble and burst into tears. "Mr. O'Reilly, it's late . . . I need to go home . . . I feel horrible. I don't know anything," he uttered in between sobs.

Seeing the young man's miserable face—the bruise under his eye, the tears—Andreas's rage dissipated. He pulled Mario close and patted his back.

"I'm sorry, I don't know what I'm doing. I'm not myself today. All this . . . was a little much." Andreas took a deep breath. "Let me take you home. Where are you going to stay tonight? With your parents?"

Mario shook his head. "No. I live by myself. My parents are gone for the week. A vacation."

"Do they know what happened?"

"No, I don't want to tell them before they get back. I don't want to spoil their vacation."

"Okay." Andreas gently tapped Mario on the shoulder. "I don't want you to stay by yourself tonight. Tell you what. We'll drive to your place, you pick up a few items, and then come with us. You can sleep in Tonio's room."

Mario swallowed and brushed away a tear. "What about school tomorrow? I have an early class."

"Skip the class, for heaven's sake. You're ill. Skipping one class won't kill you, will it? And if you insist on going, I'll take you to school. I have to pick Tonio up tomorrow anyway. Come on."

"Okay. Thanks, Mr. O'Reilly."

"And stop calling me Mr. O'Reilly. I'm Andreas."

"Thanks, Mr. . . . I mean, Andreas." Mario gave a weak smile.

They went back up to get Laura and Karla. When they came into the room, Tonio was lying in bed propped up against a pillow.

"Thank God." Karla, who was sitting on the bed, jumped up. "I thought you were going to do something really stupid, the way you looked." She slapped Andreas's arm and gave Mario a careful hug.

"Mario is going to stay with us tonight. After what happened to them, he might have nightmares alone," Andreas said.

"Good thinking," Laura said. "You can stay in Tonio's room, and when you have a nightmare, I'm right there."

"Thanks, Mama Laura," Mario said, giving a quick smile.

"You can listen to my CDs. I have a bunch of new ones. Laura knows where they are." Tonio looked almost happy underneath his bandages.

At home, Karla asked Mario if he had eaten anything. He shook his head. "No, but I'm not really hungry."

"Well, I think you should have a little something. I'm going to warm up a bowl of soup, homemade minestrone," Karla said.

"And I'll make us a relaxing drink." Laura followed Karla into the kitchen.

Andreas and Mario sat on the sofa in the living room. Mario looked tired but a little more relaxed.

"I know you probably don't want to talk about it anymore, but I still don't know what really happened. How come they beat up on Tonio so much?" Andreas asked. "You don't seem to be that badly hurt."

Mario gave him a cautious look. "Tonio seems to have inherited some of your spirit."

"What do you mean?" Andreas glared at him.

"When they first began to insult us, I told Tonio to keep on walking. If we only made it through the underpass into the station restaurant, we'd be okay. They wouldn't dare to attack us inside. But Tonio, well, he turned around and told them to fuck off. They were just waiting for something like that. So they started beating him up. I really tried to help him, but they were just too strong . . ." Mario's voice faltered.

"It's okay, Mario. It's not your fault. Tonio obviously isn't very streetwise yet. But you got a point there. I probably would've reacted the same way. The difference is, I'm a little stronger than Tonio." He gave a short laugh.

Karla and Laura brought in the soup and four glasses. They all sat at the table.

"What the heck is this?" Andreas asked Laura, pointing at his glass.

"Try it," Laura said with a grin.

Andreas took a sip. It was hot and sweet and had a fair amount of alcohol in it. "Rum?" he asked.

"Yep. Tea spiked with sugar and rum. Will help us sleep." Laura handed a glass to Karla. "This is without the alcohol."

Mario finished his soup. "Thanks, you're such a good cook," he said to Karla. "And after this, I won't be awake enough to have nightmares." He took a sip of tea.

"That's the point," Laura said.

"I'm so glad you invited Mario," Karla said when she and Andreas were finally lying in bed.

Andreas sighed. "I couldn't help it. He looked so miserable. I was too hard on him." He felt Karla's hand on his face. "He's a decent guy."

"That's the first kind thing you said about him."

"Yeah, I guess so." Andreas chuckled. "I always thought Tonio took only after you. Now, I realize he inherited some of my qualities as well."

"Which ones?" Karla asked, snuggling up to him.

"He blows up at the wrong time." Andreas told Karla what Mario had said to him about the fight and Tonio's mouthing off to the bullies.

"Well, one thing is for sure," he added. "Tonio is going to take some martial-art lessons or boxing or something to toughen him up, even if I have to drag him there."

"Okay, but let him recover first," Karla said.

"Sure." Andreas scooted close to her and put his hand on her swollen belly. "To think that we'll have to worry about another one soon. At least it's a girl."

"You think a girl is going to be less trouble?"

"I hope so." After a pause, he said, "I still don't know what I'm going to do about those jerks. I really feel like giving them a taste of their own medicine."

"You're going to do no such thing," Karla said, alarmed. "You're going to let the police handle this. I don't want to end up with a dead husband or one in jail."

"That won't happen." Andreas yawned.

"Andreas, I mean it."

"All right, all right. Don't worry."

In spite of the late hour and his exhaustion, Andreas couldn't fall asleep. One of the scenarios he had worried about had happened. His gay son was a target for bullies and violent thugs, just because he was different. And there wasn't much Andreas could do except give him as much support as he could. Martial-art and self-defense lessons? Pepper spray? Andreas sighed. He slid to the edge of the bed and tried to get up without waking Karla.

"Where are you going?" she asked.

"Living room. Go back to sleep."

Andreas stood by the window and watched as the first signs of dawn trickled down from the ridge of the mountains. Feeling a movement behind him, he held out his hand. Karla put her arm around him. "What are we going to do?" he asked.

Karla hugged him. "I don't know, honey. Fortunately, this kind of thing doesn't happen a lot here. Let's hope it's just a single incident."

They stood by the window, their arms around each other. Most of the snow had melted. A patch of yellow crocuses in the flower bed in front of the house and the tiny buds on the hazel bush were the first harbingers of spring.

Andreas felt Karla shiver a little. He pulled her toward the sofa. They sat down and he grabbed a blanket and wrapped it around her.

"All we can do is love him," Karla said in a soft voice.

"Yes." He tensed his jaw. *But I'm going to do more than that.*

Chapter 17: Tonio

Mario grabbed Tonio by the hand and pulled him up the last stretch of a short, steep hill. Tonio groaned and bent over, holding his chest.

"I'm sorry," Mario said. "The ribs?"

Tonio nodded. "Yeah, any kind of wrong movement." He breathed gently in and out. "It's okay now."

Laura put a hand on his shoulder. "Want to rest?"

"Let's sit down for a while," Stefano said.

"How is your leg?" Laura asked.

"Okay. I can still feel it a little."

"Two injured guys, sounds like an outing of invalids." Mario grinned.

They all sat on a flat slab of granite next to the path. Below them, down in the valley, the morning fog began to lift and the meadows underneath were full of wildflowers. It was a glorious early-spring day.

They were on a leisurely hike on the Gardada, a mountain above the Maggia Valley. Stefano had planned the outing, since he needed to train the muscles in his injured leg. They had taken the cable car from Locarno and then walked along a mostly even path with only a few steep hills. It was a Saturday and the easy-to-reach mountain was a favorite tourist spot. They had left early in the morning and hoped to be able to beat the crowds.

Stefano turned to Tonio. "How are you doing? In general, I mean."

"Getting better," Tonio said.

"He's still scared. He doesn't want to go anywhere," Mario said.

"I still dream about the guy slugging me."

Tonio's physical wounds were healing. The bruises on his face had almost faded. The cracked ribs would take a few more weeks. The emotional hurt, however, was still there. He had nightmares, waking up soaked in sweat and with his heart thudding. The cocoon of his safe world he had grown up in had been crushed. He realized for the first time that there were people out there who hated him not for anything he had done but simply for who he was. His emotions ranged from depression to intense anger and fear. The one guy who had beaten him up the most had not been caught. The police suspected he had returned to Italy.

Since the day of the fight, Tonio hadn't been out at night. He and Mario spent a lot of time at the O'Reillys. With his family, Tonio felt safe.

"You need to get your self-confidence back," Laura said. "I know, it's easier said than done, but it's the only way."

"Yeah, yeah, everybody says that. I wonder how *you*'d feel in my position," Tonio grumbled.

"She's right, Tonio," Mario said and put his arm around him. "You got to snap out of this. You've been behaving like the living dead ever since. I suggest we start going out again. What about going to the coffee shop on Monday after class? It's at least a start."

"Are you kidding? That's where those guys started the whole mobbing thing."

"Tonio, they've been caught. There hasn't been a problem since."

"Except for the huge guy. He's still at large. No thanks." Tonio glared at Mario.

"He's gone, Tonio. What do you want to do? Hide at home with Mama and Papa the rest of your life?"

"Why not?" Tonio said in a defiant tone. "Sounds okay to me."

"Tonio, it was a single incident. We were at the wrong place at the wrong time. It could've happened to anybody."

"But it happened to *us*." Tonio clenched his jaw.

Mario threw up his hands. "For God's sake, then go on and play the victim. I think you like that role. What a wimp."

Tonio punched Mario so hard that his boyfriend almost fell off the stone they were sitting on. "Don't you call me a wimp," he screamed, tears of anger welling up in his eyes. The exertion sent a stabbing pain through his chest and he folded over with a groan.

"Come on, guys, easy now," Stefano said. "I don't think either of you is ready for another fistfight."

"Asshole," Tonio hissed.

"That's better," Mario said, rubbing his arm. "At least you're angry instead of feeling sorry for yourself."

"It's okay, Tonio. It's okay to feel bad, but Mario is right." Laura hugged him carefully. "We'll plan something. We'll all go out together to the movies, a play, or just dinner. You won't be alone."

"We'll be your bodyguards," Stefano said. "We'll show those guys." He got up, pounded his chest, and stamped his foot. "Ouch." Stefano held his injured leg.

"Yeah, great, some bodyguards. I can just see it." Tonio chortled, then grimaced and held his chest. "Darn, can't even laugh."

They all burst out laughing, except for Tonio, who suppressed the urge.

"Let's go, guys. I smell that prosciutto," Stefano said. "No more climbing. It's all flat from here on."

They walked along a trail through chestnut and birch forests, past beautiful stone formations and a small pond. The sun had dispersed the rest of the clouds and revealed Lake Maggiore at the bottom of the mountain, the Centovalli valley, and the Monte Rosa in the distance.

At the inn, they secured a table on the patio at the edge of the terrace. It was midmorning but the place was already filling up. After ordering a plate of salami, ham, cheese, bread; a jug of red wine; and a bottle of mineral water, they relaxed in the sun.

"This is the life," Mario said and put his arm around Tonio.

Tonio leaned his head against Mario's shoulder and closed his eyes. He inhaled the fresh mountain air and the scent of Mario's sweater and enjoyed the warm sun on his face. It was great to be out again. Here, on the sunny terrace of this mountain inn, among friends and relatives, he felt safe. The people around him were peaceful, families with children, young and older couples, having a good time, enjoying the food and the view. For the first time in weeks, he felt good and at peace again.

"Perhaps you're right," Tonio said and sat up. "Let's go to the coffee shop on Monday."

The waitress came with a large plate of cold meat, fresh dark bread, and butter. She poured them glasses of Merlot del Ticino, the wine of the area.

"That's the spirit," Mario said after the waitress had left. He toasted Tonio, who smiled. It felt unfamiliar at first, as if his facial features had frozen during the past weeks.

Chapter 18: Andreas

"I'm going to the coffee shop after school for a while," Tonio said as he tossed a few papers into his briefcase.

"Oh?" Andreas peered at him while sipping his coffee. "By yourself?"

"No, with Mario," Tonio said.

It was early Monday morning. Andreas and Tonio were getting ready to drive to Lugano. It was Andreas's day at the workshop in Lugano, so he would give Tonio a ride to his school.

"I'll take the train home or Mario is going to give me a ride," Tonio said. "That way you don't have to wait for me."

Andreas noticed the hesitation in Tonio's voice. He could tell Tonio was still afraid. This was the first time since his being beaten up that he dared to go somewhere after school.

"I'll wait for you, no problem," Andreas said.

"You don't mind?" Tonio seemed relieved.

"No, I'm behind with my work anyway. That way I can catch up."

A very pregnant Karla came into the kitchen, yawning and brushing her hair out of her face. She pushed the knob on the espresso machine and put a cup under the spout. "Well, how are my two favorite men this morning?" She hugged Tonio and gently massaged his rib cage. "How is my baby?"

Tonio rolled his eyes but smiled. "Please, Mama, get a hold of yourself."

Andreas grinned. "You're chipper this morning."

"I'm just happy it's spring." She patted her bulging belly. "Only one more month before this hump comes off. I may even be able to wear a bathing suit this summer again."

Andreas hugged her and smiled. "That's my girl." He kissed her and inhaled her light lavender scent. "New perfume?"

"Okay, lovebirds, we need to hit the road or I'm going to be late for class." Tonio brushed through his hair.

Andreas noticed the absence of the colorful strands in his hair. He also felt Tonio had been wearing less flashy outfits lately. It was unlike him; it seemed as though he wanted to blend in more. Andreas liked his somewhat more subdued look, but he was concerned about Tonio's state of mind. He seemed listless and lacked self-confidence. Andreas had been down on him for his occasional bad attitude, his talking back, his coming home after eleven during the week, ignoring his father's "curfew" as Tonio called it. Now, Andreas wished his son showed some of his earlier cockiness.

He turned to Karla. "We may be home late. Tonio is going out with Mario and I have some catching up to do."

"Are you going to be home for dinner?" Karla asked.

"Of course we will," Tonio said. "School is out at three o'clock today and we won't stay at the coffee shop very long."

"Well, you may want to do something else later, a movie or something?" Andreas was glad his son showed some initiative again.

Tonio shook his head. "No, just the coffee shop, that's enough."

"Well, all right," Karla said. "If you change your mind, give me a call." She gave Tonio a hug. "Have fun."

He pulled his mouth into a lopsided smile. "Thanks."

Andreas and Karla kissed goodbye and Andreas motioned at Tonio, who picked up his briefcase and strolled out the door. "About time he shows a little more pizzazz again," he whispered.

They got into the car and Andreas tried to start the Fiat. It died on him a couple of times, then gave a hesitant roar and began to roll down the hill. Andreas and Tonio looked at each other and grinned.

"I got to take it in this Saturday," Andreas said. "It needs a real overhaul."

"Why not get a new one? I think this old horse has seen its better days," Tonio said.

"We'll get a new one, but I want to hang on to this one as well. You'll soon take driving lessons and this would be a perfect set of wheels to practice on. Besides, Laura needs a car as well."

"I guess it's better than nothing," Tonio said in a mocking tone.

"Damn right it's better than nothing, you spoiled brat." Andreas peered at his son. *He is a little more argumentative again; I guess that's a good sign.*

It was quiet in the car for a while. They were driving on a narrow road along the Maggia. It had been raining quite a lot the past few weeks and the river, swollen from spring snowmelt, had turned into a raging current. Water tumbled across boulders, creating tiny waterfalls, and white foam jumped high up into the air.

"Thanks, Papa," Tonio murmured.

Andreas glanced at him. "For what?"

"For offering the car . . . and for waiting for me today."

Andreas put his hand on Tonio's shoulder and gave him a light squeeze. "I want you to feel better again."

"I'm getting there."

"Don't let those jerks ruin your life. Okay?"

Tonio shook his head. "No, I won't."

After dropping Tonio off at school, Andreas went to his workshop. He needed to finish several tombstones. The workshop was located in a fairly quiet side street. He unlocked the sturdy wooden door and left it open to air out the two large rooms. The scent of dry stone dust was displaced by the fragrance of freshly brewed coffee from the coffee shop next door.

A waiter stepped outside and waved at him. Andreas walked over and got a cup of coffee to go, then went back inside. After airing out the rooms, he closed the door and turned on the electric heater. Although they had had a few sunny, warm spring days, it was still chilly inside the stone buildings.

He spent the next few hours cutting and carving a tombstone. When he looked at the piece of paper with the name and dates of the deceased he was going to carve into the stone, he realized that the stone was for a young man. He had been killed in a motorcycle accident. Andreas remembered his father coming by and ordering the tombstone. In spite of the many years Andreas had been carving tombstones, he had never gotten used to the pain and sadness of a parent who had to bury his or her child. He couldn't help thinking of his own children and how impossible it would be for him to go through what these grieving parents had to go through. They somehow survived and moved on. He didn't know if he could handle it. Andreas put down the chisel and pulled the dust mask from his face.

It was difficult enough dealing with healthy children. He couldn't imagine how it would be if they got seriously ill or, God forbid, even died. He shook his head. Why was he thinking of all this right now? He sensed it had to do with Tonio and his trouble and his own difficulty dealing with his son being different.

He continued to chip away at the stone, then sat back again. Cutting and carving—that's what he had been doing all his adult life. Chipping away the surface of a piece of rock to uncover its inner self, its beauty, its intrinsic form.

Lately, he had had to do a lot of chipping away in his own life as well. Chipping away at the image he had of himself. He had always felt he was an open and tolerant and progressive person. He was old-fashioned and old-school in many ways, but he didn't see himself as biased. Having to deal with his son's homosexuality had made him aware that underneath the shiny surface of tolerance lay hidden a prejudiced being. He had nothing against gays, but he resented the fact that Tonio was gay. He still felt a certain hostility toward Mario, thinking he had seduced Tonio, that it was somehow his fault. He couldn't imagine what it meant being in love with another man. He shuddered inwardly at the thought of two men making love to each other. It was unnatural, wasn't it?

Or was it?

Thousands, perhaps millions, of men and women were either gay or lesbian. They were in the minority, but still they were part of humanity, part of nature. So what was natural? What was acceptable? Opinions on that changed over time, people's attitude's changed, laws changed.

Andreas put the chisel down. He got up and took another sip of coffee, then made a face and put the cup back down. The coffee was cold. He turned on the small espresso maker at his desk and made himself a fresh cup. He inhaled the fragrance, took a sip, and stepped up to the window. Across the street an old lady wearing a black scarf was pulling at the knob of a heavy wooden door. A young man hurried up the stairs and opened the door for her.

Whichever way he looked at it, it was uncharted territory for him. He couldn't figure it out in his mind. Tonio being gay hadn't changed his feelings for his son. He loved him with all his heart, and ever since seeing him battered and broken in the hospital, he felt very protective of him. He wanted to keep him close, to save him from harm and disappointment, but he knew he couldn't. He had to let him go; his son had to live his own life, make his own decisions, and learn from his own mistakes. But he wanted Tonio to know that he would always be there for him, no matter what.

Andreas rubbed his forehead. He would meet Tonio at the coffee shop and have a cup of coffee with him and his friends. He wanted to get to know them better. He pulled on the mask, picked up the chisel and hammer, and continued to work.

Chapter 19: Tonio

"Well, look who is here!" Fred called, a smile on his face, as Tonio and Mario stepped into the coffee shop. "Just in time for homemade chocolate cake."

A few of their friends came over and greeted them. Tonio winced when one of the guys hugged him a little too tight. Although he could barely feel his cracked ribs anymore, he still bent forward and instinctively protected his chest and belly whenever someone came too close.

"It's been ages," Fred said, brushing strands of blond hair out of his face. "Cappuccino, as usual?" he asked. He waved at the barista behind the counter and placed their order.

Tonio inhaled deeply, savoring the scent of coffee permeating the room. "Good to be back," he said to Mario. A couple of their friends, two young men about Tonio's age, came over and sat at their table.

"So, tell me, where have you guys been hiding?" One of the men, a lanky young guy with a ponytail, patted Mario's shoulder.

"Oh, you know, just . . ."

Tonio glanced at Mario, who had stopped talking and stared at something behind Tonio. "What's the matter?" Tonio asked and turned his head.

"It's him," Mario whispered and put his hand on Tonio's arm.

Two men entered the coffee shop. Tonio felt the blood drain from his face. His heartbeat doubled. He recognized the taller one right away, the one with the stringy black hair that framed his pudgy face. He was wearing a leather jacket, boots, and a black top with a shiny logo.

It was him, no doubt. His hair was longer, but Tonio would never forget that face, the mean small pig eyes, the arrogant jaw. He didn't recognize the second man, a skinny young guy with a shaved head.

It was several months after the attack. The police hadn't been able to find the attacker. He had just disappeared, probably left the country. But he was back.

The two guys looked around the room, squinting their eyes. Tonio's first reaction was to bolt out of the coffee shop, but then they would see him. He slid down in his chair as low as he could without falling under the table.

Fred came out of the kitchen area and glanced at the two newcomers, then at Mario and Tonio. Mario put his hand to his ear, making the sign of a phone call. Fred gave a slight nod, reached into his pocket, and went back into the kitchen.

"He'll call the police," Mario whispered. "He recognized them, too."

"We shouldn't have come here," Tonio whispered, his voice constricted by fear.

Mario put his hand on Tonio's arm and squeezed it gently. "Just try to be calm. They may not notice us."

The two guys sat at a table near the exit and scanned the room. Fred came back out from the kitchen and went up to them. "What can I get you?"

The heavier guy looked him up and down. A vicious grin curled his lips. "You can't get us anything, you slime bucket. We'd probably choke to death on your dirty coffee." His belligerent voice attracted the attention of the other customers, most of them young men. They turned around and stared at him.

"Then why are you here?" Fred asked. A slight tremor in his voice belied his outward calm demeanor.

100

"Yeah, why are we here?" The guy almost spit out the words. "Just wanted to show my young friend here what the scum of the earth looks like." He slapped his friend's back. The younger man gave an uneasy smile.

"I have to ask you to leave," Fred said.

"We'll leave when we're ready, asshole."

"I called the police. They'll be here any minute."

"Oh, yeah? You're just one big bluff." The tall guy got up and took a step toward Fred.

"Let's go, Carlo." His friend, who had been silent so far, seemed increasingly uncomfortable.

Tonio watched the scene, terrified, taking it all in while trying to think of a way out. Why was this happening? Then he thought of his father, who was working nearby. He slid his hand into his pocket and pulled out his cell phone.

At that moment, he saw Fred topple over, holding his stomach and trying to catch his breath. The guy had slugged him. Mario got up.

"Don't," Tonio whispered, but it was too late.

Mario walked over to Fred and stood next to him. He stared at Carlo. "Get out of here. There's a warrant out for your arrest."

Carlo's face stretched into a vicious grin. "Don't I know you? You're the fag we took care of before. You must have liked it, you pervert. Coming for more." He slapped Mario across the face and pushed him back. Mario stumbled and fell against a table. When he got up, blood trickled from his mouth. A few of the other guests left, afraid of getting involved in a fight.

Red-hot rage surged through Tonio when he saw Mario bleeding, a rage that was stronger than his fear. He got up and rushed over to the guy. "You son of a bitch," he screamed.

Carlo turned around and stared at Tonio. Face-to-face with the man who had done so much damage to him, Tonio felt his heart almost give out. For a moment, anger and fear battled within him.

Then there was the sound of the doorbell. Carlo seemed distracted for a split second and Tonio pounced at him and slug him in the face. The punch hurt his fist, but the cracking sound told him that he may have done some damage to his enemy.

"What the hell is going on here?"

Tonio's heart leapt with relief at the dark, familiar voice. With all the action going on, nobody had noticed the tall, sturdy man entering the coffee shop.

Chapter 20: Andreas

When Andreas opened the door to the coffee shop and saw Mario bleeding and another young man toppled over trying to catch his breath and his son punching a tall dangerous-looking guy in the face, he knew he had arrived just in time.

He glanced at Tonio, who winced and rubbed his fist but seemed okay. *The boy needs to learn how to fight properly.* The thought flashed through his mind as he grabbed the bully by the shoulder and yanked him around.

"Sir, what do you think you're doing?" Andreas addressed him in a calm voice.

Carlo, misinterpreting Andreas's cool, almost friendly demeanor, gave a vicious grin. "Just beating up some scum-bags. Want to join in?"

Andreas, outwardly calm and not looking at his son, asked, "Tonio, is this the guy?"

"Yes," Tonio said.

Andreas, still holding the man by the shoulder, stared at him coldly. "Well, let's do it, then. Let's beat up some scum-bags."

There was a shocked gasp in the room as Andreas threw a perfect punch to the chin of the man, which sent him flying several feet. The guy flailed his arms, trying to regain his balance, and hit a table, toppling it. Cups, saucers, spoons, and pieces of cake tumbled to the ground. Coffee and water spilled, forming small puddles on the floor.

Andreas went after the man, grabbed him by the hair, and yanked him to his feet. The bully yelled out in pain and looked at him, stunned and confused.

"That was for beating up my son," Andreas said, trying to suppress the rising rage. He knew he couldn't lose his head, or he would be able to kill the man. "And this is for hurting his friend." Another powerful punch to the stomach did the rest to bring the man down. He was on his knees, heaving and spitting, holding his stomach, then collapsed on the floor.

Hoots and clapping erupted around Andreas. The cheers, however, were drowned out by the sound of sirens blasting.

"Let's get out of here, Carlo." His friend, who had withdrawn into a corner of the coffee shop, rushed up to the man on the floor and tried to help him up.

"Oh, no, he's not going anywhere." Andreas held the younger man back and pushed Carlo to the floor again with his foot.

"What's going on here?" a voice shouted. Andreas turned around. Several policemen entered the coffee shop. A heavy-set cop with curly brown hair and piercing dark eyes, his hand on his holstered gun, told Andreas to step back. He looked vaguely familiar to Andreas, but he couldn't place him.

"He's the one who started the fight," a skinny young man with a small golden ring in one ear and strands of purple in his blond hair said, pointing at Carlo. "I'm Fred, the manager of the coffee shop. I called you."

"Okay, everybody calm down. Nobody leaves. I said, nobody!" the heavyset man, who seemed to be the officer in charge, yelled at

103

Carlo's friend as he was trying to sneak out. One of the policemen held him back.

In the meantime, Carlo had managed to raise himself to his knees. Two of the policemen helped him on his feet. One of the cops began to check the identities of Andreas and the two men involved in the brawl. He wrote down the information and went outside, while the officer in charge turned to Fred. "Care to fill me in?" He pulled out a small notepad from his pocket. Fred told him what happened and the officer made some notes.

The cop who had left with the sheet of paper with the names came back, whispered something to the officer in charge, and handed him the sheet. The officer nodded and the cop took Carlo by the arm, telling him that he was going to be arrested because there was a warrant out for him. Carlo made a desperate attempt to escape, but a few seconds later he was handcuffed and kneeled on the floor. Two cops handcuffed Carlo's friend and led the two men outside.

As the officer in charge perused the piece of paper with the names, a smile curled his lips. "Andreas O'Reilly, is that you?" He looked up.

"Yes, do I know you?" Andreas asked.

"Well, yes, we used to shoot paper planes at each other in school." He snapped his ID badge open and showed it to Andreas, who suddenly remembered him. He had been a skinny young kid who constantly got into trouble in school.

Andreas smiled. "Fernando? Jesus, you did look familiar, but I never would have guessed . . ."

"Yeah, I've put on a few pounds," Fernando said, patting his protruding belly. "So it seems you still have a powerful right one."

Andreas shook his head and gave a quick chuckle. "Not anymore. My hand is going to hurt for days." He was rubbing his right fist, which felt sore. *I'm getting too old for this.*

"What are the police going to do about protecting this place?" Andreas waved his hand, motioning around the coffee shop. "This isn't the first time these people had trouble. My son and his . . . friend got beaten up without provocation by these hoodlums."

"Exactly," Fred said, "and they have trashed the place before. I've called the police and they don't seem to care. Perhaps we're just not important enough. Who gives a hoot about a bunch of fags?"

Fernando looked him up and down, then shook his head. "We are here to protect everyone, but we can't be everywhere at all times. But I can assure you, you won't see the big guy for a while. Beating up on people is just one of his crimes. Last time, he went too far. He beat up someone who had a weak heart and died. He is wanted for manslaughter."

Jesus, Andreas thought. *I just punched a killer.*

"He's not coming out anytime soon," Fernando continued. "But I'll make sure one of our people is in the area, just in case. And if you have any more problems, here is my phone number."

Fred looked at him, surprised. "Thanks," he said, taking the cop's business card.

Fernando nodded at Andreas and gave a brief smile. "Let's get together when I'm not on duty," he said, then put his hand to his head in a salute and left.

After the police had left, a sigh of relief swept through the coffee shop. Andreas looked around, assessing the damage. It wasn't too bad: a bunch of broken cups and saucers, a few pieces of cake crumbled on the floor, and some coffee spilled. Mario had a swollen lip but seemed all right. Fred had recovered from his punch to the belly.

"Sorry about that," Andreas said to Fred, pointing at the mess on the floor. "I should've pushed him in the other direction."

"Who cares about a few broken dishes? You're a hero, you saved us," Fred said. "That was awesome." He went up to Andreas and wrapped his arms around him.

105

Feeling overwhelmed by the young man's enthusiastic response, Andreas stiffened a little, then gave a quick smile and cleared his throat. He turned to Mario. "You should put some ice on your lip."

"I'll get you some," Fred said and went into the kitchen.

Andreas took a deep breath. It was only now, after the action was over, that he became aware of what could have happened to Tonio if he hadn't arrived in time. He tapped Tonio's chest with his finger. "Son, you need to be little more streetwise. What were you thinking, attacking a guy who is that much taller and stronger than you?"

"He hit Mario and I lost it."

"That's how you get yourself killed."

"What should I have done? Just let him beat up Mario? I'm tired of being a coward." Tonio's voice trembled.

Andreas pulled him close and gave him a brief hug. "You're not a coward. But don't mix up being foolhardy with being brave."

"Where did *you* learn how to fight?" Tonio asked.

"Nowhere. All I know is street fighting. When I was your age, I hung around a bunch of rough kids, so I had to learn to defend myself. Being tall and fairly strong helped."

"Karate, that's what we need," Fred said as he came back with ice cubes wrapped in a washrag. He did a couple of pretend punches, which made him look more like a ballet dancer than a martial artist, then handed Mario the towel. His assistant brought a couple of brooms and they began to clean up the mess.

"He's right," Mario said. "I know of someone who is really good. I wouldn't mind taking some lessons."

"I think that's a great idea," Andreas said.

Tonio shrugged. "I guess so."

"Martial art teaches you above all how to avoid a fight. That's what my friend told me," Mario said, dabbing his mouth with the washrag.

"Well, I think it's time for some fun and relaxation. What do you say, we'll have a cup of excellent java and some chocolate cake? On the house. *Signor* O'Reilly, you're officially hired as bodyguard for our illustrious establishment." Fred bowed with a flourish.

Andreas gave a quick smile. "Call me Andreas, but I think you'll be okay without me."

After everybody helped to pick up the broken china and swept the floor, they all sat down. Fred and the waiter prepared macchiato and espresso and brought a plate with chocolate cake. The fragrance of fresh coffee filled the place. Soon, everybody drank coffee and enjoyed a piece of cake.

"Ouch," Mario said as he took a sip of the hot beverage and touched his lip.

"Want a straw?" Fred asked. "Bring our invalid a straw," he called to the waiter.

"Very funny," Mario said with a sneer, but he accepted the straw and was able to drink his coffee.

"Let me make it better," Tonio said and bent toward Mario. He kissed him gently on the mouth.

Andreas glanced at the two, trying not to show his discomfort. He noticed that Fred observed him.

"Hey, guys, no hanky-panky here. This is a decent establishment." Fred grinned and tossed a paper napkin at Tonio, then turned to Andreas. "Feel a little uncomfortable around a bunch of gays?" Fred winked at him.

At first Andreas wanted to deny it, but then he said. "Well, perhaps a little. I'm getting used to it, though."

"I know, it's not easy. You're really cool. When my father found out I was gay, he didn't talk to me for months. He's come around a little, but I don't think he'll ever fully accept it . . . or me." Fred looked at Andreas. There was a touch of pain in his blue eyes.

"I'm sorry," Andreas said.

Fred shrugged. "*C'est la vie.*"

Andreas felt Tonio's eyes on him. He turned to face him and put his hand on his shoulder, squeezing it. Tonio smiled and there was a slick of moisture along his lower eyelashes.

"Ready to go home?" Andreas asked.

Tonio nodded.

"Come with us, Mario," Andreas said. "Unless you guys want to stay at Mario's."

Mario and Tonio exchanged a quick glance. Andreas could tell they were surprised. Up till now, Andreas had raised no explicit objection of them spending the night together, but he hadn't encouraged it, either. He couldn't deny it. The event at Fred's coffee shop had made its mark on his feelings. Something had changed not just in his relationship to Tonio but in the way he saw these young men. So far, they had always struck him as exotic at best, and strange or unnatural at worst. Now, they were just like other young men, trying to live their lives and enjoy themselves. He felt he had made a few new friends.

As they were driving along the Maggia River on their way home, Andreas cleared his throat. "Is there any chance I can convince you guys not to tell Karla what happened? She's been really worried about me doing something stupid, like beating up on those bastards."

"Papa, you can't be serious. You were defending us. Mama couldn't object to that, could she?"

"I don't know. You know your mother has been in a somewhat . . . well, shall we say, delicate mood. She blows up easily. I know it has to do with her pregnancy. I just don't want to upset her more than is necessary." *And she's going to kick my ass if she finds out I slugged that guy.*

"Then how are we going to explain Mario's swollen mouth?" Tonio said.

"Well . . . he could've have fallen and hit his head. Oh, I know, it's ridiculous. We'll have to tell her." Andreas sighed.

"That's so funny," Tonio said. "You're not afraid of a bunch of criminals but you're afraid of Mama?"

Andreas chuckled. "Oh, you know how women are sometimes."

Tonio and Mario burst out laughing. "No, we don't, and that may be a good thing," Tonio said.

Andreas shook his head but smiled.

It smelled of pesto sauce and burning wood when they arrived at home. The evenings and nights in early March were still cool. Karla had built a fire in the fireplace and was stirring the sauce. She glanced at them and smiled when they came into the house, then looked at Mario shocked.

"What happened to you?" she asked and put down the wooden stirring spoon.

Andreas went up to her and kissed her, then motioned at Tonio and Mario. "They'll tell you all about it." The two didn't need any encouragement. They described the incident in great detail, playing Andreas's prowess up sky-high. Andreas went into the living room and put a few more logs on the fire. When he came back into the kitchen, Tonio was demonstrating to his mother how Andreas had given the bully a perfect blow to the jaw.

Karla glanced at Andreas, then back at Tonio. Her face was grim, but Andreas couldn't tell if it was because of the event itself or of the role he played in it. "They exaggerate," he said. "It wasn't such a big deal. I just came at the right time. We called the police and they arrested and booked them. I hope that's the end of it." He figured mentioning the police would give his involvement in the fight the desired legitimacy.

"Well, I'm sure glad you're not hurt any worse," Karla said to Mario. "Want me to give you some ice for your lip?"

"I had some already. I'm fine right now. Perhaps after dinner," Mario said.

During their dinner of spaghetti with pesto and a mixed salad Mario and Tonio continued to talk about the event. Andreas and Karla were quiet. Every once in a while, Andreas glanced at Karla, but she didn't pay any attention to him.

"We'll both take martial-art lessons," Tonio said at one point.

"That's excellent training, even if you never have to use it," Andreas said. "Good exercise all around, don't you think so?" He hoped to get some reaction out of Karla.

"I'm sure it is," she said without looking at him.

They finished their dinner and had a cup of espresso in the living room. After everybody had helped clean up the kitchen, Tonio and Mario turned in for the night, exhausted after their turbulent day.

When Andreas stepped out of the bathroom, Karla was putting on her nightgown. She sat at the edge of the bed and opened a bottle of body lotion. She still didn't look at him.

"All right, Karla, let's have it out. I know you're upset. We might as well get it over with."

She finally looked up and stared at him.

"I didn't start that fight, you know," Andreas continued. "I would've called the police and not gotten involved if there had been any chance I could've avoided a bloodbath. This jerk had just clobbered Fred and Mario, and Tonio, our crazy son, punched him in the face. What was I supposed to do? Watch them get killed?"

Karla looked down at her hands in her lap. Her shoulders were trembling a little. Then she shot him an amused look and laughed. "I just wish I could've have seen you punch out that guy."

Andreas breathed a sigh of relief and sat next to her. "So you're not mad?"

"What good would it do? No, I'm not mad. I just don't want to think about what could have happened to you."

"Well, it's over with. They're going to be behind bars for a while, I'm sure." Andreas didn't tell Karla that one of the guys had

110

killed someone. It would just upset her. "Let me do that," he said, and took the bottle with the body lotion out of her hand. He squeezed some into his hand and began to rub her feet with it.

Karla leaned against the backrest of the bed, lifted her legs on top of the sheets, and closed her eyes. "That feels wonderful," she moaned, as Andreas massaged her feet, rubbed more lotion into her legs, and stroked the inside of her thighs, moving his hand up to her crotch and pulling her panties aside. He bent down to kiss her large, swollen belly. Karla gave a sigh of pleasure, slipped off her underwear, and curled up on her side, her back to him. "Careful," she whispered.

"I'll be careful," he said, his voice hoarse.

Chapter 21: Laura

Laura woke up to the singing and chirping of birds outside Stefano's cottage. The garden with its trees, shrubs, plants, and flowers attracted every conceivable feathered friend. They started their concert at dawn and were the perfect natural alarm clock during the week and a nuisance on the weekends when the residents would have liked to sleep in.

Stretching and yawning, she looked over at Stefano, who was still asleep. He lay there turned toward her. He looked peaceful and innocent, and Laura was tempted to muss his mop of curly brown hair but didn't want to wake him that early.

She got out of bed and stood by the window, pushing the curtain aside. Dawn was spreading and it looked as if it was going to be a sunny April day. A few heaps of billowy white clouds grazed the mountain ridge. In the east, the sky was a mixture of deep purple and orange. She opened the window a crack and inhaled the sweet fragrance of a patch of pink hyacinths at the corner.

In the kitchen she filled the espresso pot with finely ground coffee, added water, and turned on the stove. Her cell phone was playing its musical sound. She grabbed it and saw her father's name on the display. Surprised and a little concerned that he would call so early, she pushed the answer button.

"Good morning, sweetie, did I wake you?" Fortunately, his voice sounded cheerful.

"No, I just got up. How are you?"

"Great. Listen, you have a new baby sister. Little Emilia just arrived, healthy, three kilos, and all her tiny toes and fingers are perfect. Mama is exhausted but okay." He gave a throaty laugh.

"Oh my God," Laura exclaimed. "How wonderful, but it's a little early. She was due in a week or so."

"Well, the little girl was in a hurry. Mama had contractions, but the baby was still in a breech position, so the doctor decided on a C-section."

"Oh, really? How is she feeling?"

"She is doing fine. Tired but happy."

"Yippee," Laura called out, as the news began to sink in. "Are you at the hospital now?"

"Yes, I'll be here for a while. Mama is asleep . . . oh, no, she just woke up. Here she is."

Laura heard a mumbling sound, then her mother's tired voice. "Hi, honey."

"Mama, are you okay?"

"I'm fine. She's so cute. I'm getting ready to nurse her."

"We'll be right there," Laura said. She put the phone down and rushed into the bedroom. Stefano was sitting up, rubbing his eyes.

"Come on, sleepyhead, get up." Laura jumped on the bed and hugged him.

"What's the matter?" he said.

Emilia

"The baby is here." She pulled on his arm. "Get ready, we're going to the hospital."

"Oh? Really? Uh, great." Stefano got out of bed, scratching his head and yawning. "Any coffee?"

"In the kitchen, but hurry."

Laura, followed by Stefano, stepped into a hospital room full of flower bouquets and visitors. Tonio, Mario, her father, her father's aunt and uncle, as well as Grandma Emilia, after whom the new baby was named, were there. Her mother was sitting in bed, holding the little bundled newborn in her arms. She looked tired and there were dark shadows under her eyes, but she smiled.

Laura went up to her and hugged her. Little Emilia was tiny but very pretty for a newborn. Her skin was smooth and she had long eyelashes and a thick fuzz of blond hair. "It's going to fall out after a while and probably get darker," her mother said and gently stroked the baby's head. She yawned. "Want to hold her?"

Laura nodded and gently lifted the little bundle with her new baby sister. A feeling of warmth and love flooded her and tears gathered in her eyes as she gazed at the sleeping child. The baby opened her eyes for a second—they were a deep blue—then closed them again and yawned.

"Isn't she cute?" Stefano put his arm around Laura and winked at her. "Want one, too?"

"Maybe," Laura said and smiled at him.

"I think you guys better wait awhile with that," her father said. He took Emilia in his arms and kissed her forehead. "She *is* cute, isn't she?" He carried her over to his seventy-five-year-old mother. "Well, Mom, here is your namesake and—definitely—last grandchild."

Grandma Emilia, a petite woman with curly grey hair and clear blue eyes, hugged Andreas, then took the baby into her arms. "She is just perfect. Well done, Karla and Andreas."

"You can say that, all right," Uncle Alois said, and he and Aunt Maria fawned over the baby.

Laura looked at her mother, who had fallen asleep in the meantime. Her father chuckled. "She's in and out. She's still groggy from the surgery."

"How long does she have to be in the hospital?" Tonio asked, arranging some flowers in a vase.

"They'll keep her for about three to four days, depending on how she feels," Andreas said.

"Doesn't she need help while recovering at home?" Mario asked.

Andreas nodded. "Yes, the county nurse will come every day in the beginning. I'll help, too, of course."

"I'll be at home as well," Laura said. "I can help take care of her and the baby."

"We can help as well," Tonio said.

Mario agreed. "Yeah, that would be fun."

Andreas laughed. "I guess little Emilia will be the best-cared-for baby of the valley."

"We'll all help," Aunt Maria said, and Uncle Alois and Grandma Emilia nodded with enthusiasm.

"That's so kind of you, but you guys live a little too far away for everyday care. But we'll have you babysit one of these days. Don't worry," Andreas said.

"Where is my baby?" a tired voice sounded from the bed. Karla had come out of her catnap.

"Here she is." Andreas put little Emilia into Karla's arms. The baby started to cry and Karla pushed aside her nightgown a little. Emilia latched on to her nipple and quieted down.

"Well, time to let mother and child have some privacy," Uncle Alois said. He and Aunt Maria waved and Grandma Emilia threw a kiss.

After everybody except for the immediate family and boyfriends had left, the nurse came in and picked the baby up for a quick checkup. As soon as Emilia was away from her mother, Karla leaned her head back onto the pillow and fell asleep again.

"Poor Mama, she's so tired," Laura said. "I hope this isn't all too much for her."

"It's the surgery more than anything that wiped her out," her father said. He gently pulled the cover over Karla's chest, then bent down and kissed her forehead. Her eyelids fluttered and she gave a little smile. "She'll be okay," he added.

"Time to go, huh?" Stefano said. "She needs to rest now."

"Yes, I'll be leaving soon as well," Andreas said.

"I'll be home," Laura said to her father and hugged him. "I'll cook us some spaghetti tonight."

"Forget it, honey, you're not cooking. We are all going out. Come on, guys, I invited Lena and Luigi as well. We have something to celebrate after all."

The following few weeks Laura spent at home, helping her mother. She recovered faster than anticipated, at least physically. However, she had a case of the baby blues, feeling depressed a lot. She would cry for no apparent reason and Laura and her father worried about her state of mind.

After about a month, Laura noticed an improvement in her mother's mood. She breathed a sigh of relief when she came inside one day and inhaled the smell of paint. Karla had prepared a fresh canvas. Dressed in her painter's apron, she almost looked like her old self again. The painting was an acrylic of Laura holding Emilia, and she gave it to Laura once it was finished.

Chapter 22: Karla

"Already?" Karla glanced at her watch, then added a few more brushstrokes to the canvas and put the brush into the bowl of water. The sound of crying came from Emilia's bedroom. The three-month-old baby had woken up from her nap and wanted her attention. Karla stepped back, squinted her eyes and studied the canvas, then sighed.

"Coming, sweetie," she called. Her daughter did not like to take long naps during the day. Unlike her older siblings, who had usually slept a solid two hours or more and given Karla enough time to get some work done, Emilia took little catnaps for about thirty minutes, sometimes less, all through the day. It wasn't enough time for Karla to concentrate fully on her painting.

As soon as Karla came into the bedroom, the baby stopped crying and cracked a smile, a few last tears glistening in her large blue eyes. Karla picked her up, kissed her soft face, and gently brushed her hand through the girl's silky light brown hair. Emilia didn't look anything like the rest of the O'Reilly brood, as Andreas sometimes called their family. All the other members had thick dark hair and either brown or green eyes. "Are you sure it wasn't the milkman?" Andreas sometimes teased Karla.

Karla changed Emilia's diaper and carried her into the living room. While nursing the baby, she glanced at the photos on the mantelpiece above the fireplace. It showed a few pictures of Emilia next to a photo of Karla's mother as a baby. Karla, who had lost her mother at five years of age in a car accident, only vaguely remembered what she had looked like. However, when Andreas put the photos next to each other, she discovered how much the babies resembled each other: the same shape and color of the eyes, the small nose, and the silky hair with the reddish highlights. It was almost eerie.

"Perhaps Grandma Laura has come back," Laura, her daughter, had said. "You know, something like reincarnation."

Karla gave a wistful smile at the picture. Her memories of her mother, whom she had missed terribly as a child and young girl, had been fading with time. Her mother had become a stranger to her, a distant relative she had loved but wasn't thinking about much anymore. And sometimes Karla felt that even Emilia didn't quite fit into her life.

Right after Emilia was born Karla had gone through a difficult time. Instead of the deep joy she experienced after her older children were born, she felt strangely removed from the little bundle lying in her arms. During the first few weeks she went through the motions of taking care of Emilia, breast-feeding her, changing diapers, whispering endearments, trying to conjure up the feelings of joy she had felt when Laura and Tonio were born. Sometimes, she was overcome by panic. What if she didn't love the child enough? What was wrong with her?

Her doctor attributed her feelings of depression in part to the aftermath of the surgery. Fortunately, the "baby blues" disappeared after a few weeks and she began to enjoy her role as mother more. The fact, however, that Emilia wanted to enter the world upside down or feet first felt like a strange sign to her. There were still times she looked at her child and smiled, wondering if this dainty, silky-haired wisp of a girl was really hers.

Emilia had finished feeding and made little gurgling sounds. When Karla got up and carried her around to burp her, Andreas came into the room. "She's up already?" he asked and kissed the baby, making little sucking sounds. Emilia gave a little squeal.

Karla sighed. "Yeah, just another catnap."

"Did you get any work done?"

Karla shook her head. "Not much."

"Well, at least she almost sleeps through the night," Andreas said. He took Emilia out of Karla's arms.

Karla nodded. "That's one good thing, yes. Perhaps I should start painting at night. It wouldn't be a bad idea, if I wasn't so darn tired all the time." Her voice trembled.

"Tell you what," Andreas said, hugging her. "I need to drive to Locarno to run some errands. I can take her with me. You know she always falls asleep in the car. That way you can get some painting done."

"Oh, that would be great. Are you sure that's not too much trouble?"

"No, no problem. Come on, little princess, you can come with Papa to the big city," he cooed.

Karla dressed Emilia in a jumper and light sweater. It was July and quite warm outside. Andreas carried her to the car and put her in the car seat. Emilia smiled and made baby noises. When Andreas got into the driver's seat, Karla handed him the diaper bag, bent down, and kissed him. "Thanks, honey."

He waved and left. Karla watched the car drive away and sighed. *Thank God for a perfect father.* She took a deep breath and went inside. On the way to the studio, she pushed the button on the espresso machine and made herself a cup of coffee.

Standing in front of the canvas, she picked up the brush and studied the painting. Her concentration was gone, but she forced herself to continue. She needed to take advantage of any free time she had. Having to take care of an infant again after all these years proved to be more difficult than she had anticipated. She wasn't used to breaking up her working day into small stretches anymore. Andreas was a big help, and so were Laura and Tonio. Andreas even suggested they hire someone to take care of Emilia part of the time. So far, Karla had resisted. In spite of the difficulties, she wanted to take care of Emilia herself. She would be her last child and she wanted to savor the time they had together.

"We'll see," she mumbled, as she added one more brush-stroke to the almost-finished painting. "She'll grow up fast and it will get easier," she tried to convince herself.

Karla stepped outside and sat on the bench under the chestnut tree. It was a pleasant summer day with a clear blue sky. The air smelled clean and the breeze brought a whiff of jasmine from the shrub nearby.

In spite of the beauty around her, Karla was flooded by sadness. Such mood swings had diminished somewhat over the past few weeks, but every once in a while they hit her again without warning. She felt guilty for her moods. Everybody was so good to her, and yet she couldn't help herself. "I'm just so tired," she mumbled, trying to suppress a sob, then let go and burst into tears.

PART TWO: DEEP FREEZE

Chapter 23: Laura

Laura helped Stefano put the garden tools away at his home. They had just returned from finishing a landscaping job, and Laura had been able to add one of her sculptures. It was another one of Stefano's freelance contracts for a friend of a former client. Laura and Stefano had been working together for the past four years, doing landscaping and stonework, mostly for well-to-do customers in the affluent areas of Ascona. Laura still worked for her father and lived at home, but spent most of her time at Stefano's.

She stepped into the bathroom, pulled off her T-shirt, washed her hands, and pressed a washrag with cold water to her flushed face. It was a fairly warm spring day in April. It had rained quite a bit in late March and the soil was moist and ready for planting. It was a busy time for gardeners.

"Do you have any other jobs lined up?" she asked. She walked into the kitchen, where Stefano was busy preparing tea. He lifted the whistling water kettle off the stove and set it aside.

"No, unfortunately not. It's back to the old garden shop again for a while."

To supplement his income, Stefano had kept a part-time job at the garden center. However, he became increasingly dissatisfied with that kind of work, now that he had tasted the freedom and satisfaction he got from his more creative freelancing business. Besides, he made more money in a few days working for a well-to-do client than in several weeks at the garden shop.

"One day, you'll be able to quit altogether," Laura said, trying to cheer him up. "Just be patient. We have a few steady clients who like your work. They'll recommend you, you'll see."

"I know." Stefano carried the teacups into the living room while Laura poured the hot water into the pot. She was more of a coffee drinker, but being with Stefano, she had acquired a taste for black tea. Stefano's mother had been English and Stefano carried on her tradition of afternoon tea. Like his love of gardening, drinking tea was another way for him to honor her.

"We need to talk about something," he said and sat next to Laura on the sofa.

"Gee, that sounds ominous, are you trying to break up with me?" Laura meant it as a joke, but she couldn't help being a little concerned.

Stefano had been really busy at work. It was close to Easter and he had been swamped by clients looking for decorations and festive flower arrangements. They hadn't seen much of each other for a few weeks, and the few times they had been together he had been somewhat absentminded. Laura thought it had been because of work, but now that he looked so serious and concerned, she began to worry.

"Of course not." Stefano sounded puzzled. "Why would I want to do that?" He put his arm around her and pulled her close.

"Just kidding," Laura said, relieved. "Okay, so what else could it be? You're pregnant."

Stefano rolled his eyes. "Would you please stop joking and listen?"

"All right. What's the problem?"

"Well, not really a problem, although it could become one." Stefano scratched his head.

"Please, don't drag it out like this. You're making me nervous."

"Okay, okay. You know I've been looking for ways to further my career—I mean, my freelancing business, right?"

Laura nodded, poured some milk into their cups. Stefano added tea and sugar. He took a sip, then got up and walked to the window, taking his cup of tea with him. He turned around and sat on the windowsill, looking pensively at Laura, taking a few more sips.

"Yes?" *He can be such a slowpoke sometimes.*

"Well . . ." Stefano hesitated, then set down his cup on the windowsill. "There is this well-known garden-design school in London. They have all kinds of classes and they also have a diploma program. My father encouraged me to attend. He offered to pay the tuition for it and to help me out financially."

Stefano cleared his throat and paused. "Anyway, I just thought . . . it would be a great opportunity for me, since I don't have much formal schooling and training, except what I learn at the garden center or on my own. I just feel I need something more—"

"Stefano, that sounds like a wonderful idea. And in England of all places, your mother's home country. You don't seem to be too happy about it, though."

"Well, I'd really like to do it, but it would mean we wouldn't be together for a while."

"I know, but we would survive for a few months or weeks. I could even visit you."

Stefano sighed. "Problem is, the program I'm thinking of lasts more than a few weeks or months."

"How long?"

"One year. It's the diploma program."

"Oh, I see." Laura's enthusiasm evaporated. Thoughts twirled through her mind. *A year? But England isn't that far away. I could visit, couldn't I? Would he want me to? Perhaps he does want to break up after all. What are we going to do?* She felt her eyes sting and blinked.

"I know it's going to be hard. Maybe I should just forget about it or take one of the shorter classes. I don't want to be separated that long from you." Stefano fiddled with his hands. Laura felt his resolve waning. But this was important for him, perhaps for both of them, for their common business plans. She didn't want to hold him back.

Laura swallowed and took a deep breath. "No, Stefano, you should take the longer course. If you're going to do it, you might as well do it right."

Stefano came over to her and sat down again. He put his arm around her. "You know, England isn't that far. I could come home for weekends. You could visit me, too, or we could meet in Paris once in a while. Besides, there are several weeks of vacation all through the terms, which I'm planning to spend at home."

Laura nodded. "You're right." She felt more enthusiastic again. "That actually sounds very tempting. Paris, I've never been to Paris. That would be great."

Stefano smiled, then wrinkled his forehead. "I just hope the school isn't too hard for me."

Laura knew that Stefano lacked self-confidence when it came to his academic skills. "Come on, you'll do fine. Don't worry." She hugged him.

Chapter 24: Andreas

Andreas left his car in a parking lot near the old part of Locarno. He locked the new carving tools he had bought in the trunk and walked down the street toward the art gallery where Karla worked. It was close to lunchtime and he decided to try to have lunch with her and pick up Emilia. He would watch her in the afternoon.

Emilia, now four years old, spent half a day at the small daycare center in their village. But today was the first of May and a holiday in the Ticino, so daycare and schools were closed. During vacation, Karla took Emilia with her when she worked at the gallery and Andreas was out or busy. He watched her when he worked in his studio at home.

Emilia

It was a sunny and pleasantly warm day. Loads of fresh vegetables sat in crates before the small grocery stores in the old part of the city. The flower shop at the corner donned a colorful array of spring flowers—irises, tulips, hyacinths. The sweet honey-like scent of the freesia in a pot outside tickled his nose. He stopped at one of the small bakeries and bought a couple of cupcakes, Emilia's favorite sweets.

When he turned the corner at Via San Antonio, he saw Emilia out on the street several houses away from the gallery. He stopped, surprised. Emilia saw him and came running toward him, smiling.

"Hi there, sweetie. What are you doing here alone? Where's Mama?"

Emilia pointed back in the direction of the gallery.

"What the . . ." Andreas looked up and down street.

Karla came running out of the gallery. She spotted them and waved. "Thank God," she said. She pointed an accusing finger at Emilia. "You're not supposed to be out here by yourself, you know that." She shook her head. "I turn my back one minute and she's gone."

"Well, I guess I came at the right time." He was disturbed by the fact that his child was out on the street alone. Fortunately, the narrow street was closed to most traffic.

"I was busy with a client and Emilia was playing in the back, and the next thing I know, she's disappeared."

"Didn't you see her leave?" Andreas asked.

"No, because she left through the back door, which is normally locked. I don't know why it was open. Perhaps Silvia forgot to lock it. She was here earlier this morning."

"Anyway," Andreas said, "we'll have to watch the sneaky little thing more carefully." He playfully shook his finger at Emilia, who smiled mischievously. "I came a little early because I thought we could have lunch together, somewhere outside. It's so nice today."

"Oh, I'm sorry," Karla said. "My client just invited me to lunch. I think he wants to talk about one of the paintings. I wish I'd known . . ."

"It's okay. Just a thought." Andreas didn't want to let on that he was disappointed.

They walked back to the gallery. Inside, an elegant-looking man stood in front of one of Karla's paintings, studying it. He was tall, slender, with bleach-blond hair, wearing white pants, a white-and-blue patterned shirt, and soft leather loafers. He gave off an air of money. He turned around and his deep blue eyes flicked to Andreas for a couple of seconds, then he looked back at Karla and gave her a big smile.

Andreas disliked the man right away, although he wasn't sure why. For all he knew, the man was an important customer, getting ready to leave a big sum of money for a painting.

"Sorry for dashing off like that," Karla said to the customer. "My daughter snuck away."

"No problem." He smiled at Emilia. "Hello, young lady." He tried to tickle her chin, but Emilia wanted none of that. She shook her head, turned to Andreas, and wrapped her arms around his legs.

She doesn't like him, either, Andreas thought. He lifted Emilia up and kissed her. The man glanced from Andreas to Karla and back.

"This is my husband," Karla said. She introduced the prospective customer as "Mr. Swallow."

"Oh, call me Walter," the man said and stretched out his hand.

Andreas shook it and gave a quick smile, but didn't volunteer his first name.

"Your wife is a marvelous painter." The man stretched his face into a grin, which made him look like Ken from Ken and Barbie.

"I know," Andreas said coldly. He turned to Karla. "Well, we're off."

"Okay, I'll be home early. Bye, sweetie." Karla kissed Emilia and gave Andreas a questioning look. She obviously felt his bad mood, but he had no intention of showing more than cool friendliness.

"See you later," he said and made a hand gesture to Walter Swallow, which he meant more as a sign of dismissal than a goodbye.

"Oh, call me Walter. Oh, call me Walter," Andreas said with a reedy voice, sneering at the customer as he walked down the street.

Emilia laughed out loud at the funny noises her father made. Andreas didn't know why he felt so irritated. But the combination of Karla not watching Emilia properly while getting ready to go out to lunch with one of those stuffed-up clients when she could have gone out with her husband irked him more than he wanted to admit.

He sighed and put Emilia down. "What about going for pizza, just the two of us?" he asked her. "And cupcakes for dessert?" He showed Emilia the bag with the sweets.

"Yes. Yes." Emilia jumped up and down.

Sitting outside in the courtyard at a pizzeria nearby, Andreas watched amused as Emilia picked up small pieces of her slice of pizza he had cut up for her. Unlike many other kids her age, Emilia was a dainty eater. She looked like a little lady with her linden-green spring dress and her light brown neatly braided hair. A feeling of love and warmth spread through Andreas's chest. He bent down and kissed the girl on the nose.

"Good?" he asked.

Emilia nodded with a smile. "Can I have some ice cream?" she asked after finishing the last piece.

"What about the cupcakes?" Andreas asked.

"Ice cream," the girl decided after a quick pause.

Andreas wasn't very hungry. After finishing two small slices of pizza, he called the waiter and ordered an espresso for himself and a scoop of ice cream for Emilia.

Stirring the coffee, he thought back to the scene at the gallery. Why was he so irritated? So Emilia slipped away and was out in the street for a little while, a street that was closed to traffic. He knew the girl could be sneaky sometimes, particularly when she wanted to get her parents' attention. Karla had been busy; it could've happened to him, too.

It seems to happen more to Karla, though, he felt. She was too involved in this damn gallery. He wouldn't mind as much if it had to do with her own paintings, but she seemed to spend an inordinate amount of time promoting other artists' work, selling paintings because of the commission. He didn't even know how much time she devoted to her art anymore. He hadn't seen anything new of hers in a while. She was on the way to becoming an art dealer rather than an artist. And all that going out to lunch and dinner with those patrons of the arts, those gussied-up arrogant men.

Andreas rubbed his forehead, as if to clear away the troubling thoughts. He hated these pangs of jealousy. After all, he was a modern husband who didn't begrudge his wife her success, wasn't he?

"All done," Emilia said, interrupting his daydreaming. She had finished with her ice cream and was looking for another paper napkin.

Andreas handed her a Kleenex and called the waiter. "Time to go home; you look tired, honey." He smiled as Emilia yawned and rubbed her eyes.

At home, Andreas carried the sleeping Emilia into her bedroom and put her down for a nap. He made a cup of espresso in the kitchen, stepped outside, and sat on the granite bench on the patio. The white-and-purple blossoms on the magnolia trees in the neighbor's yard and the wildflowers in the meadow in front of the house formed a vivid contrast to the green grass and the grape vines in the adjacent field. The light spring breeze brought the sweet scent of honeysuckle. A squirrel scurried across the meadow in front of the house and raced up a tree. Nature was fully alive. Why couldn't everything be as beautiful? Andreas sighed.

Sipping his coffee, he decided to have a talk with Karla, a serious talk, not the usual arguments they had had lately, which always ended on a sour note. Their relationship was in trouble. It scared him. He loved Karla; he didn't want them to grow apart even further.

Because that's what had been happening lately. Her work at the gallery and all of what that entailed wasn't the only bone of contention between them. For the past two years or so he had felt an increasing emotional disconnect and a lack of physical intimacy between them.

Making love had always been an enjoyable and important part of their relationship. Of course, they both had slowed down somewhat. After all, they were older and had been married for over twenty years. He was almost fifty and Karla was forty-seven. He didn't expect sex to always be the fireworks they had experienced in their twenties. However, he wasn't ready for the monastery or the convent yet, and having sex every two weeks or so just wasn't enough. He couldn't understand it and wondered if he was no longer attractive to Karla.

The noise of a car engine woke him from his musing. He got up and watched as Karla parked her new shiny Mini Cooper and got out of the car. He met her halfway and took one of the grocery bags out of her hands.

"Hi," she said, giving him a cautious look.

He carried the bag into the kitchen and put it on the counter. They quietly unpacked the food and put it away.

Andreas cleared his throat. "How was work?"

"Okay," she said matter-of-factly.

"Did that guy buy anything?"

She glared at him briefly. "Yes, in fact, he did. In spite of your less than friendly behavior."

Andreas's first reaction was to snap at her, but he caught himself in time. He wanted to have an amiable discussion, not another fight.

"I'm sorry," he said. "I was upset, I shouldn't have taken it out on him."

"Upset about what?"

"About a lot of things." He turned to face her. "I want to talk about it, but in a friendly way. I don't want another argument."

"I'm not the one who argues," Karla snapped.

Andreas gave her a pleading look. "Please, could we . . ."

"All right." Karla shrugged.

They went into the living room. Karla sat on the sofa, grabbed a pillow, hugging it to her chest as if she wanted to protect herself from an attack. Andreas sat at a chair opposite her, then got up, feeling uncomfortable.

"I'm sorry I was unfriendly this morning," he said. "I was upset because I found Emilia outside alone while you were busy with that . . . guy." Andreas glanced at Karla, who stared at him, her full lips pressed together into a hostile thin line.

"I'm sorry about Emilia," she said. "I should've watched her better, but she was outside for only a few seconds. I told Silvia to always lock the back door. She apologized, she just forgot."

"This is not really about Silvia," Andreas said, getting upset at Karla's attempt to lay the blame on Silvia for her own lack of attention.

"I know." Karla waved her hand dismissively. "But had the back door been locked, I would've seen Emilia leave and this wouldn't have happened. It won't happen again. What else do you blame me for?"

Andreas lowered his face into his hands and shook his head. He looked up again. "It's not about blaming anybody. I just feel things aren't right between us and I want to talk about it."

"Yeah. I'll tell you what's not right between us," Karla said in a sharp voice. "Your constant accusations. You always blame me for not watching Emilia properly and make me feel like a bad mother. And then you come to my workplace and insult my clients, almost making me lose a sale. That's one thing that's wrong between us. You're jealous of my work, my success." She got up. Her face was flushed and her dark eyes shot daggers.

Andreas sighed. "This is ridiculous, I'm not jealous of your success. That's just plain dumb. Why can't we talk about this like adults?" He brushed through his hair and glared at Karla, trying hard not to blow up. "I wanted to invite you for lunch. I get to your place and Emilia is out in the street and you getting ready to go out to lunch with another guy. So, yes, I was upset."

"So you *are* jealous," Karla sneered. "You don't like the fact that some important men take me out and admire my art."

"Admire your art? Well, they may admire your butt, but I doubt they care about anybody else's art but their own. You're dreaming, honey."

"You're such a jerk. Now, you even belittle my art." Karla seemed on the point of bursting into tears.

"No, I'm not, you're twisting my words again. I admire your art. But I'll tell you one thing"—he pointed his finger at her and scrunched his eyes—"the time you waste selling someone else's art doesn't do much for your own painting. You are distracted too much, hobnobbing with all these hotshots in the art world. It gives you the wrong ideas—"

"How dare you?" Karla's voice trembled. "My work is important to me. I meet interesting people, nice people, people who respect me. Unlike my husband, who only puts me down all the time."

"I didn't . . . Oh, for heaven's sake, what's the use?" Andreas punched one of the pillows.

"Well, to put your mind at rest about the guy I went to lunch with today. He is gay, so he has no interest in jumping into bed with me," Karla said.

"Oh, he's gay, so that explains why he wiggles his hips like a friggin' woman," Andreas blurted out, regretting it instantly.

"Andreas, you seem to have forgotten, you have a gay son," Karla said.

"Sorry, I didn't mean to say anything against gays."

"Oh, yeah?"

"Yeah." He felt he was losing it. "Well, if you jumped into the sack at home more often, I wouldn't have to get jealous. When was the last time—"

"That's such a low blow. No wonder I don't feel like it anymore." Her voice broke.

Andreas glared at her. "What the fuck have I done to deserve—"

"Mama?" Emilia was standing at the door, her blanket in one hand and rubbing her eyes with the other.

Andreas sat down, feeling drained and defeated. He watched as Karla pulled Emilia close and put her on her lap, hugging her. Emilia leaned her head against Karla's chest and sucked her thumb. This kind of mother-and-child scene normally made him feel warm inside. Now, it angered him even more. He got up, left the house, and walked over to his studio. He sat on his chair and picked up one of the tools, then put it down again. He felt like crying.

Chapter 25: Karla

Karla tried to hold back the tears as she continued to hug Emilia. She felt desperate. Why did every conversation they had turn into an ugly argument? She heard the door again and wondered if he was coming back.

"Hi, Mama." Laura smiled at her as she came into the room. "And how is my little sister?" She bent down and kissed Emilia, then gave her mother a probing look.

"What's the matter? You look upset. Have you been crying?"

Karla shook her head. "No, but I feel like it."

"Why? Did you and Papa have another fight? He looked really sad when I saw him in his studio just now."

"Yeah, we had an argument." Karla sighed.

"What is the matter with you two? Seems like you've been fighting a lot lately. You're not breaking up, are you? Please don't," Laura said.

"I don't know. He's angry all the time. He blames me for all kinds of stuff." Karla put her head in her hands.

"Perhaps you need to see someone, you know, like a counselor."

"Perhaps." Karla got up. "I'll try to talk to him again."

"Why don't I take Emilia with me?" Laura said. "Stefano and I just finished a job and I have the rest of the day off. We could go for a walk. It's so nice out now."

"That would be great," Karla said. "Give us some time to ourselves."

Laura came up to her and hugged her. "Mama, why don't you two make up?"

Karla sighed. "Trying to."

"Well, Emilia and I are going to have fun, aren't we? But first you need to get dressed."

"She just had a nap. Her clothes are in her bedroom. Thanks again, honey."

Laura pointed her finger at her mother and scrunched up her face. "You go out there and straighten things out, you hear me?" She took Emilia's hand and walked her to her bedroom.

"Yes, ma'am." In spite of everything, Karla had to laugh. Laura looked so much like Andreas when she was worried or angry.

Karla walked outside and took a deep breath when she approached Andreas's studio. She wanted to make every effort not to say anything to hurt him, even if he tried to insult her.

"Hi," she said as she entered the studio. He put his tool down and turned around. She sat on a bench next to him. "Laura just came. She's going to take Emilia for a walk. Perhaps . . . we can talk without hurting each other." Karla's voice broke. She wrapped her arms around Andreas. He stiffened at first, but after a while he hugged her back.

"What are we going to do?" Karla wiped a tear away.

"If we could reach a point where we can talk like two people who love each other rather than enemies, that would be a start," Andreas said.

Karla nodded. "I don't want all this fighting, either. But I also want to live my own life. It seems . . ."

Andreas sighed. "I don't mean to bully you, although sometimes it may seem that way."

"Okay, you guys, we're leaving. And I want you two to be lovey-dovey by the time we get back." Laura stood at the door, her fists propped on her sides, as she had done often as a child when she wanted to assert herself.

"We'll try," Karla said and managed a quick smile. "Laura is worried about us," she said after Laura and Emilia had left.

Andreas nodded. "I am, too."

Karla sighed. "I have the feeling you're only going to be happy if I quit my job at the gallery and stay home full-time."

"No, that's not true," Andreas said. "I just wish you'd find a better balance between your job and spending time with Emilia . . . and with me. And what about your painting? I don't know if you even have enough time for your art anymore. You seem to focus entirely on selling other people's stuff."

"I paint. I paint all the time at the gallery," Karla said.

"Maybe. I just haven't seen anything new of yours lately."

"Don't worry about my art," Karla said. "I don't think this is about my painting, or even about Emilia. Emilia is well taken care of. I know I don't have as much time with her as I did with Laura and Tonio. But lots of parents work full-time and their children are all right. I think it's about us." Karla's heart was beating fast as she admitted, perhaps for the first time, that they had real problems.

Andreas nodded. "Yes, it is. What are we going to do about it?"

Chapter 26: Laura

"What is this?" Laura asked, turning the small, neatly wrapped package in her hands.

"You won't know unless you open it." Stefano smiled at her.

"Is that what I think it is?" Laura's hands were shaking a little as she opened the box. Stefano had never given her jewelry. He had brought her flowers and candy and such things. A few days ago, they had gone shopping and Laura had admired a pair of earrings in one of the stores. Stefano had encouraged her to try them on, but they were in a rush and Laura said she would come back later.

When she opened the box and peeked inside, her heart leapt. It wasn't earrings; it was a ring, a silver band with a small sparkling emerald. It looked like an engagement ring. "Stefano?"

"Do you like it? I hope it fits—it can be adjusted if it's too big."

"Stefano, what . . ."

"You don't like it? We can always exchange—"

"Of course, I like it, it's beautiful, gorgeous," Laura exclaimed and held the ring toward the window, watching it sparkle in the May sun. Her heart fluttered a little. "Is this an engagement ring?"

"Kind of." Stefano grinned.

"What do you mean, 'kind of'?"

"Well, it is an engagement ring and I hope you accept it. But I want it to be more than that. I . . ." He rubbed the top of his head, which he always did when he was embarrassed or nervous. Then he sat next to Laura and put his arm around her. "Laura, I want us to get married before I leave for England."

"What?" Laura stared at him. "Stefano, isn't this a little sudden? I mean . . . I'd love to get married, but why in such a rush?"

"Well, I just wanted it to be settled before I leave. It would be great to know we belong together for sure."

"But . . . we don't need to get married to know we belong together. This would mean we'd have to get married in . . . four weeks at the latest." Laura wrinkled her forehead, then held up her hand with the ring again. "I don't think that's possible."

"We can do it." Stefano sounded excited and got up. "I asked at city hall. We could file right away and there may be enough time. It takes two to six weeks. Even if it takes more than four weeks, I can come back for a few days."

"I don't know, Stefano, this all sounds so rushed. I want to be able to make some preparations for a wedding, have a nice dress, invite people, arrange it all. And what about church? My parents would be so disappointed if we didn't have a church wedding. And there is no way we can arrange that before you leave."

"Well, we could get married at city hall and then have a big wedding in church once I get back."

"Have the church wedding a year later? That doesn't sound like a good idea."

"Or a few weeks later. Perhaps you guys can prepare the wedding and I'll come back for a weekend. We can do it."

"Honey, I don't know. It's just . . . getting married is a big deal and I want to be in the right state of mind for it. I don't want to be pushed into it."

Stefano's facial expression changed from excited to disappointed. "I expected you to be a little more enthusiastic. Don't you love me?"

Laura sighed. "Of course I love you. And getting married sounds great. But not so soon. This is so unexpected, I need a little time for it to sink in." She got up and put her arms around him. "Please don't be disappointed. I want to get married and I love this ring. Why can't we just be engaged and then get married when you come back? We can have a nice little engagement party with the family before you leave. What do you think? Don't look so gloomy."

Stefano exhaled deeply. "Well, I guess so." He still sounded disappointed.

"Stefano, I love you and this is a really beautiful ring." Laura stretched out her hand and looked at the shiny green stone. "Please, let's make this fun." She hugged him again. He behaved a little stiff at first, but then hugged her back.

Laura was torn between confusion and happiness. She was overwhelmed by Stefano's profession of love, but couldn't understand his urgency. Or was she being too cautious, not spontaneous enough? He went through all this trouble to surprise her and he was dead serious about getting married. He even went to inquire about the legal procedures. He must feel rejected and it hurt her, but she couldn't help herself. Listening to her parents' increased fighting over the past couple of years didn't exactly encourage her to rush into a permanent relationship herself.

Chapter 27: Karla

When Karla and her client came back from lunch, Silvia waved at her. "Andreas called."

Silvia's concerned tone made Karla uneasy. Then it dawned on her. She should have picked Emilia up at daycare. *He's going to be furious.* She turned to her client, a middle-aged patron of the arts who had just bought one of the paintings and whom she had treated to lunch at an expensive restaurant in Locarno. "Excuse me for a moment, I need to make a quick phone call."

"No problem, I have to scoot anyway. I'm going to meet a few friends and do some shopping while I'm in town," the elegantly clad man said. "We'll talk about the shipping of the painting later. Thank you very much for your company. It was charming." He kissed her hand, then waved at Silvia and left, the scent of his expensive eau de cologne trailing behind him.

Karla wrinkled her nose. He was a charming man, but she disliked men who doused themselves in perfume. With a big sigh, she turned to Silvia. "Was he mad?"

"He didn't exactly sound happy, you were supposed to pick up Emilia at daycare. He had to drive home from Lugano to get her himself. Yeah, he was a little upset."

Karla's heart sank. "A little? I bet he's livid. I'll get it tonight. We changed our schedule last week because he needed to be in Lugano today. Normally Wednesday is his day to pick her up and I totally forgot about it. Why didn't he remind me this morning?"

"He'll calm down," Silvia said. "It was a misunderstanding, after all."

"Well, knowing Andreas, he'll use it as another reason to blame me for working out of the house too much and running around with elegant men while neglecting my lord and master and my motherly duties." Karla rolled her eyes, then picked up her cell phone and tried to call Andreas. There was no answer and she left a message apologizing for having forgotten about their changed schedule. "I wish you had reminded me this morning. I'm really sorry."

Karla put the receiver down and browsed through the papers for the day. She had done well, selling one of her own paintings and one for a well-known artist from Italy. In addition, she had received the confirmation for her participation in an exhibition in France. A few years before, she would have rushed home in order to tell Andreas about her success and they would have celebrated. Now, however, she dreaded facing him tonight. He would be angry and she was so tired of his reproaches. Had things gone so sour between them?

On the way home later that evening, she stopped at the grocery store and bought the ingredients for Andreas's favorite dessert, chocolate *panna cotta*, a sweet made of cream, sugar, and chocolate. Instead of looking forward to surprising him with it, though, she felt resentful that she had to bribe him into a passable mood. What right did he have to make her feel so guilty about a small mistake?

As she parked the car and walked across the patio, the house looked deserted. She went inside and put the groceries away. On the kitchen table, there was a note. Andreas and Emilia had gone out to the grotto, the restaurant in town, for pizza. What did that mean? Were they bringing it home or were they eating there? She had prepared lasagna the day before and had planned to heat it up for dinner. After waiting for a while, she decided to walk to the restaurant.

It was May and pleasantly warm. The guests at the grotto were sitting outside under the chestnut trees. A fire was burning in the open fireplace. She saw Andreas and Emilia sitting next to Lena and Luigi, their neighbors and good friends. Karla was relieved when she saw them. Andreas wouldn't be able to yell at her with their friends present. Emilia waved happily at her.

"I'm going to the zoo with Tonio," the girl said, sounding excited.

"You are?" Karla asked. "That's wonderful. When are you going?"

"Saturday," Emilia said and put a small piece of pizza into her mouth.

Andreas gave her a quick glance; he looked serious but not hostile, but that didn't mean anything. He would never berate her among friends.

"You saw the note?" he asked.

"Yes, I was surprised. We actually planned having lasagna tonight," Karla said as she kissed Emilia, who smelled of garlic and tomatoes.

"Well, plans changed," he said. "They often do around here." The sarcasm wasn't lost on Karla, although Lena and Luigi didn't seem to notice.

They had a pleasant dinner together, but Karla didn't feel at ease. The tension between her and Andreas felt like a thick, poisonous cloud and robbed her of her appetite. She only nibbled on her salad. Soon, Emilia began to yawn and they decided to leave. They walked back in silence with Lena and Luigi, who did all the talking.

At home, alone in the living room after Emilia had gone to bed, Karla tried to lighten the mood. She quickly prepared the dessert and brought it into the living room. "A peace offering," she said.

"I'm really sorry about today. I totally forgot our change in schedule. I hope it didn't upset your whole day."

Andreas glanced at the dessert. Normally, he would have had a big smile on his face and dug in right away, but nothing was normal these days. He let the plate sit at the table and faced her. "Well, it did completely destroy my plans for the day. I had to cancel an important meeting and rush home." He spoke calmly, but the anger that hung in the air was palpable.

"Anyway, I made some different arrangements for the future," Andreas said. "I talked to Lena. She volunteered to pick up Emilia at daycare from now on, since we don't seem to get our schedule straight. I offered to pay her, but she refused to take any money."

We don't seem to get our schedule straight. What you really mean is that I don't get my schedule straight. Karla was mortified. "It's not as if this kind of thing happens all the time."

Andreas glared at her. "Karla, you don't seem to understand how serious this is. It's not just about picking Emilia up at daycare. You let her walk out alone on the street in Locarno. I understand that your job demands all your attention. But I'll be damned if I'm going to risk my child's well-being because you can't be a proper mother." He got up and walked toward the door. "I'm going to bed."

Karla was too stunned to say anything. She stared at the window, into the dark. The tears dropping on her hands made her realize she was crying. Never in their life together had he been so cruel and unfair. She spent the next hour sitting on the sofa, crying.

At about midnight, a more subdued Andreas came into the living room. "I'm sorry, I was out of line. I didn't mean you're not a good mother. My anger about the missed meeting got the better of me. I guess I should've reminded you this morning."

But his words didn't do much to alleviate her pain. "That's exactly what you meant. You've said it more than once, just not in such a direct way." Andreas sat next to her. She held up her hands in a defensive gesture. "Please don't touch me. Don't say anything, just leave me alone."

She covered her face with her hands. A few seconds later, she felt him get up and leave the room.

Chapter 28: Tonio

Tonio lifted Emilia onto the stone bench in front of the monkey house so she could see better. "Your brothers and sisters," he said, pointing at a group of young spider monkeys who were wrangling and chasing each other.

Emilia giggled. "Not my brothers."

"No?" Tonio kissed her. "Don't you play like that with your friends?"

Emilia put her arms around him. "No."

"Oh yes, I think so," Tonio insisted.

Mario patted Emilia's back. "I think these are Tonio's brothers and sisters."

"Yeah." She gave Tonio an impish look.

"Well, I think they are all our brothers and sisters . . . actually, our cousins," Tonio said. "Let's go and see the penguins now."

Tonio and Mario had taken Emilia to the zoo in Zurich to see the baby animals. It was late spring and the zoo had several new inhabitants—among others, three young tigers and baby elephants.

It had been Mario's idea after Tonio told him that he felt his parents needed a little time to themselves. Mario loved children and he was fond of little Emilia.

"She is such a little lady," he whispered to Tonio as they followed her along the path past the enclosure for the bigger monkeys.

Emilia was wearing a flowery skirt, matching blouse, and black patent-leather shoes.

"She insisted on wearing a dress and her new Sunday shoes to the zoo," Tonio said.

When Tonio had picked Emilia up, Karla had told him there was no way she could convince her to wear jeans and a T-shirt. The child had insisted she needed to dress up because she was going out with Tonio.

"She may have inherited your love of fashion." Mario put his arm around Tonio.

They arrived just in time at the enclosure where the penguins lived to see them march single file toward the water and dive in. Emilia was excited, watching their antics. Mario lifted her up and put her on his shoulders so she could watch over the heads of the people in front of them. Tonio snapped a few pictures.

After a while, they went on and decided to take a break and have lunch at one of the restaurants at the zoo. The restaurant had a large patio and the warm early-May sun allowed them to sit outside. A whiff of fried meat, sausages, and onions came from the kitchen, making Tonio feel hungry. He and Mario ordered hash browns and bratwurst, a specialty in the German Swiss part. Emilia's choice was "frie fries," her term for French fries, and a Coke. The two men chuckled as they watched the little girl's dainty eating habits. She picked up one French fry after the other, dunked it in a little bit of ketchup, put it in her mouth, and wiped her fingers on the paper napkin.

"I wonder if she was a princess or other royalty in one of her past lives," Mario said.

"My mother claims she is a reincarnation of her own mother. According to the photos, they do look alike," Tonio said.

Mario put his hand on Tonio's shoulder. "Have you ever thought about adopting a child?"

Tonio looked at him, startled. "Not really, although . . . I don't think it's possible for two men." He gave Mario an inquiring look. "What brought that on, anyway?"

"Well, I've been thinking about it. Registered partnerships for same-sex couples already exist and there is a petition in the Federal Council that would grant us the adoption of children. Of course, it may take years to get it through the National and States Council. I think it's just a question of time."

"Maybe," Tonio said.

"I'm done," Emilia said as she folded her napkin. "Can we see the elephants now?"

"I think that's a great idea," Tonio said. He turned to Mario. "Let's have coffee later, I don't think they have decent espresso here."

They took a leisurely walk toward the area with the elephants. Mario took Tonio's hand and squeezed it, then let go. "I think we should think about registered partnership."

Tonio's heart picked up speed and he looked at Mario, startled. "Did you just propose to me?"

Mario gave him an embarrassed look. "I guess so, something like that. Actually, I wanted to ask you at a slightly more romantic place than the zoo."

Tonio stopped. "I . . . I'm surprised. I . . . isn't this a little fast?"

"We've known each other for over four years. Isn't that long enough?"

"I guess it is." Tonio was flustered and felt a little over-whelmed.

Mario put his arm around him. "Just relax. We'll talk about it later. I shouldn't have sprung it on you like this."

They walked in silence for a while. "I hope our relationship will last," Tonio said. "So many of our friends are divorced or separated."

"We just have to make it work," Mario said. "Problem is people have this inflated idea of marriage. And when that fairy-tale image they had of their partner fades and a real human being emerges, they can't handle it."

Tonio chuckled. "Yes, Mr. Philosopher."

"We love each other, we'll make it work," Mario said.

Tonio wrinkled his forehead and sighed. "My parents love each other, at least I think they did in the past, but lately they have been fighting a lot. Something is wrong. They seemed generally unhappy. I don't know what happened. I'm beginning to think they shouldn't have had another child."

"What do you mean? They love Emilia." Mario looked at him, surprised.

"Sure they do. But let's face it. Having another kid after eighteen years, when the older siblings are already grown, is a little unusual. I mean, they're almost ready for grandchildren. Now, they have to raise another child. My mother struggles to advance her career as a painter. I think she's having some kind of midlife crisis. She's afraid she's running out of time or something. And my dad keeps harping on her to spend more time with Emilia. Then she calls him a macho and a bully." Tonio brushed through his dark longish hair.

"Hmm, is it really the child, or do they have other problems?" Mario said pensively. "My parents almost got divorced a few years ago. They've had a rocky relationship all their lives, but it got worse after we kids moved out. They kind of worked it out, but my mom once told me that after we children left and she and dad were alone, they had a difficult time. So perhaps it's the same with your parents."

Tonio nodded. "Possibly. I think part of the problem is that my father is worried about his business and the fact that my mother sometimes makes more money than he does. You know he's a great guy, but he has some old-fashioned ideas about partnerships. Mom stays home and Dad makes the money. And my mother isn't exactly the stay-at-home-mom type." He sighed. "I just hope they'll work it out. It would be devastating if our family fell apart."

"Well, we'll have to help them. We'll offer to babysit Emilia more, encourage them to take a vacation all by themselves. Let them have a second honeymoon or something. And we could get used to eventually having a child of our own."

Tonio gave him a playful punch. "You're serious about that, aren't you? Would you mind letting up on this adoption business a little bit? I'm just too young to be a father."

"All right, all right, calm down, for heaven's sake." Mario held up his hand and gave an irritated snort.

"We can still babysit Emilia more," Tonio said, trying to appease him. "Laura does most of it and she could use a break once in a while. Besides, I'm not against adopting a child, but let's take this a step at a time."

"Baby elephants," Emilia screamed as they approached the enclosure with the elephants.

"Well, look at that." Mario lifted Emilia up and hugged her, then sat her on top of the railing. "See, everyone is having young ones." He winked at Tonio, who rolled his eyes.

"Yes, Daddy."

Chapter 29: Laura

Laura felt her father's eyes on her. She was supposed to take care of the accounting, but had been daydreaming instead. She sighed and tried to focus on the Excel sheet on the laptop.

"You look a little gloomy today," he said. "What's the matter? Bored with the paperwork?"

Laura shook her head. "No, not really."

"You don't need to finish today. Take a break and work at your sculpture." He pointed at the half-finished marble figure on Laura's worktable.

"It's not that," Laura said and pushed her chair back. She faced her father. "Stefano wants to get married."

"Oh?" He lifted his eyebrow, then smiled. "Well, you're engaged." He motioned at her ring. "That should make you happy, so what's wrong?"

"What I meant is, he wants to get married before he leaves for England."

"Why the rush? That's in two weeks, I don't think that's possible." He frowned.

"I know and I told him I didn't want to rush into something so important. I want to be able to prepare a nice wedding. I mean . . ."

"Of course you do, honey. What's gotten into him? Why can't you guys wait until he returns or at least until we had time to prepare a wedding? What . . ." He peered at her. "Is there a valid reason for the rush? You're not pregnant, are you?"

Laura shook her head. "No. He just feels he needs to solidify our relationship, you know, to demonstrate publicly that we belong together. It's so dumb. We love each other, why can't we wait with getting married until the time is right?"

"I agree with you." Her father got up and sat next to her. "Hmm. He may feel insecure, leaving you alone."

"I thought about that. But that's absurd. Besides, if he is that insecure . . ."

"Oh, you know, people sometimes act irrational when it comes to matters of the heart." He chuckled. "Well, what did you guys decide?"

"I told him I didn't want to rush into this. He finally agreed, but ever since then, he's been acting kind of funny. Every once in while he drops a hint that I may not love him enough and that he's afraid

I'd want to meet someone else while he was gone. It really hurts me that he has so little confidence in me. . . . We had a big fight yesterday." Laura's voice trembled.

Her father put his hand on her shoulder. "Laura, don't let him bully you like this. He's obviously very insecure and has a tendency to be jealous. That can be bad for a relationship. He doesn't own you."

"I just hate seeing him hurt. At the same time, he makes me very angry for being so distrustful."

"You know what? It may not look that way right now, but I think this temporary separation is a good thing. It gives you both time to be by yourself and evaluate the relationship and how you feel about each other. And if it turns out that it doesn't work, then it's better to know it before you get married. Right?"

Laura nodded. "I don't want to lose him, though."

"Giving in to his unreasonable demands so you won't lose him? Does that sound like something you want to do?"

"No, certainly not," Laura said with conviction. She sighed. "Why is love so difficult?"

Her father hugged her. "My poor little girl. Yeah, love is difficult sometimes, as you can tell with Mama and me."

Laura wrapped her arms around him and put her head on his chest. "Papa, are you and Mama going to be okay?" She lifted her head and tried to read the expression in his eyes.

He looked at her, then lowered his gaze. "I hope so, sweetie. Don't worry about us, though. Look, we've been together for a long time and we've been through difficult times before. We'll manage, somehow."

"Did you ever regret having married?"

He shook his head. "No. Never. Not even during our most trying times. But this isn't about Mama and me. This is about you. You have to do what your heart tells you because you have to live with your decision for a long time." He put his hand under her chin and lifted her head. "If Stefano loves you, he'll let you be yourself and he'll respect your feelings. Else, he doesn't deserve you. Okay?"

Laura nodded. *It sounds so right when you talk about it, but when I'm by myself . . ."*

Chapter 30: Karla

Karla made a few minor changes to a painting, stepped back, and studied it with half-closed eyes, then took a deep breath and gave a satisfied sigh. She dropped the brush into the bowl of paint thinner. She liked what she saw.

The picture showed a landscape that she had painted out in nature, or, in the language of the painters, in "plain air." Although it looked realistic at first sight, it wasn't a naturalistic representation. What she tried to achieve was to show the environment around her not at a specific moment, as in a photograph, but over a longer period of time. The painting showed the transition from one point in time to another in one painting. Sunrise, midday, and sunset were mixed together and the effect was stunning. The picture was part of a series of paintings she had begun a few weeks ago and hoped to finish for the upcoming exhibition the following year in France.

It was a quiet day at the gallery; hardly any customers or visitors had shown up. Silvia, who was doing some paper-work, got up and the two of them looked at Karla's new picture.

"I still think Andreas has developed some macho tendencies about me staying home and fulfilling my familial and motherly duties," Karla said. "But I want to make an effort and meet him halfway. And I have to admit that he was right about me neglecting my painting. Since I focus more on it again, I feel more satisfied."

After she and Andreas had made up again following their last ugly fight, Karla had decided to cut back her hours at the gallery and spend an extra day at home. Silvia had agreed to accommodate her.

"I understand," Silvia said. "I don't know how justified your hubby is about familial and motherly duties. But I don't want your work here to cut into your art. I'll try to find someone for the extra day." She put her arm on Karla's shoulder. "This painting is amazing. I want it in the gallery after the exhibition."

Karla nodded. "You'll get it." She sighed. "I have to admit, I'll miss the extra cash, but I guess my marriage and my art take precedence."

"I hope so," Silvia said. "Well, talk about hubby." She motioned with her head at the shop window.

"Oh, he's probably coming to check on me, making sure I don't run around with one of my handsome male customers," Karla said, then became serious. "But why is he here?" She glanced at her watch. "He's supposed to pick up Emilia at daycare." Karla peered at Andreas, who came inside and gave a quick welcome nod to Silvia. She saw right away that something was wrong. He looked worried and a deep line had formed between his eyebrows. As he stepped up to Karla, he put his arms around her.

"Honey, I have some bad news."

Karla pushed him back and stared at him. Her heart was throbbing. "What? Something happened to Emilia?"

He shook his head. "No, she's fine."

"Then what? Tonio? Laura?"

"No. It's your father. He had a heart attack—"

"What?" Karla felt as though the air had been knocked out of her. She began to tremble. Andreas held her. "Is he . . . did he?"

"He's in the hospital in intensive care. The doctors are mildly optimistic he's going to make it."

"Oh my God." Karla was wringing her hands.

"Calm down, honey, it's going to be okay. We made reservations for you." He turned to Silvia. "Can you—"

"Don't worry," Silvia said. "She should definitely go and see him."

"I can't just . . ." Karla's face was pale and her eyes darted around the room.

"Yes, you can. I'll take you to the airport tomorrow. Let's go home right now and pack."

"Okay," Karla whispered and began to walk to the door as if in trance. She turned back. "I'm sorry, Silvia."

"Don't worry, please. I'll take care of everything here. You just focus on your dad now, okay?" Silvia walked them to the door. "I'll pray for him."

On the way home, Karla barely noticed anything around her. She clenched her hands together and tried to calm her labored breathing. Every once in a while Andreas put his hand on hers.

"How did you find out?" Karla asked after having calmed down a little.

"Rosa called," Andreas said. "I just got home with Emilia from daycare."

"Where is Emilia now?"

"At home, Laura is there and Tonio should be home anytime soon."

"What about Emilia? I don't know if I can take her along." Karla's mind was reeling and she didn't know what to focus on first.

"Leave Emilia with us, Karla. You'll have no time and energy to worry about her. Also, we don't know how she'll react to the high altitude of Cusco. She has never been that high up."

"How is she going to feel when I leave?" Karla asked.

"She'll be fine. You won't be gone for that long. Hopefully, your father will improve fast, or . . ." Andreas obviously didn't want to express the thought that had been on Karla's mind as well.

"We should've gone back more. I haven't seen him for so long." Karla's voice broke and tears rose to her eyes. "If he dies before I get there, I'll never forgive myself."

"Don't think the worst. He's going to make it, he's tough." Andreas touched her arm. "You don't need to feel guilty, it's not your fault. This is life. Your dad is a certain age and . . . anyway, he's going to be fine."

At home, Laura and Tonio were trying to calm Emilia, who was fussy and tearful, feeling that something was wrong. Karla went up to her and hugged her. "Mama will be back real soon, okay? You know, Grandpa is sick and I have to go and help take care of him."

"I want to go, too, I want to see Grandpa," Emilia said.

"It's too far, sweetie." Andreas lifted her up. "Besides, you have to stay with Papa and Laura and Tonio or we'll be all alone." He motioned to Laura. "Go help Mama pack." He continued to hug Emilia. As Karla retired to her bedroom, she looked back and saw Tonio making funny faces at Emilia, who gave a hesitant grin.

Laura followed her. "She'll be fine with us. Don't worry, Mama. I'm so sorry about Grandpa."

"Did you talk to Rosa?" Karla asked, opening the closet and pulling out a suitcase.

"No, Papa did."

"I should call her," Karla said. She began to sort through her closet and chest of drawers, then sat on the bed, defeated. "I don't even know what to pack. What's the season in Cusco?" She wiped the tears from her face.

"Well, it's June here, beginning of summer, so in Cusco it's beginning of winter. Better pack some warm stuff." Laura pulled out a couple of pants and sweaters from Karla's closet.

Together, they managed to pack a suitcase. Karla checked her passport, which fortunately was still valid.

Emilia

Karla wasn't able to settle down that night. Images of her father and her Peruvian family kept circling in front of her eyes whenever she tried to close them. Andreas gave her a soothing massage and she eventually fell into a fitful slumber.

The following morning Andreas drove Karla to the airport in Zurich. Emilia and Laura accompanied them. Andreas and Karla felt that letting Emilia watch the many planes land and take off from the visitors terrace would take her mind off her mother's departure for a while. As it turned out, the farewell was less painful for Emilia than it was for Karla. She cried a little when Karla went through passport control, but when Karla turned around to wave, the little girl waved as well. Karla watched as Andreas picked her up and he and Laura made their way toward the outside terrace.

As Karla walked along the gangway to the plane, she got a glimpse of her family on the visitors terrace. Andreas waved his jacket back and forth. She took a deep breath, waved back, and blinked away the tears. Inside, she stowed her carry-on bag in the upper bin. She pushed an art magazine into the seat pocket in front of her and sat down. While waiting for the plane to leave, she pulled out the magazine and paged through it, looking for an article about Gustav Klimt, the Austrian painter whose work she loved. She began to read, then dropped it into her lap with a sigh. She wasn't able to concentrate.

When she arrived in Madrid, where she had a two-hour wait, she called Rosa again. "He's still in intensive care," Arturo's wife said. "But things are looking better. They'll move him tomorrow if his condition remains stable."

The news made Karla feel a little better again. "Tell him I love him and I'm on my way." Back on the plane, she ordered a glass of red wine when the flight attendant came by with the drinks. Normally she didn't like to drink alcohol while flying, but today she hoped it would help her sleep.

The wine, however, wasn't able to squelch her anxiety. The uncomfortable airline seats didn't help matters much, so Karla spent the time between Madrid and Lima nodding off at times, and thinking about her family in Switzerland she left behind and the one in Peru awaiting her.

Would Emilia be all right without her? Her four-year-old daughter had become a little more independent during the last year spent in daycare. She was secure and happy with Andreas and she loved being with Laura and Tonio and their partners. They would help her get over the separation. Karla gave a wistful smile at the thought of her "little princess," as Tonio called his younger sister.

Andreas? She missed him, and at the same time she was relieved to put some distance between them. Perhaps it would help her clear her mind and clarify her feelings for him. Things hadn't been good between them. They seemed to have argued more often and more bitterly the past couple of years than in their whole married life combined.

Before Emilia was born, they had shared the upbringing of the children as well as their careers as artists. But then something changed. Andreas became increasingly critical of her work at the gallery. At first, they both enjoyed the little extra money Karla made, which was a welcome addition to Andreas's income.

His tombstone business had gone through some tough times and his income was down from the years before. Part of it had to do with the difficult economic situation. On top of this, more and more people opted for cremation for their deceased relatives and for smaller and cheaper memorial plates instead of full-sized gravestones.

At the same time that he was struggling, Karla's income from her art dealings and the sale of her paintings had risen incrementally. There were months she made more money than he did.

Emilia

He always denied it, but Karla suspected that his criticism about her spending too much time at the gallery was at least in part due to jealousy and insecurity. Not only was he no longer the main provider, he also wasn't as successful in the art world as Karla had been the past few years. He was in a phase of reduced creativity and Karla knew from experience what that felt like. She had had her share of painter's block and times of creative paralysis. And he was a man and, of course, would never admit to needing help. He'd rather project his lack of artistic endeavor onto Karla, claiming that her art had stagnated because she was hobnobbing with elegant collectors and patrons.

The flight attendant walked by with a tray of beverages. Karla grabbed a glass of orange juice. After sipping the cool liquid, she leaned her head back and closed her eyes with a sigh. Andreas could be such a grouch sometimes. But she loved him and she wanted their relationship to improve again. It was important not just for Emilia but also for her older children.

The week before, Laura had taken Stefano to the airport. It had been hard on her—on both of them. The pressure of the past few weeks when Stefano prepared for his departure and his disappointment at her refusal to marry him before he left had weighed on Laura's mind. Once he was gone, she felt both sad and relieved. Now, she would have more time to herself and would be able to help take care of Emilia while Karla was gone. She was going to visit Stefano in a few weeks, once he had settled in somewhat, and he planned to spend his vacation at home.

And Tonio and Mario were going to apply for joint partnership. Karla and Andreas felt Tonio was a little young for such a commitment but accepted his decision. She suspected, though, that her son wasn't as eager to tie the knot as Mario was. Mario was six years older than Tonio and ready to settle down. When Karla voiced her reservation to Andreas, he had said that he felt that Mario was a good influence on Tonio because he was a little older and more mature. That was a far cry from his initial reaction to Tonio and Mario's relationship. Andreas had come a long way in that respect. He was a good man and Karla didn't want to lose him.

She sighed, thinking of her Peruvian family. *Hang in there, papá,* she begged silently. Karla's father hadn't been around when she was growing up in Switzerland. Karla had been the result of a passionate but short-lived fling between Karla's mother and her father. Although Arturo had tried to develop a relationship with his daughter abroad, it took Karla a long time to fully accept him as her father. Now that she loved him, he was in danger of being snatched away from her again.

Chapter 31: Andreas

Andreas and Laura were sitting on the patio, watching the sky darken. The sound of crickets and an occasional hoot of an owl nearby interrupted the calm of the evening from time to time. It smelled of freshly cut grass. Emilia was curled up in Andreas's arms, trying to stay awake.

"Time for you to go to bed," Andreas said, but Emilia shook her head.

Laura and Andreas glanced at each other and smiled.

"Where is Mama now?" Emilia asked and yawned.

"Hmm, somewhere in the sky over the Atlantic Ocean," Andreas said.

"Where is the Atlantic?" Emilia yawned again.

"The Atlantic Ocean is the big lake between Europe and America," Andreas said. "But you're tired, honey, you really should lie down."

"You have to lie down, too," Emilia said.

"Want me to tell you a good-night story?" Laura asked and brushed through Emilia's silky hair.

Emilia nodded. "Yes, about Nemo." A few days before, she had watched the DVD with the story *Alla ricerca di Nemo*, or *Finding Nemo*.

"All right, let's go." Laura got up and took Emilia by the hand.

Emilia held on to Andreas. "Papa has to come, too."

"Okay, let's all listen to Laura's story about Nemo." Andreas smiled at Laura.

She rolled her eyes. "I don't even know the story, I haven't seen the movie yet."

"Oh, just make something up; she's already half asleep anyway." Andreas picked Emilia up.

"No, I'm not," the girl protested.

After Emilia was lying in bed, hugging her plush bunny rabbit, Andreas and Laura sat on the bed next to her. Laura began telling a story about a fish by the name of Nemo. After the second sentence, Emilia's eyelids began to droop, and soon she was fast asleep. Andreas covered her with a lightweight comforter and opened the window, since it was still warm after a hot day in June.

They tiptoed out of the room and sat back down on the patio. In the meantime, it had gotten dark and a pleasantly cool breeze came from the Maggia River.

"Want some tea?" Laura asked.

"Hmm, I feel more like a glass of Prosecco," Andreas said.

"Oh, we have Prosecco?"

"Yes, it's in the refrigerator. Let me get it." Andreas got up and walked into the kitchen. He came back with a bottle and two glasses. "I was going to open it last night, but then all the commotion started with Mama packing and I forgot all about it."

Laura lit the oil lamp on the granite table and Andreas opened the bottle and poured them both a glass of bubbly white wine. He toasted Laura, who smiled at him. Flickering lights from the candle flame danced across her face.

"I'm so glad you're here, honey," Andreas said. "I'd feel very lost without you."

Laura put her hand on his arm. "I really hope Grandpa is going to be okay."

"So do I," Andreas said. "The latest news from Rosa is quite encouraging and I'm sure having Mama around will cheer him up as well." He took a sip of wine and glanced at her. "How are you and Stefano doing?"

"Good," Laura said. "We talk on the phone every day and send each other text messages. He is doing really well and he loves his classes and the teachers." She paused. "I miss him, of course, but . . ."

"But?" Andreas asked.

"Well, to be honest, I'm also a little relieved to be by myself again. I can focus more on my work and my own life. Things had been pretty intense with Stefano's harebrained idea about rushing to the altar." Laura chuckled.

"Yeah, I understand. Sometimes, a little distance helps us clarify things." Andreas took another sip of wine. "Although, I already miss Mama."

"Well, that's a good thing, isn't it?" Laura said.

Andreas nodded. "I guess so." He sighed. "Question is, does she miss me as well?"

"I'm sure she does," Laura said.

"I hope so." Andreas said matter-of-factly. He glanced at Laura, who yawned and stretched. "But you're tired, honey, you should turn in as well."

"Okay, Papa," she said and got up. "If you hear from Mama, call me." She bent down to kiss him.

She walked across the patio to the bedroom cottage. Andreas looked after her, then gazed at the dark forest to the left of their property. He took a deep breath, inhaling the scent of freshly cut grass, and thought about the upheaval of the previous couple of days, the news of Arturo's heart attack and Karla's rushed departure. He was glad that the turmoil was over for the time being and that he had some peace again.

Andreas was sure he had dreamt of Karla when he felt a light touch on his arm.

"Papa?" a voice whispered, and he felt a warm breath on his ear.

He lifted his head. "What's the matter, *cara*?"

Emilia's small frame in her nightgown lit up against the light of the almost-full moon shining through the open window. "Can I sleep in Mama's bed?"

Andreas sat up. "Did you have a bad dream?" Sometimes Emilia crawled into bed with them when she dreamt of something that scared her.

"No, but I don't want to sleep alone," she said in her wispy voice.

"All right, come on." Andreas pushed the light comforter back and Emilia walked around the bed and climbed up on Karla's side. She scooted close to Andreas and he put his arm around her.

"Better?" he asked.

"Uh-huh," she said. She snuggled up to him and yawned.

Andreas smiled. "That's good, now Papa isn't alone anymore, either."

There was no answer, just a light snoring sound. Lying on his back and listening to Emilia's even breathing, he realized that in the past twenty-five years of his life he hadn't slept alone except for a few times when one of them had been ill and needed to recover. There had always been a presence next to him.

Karla and he had never even considered sleeping in separate rooms, as was the case with a few other couples they knew who had been married for a long time. They had slept in the same bed even at times they had been at odds with each other, sometimes back to back and with a large gap between them. He sighed, thinking back to the times when there had been no distance, just two warm bodies with their arms around each other after making love, slowly drifting off to sleep.

He carefully slid to the edge so as not to wake Emilia and got up. Standing at the window, inhaling the mild night air and the sweet scent of the few rose bushes Karla had planted in the spring, he wondered if she, too, was sleeping alone in her room in Cusco, now that her two half sisters and her brother had married and moved out. He pictured her in her bed, wrapped in a bunch of alpaca blankets against the freezing nights in the Peruvian Andes.

He shook his head; he had forgotten the time difference. Karla was probably up, busy with her father and her family. She had no time to miss him. What if she decided to stay and not come back? It was a ridiculous thought; she would never do that. Even if she didn't miss him that much, she'd never leave her children. But such fleeting thoughts made him aware how tentative and troubled their relationship had become.

Leaning his head against the window frame, he closed his eyes. *Dear God,* he silently prayed, *help us keep our family intact.*

PART THREE: A LONG JOURNEY HOME

Chapter 32

Tonio was busy putting away a few shirts when the bell at the front door of the boutique chimed.

"Well, look who is here, sister of mine." He stepped from behind the counter and sauntered toward the door. "How may I help you, pretty lady? Looking for something chic for your *beau* in England?"

Laura smiled and shook her head. "No, I was shopping for some carving tools and I wanted to see if you felt like having lunch somewhere. It's nice and cool along the lake."

Tonio glanced at his watch. "If you can wait for a few minutes until my help gets here, I'll join you."

"Isn't Mario here?" Laura asked.

"Nope, my partner in crime is in Italy. He and his dad are visiting some of our suppliers, finalizing purchases for the fall fashion. So I'm holding down the fort."

"They didn't take you along?" Laura asked.

"Well, I get to go next time together with Mario to get ready for the spring season. That's actually more fun, we get to pick out the more colorful outfits for spring and summer. But here is Ernesto." Tonio waved toward the door, where a slender young man with dark eyes and wavy hair entered. He gave them a big smile.

Laura smiled back. "Hey, Ernesto."

"Hi, sweetie." The young man hugged her. He smelled of an expensive aftershave.

"Just in time," Tonio said and looked at himself in the mirror, combing his fingers through his hair.

"Am I ever late?" Ernesto said, giving Tonio a stern look.

"Of course not, sweetie pie." Tonio put his arm around him and kissed him on the cheek. "I didn't mean it that way, but I'm going out to lunch with a lovely young lady."

Ernesto put his hand on his hip and wiggled in a suggestive manner. "What? I'm going to tell your sweetheart about that."

Laura rolled her eyes. "Please, you two, give me a break."

They all laughed. Tonio put his arm around Laura and the two left the store. They walked down to the lake and sat on the patio of one of the restaurants.

It was a warm day in June and Tonio enjoyed the invigorating breeze from the lake. Back in the boutique, the air tended to be stuffy. He watched as Laura turned her face toward the sun and closed her eyes. She was a little paler than usual and seemed to have lost some weight.

"Are you all right? You look skinnier."

Laura opened her eyes and smiled. "I'm trying to slim down a little."

"Ah, getting ready for a hot and juicy night with your *amante* in England." Tonio winked at her, then turned serious. "You know you don't need to slim down. You have a perfect physique. I used to kid you about being a heavyweight champion, but you're attractive and well-proportioned. So stop worrying about your looks."

"Well, thanks for the encouragement, but you haven't seen the number on the scale. I did gain weight. I know why, too. Ever since Stefano left, I've been eating more than usual, snacking and so on."

Tonio nodded. "Loneliness fat—you're trying to compensate for the lack of sex."

Laura playfully punched his arm. "Sex. Is that all you can think about?"

"It's the breath of life, what can I say?" Tonio lifted his hands in a resigned gesture. "But anyway, when are you going to see him?"

"He has some time off in July and early September before the fall term starts. So we made plans to get together in England and perhaps in Paris. But now with Mama gone, I don't know."

Tonio wrinkled his forehead. "What do you mean? You're not thinking about canceling your plans just because Mama is gone?"

"Well, I hate to leave Papa having to take care of Emilia all by himself."

"Oh, for God's sake, stop that nonsense."

The waiter came by with two plates of pasta, salads, and two glasses of red wine. After he had left, Tonio stared at Laura. "Laura, Papa is very well capable of taking care of Emilia. Besides, I'm here, too, have you forgotten? You don't have much confidence in my motherly or fatherly abilities, do you?"

"Of course I do. You're wonderful with Emilia. But you don't live at home anymore and you have your own life. I don't—"

"You have your own life, too, and I don't want you to change your plans. You're going to see him and that's that. Mama should long be back by then. Besides, Mario and I can help Papa. In fact, it might be a good thing." Tonio chuckled. "We'll have Emilia with us and Mario can get a feel for what it means to take care of a child. Perhaps it will dampen his enthusiasm about wanting to adopt one."

"You don't seem too enthusiastic about it," Laura said.

"Oh, I don't know." Tonio shrugged. "Sure, it would be great to be able to adopt a child eventually. I love children, too. But I'm afraid Mario has set his heart and hope on this initiative floating around the federal government that would give same-sex couples the right to adopt children. It's not going to happen right away." Tonio took a sip of wine. He put the glass back and glanced at the lake.

The breeze had picked up somewhat and the whitecaps on the surface glimmered in the sunshine. A thin layer of mist enveloped the mountains behind the lake.

Tonio glanced at Laura. "It will pass eventually, but there are still enough people against it. I'm just afraid Mario is going to be heartbroken if it gets turned down."

"And you?" Laura asked.

"I'm fine with or without children. Besides, I'm only twenty-two, for Christ's sake. There is still a lot I would like to do by myself and with Mario before settling down with a bunch of kids."

"That I can understand," Laura said.

"What about you, Laura? Have you thought of children?"

"Sure, eventually I would love to have children, in the future sometime. We're not even married yet."

Tonio watched her; she seemed preoccupied. "You know, I think we have the same problem," he said.

"What's that?" Laura glanced at him, then continued to gaze at the lake.

"We have significant others who put us under pressure. They feel more certain about the relationship than we do."

Laura wrinkled her forehead. "You may have a point. I mean, I love Stefano, but I'm just not in such a rush to get married. What's wrong with waiting a little? We belong to each other without that piece of paper."

"I know. It's the same thing with registering for partnership. Mario is gung ho about it. It's okay with me, but it just doesn't make that much of a difference to me. Why rush into something like that?"

Laura looked at him, her green eyes lighting up in the sunlight. "That's what Papa said, too."

Tonio took a deep breath. "Do you think we hesitate because we're afraid the relationships won't last? Or are we just too chicken? I mean, our parents don't give us much encouragement right now about relationships with all their fighting and disagreements."

"Could be. Then again, their relationship seems to have been okay for many years. It's just recently that they don't see eye-to-eye," Laura said.

"Well, the 'recently' is going on for about two years, or longer," Tonio said in a low voice.

"I just hope things will improve when Mama comes back from Peru," Laura said. "Right now, they are all lovey-dovey on the phone, claiming they miss each other." She waved at the waiter. "Want some espresso?"

Tonio nodded. "It may help—the separation I mean. Perhaps they'll realize what they would lose not being together. Then again, Mama sounded really happy when I talked to her on the phone. She doesn't give me the feeling she misses us."

"Well, think about it. Her father, who she thought was going to die, is recovering. And she is together with her Peruvian family after many years. Of course she's happy. I'm sure she misses us, too."

"I guess you're right," Tonio said.

The waiter brought two cups of espresso. Laura paid the bill, shaking her head when Tonio wanted to pay. "I invited you."

Tonio emptied his cup, then glanced at his watch. "I better get back."

"Yes, and I need to go home," Laura said.

They both got up and Tonio pointed his finger at Laura. "And Laura, you *are* going to England or France, okay? If not, you're going to be in big trouble with me."

"Yes, my little brother. I wouldn't want to risk that." Laura smiled at him and waved as she walked away.

Tonio looked after her for a while, then walked back to the boutique. *She takes her role as older sister too seriously. She needs to loosen up and Mama needs to get back.*

Chapter 33: Karla

Karla put down her drawing pad and glanced at her father, who was resting comfortably on the easy chair next to her. They were sitting on the patio of Arturo's home in the San Blas area of Cusco. Although it was winter in the southern hemisphere, the late-June sun was pleasantly warm in the afternoon. The sky above Cusco was a clear blue and the air smelled of dry grass and dust. The hills next to the house were a yellow-brown color.

Karla was sketching the outline of the mountains nearby. Ever since she got here and her father started feeling better, she had felt a surge of creativity. The environment with its colors and hues was perfect for the new kinds of paintings she had begun back in Switzerland. She had to admit, she was happy here, happier than she had been in a long time. It was wonderful to be able to relax without the pressure of a demanding husband and all the family obligations. She missed Emilia, Laura, and Tonio, and sometimes also Andreas, but she talked to them on the phone every day. They seemed to be getting along really well without her. Even Emilia, who had missed her in the beginning and had sometimes cried a little on the phone, was now always cheerful. When she was busy playing or listening to a story Laura, Tonio, or Andreas told her and Karla happened to call, she didn't even want to talk to her. "Hi, Mama, I'm busy. Talk to you tomorrow," she would call to the amusement of everyone around.

At first, Karla was a little put off that they all got along so well without her, but she was more relieved than jealous. It gave her the freedom to be herself for a while. Over the years she had forgotten what it felt like to be in charge of her own destiny. It was almost like being single again without any pressing obligations except for keeping her recovering father company, something she really enjoyed. Arturo was so grateful for every little sign of attention.

She also loved being with the rest of the family. She visited with her half sisters, Manuela and Maria, who had married and moved out, and with Antonio, her youngest brother, who lived at home. He worked in his father's business and practically ran it himself since Arturo's heart attack. With Rosa, Arturo's wife, she spent hours talking, laughing, shopping, and helping her cook. She was the beloved daughter again and she had to admit, she enjoyed that position tremendously.

And then there was Julio, her handsome cousin, the son of Uncle Guillermo, who had died many years before. Julio was about her age and a widower. He had lost his wife to cancer two years before and was still mourning her. But he seemed to enjoy taking his cousin around in his car. He drove her to places where she painted and kept her company. And Karla liked being with him. He was a serious, sometimes somber, sensitive man, and he treated her with kindness and respect. She couldn't help but compare his behavior to that of Andreas, and Andreas didn't fare very well in that comparison. She didn't see Julio as a rival to Andreas. After all, he was her cousin and there was a blood relationship, although a distant one. But she simply enjoyed being with someone who treated her well and admired her painting.

Am I being selfish? she asked herself occasionally. But then again, didn't she have the right to be happy? And Emilia and everyone in Switzerland was well taken care of. Besides, she would return soon. Her return ticket was for the end of July, but the thought of extending it had crossed her mind occasionally.

Her father stirred and got up. He came over, put his hand on her shoulder, and looked at her drawing. He smiled and kissed her hair. "Want some tea?"

Arturo was on a strict diet, which meant no caffeine—just herbal tea. Although he complained about having to drink this "watery liquid," he slowly got used to it. However, he refused to give up his glass of beer in the evening. "Alcohol is good for the heart," he claimed.

Karla got up. "That would be nice. I'll get it," she said.

"Oh no, I'll get it. I'm not an invalid yet, you know," Arturo said. He walked somewhat slowly across the patio and went inside.

As Karla followed him with her eyes, she became aware once again how frail he still looked. He was improving every day, but he was getting old. There was no doubt about that. She didn't know how much longer she would have him. The thought made her wish to stay on even more pressing. His seventy-fifth birthday was at the beginning of August.

What would Andreas think if she stayed? And she couldn't stay away from Emilia for that long. It would be great if Andreas came and brought her along. Karla took a deep breath. She would suggest it to him. That way Arturo and the family would finally get to meet Emilia and they could all celebrate Arturo's birthday together.

Chapter 34: Andreas

"Come on, sweetie," Andreas called to Emilia, who stood by the side of the road, holding on to her doll stroller. The doll had long light brown hair and the same green-and-yellow patterned dress as Emilia was wearing.

Andreas walked a few steps back and tried to help her push the stroller, but she insisted on doing it herself. Only when they got to the uneven unpaved part of the road and the stroller got stuck did she let Andreas carry it while she held the doll in her arms.

Emilia

"Independent little creature, aren't you?" Andreas said.

"Yes," Emilia agreed matter-of-factly.

Andreas grinned as he watched the little girl who had developed a mind of her own and was a lot less needy than she had been just a year before. She wasn't as attached to her mother anymore and quite happy to stay with other people once in a while, which was a great relief to Andreas now that Karla was gone. He shared the babysitting with Laura, and sometimes Tonio and Mario picked her up for an outing. Today, Laura was working at Andreas's studio and Andreas took the time off to be with Emilia, since preschool was out for a few weeks.

At the top of the hill there was a children's playground with a slide, a small merry-go-round, and monkey bars. Andreas was surprised when he saw a man and a young woman sitting on one of the wooden benches and a little boy playing on the monkey bars. Normally the playground was deserted, since it was vacation time and the few families with little children in the small village were on vacation. Some of them took their kids to the larger entertainment parks along the lake in Locarno.

Andreas didn't recognize the visitors—a man, probably in his fifties, and a young woman who couldn't be more than in her mid-twenties. She was pretty, with long, dark hair and a slender figure. She was dressed in jeans and a short yellow top that covered a nicely shaped bosom and left the smooth tanned skin of her flat stomach exposed. Andreas noticed this in the few seconds while the girl got up and removed a small cooler from the bench so Andreas could sit down.

They greeted each other and Andreas thanked her and sat down, while Emilia sauntered across the playground to the merry-go-round.

"Push me, Papa," she called after she settled down inside, her doll in her lap.

Andreas was getting ready to get up when the little boy jumped down from the monkey bars. "Want me to push you?" he asked. He was about six years old, skinny, with curly dark hair, dressed in shorts and a T-shirt.

Emilia gave him a hesitant look, then glanced at her father.

"But be careful, Paolo," the young woman said. "Push her slowly."

"I will," the boy said. "May I?" he asked Emilia, and held on to the railing.

"Let him push you," Andreas called.

Emilia nodded and Paolo began to turn the merry-go-round, then jumped inside and showed Emilia how to turn the wooden wheel in the middle. Now, they both turned the wheel and Emilia was giggling as they swooshed around.

Andreas and the visitors looked at one another and smiled.

"I'm Andreas," he said, and shook hands with the man and the girl.

"Giorgio," the man said, "and this is my daughter Susanna. And the little tyke over there is Paolo, my grand-son."

"You're not from here, are you?" Andreas said.

"No, we live close by, in Cordevio, but we don't have a playground there. I found out about this one from a friend of mine, and since we don't always want to drive to Locarno, we thought we'd check it out."

"Yes, it's convenient. We bring Emilia here quite often," Andreas said.

"How old is your granddaughter?" Giorgio asked.

"She's my daughter and she is four."

Giorgio put his hand on his mouth. "Oh, I'm sorry."

"Don't be." Andreas laughed. "I could be her grandfather as far as age goes. We have two grown children, and Emilia here came along much later. She was quite a surprise."

"Well, she sure is a cute surprise," Giorgio said.

"Thanks, yes, we're quite happy. Being a father at my age keeps you young a little longer, I think."

"What about your wife? I assume she's quite a bit younger than you are." He waved his hand. "I'm sorry, I'm such a gossip. It's none of my business."

"Dad, you should think before you talk." Susanna gave Andreas an apologetic smile, which made her beautiful face even more attractive.

"I know, I know. Forget I asked."

"Don't worry, no problem. My wife is only three years younger than I am. She was forty-four when Emilia was born. To be honest, she wasn't too happy about being pregnant again after all that time."

"I can imagine. That must have been quite an adjustment," Giorgio said.

Andreas nodded. "Yes, it was. Fortunately, our older children are a real help and I enjoy taking care of Emilia, as well. So we manage."

In the meantime, the children had left the merry-go-round and were heading for the slide. Again Emilia called on Andreas to catch her at the bottom. She didn't want to fall off and get her dress dirty.

The three adults laughed. "She is such a dainty little thing," Andreas said. "My older kids were real rambunctious when they were little." He called to Emilia. "Don't worry, if your dress gets dirty, we can wash it."

"Will you wash it for me?" Emilia asked.

"Sure I will," Andreas said with chuckle.

"Tell you what," Paolo said to her. "I'll slide down ahead of you and catch you at the bottom."

"There you go," Andreas said as he watched Paolo sit on the slide and Emilia behind him. The two of them scooted down and Paolo stopped her at the bottom. Andreas turned to Susanna and Giorgio. "Looks like my daughter found a little gentleman."

Giorgio laughed. "Sounds like the perfect pair."

"How old is Paolo?" Andreas asked.

"He just turned six," Susanna said. "His birthday was in May."

Giorgio wrinkled his forehead. "Unfortunately, he doesn't have a caring father like your daughter does," he said in a subdued tone.

"Oh?" Andreas glanced at Susanna.

"I'm a single mother," she explained. "Unfortunately, his father doesn't take much of an interest in him."

"That's too bad," Andreas said. "I could never understand that."

"Neither can I," Giorgio said. "How can a man not like a darling boy like Paolo?"

"It's not that he doesn't like him," Susanna said. "He just hasn't accepted full responsibility for his existence. He tries."

Giorgio put his hand on Susanna's shoulder. "She is too nice, she always defends him."

"Well, I still hope he'll come around. Paolo adores him and I don't want to create unnecessary friction," Susanna said.

Andreas observed her quietly. She seemed to be very mature for her age. And she was attractive and a nice person. She could find another man.

"Besides," Susanna continued with a smile, "he may not have a perfect father, but he does have a wonderful grandfather and grandmother." She hugged Giorgio and he patted her hand.

"That's worth a lot," Andreas said.

"He is our pride and joy," Giorgio said, then glanced at his watch. "But I'm sorry to break up our little gathering. We should be going soon, if you still want to do that shopping."

Susanna nodded. "Yes, I guess so. He really does need some new clothes, he is growing so fast," she said and got up. She waved at Paolo. "Time to go, honey. Say goodbye to your new friend."

The kids came running toward them. Emilia looked sad. "I don't want him to go," she said to Andreas and grabbed Paolo's hand.

"Well, it looks like a romance is developing." Giorgio winked at them.

"Perhaps Paolo and his mom can come back another day," Andreas suggested.

"We'd love to," Susanna said. "Right now, he's not in school, so yes. Would you like that, Paolo?"

"Yeah, sure," the little boy said nonchalantly.

"Tomorrow?" Emilia asked eagerly.

"Tomorrow would be good for me," Andreas said. "The rest of the week, I'll be in Lugano and my daughter watches Emilia. But, of course, she could bring her as well. My wife is in Peru right now, visiting her family. Her father was in bad health."

"Oh, I hope he's okay."

"Yes, he's getting better."

"Tomorrow sounds good to me, too," Susanna said.

"Great." Andreas felt happy.

"Oh, good," Emilia piped, clapping her hands.

"Well, a happy ending to a good day." Giorgio shook Andreas's hand. He gently brushed over Emilia's hair.

As the two departed, Andreas looked after them. Susanna turned around and waved. It would be nice to have some company babysitting Emilia, he thought. And such charming company on top of it. He smiled.

After Paolo left, Emilia didn't seem to have any interest in the playground. She undressed and dressed her doll for a while, then wanted to go home.

"Time to go," Andreas said. "We'll go out for dinner to-night, so Laura doesn't have to cook. How does that sound?"

Emilia nodded wistfully. Andreas bent down and kissed her. "You'll see Paolo again soon."

Chapter 35: Laura

Laura hung up the phone and smiled. Stefano had just passed an important exam and had been bubbly and overjoyed. It seemed that his fear of not having the academic qualifications for higher education had dissolved. So far he had been doing really well. Not even Laura's remark that she had second thoughts about visiting him in case her mother wasn't back by then seemed to dampen his enthusiasm.

"Don't worry. If you can't come, I'll spend my vacation in Switzerland. In fact, I'll have a long weekend two weeks from now. I can hop on the night train and visit. Or, we could meet in Paris. I'm sure they can spare you for a weekend," he said, then went on telling her about the school and some of the friends he had made.

Laura was glad Stefano was so full of enthusiasm. He sounded more confident and less needy and he hadn't mentioned the wedding in a while. Relieved that the immediate pressure was off, she at the same time wondered what caused his backing off. Perhaps a good-looking English girl? When she mentioned it jokingly, he laughed.

"Well, there are a few hot babes in my class," he said. "But don't worry, I'm so busy with school and homework, I don't have much time or energy to lust after them," he teased her.

"What about you?" he went on. "Any handsome hunks I should be worried about?" However, he didn't sound worried at all.

Putting away the washed dishes in the kitchen, Laura began to wonder if he really was that busy. He had mentioned once that he and a few friends occasionally went to the pub after class, and he had also talked about a few trips to downtown London on the weekends to see some shows. He may be working hard, but he seemed to play equally hard. Well, it was okay that he was enjoying himself, wasn't it? But he could've sounded a little more like he missed her.

Laura took a deep breath. "You don't make any sense, girl," she said to herself. "First, you complain that he is too clingy, and now, you don't like the fact that he is not pining for you enough." Tonio was right when he said the other day that women didn't make sense.

As if her thoughts had conjured him up, Tonio entered the kitchen, followed by Mario, who carried a large pizza box. Tonio put two grocery bags on the table and hugged Laura.

"Sweetheart, you may congratulate us, we filed the papers."

"Oh? I thought you wanted to wait until Mama gets back," Laura said.

"Well, we have to wait for a few weeks anyway until it's final. We'll celebrate properly once she is back. This here is just a little prenuptial celebration."

"Pizza, oh goodie," Emilia shouted as she came rushing into kitchen.

"What are we celebrating?" Andreas, who followed her, asked. He pointed at the grocery bags and the bottle of wine and lemonade Tonio unpacked.

"Marriage," Tonio said to him. "I mean, we're celebrating having filed the papers for registered partnership."

"I see," Andreas said. "Aren't you a little bit young for this?" He lifted his eyebrow and scrutinized Tonio.

"Well, it'll take a while for this to be approved. There is still time to back out." Tonio poked Mario teasingly.

"You're already thinking of backing out?" Mario scowled at him.

"Just kidding, relax." Tonio turned to Andreas. "Anyway, Papa, what do you think? You're okay with it?"

"You have to know what's best for you. Besides, what say in the matter do I have anyway?"

Tonio sighed. "Believe it or not, Papa, I value your opinion."

"You do? Well, in that case, I guess I approve. You already live together, you might as well make it official."

"Thanks." Tonio hugged his father.

Andreas hugged him back and gave a quick smile. "Okay, now what about dinner?"

"Can I have some ice cream?" Emilia asked.

"Later, for dessert," Laura said and took a large salad bowl out of the cabinet.

"I want some now." Emilia eyed the large tub of chocolate-and-marshmallow gelato Tonio was putting into the freezer.

"The answer is no," Andreas said. "Stop whining."

Emilia gave him a dirty look and went over to Mario, who greeted her with an exaggerated bow. "Do you think you could show me how to set the table, Your Royal Highness?"

They decided to eat outside at the granite table, since the evening was warm enough. The summer breeze from the Maggia brought the scents of jasmine and lavender. Mario opened the bottle of red wine and poured everybody a glass.

"To us," Tonio said and raised his glass. Laura, Andreas, and Mario followed.

"May you be happy together," Andreas said.

Tonio's facial color deepened and his eyes misted over. Laura was happy to see that her father approved of their union. She knew his favorable opinion meant a lot to her brother.

For a while it was quiet as everybody ate. Emilia decided she didn't want any salad, instead saving her appetite for dessert. Andreas gave her a stern look. "No dessert unless you eat your salad."

Emilia

Emilia made a face and began pushing pieces of lettuce and carrots around her plate.

"Don't play with your food," Andreas said.

"Uh, Dad is getting tough with the little princess." Mario winked at Emilia.

"We're spoiling her too much as it is. By the time her mother gets back, she'll be unmanageable," Andreas said.

"Talk about Mama," Laura said. "Any news?"

Her father gave her a quick glance. "We talked yesterday. I think she wants to stay on."

"Oh? I thought she might want to," Laura said. "Now that Grandpa is feeling better."

"For how long?" Tonio asked.

Andreas put a small slice of pizza on Emilia's plate. He began to cut it, but she said she wanted to do it herself. "Until sometime in August—she wants to be there for Arturo's birthday."

"That long?" Tonio wrinkled his forehead.

"I guess it's okay," Andreas said. "She hasn't seen her Peruvian family for quite a long time and she almost lost her father. I can understand her wanting to spend some time with him."

Laura felt her father was trying to convince himself that it was okay. The tension in his voice, however, gave him away. Laura was startled to hear of the sudden change of plans. When she had talked to her mother last, she had said "See you in a little while." Now, it would be almost two months if she waited until Grandpa's birthday. Laura wondered what such a long absence would do to Emilia. At the moment, the little girl seemed more interested in a dessert than her mother.

"Papa, I ate all the pizza . . . and the salad. Can I have some ice cream now?"

Andreas's somber face turned into a smile. "All the salad? But I still see a few leaves of lettuce on your plate."

"But it's almost all gone," Emilia said. Her voice quivered and tears began to form in her eyes. Did the talk about her mother affect her after all?

Andreas hugged her. "It's okay, sweetie, you did do a good job."

Laura got up. "Come on, Emilia, let's get the ice cream. You can help me."

"We'll help, too," Mario said, and he and Tonio got up. "Come on, princess, we'll get the royal ice cream." Mario lifted Emilia up and put her on his shoulders. He sauntered toward the house, pretending to be a horse. Emilia laughed out loud.

Later that evening, after Tonio and Mario had left and Emilia was asleep, Laura and her father cleared the table and washed the few dishes. Laura turned on the coffee machine and poured them each an espresso. They went back outside, where it was still pleasantly warm.

After drinking the strong fragrant liquid, Laura put down her cup. "What's the story with Mama?"

Her father glanced at her, then looked down at his coffee cup. "I encouraged her to stay longer, but I didn't expect it to be that long. She asked me to come over and bring Emilia with me, but I really can't right now. I just began to work on a large project. I was going to tell you about it, but I haven't had a chance yet. I want you to help me with it. You could have a couple of your own sculptures in an important exhibition in Italy. And for me, it's the first major deal in a while. A trip to Peru would be bad timing."

"Oh, Papa, that's wonderful. I'm so happy for you, and boy, I sure would love to participate." Laura hugged him. "When is the deadline for submitting the work?"

"The exhibition is next spring. I have a few old pieces I can use, but I will have to create quite a few new ones. I haven't produced that much new stuff lately, but I have some ideas for a whole new series."

Laura felt her father's renewed enthusiasm for his art. She knew he had had a hard time with his more creative work. "Listen, Papa, you know I can take care of most aspects of the tombstone business for a while. I wouldn't mind. That way you can concentrate on sculpting."

"What about *your* sculpting?" he asked.

"I already have a few pieces I would love to have in a show. I have enough time. Besides, I don't need to go to England. Stefano said he would spend his vacation here."

"Oh, no, you're going," her father said. "No way are you giving up your plans just because your mother and I don't seem to get it together." He pointed his finger at her. "It's good for you to get out of the country and have an adventure. You've been giving up enough of your own life to help me with Emilia and everything."

Laura put her hand on his arm. "It hasn't been a sacrifice, I enjoy taking care of Emilia. Besides, I have to practice having a family of my own, you know."

"You're such a wonderful girl, Laura. What would I do without you?" Her father's dark voice trembled a little.

"You're a wonderful father, too, Papa. You know that?" Although it was almost too dark to see, she thought she detected a few more grey strands in his hair. It made her realize that he had aged, that her parents were getting old, or at least older. She grabbed his arm and squeezed it.

"Papa, I still think you should take a couple of weeks at least and go to Peru. I think it's important. Besides, Grandpa hasn't seen you in a long time and he has never seen Emilia. You have enough time. Do it for me, for us, for the family."

Her father looked at her pensively, then nodded. "I know, I'll think about it." He took the last sip of coffee and smiled at her.

Laura observed him quietly. There was something he wasn't telling her."

Chapter 36: Andreas

After Laura had gone to bed, Andreas sat outside, enjoying the summer night. In the meantime, an almost-full moon had risen and bathed the trees and bushes in its silvery light. It was still warm in spite of the late hour. After a while, however, a cool breeze kicked up and a bank of dark clouds sailed across the sky, hiding the moon for a while and casting shadows on the meadow in front of him. The summer wind brought a whiff of honeysuckle from the shrub in the corner of the patio.

Andreas scanned the sky to the north, wondering if it was going to rain the following day. He was supposed to meet with Susanna and Emilia's little friend Paolo. They had decided to take the kids for a picnic and a play-day down at the Maggia River. Andreas had invited Laura to join them after she had teased him about hanging out with another woman while her mother was gone.

"You can be our chaperon," he had said, laughing. "And you don't need to worry, she's much too young for me—or, rather, I'm too old for her."

Thinking of Susanna, he smiled. She was a pleasant companion, a kind and sensitive young girl. It warmed his heart to see how devoted she was to her son. It must not be easy to raise a child all by herself. She had asked him once how long Karla would stay in Peru. When he told her it wasn't certain yet when she would return, she had given him a puzzled look. "I couldn't be away from Paolo that long." He had explained the situation to her, the fact that Karla's father had been ill and that she hadn't seen her family in a long time—the usual explanation he gave when people asked him about Karla.

Every once in a while, however, he asked himself the same thing. How could she stay away for weeks? Then he told himself he was being unfair. He had encouraged her to stay for a while, and she had asked him to come over and bring Emilia. Perhaps Laura was right; he should make an effort and take a couple of weeks off. He remembered how inspired he had been during his very first trip there as a young man when he and Karla had visited her Peruvian family. The pre-Inca carvings out in the desert near Arequipa and the many sculptures and the stonework all over the country had fueled his creativity. That experience had been the source of a group of carvings that had launched his first major exhibition back home. From what Karla had told him on the phone, the Peruvian landscape had renewed her inspiration as well and she was working on a new series of paintings.

Throughout their life together, it had always been their joint enthusiasm for their art that had united them and helped them through difficult times. He glanced at his watch. It was ten o'clock, which meant it was four o'clock in the afternoon in Peru. A good time to call; she might be home. He dialed the number and soon heard the familiar *"bueno"* and Arturo's voice. After talking for a while about the family and Arturo's improving health, Andreas asked for Karla.

"Unfortunately, she is out right now," Arturo said. "*Salió con Julio*—she went out with Julio. I think he took her shopping to buy some art supplies. They should be home soon. I'll tell her to call you back."

"Don't worry, it's nothing important," Andreas said. "I just wanted to see how she was. I'll call again tomorrow. She doesn't need to call me back. It's late here already and I'm going to bed. Just tell her I said hello."

Disappointed that he had missed her, he put the phone down. It was the second time he had called and she had been out with her cousin. She seemed to be having a darn good time over there. Wasn't she supposed to entertain her father? What was she doing gallivanting all over the place with another man? Okay, so it was her cousin, but still.

He shook his head and pushed the rising irritation aside. He glanced at the sky again and noticed that the dark clouds seemed to have evaporated. It would be a sunny day tomorrow. He was looking forward to the outing with Susanna.

Chapter 37: Karla

The sun was sliding behind the hills. Karla added a thick blotch of paint to the canvas, smoothed it somewhat with her gloved hand, then stepped back and squinted her eyes. Julio, who had been sitting on a stone nearby, got up and stood next to her. Together they studied the progress in her painting.

"You're cheating," Julio said.

"Cheating?" Karla looked at him. He tried to keep a serious face, but his dark eyes showed a humorous glint. He brushed his hand through his short dark hair.

"Why cheating?" Karla asked and dunked her thick brush into the bowl of paint thinner.

"From far away, your painting looks realistic. I thought you were painting the scenery in front of you. But now?" He got close to the picture and scanned it carefully. "It kind of looks like the trees but not really, more like . . . abstract, no?"

"You're right," Karla said. "I'm not trying to paint a realistic scene, but rather capture the colors, the shapes, and the mood." She laughed. "Perhaps I *am* cheating."

"It's beautiful though. I like it," Julio said. "The colors are so rich. And the shapes, so wild."

Karla smiled at Julio's enthusiasm. Having no training in painting or art in general—he was a computer analyst and electronics aficionado—he always seemed to pick up something significant in Karla's painting.

They were about half an hour away from the city of Cusco, along the Valle Sacrado. Karla had always wanted to paint the trees and shrubbery of the forests along the mountain road. However, being out on her own, particularly late in the day or early evening, would have been too dangerous, so Julio was her self-appointed bodyguard.

As the sun disappeared behind the hills, the temperature dropped almost instantly and Karla began to shiver, and she put on her thick alpaca-wool jacket.

"I think it's time to go," Julio said. "It's getting late. We can come back tomorrow."

Karla nodded. "Don't you have to work tomorrow?"

"No, I took a few days off so I can drive you around and play painter's apprentice." He smiled at her, his high cheek-bones lifting and the few wrinkles around his eyes deepening.

"This is so kind of you. I hope that doesn't cause any problems with your job."

"No problem. That's the beauty of working for myself. I can take time off without having to report to a boss. It's been kind of slow anyway. It'll pick up in a month or so, but right now, I enjoy doing something different, like entertaining a beautiful lady."

Karla smiled and her face grew warm. Was he flirting with her? He gave a quick smile, then got serious again. "Let's clean up here." No, he was just being his usual charming self.

They gathered the painting utensils and the easel and stowed them in the back of Julio's SUV.

"Are you hungry?" he asked, as they drove along the curvy road toward the city. "We could have dinner at Heidi's."

Heidi was the name of a restaurant owned by a German that served a wonderful quinoa soup and other delicacies. Karla had discovered the restaurant by chance and decided to try it out, since the name reminded her of the famous Swiss children's book. She and Julio had become regular visitors there.

"Why not?" Karla said. "Let me call Rosa to tell her I won't be home for dinner." She pulled out her cell phone and dialed the number. Arturo answered the phone and told her that Andreas had called about an hour before. He would call again the following day.

"Too bad, I missed Andreas's call," she said to Julio after punching the disconnect button.

"You must miss your husband and children," Julio said. "It's been a few weeks already. How are they doing?"

"I think they're fine. Yes, I miss them, particularly Emilia. I feel guilty for leaving her back home. But I left in such a confused state of mind and it was all so rushed, I couldn't have taken her with me. And now, I've been in such a creative mood ever since I got here that I just want to finish the series of paintings I started. It's so refreshing having all the time in the world to devote just to my painting." She sighed. "It's always the same, having to balance my role as wife and mother with my professional life. If I don't spend enough time with my family, I feel guilty. If I don't devote enough time to my art, I feel guilty, too." She chuckled. "It's ridiculous."

"Sounds very Catholic to me," Julio said. "The guilt feelings, I mean."

"I guess so. Anyway, I really hope Andreas changes his mind and comes for a visit with Emilia. I would so much like to have Arturo finally meet her. And we could celebrate his birthday together."

"Yes, he would love that," Julio agreed. "Whatever you do, though, don't leave your husband alone for too long. Men don't do that well by themselves."

Karla glanced at him. The cheerfulness had disappeared from his face and he looked sad. He must be thinking of his wife. She put her hand on his arm and squeezed it a little. They drove on in silence. Karla gazed out the window, savoring the last moments of the beautiful Sacred Valley, with its eucalyptus trees, shrubs, and plants that stayed lush even through the dry season. The many shades of green complemented the dark-brown and reddish bark of the trees and the purplish and orange tones of the rocks.

She inhaled deeply. "I love the scent of eucalyptus. It's so invigorating."

Julio glanced at her and smiled. "You are an artist, you live through your senses."

Chapter 38: Tonio

Tonio wrinkled his forehead as he scanned the display on the phone. He recognized the number. Why was his mother calling him at the store? Something happened to Grandpa?

"Mama? What's wrong?"

"Nothing, don't worry," Karla said. "I won't be long, I know you're at work. But I tried to call Papa and Laura and neither of them answered. Do you know where they are? Papa tried to call me yesterday."

"I know that Laura is in Lugano at Papa's workshop. And Papa is out with a beautiful young woman." He covered the receiver and winked at Mario, who shook his head and rolled his eyes.

"What?" Karla said.

"Just kidding, Mama. He and Susanna—you know, the mother of Emilia's little boyfriend—have taken the kids down to the Maggia."

"Susanna?" a puzzled voice asked.

"You mean, you don't know about Susanna and Paolo? Papa and Emilia met them at the playground near our house. Emilia and Paolo, Susanna's six-year-old son, became great friends, and I think they sometimes get together. I was just joking about the other stuff. Don't get any wrong ideas."

There was a pause at the other end. "Okay, just strange he didn't mention anything, but then again, we haven't talked in a while. We keep missing each other. How long has this been going on—I mean, him being with . . . Paolo and what's her name? Susanna?"

"Just a couple of weeks, I think. Hey, Mama, this is purely platonic. The kids may be in love with each other, but not the adults." *At least, I hope not.*

Another pause. "Well, just tell him I called." Her voice sounded subdued.

"Okay, Mama, I will. I'm sure he'll try to call again. You know, you should set a time when you call each other. It's difficult with the time difference."

"Yeah, I know."

"Besides, you've been out quite a bit yourself from what I hear, with a man named Julio," Tonio said.

"I've been really busy painting. I paint outside and Julio drives me around. You met Julio the last time you were here, didn't you? He's my cousin, the one who lost his wife."

"Yeah," Tonio said. "I think I've met him once, but that was a long time ago. Anyway, have fun with Julio."

"Thanks, and this *is* purely platonic. He's my cousin, after all. So don't make any dumb remarks to Papa." She sounded irritated now.

"Sorry, Mama. I was just kidding. Nothing to worry about."

"All right, talk to you later."

"Hey, Mama, when are you planning to come back? I heard you—" There was a click at the other end.

Tonio put the phone down. "She just cut me off. I think she's pissed."

"Well, I don't blame her," Mario said. "Why did you make that dumb remark anyway?"

"Jesus, how could I have known that my father didn't say anything about Susanna and her son? Don't they talk to each other? Perhaps there *is* more than he lets on." Tonio gave the phone a pensive look.

"Uh, I smell problems," Mario said.

"As if they didn't have enough problems already without false suspicions. Well, then again, being jealous may be a good sign. Means they still care," Tonio said.

"Probably," Mario said. "By the way, we need to talk about the next trip to Milano. We're both going this time."

"Yeah, right, great. That should be fun," Tonio said, but his mind was still on his father. "I need to warn him that my mother knows he's meeting Susanna. That way he can tell her before she yells at him."

Mario put his arm on Tonio's shoulder. "You should stay out of your parents' affairs. You're making things worse."

Tonio sighed. "I guess you're right. Besides, it's his own fault for not telling her."

Chapter 39: Andreas

It was a clear, sunny day and already quite warm at nine in the morning when Andreas, Susanna, and their children walked the short path down to the Maggia River. It was Sunday and there were quite a few people camping along the river. The place where Andreas was heading was a wide stretch of sand and stones, where the river veered off and deposited sediments. It was an ideal spot for children, away from the more turbulent part of the mountain river.

Andreas and Susanna were dressed in shorts and the children were wearing their bathing suits. Andreas couldn't help but admire Susanna's long, shapely legs and her smooth, flat belly underneath her tank top, although he tried not to stare. Having been a bachelor for several weeks, he felt starved for physical contact. He forced his eyes in the direction of the children, who were playing in the shallow pools of the river, collecting stones and other things, like a discarded beer bottle here and there or pieces of driftwood. Screams and laughter filled the air as they splashed around.

Having found a shaded spot at the bank of the river, Andreas spread out a blanket and a few towels and Susanna took two bottles of lemonade out of the cooler she had brought. She handed Andreas one and they settled on the blanket, sipping lemonade and watching the children, who were soon joined by a young dog. It was a puppy, probably a golden retriever, with a shiny fur, lumpy ears, and a constantly wagging tail. Excited, the kids began to play with the dog.

"Uh-oh," Andreas said. "Now, I have to listen to Emilia nagging me about wanting a puppy for the next few weeks."

"Yeah, I know what you mean," Susanna said. "Paolo would love a dog as well. It's just not convenient right now. I work all day and you need time for an animal. Fortunately, my father and mother have a dog, so Paolo gets to play with Snoopy on weekends."

Andreas raised his eyebrows. "Snoopy? After the *Peanuts* character?"

"Yeah." Susanna nodded and smiled. "My mother named him."

"I guess it belongs to them." Andreas motioned to a camper parked on the side of the road not too far from them. A family of three, a man and a woman with a young boy about Paolo's age or a little older got out. The man called the dog, but the puppy was too busy being entertained by the kids to mind him. The little boy whistled a few times and the dog finally ran back to him.

"Sorry about that," the man said to Andreas and Susanna. "But she's good-natured and she loves kids."

"Oh, I don't mind," Andreas said. "My daughter loves dogs, animals in general. I was just telling my friend that she is going to drive me nuts, begging me to get her a puppy."

The woman nodded knowingly. "Yeah, I can understand that. My son is crazy about Ginger."

In the meantime, Emilia, Paolo, and the young boy came walking toward them, the puppy running, barking, and jumping up on them. At one time, he almost knocked Emilia down.

"Georg, hold the dog," his father said.

Georg got hold of the puppy's collar and held her still for a while. Emilia, however, wasn't afraid. She wrapped her arms around the dog, which kept licking her face. "Isn't he cute, Papa?" she called.

Andreas chuckled. "Here it comes. Yes, sweetie, she's very cute. It's a girl, Emilia."

"Papa, I want a puppy," both Emilia and Andreas said in unison, Andreas imitating Emilia's voice.

"I know, but you're still a little too young for a pet," Andreas said. "When you're a little older and can take care of it, we'll talk about it."

"I can take care of it, I can. Really," Emilia asserted with the complete conviction of a four-year-old who had set her heart on something.

The adults laughed and the man said to Emilia, "Why don't you play with Ginger? Georg will show you how she can catch sticks."

The children ran off again and continued to play with the dog. The adults introduced themselves and Andreas found out that the family came from the south of Germany, from the Black Forest region. They spent a few weeks in the summer camping along the Maggia River.

"We've been coming here for a few years. We love the southern climate. The Vallemaggia is one of our favorite vacation spots," Heinz said.

Verena, his wife, nodded enthusiastically. "It's beautiful here. You have everything, the water, the mountains, the sun."

"And the good food," Heinz added, patting his slightly protruding belly.

While the children were playing with Ginger, Andreas pointed at the large camper. "This looks like a house. How can you drive this thing? It's so big."

Heinz laughed. "It takes a little getting used to, but it's very convenient." He invited Susanna and Andreas to have a look at the inside.

The RV consisted of two parts, a larger area with a kitchenette, a tiny bathroom, bunk beds, and a small sitting area. There were cute curtains in the windows.

"Amazing," Andreas said. "Looks like you have everything you need to be comfortable."

"Yes, exactly," Heinz said. "And you don't have to worry about hotels. We actually got the idea on our trip through the United

States. They have a lot of campers such as this." He opened the connecting door in the back of the camper, which led to a smaller area. "And here is Ginger's room." He pointed at a large comfortable-looking dog basket next to some food bowls and a bunch of toys. "She has her own little house, and she even has a separate entrance." There was a small door leading outside.

"We were just getting ready to have some coffee," Verena said. "Would you like to join us?"

"Thanks," Andreas said. "We didn't mean to intrude, though."

"No problem. Take a seat." Heinz pointed at the table.

While the adults drank coffee, the children and Ginger came running back. Ginger, a little winded from her running around and jumping and up and down, retired to her room and stretched out in the dog basket. Emilia followed her and gave little shrieks of delight. "Papa, look how cute." She was lying down in the basket next to Ginger, hugging her and putting her head on her belly. Ginger generously tolerated the little intruder. The adults and Georg laughed. Heinz got up and grabbed his camera. "That's a perfect shot," he said as he snapped a picture of Emilia and the puppy.

"Okay, Emilia, come on now," Andreas called her. "Are you guys thirsty?" he asked the children. "We have lemonade."

"I also made sandwiches. I think there are enough, if you would like to join us," Susanna said to Heinz and Verena.

"Thanks, we just had lunch, but we'll bring the coffee outside. It's too nice to be cooped up in here." Heinz and Verena grabbed the coffeepot and cups and they all went outside and sat on the folding chairs. Susanna unpacked the sandwiches.

"Gee, you made enough for an army," Andreas said. "They look delicious. Thanks for making these."

"Well, you know, little boys are always hungry," she said, and handed a sandwich to Emilia and Paolo. She offered one to Georg as well, who decided he was still a little hungry after lunch. "You sure don't want to join us?" she asked Heinz and Verena.

"I'm fine, thanks," Verena said, "but I have some dessert we can share." She went inside and brought out a large German chocolate cake.

"Wow, this is a feast for kings." Andreas took a bite out of his sandwich. "Prosciutto, excellent."

"Well, okay, I can't resist. I'll try a little bit," Heinz said. "I have no willpower."

Susanna handed him a sandwich.

The rest of the afternoon they spent eating, talking, and watching the children play. When it was time to leave, Andreas was barely able to pry Emilia away from Ginger. Heinz assured her that she could come back every day and play with the dog, until they leave.

"We'll be here for another ten days," Verena said.

On the way back to Andreas's house, Emilia sighed. "I wish Ginger could stay with me."

"I know, sweetie, but then Georg would be sad and Ginger would miss Georg, too," Andreas said.

"Georg could stay, too," Emilia volunteered.

Andreas and Susanna looked at each other and smiled.

"You can play with my grandfather's dog," Paolo said. "It's a boy and he's pretty cool."

"Yes," Susanna said. "He's very gentle, you'll like him."

"Okay," Emilia said hesitantly. She kept looking back to the river. "What's his name?" she asked Paolo.

"Snoopy," Paolo said.

Emilia laughed. "That's a funny name." The mention of another dog did seem to have an invigorating effect on her, though. "Catch me," she said to Paolo and began to jog up the hill. He ran after her.

As Andreas and Susanna approached the house, Andreas saw Tonio's and Laura's cars parked in the driveway. "My older kids are home," he said. "We're going to have dinner at the grotto here. Would you like to join us? I'd love to invite you. You prepared such a wonderful picnic today."

"I wish I could," Susanna said. "But my parents invited us for dinner."

"Oh, well, some other time, then," Andreas said.

"Yes, that would be fun." Susanna smiled at him; her blue eyes sparkled. Andreas noticed again how lovely she looked.

Laura and Tonio were sitting outside on the bench under the chestnut tree. "Here you are," Laura called as she got up. She looked different and Andreas tried to figure out why. Then he saw it. She was wearing a dress, a light-green skirt and matching top, which made her look slim and more feminine. The color of her outfit lit up her eyes.

Andreas hugged her. "Hey, I can't remember the last time I saw you in a dress," he said. "You look lovely."

"Thanks." Laura smiled, her face getting flushed. "Tonio picked it out for me."

"She needs a somewhat more enticing wardrobe when she goes to visit her fiancé," Tonio said. "Those torn dungarees just won't do. She takes too much after you when it comes to fashion." Tonio looked Andreas up and down. "You don't look too shabby today, though. He seems to make an effort when he goes out with respectable people." He winked at Susanna.

"Ah, my son is the fashion aficionado in the family," Andreas said and squeezed Tonio's shoulder. Tonio was dressed in his casual chic: bottle-green pedal pushers and a patterned button-down short-sleeve shirt. His hair was shorter, brushed into a kind of windswept look.

Andreas introduced Susanna and Paolo, then turned to Laura and Tonio. "Well, are you guys ready for dinner?"

"We sure are, I'm hungry," Tonio said.

Susanna checked her watch. "We're on our way. Say goodbye, Paolo." She turned to Andreas. "Thanks for a beautiful day, we really enjoyed it. Oh, and we will be gone for a few days. My parents invited us to go on a brief vacation with them. We'll be back next weekend, though."

"That's right, you mentioned it," Andreas said. "We'll miss you guys, won't we, Emilia?"

"Yeah," Emilia said, giving Paolo a forlorn look.

"Well, you'll have Ginger and Georg to play with," Susanna said.

"Yeah," Emilia said, this time with more enthusiasm. Her eyes sparkled.

"Ginger? Georg? What's going on here, princess?" Tonio grabbed her and lifted her up. "Who are you meeting behind my back? I want to know everything."

Emilia didn't need much encouragement. She proceeded to tell Tonio about the wonderful puppy she and Paolo and Georg played with all afternoon.

Susanna turned to Laura and Tonio. "It was great meeting you all. Enjoy your dinner."

Andreas accompanied Susanna and Paolo to her car. "Have a wonderful time, and I look forward to seeing you again at the playground," Andreas said and gave Susanna a quick hug.

"We'll be there," she said and opened the car door. She rolled down the window. "You sure have a nice family," she added with a serious face, then started the car.

"Yes, I know, I'm very lucky." Andreas waved at her as she and Paolo drove away.

Chapter 40: Laura

"Nice people," Laura said, as the four of them walked on the cobblestone path toward the restaurant at the end of the village. Emilia skipped ahead with one of her preschool friends she had met on the way.

"Well, *she* is more than nice, I'd call her hot," Tonio said. "You know I'm not into women, but I have to admit, she is one good-looking babe." He gave their father a playful punch. "No wonder you hang out with her all the time."

"I get together with her because the children are friends," Andreas said.

"Oh, yeah? And that's the only reason? You're sacrificing yourself for the sake of Emilia? How very generous of you."

Andreas glared at him. "What other reason could there be? Of course, she is a nice person, and yes, she's good-looking. She is also a lot younger than I am. So what are you getting at?"

Tonio winked at Laura. "Nothing at all, but why are you so defensive?"

"I'm not defensive, I just don't like where this conversation is going. Susanna is a kind young woman and we get together with the children. There is no hidden motive."

"So why haven't you told Mama about Susanna and . . . what's her son's name? Paolo?"

Andreas came to an abrupt stop and faced Tonio. His facial color darkened and the groove between his eyebrows showed his growing anger. "Because I haven't had the chance yet. I haven't talked to Mama much lately. She is out all the time. There's no reason I wouldn't tell her and I'll do so when the time is right.

Anything else? What is this, anyway? An interrogation?" He glared at Tonio, then continued to walk. "And, besides, how do you know I haven't told her?"

Tonio cleared his throat. "Because I mentioned it and she said she didn't know anything about it."

Andreas stopped again and stared at him. "What exactly did you tell her?" There was a hostile undertone in his voice.

Laura, feeling that this conversation was leading to an outright argument, put her hand on her father's arm and gave Tonio an imploring look. "Come on, guys, no fighting." Her father brushed her hand away and continued to glare at Tonio.

Tonio lifted his hands in a gesture of innocence. "I just told her the truth. She called me this morning at work and told me that she had tried to call Laura and you and neither of you answered. She just wanted to know if everything was all right. I told her that Laura was in Lugano and you were on an outing with Susanna and Emilia's little friend. How was I supposed to know you haven't told her?"

"So what did she say?" Andreas said, sounding a little calmer.

"She just said that she didn't know anything about it. So I explained to her that Emilia and Paolo were friends and that you hang out with each other sometimes. What's wrong with that?"

"Nothing," Andreas said. "So what was her reaction?"

"She seemed a little pissed, particularly since I was joking, saying you were out with a beautiful young woman." Tonio folded his hands in an imploring gesture. "Don't hit me, Papa, I won't do it again." Then he burst out laughing.

"Tonio, you're such an idiot. I just wish that once in a while you'd think before you talk. It would make life so much easier for everybody."

"It was an innocent little joke. Had I known that Mama didn't know about Susanna, I wouldn't have said anything. I'm sorry, okay?"

Andreas waved his hand. "Oh, who cares? I'll explain it to her." He looked around. "Where's Emilia now?"

"Over there." Laura pointed at one of the tables where the family of Emilia's little friend was sitting. Laura waved at them and Emilia came running back.

They sat at a table underneath a wooden trellis covered with grapevines. It was a warm and pleasant evening and the grotto was quite busy. After everybody had decided what they wanted to eat, Andreas called the waiter. Having ordered spaghetti for Emilia and Laura and stew, risotto, and vegetables for Tonio and himself as well as lemonade and a jug of red wine, he pulled his cell phone out of his pocket and began to punch in numbers.

"Calling Mama?" Laura asked.

Her father nodded. Laura glanced at Tonio, who raised his eyebrow and gave her a barely perceptible wink.

The waiter brought the drinks and the food, poured Emilia some lemonade and the adults a glass of red wine. Laura handed Emilia a spoon and asked her if she should cut the spaghetti for her. Emilia shook her head, wanting to do it herself. Her father took a sip of wine and waited for the connection.

"Hi, Rosa, how are you doing?" He talked to Arturo's wife, asking about Arturo and the family. When he asked to talk to Karla, the smile disappeared from his face. Laura's heart sank; she had really hoped her mother would be available.

"What? Again? Is the woman ever home?" Her father almost shouted it, then lowered his voice. "Painting, huh? Doesn't she have her cell phone with her? Well, never mind, I'll try later." He tapped his fingers on the granite table and went on making small talk, but his mind was obviously elsewhere. Rosa seemed to do most of the talking.

"Okay, fine," Andreas said. "Say hello to everyone. Bye."

Laura motioned to him that she wanted to talk to Rosa, but he had already pressed the disconnect button.

"Sorry," he said. "Want to call her back?" He handed her the phone, but Laura shook her head. "Later, perhaps."

"Not home, huh?" Tonio asked.

"No," Andreas answered in an abrupt tone. He scrunched his forehead and glared at Emilia. "What are you doing? Stop playing with your food."

Emilia, who had been trying to roll spaghetti on her fork, which kept sliding off, looked at him with big eyes, which quickly filled with tears. She was obviously shocked at her father's unusually harsh tone. So was Laura.

"Let me cut the spaghetti for you. If you go on like this, it'll be cold by the time you can eat it," Andreas said in a gentler tone.

Emilia put her fork down. "I wanted to make ringlets, like Laura does," she said and burst into tears.

"I'm sorry, sweetie, I didn't mean to yell at you." Andreas got up and lifted Emilia onto his lap, hugging her. "Papa is sorry, okay?" Emilia nodded and wiped her face. "Let me show you how to do it," he said and put her down next to him. He took her fork, rolled up a few spaghetti strands, and handed the fork to Emilia. She put it into her mouth and chewed, wiping the last tears away.

The rest of dinner was a quiet affair. Laura observed her father. He wasn't eating with his usual appetite, taking a few bites here and there while continuing to help Emilia. Laura felt sorry for him, but soon her sympathy turned into anger.

Why couldn't her parents treat each other with respect? They acted like a couple of kids. She had hoped the separation would make them realize how much they meant to each other, but it seemed that things were getting worse. Her mother was out all the time with who knows whom, and her father seemed to spend quite a bit of time with an attractive much-younger woman. Her family was in serious trouble.

Later that evening, Laura and Tonio were sitting on the stone patio in front of the house. They sipped espresso and watched as the night settled slowly over the fields and trees nearby. Orange and purple clouds hovered above the mountaintops. The peaceful summer evening reminded Laura of days in the past, when the whole family would sit outside on Sunday evenings, enjoying the peace and serenity before heading off to school and work the following day.

Where had that time gone?

She turned to Tonio, who gazed at the mountains, his profile with the firm chin and straight nose fading into the dark. "What are we going to do?"

Tonio sighed. "I don't know, Laura. All we can do is live our own lives. We can't live it for them."

"What's going to happen to Emilia if they separate?"

Tonio was quiet for a while. "The same thing that happens to all the children whose families break up. They would probably have joint custody and Emilia would be shuffled from one to the other. . . . What are you talking about? They won't break up. They can't." There was a note of desperation in his voice.

"Let's hope not," Laura whispered.

Chapter 41: Karla

"You're in trouble, *preciosa*," Arturo said as Karla came inside carrying a large canvas. "Your *esposo* called and he seemed pretty upset that you were out again."

"Oh no, I missed him again." Karla leaned the canvas against the wall. "I tried to call him on my cell, but I couldn't get a connection. Why can't he call me later? He knows I'm out painting during the day. Did you talk to him?"

"No, Rosa did." Arturo motioned at his wife, who entered the room.

"Beautiful painting," Rosa said and pointed at Karla's canvas. They all studied it for a while. "Gorgeous colors," she added.

"Thanks," Karla said. "You talked to Andreas? He was upset?"

Rosa nodded and patted Karla's arm. "Yes, he sounded a little put off, but why don't you call him back?" She glanced at the clock. "It's only eleven there."

"I can try," Karla said. She dialed the number but only got the answering machine. "He's either out or already asleep . . . or he doesn't want to talk to me."

Arturo shook his head. "I'm sure he wants to talk to you, he misses you, *mi hija*."

"I don't know about that," Karla sneered. "From what Tonio told me, he seems to spend quite a lot of time with a beautiful young woman."

"*Cómo*?" Arturo asked.

Karla told them about her phone conversation. "It's the mother of a playmate of Emilia's. They went on an outing together and they seem to hang out quite a bit."

"I'm sure that it is innocent," Arturo said. "Andreas wouldn't do anything improper."

"Well, I don't know about that," Rosa said. "You know how men are."

"Wait a minute," Arturo protested. "Not all men."

"Oh, I didn't mean you, *cielo*." Rosa patted Arturo's shoulder.

"I wouldn't think anything of it if Andreas had told me about that woman and that he was doing things with her and the children," Karla said. "I just find it strange he never said anything. Wouldn't that be something he'd share with me? I mean, Emilia told me about Paolo, her new friend. But I thought that it was someone from her preschool group. Andreas never mentioned his mother and how they met." Karla folded her arms in front of her chest and looked at Arturo pensively.

Her father got up and put his hand on her arm. "I told you, it's not good to leave a husband alone for too long. They don't do well by themselves."

Karla rolled her eyes. "Yeah, Julio said the same thing. I'm trying very hard to get Andreas to come here and bring Emilia, so you all could finally meet her. It would be perfect now that I'm already here. But he sounds so lukewarm about it. He claims he just got this new project and is swamped with work. That doesn't seem to prevent him from going on outings with this young woman. Interesting, isn't it?"

Karla was getting irritated. Everybody seemed to blame her for her and Andreas's estrangement. "Anyway, I'm going out with Julio tonight. He invited me to go dancing at the Plaza de Armas." She noticed the quick exchange of looks between Rosa and her father. "What? What have I done now? It's just an outing between friends. If Andreas can go out with another woman, I can at least hang out with a relative of mine."

"Calm down, Karla," her father said in a serious voice and motioned her to sit down again. He sat across from her.

"Let me just say this as your father. I have no intention of interfering with your life. Your relationship with Andreas is your business. I just want to remind you of one thing. Julio has been hurt very badly by the death of his wife. I noticed that he has become more cheerful since you got here and the two of you have been doing things together. This is a good sign. However, I just hope that you're aware of how vulnerable he is. As long as you are friends and cousins, that's fine. But should he suspect that he means more to you or if he develops feelings for you that go beyond friendship, think of what it would do to him."

He linked eyes with Karla and she felt the blood rush to her face. She averted her eyes first; she couldn't outstare him. "Don't hurt him, Karla." His voice was calm but intense.

Anger flooded Karla. How could her father suspect her of something like that? "I'd never—"

The door opened and Julio entered. *"Hola."* He kissed Rosa and patted Arturo on the back. *"Cómo estan?"* He gave Karla a bright smile. "Ready?"

"Not quite," she said. "We've been talking all this time, I haven't had a chance to change. It won't take me long, though."

"No problem, take your time." He sat down and Karla went to her bedroom.

She sat on the bed and felt miserable. Had her father any reason to suspect more than friendly feelings between her and Julio? Yes, she liked being with Julio. He was charming and kind, and she liked the little flirtation without taking it seriously. It was the Latin way, she thought. She took a deep breath. Then again, perhaps Arturo had a point. Perhaps there was more behind Julio's compliments about her beauty than simple Latin charm.

Karla didn't feel like going out anymore. Had she made a mistake? Had she encouraged him in some ways? She didn't think so, but how did she know how he felt? She had made some remarks about her marriage problems. Did he think he had a chance? She needed to set him right. She may have made many mistakes in her life, but she wasn't a tease. She liked Julio too much to want to hurt him. And if that meant not being with him alone anymore, she'd do it.

She took a deep breath, pulled off her jeans and top, and put on a nicer pair of pants and a blouse. She grabbed her thicker jacket, since the night would be cool, and a small purse she could wear across her shoulder while dancing. She had been looking forward to this lighthearted entertainment. She couldn't back out now. They just needed to talk.

When she entered the living room, her father, Rosa, and Julio were laughing and talking. The mood was easygoing, as if their former serious conversation hadn't taken place.

"Okay, let's go," Julio said. "You look lovely."

"Thanks." Karla blushed, then faced her father. "I'll be home early," she said.

He got up and gave her a hug. "Have a good time. You'll have fun. Julio is an excellent dancer." He seemed to want to put her at ease.

She nodded and waved goodbye to Rosa.

Julio and Karla walked down the steep road from San Blas toward the Plaza de Armas. Karla put on her jacket. With the sun going down, it was getting cold.

Julio put his hand on her shoulder. "You'll get warm dancing," he said. "We're early, we have time for a bite to eat. Let's go to one of the restaurants on the balustrade facing the plaza. My treat."

"Oh no," Karla protested.

Julio glanced at her, surprised. "You don't feel like eating?"

"No, I mean, yes, of course, but this time it's *my* treat," Karla said.

"No way," Julio protested.

Karla stopped and told him in a firm voice: "Yes, Julio. Else I won't come."

Julio raised his hands. "All right, all right, modern lady. I'll let you pay." He held her arm and the two continued in silence.

"You seem preoccupied," he said. "What's on your mind?"

"Oh, I kind of had an argument with my father."

"Uh-oh. About what?"

"I'll tell you at dinner." Karla felt it was a good time to broach the subject she and Arturo had talked about.

Sitting on the second floor of one of the restaurants along the Plaza de Armas, they watched the sun go down and the plaza fill up with people. There were quite a few tourists as well as natives who

207

went for a drink after work, for dinner, or for one of the nightclubs. The cathedral across the plaza was lit and parishioners entered the church for evening mass or left after a visit to the confession booth or a quiet, private worship. Different aromas of food and spices from the many restaurants along the upstairs gallery that surrounded the plaza wafted through the air.

After the waiter asked for their order and brought some appetizers and a jug of wine, Julio poured them each a glass. "So, tell me, what were you arguing about with Uncle Arturo?"

Karla took a deep breath. "It wasn't really an argument." She lifted her glass and they toasted each other. She took a sip of wine. "We were talking about you . . . well, us, really."

"Oh?" Julio raised an eyebrow and smiled. "I hope good things."

Karla began to feel embarrassed. "How shall I put this? My father is worried that . . . oh, this is so silly." Her face felt warm and she knew she was blushing. "He is concerned that we're together too much, that we might develop feelings for each other and that you might get hurt again. After all, I'm married and we're cousins and . . ." Karla glanced at him.

Julio lifted his glass, took a sip, then put it down and gave Karla a probing look. "Well? Are we? Developing feelings for each other? I assume he means inappropriate feelings."

"I don't know . . . I mean, Julio, I really like you. I enjoy our outings and all that, but I see us as friends and I really hope I didn't do anything to encourage you to think otherwise."

To Karla's relief, Julio chuckled. "That's normally the kiss of death for a man who is in love with a woman and she tells him they are merely friends." He put his hand on Karla's arm and grinned. "Karla, you are a stunningly beautiful, attractive, and lovely woman. I enjoy being with you and I had a great time being your painter's assistant. However, I would never let myself get involved with a married woman who is also my cousin. What a mess that would create, and I've had my share of messes in my life." His face clouded over a little. Then he smiled again. "Uncle Arturo is such a worrywart, no wonder he had a heart attack."

In the meantime, the waiter had brought their first course, two bowls of quinoa soup with vegetables. It smelled delicious and Karla was hungry. With the uncomfortable issue seemingly resolved, she was able to relax.

"Besides," Julio said, "I'm dating a woman for the first time again since Gloria's death." He began to eat his soup.

"Oh, that's wonderful," Karla said. "Who is it?"

"She's a woman I met back in Lima. We've been seeing each other for a few weeks."

"You have to tell me about her," Karla said. "Now, we can at least put my father's overactive imagination to rest."

They ate quietly for a while, enjoying the delicious food. The soup was followed by a plate of seafood, rice, and vegetables.

Picking up the conversation again, Julio said, "Tell me, you mentioned you might stay on and celebrate Arturo's birthday. Have you decided?"

Karla sighed. "No, not really. I'd love to."

"What about Andreas?"

"Well, what about him? That's an open question," Karla said with a slight smirk.

Julio gave her a puzzled look. "You don't miss him?"

"Yeah, I guess so."

Julio didn't say anything, waiting for her to continue.

"I'm still trying to convince him to come over for a couple of weeks and bring Emilia." Karla's good mood was beginning to fade. "He claims he has a lot of work and it would be difficult to get away right now. If he doesn't come, I'll have to go back. I can't stay away from Emilia that long."

"I understand," Julio said. "Well, you were able to spend a nice long time with Uncle Arturo. I'm sure he wouldn't want you to stay on if that might endanger your family life back home. You, Andreas, and Emilia can always come back another time."

"I know, but it would just be perfect right now. And I don't know how many more birthdays I can celebrate with my father."

"Ah, he's tough. He'll be around for a few more years," Julio said. He took another sip of wine, then touched her hand briefly. "Focus on what's important, like your children and your relationship with your husband."

"I don't think our relationship is just up to me alone," she said, anger rising in her.

"Karla, there are difficulties in all relationships. And sometimes, it's only after you lose someone that you realize how precious that person really was. My wife and I had our fights, and ours wasn't a marriage made in heaven, either." He took a deep breath and his voice trembled slightly. "But, believe me, I would gladly relive every single argument we had, and even let her win them, if I could have her back."

Karla nodded. "I believe you."

It was quiet and they both gazed at the plaza, where darkness descended quite rapidly, as was the case so close to the equator. The golden glow from the old-fashioned streetlamps and the twinkling lights on the hills created a festive atmosphere.

Julio drank the last few drops of his wine. "Anyway, let's forget about problems and have fun. It's time to go dancing." He waved at the waiter, who brought the check.

Karla grabbed it before Julio was able to get hold of it. They both laughed and Julio shook his head. "You're a determined woman, aren't you?"

They left the restaurant and walked to one of the dance clubs Julio knew about in a side street off the Plaza de Armas. It had a live band of excellent musicians who played salsa as well as other Latin rhythms. A hangout mainly known by locals, it wasn't as crowded as the places along the plaza.

When the music started, they began to dance and Karla found out that Arturo's assessment of Julio's dancing was accurate. He was an excellent dancer. As he was holding her and guiding her across the dance floor, Karla remembered how, many years before, she had danced in Cusco with Andreas during their first trip to Peru.

Where had the time gone? Julio was right. You only become aware how precious something was after you lose it. She didn't want to lose Andreas. Not really, despite all their disagreements.

Chapter 42: Andreas

The week after Susanna and Paolo's vacation, Andreas and Emilia trudged up the hill to the playground. Andreas was looking forward to their companionship. He was also relieved to get a break from having to take Emilia down to the Maggia to play with Ginger. She was barely up in the morning when the begging started. Sometimes Laura helped out and took her down. Normally, though, Andreas brought her and left her with the family for a couple of hours. They were kind enough to watch her and she bonded not just with Ginger but with Georg as well. Although Andreas liked the people, he was also glad when they told him they'd be leaving in a couple of days.

"I'm so glad you're back," he said to Susanna as he met her at the top of the hill. And he meant it in more than one way. He had missed her company and he hoped Paolo would take Emilia's mind off "her puppy," as she already called Ginger.

Susanna laughed when Andreas told her about his week of puppy talk.

"Are you thinking of getting her one?" she asked him.

"Well, once my wife gets back, we'll talk about it. She's still awfully young and neither my wife nor I have a lot of time or energy for training and caring for a puppy. My uncle used to have a dog, and it's a lot of work."

"I agree," Susanna said. "Then again, pets make wonderful companions for a child and they teach them responsibility."

"True, we'll probably get her one when she's a little older, if she is still as crazy about it."

"Paolo, be careful," Susanna called to her son.

Both children were playing on the monkey bars. Emilia couldn't climb all the way to the top yet. Paolo was on top and obviously wanted to impress the girl with his superior climbing feats.

"Watch me," he called as he swung from one bar to the next. At that moment, he slipped and fell, hitting his head hard on one of the lower bars.

Susanna and Andreas jumped up. At first, Paolo's face turned white and he seemed to lose consciousness. Susanna held him and called his name in panic. Emilia began to cry and Andreas quickly lifted her down. He kneeled down next to the trembling and sobbing Susanna and carefully touched Paolo's face. Paolo opened his eyes and sat up with the help of Andreas, who put his hand on the boy's forehead, carefully supporting him while the boy wretched and coughed. After a while, Paolo stopped and said that his head hurt.

"Calm down," Andreas said to Susanna, who seemed to be close to an outright panic attack. "He's going to be okay. He may have a slight concussion, but I don't think it's serious. But we should take him to the doctor."

Susanna took a few deep breaths and gained back her composure. "I am sorry, I freaked out," she apologized.

"Don't worry," Andreas said. He carefully lifted Paolo up and carried him to Susanna's car. He didn't have his own car with him, since he and Emilia had walked to the playground.

"Sit in the back with him so you can support him," he told Susanna. "I'll drive."

He strapped Emilia, who had calmed down a little in the meantime, into the seat belt. He knew it was against the law to have a four-year-old child in the front seat, but there was no time to worry about it. Since Susanna's regular doctor was in Locarno, they decided to take Paolo to Andreas and Karla's pediatrician, whose clinic was close by.

As Andreas had suspected, Paolo had a slight concussion. The doctor gave Susanna some medicine for headaches and advised her to keep Paolo in bed for a few days and at home until the symptoms disappeared. When they left the doctor's office, Paolo felt a little better. He still had a slight headache but didn't feel nauseated anymore.

"I don't know how to thank you." Susanna touched Andreas's arm. "I'm sorry I panicked. I shouldn't have done that. What if I had been alone? I was just so afraid when I saw his pale face and he didn't react anymore." Her voice broke and she was close to tears.

"You don't need to apologize. Your reaction was natural. Who knows how I would have behaved had it been Emilia?" Andreas tried to reassure her. "Anyway, I'll drive you home."

"That's nice of you, but I don't want to inconvenience you even more."

"It's not an inconvenience. I don't think you should drive right now and I want to make sure you get home all right. It's not far anyway."

On the way to Susanna's home, Andreas stopped at his house. Fortunately, Laura was at home. He dropped off Emilia, who was exhausted from the turmoil and half asleep. Paolo was tired but was able to talk again.

"What were you trying to do, Paolo?" Andreas teased him. "You know you can't fly, you're not a bird."

"I think he'll be a little more careful from now on, won't you, honey?" Susanna said.

Paolo nodded.

At Susanna's, Andreas carried Paolo into the house and laid him down on the bed. By then, the boy could barely keep his eyes open. While Susanna helped Paolo put on his pajamas, Andreas had time to look around the apartment. It was small and simple but nicely furnished. Aside from a few prints and posters, there were several photos of Paolo and Susanna and her parents on the wall. There was also a picture of Paolo with a young man. Andreas assumed it was the father.

"How is he?" Andreas asked as Susanna stepped out of the bedroom.

"He seems all right." She sounded relieved. "I gave him his medicine and he's almost asleep."

Andreas went into the bedroom to check on Paolo. The boy was still pale but gave him a little smile. Andreas put his hand gently on the boy's forehead and then bent down to kiss him. When he turned around, Susanna was standing by the door watching him. She had tears in her eyes.

"Are you all right?" Andreas asked.

She nodded. "I wish you were his father. I mean . . . I wish his father was more like you." She began to cry.

Andreas gave her a hug. As he was holding her slender body, feeling the slight tremors of her sobs, he was overcome by compassion and sympathy for the brave young woman, who in a crisis such as this must feel so alone without a husband. After a while, she calmed down and looked up at him. He kissed her lightly on the cheek. Whether by accident or intent, she moved her head so that their lips touched. The next thing he knew, they were kissing in a way they shouldn't. Her mouth tasted nutty—it reminded him of almonds—and her hair brushed gently against his cheek. He felt aroused; he wanted to kiss her more, pull off her clothes, press her soft body against his. He felt for her small, firm breasts.

Emilia. The thought of his child flashed through his mind and, with the last shred of willpower, he stepped back. "We shouldn't be doing this," he whispered.

Susanna brushed her hair out of her face. "I know. I am sorry. I was so afraid. I am so relieved and you are so kind . . . I'm sorry."

"It's my fault. You're very sweet and nice, but I'm married and . . ."

"I know." Susanna took a deep breath. "Let's forget it happened. We've both not been ourselves." She gave him an apologetic smile. "Can I offer you something to drink?"

"No, thanks, I have to leave. I need to call my daughter so she can give me a ride home." Andreas pulled out his cell phone.

"I'm so sorry for causing you all this trouble. I'd love to drive you home, but I can't leave Paolo now. But I can pay for a taxi."

"Nonsense," Andreas protested. "Don't worry. I already told Laura she would have to pick me up. Emilia wanted to come as well to make sure Paolo was okay."

Andreas called Laura and explained how to get to Susanna's place. After he hung up the phone, they sat in the living room, waiting. There was an awkward silence between them. Finally, Andreas asked Susanna if she knew of somebody who could stay with her during the night, in case she needed help with Paolo. "I don't think anything will happen, but it's better to be safe."

"My parents are out of town right now, but my next-door neighbor is a good friend of mine. I'll let her know what happened and I'm sure she'll help me if I need it."

"If you need anything, you can call us anytime. I'm not just saying this, I mean it. Here is our phone number." He gave Susanna his business card.

"Thanks, you're very kind." Susanna smiled.

There was a knock at the door. Andreas was relieved that Laura had arrived. The kissing incident had unsettled him and he couldn't wait to get away from Susanna to clear his head. When he saw the two women together, he realized with a shock how young Susanna really was and felt ashamed of his feelings for her.

Emilia, who had recovered from the day's turbulence, wanted to see Paolo. Susanna took her into the bedroom.

"He's asleep," Emilia whispered as she came back.

"He'll be okay," Andreas said.

On the way home, Andreas was quiet. He was angry at himself; he had come that close to betraying Karla and he may have stirred up feelings in Susanna and hurt her. He had also endangered Paolo and Emilia's friendship. *What an idiot I am.*

"What's the matter with you, Papa? You look upset," Laura said.

Andreas shook his head. "It's nothing. It was just a difficult day with Paolo's accident. I'm a little worn out."

"I hope you're not too worn out to enjoy some company," Laura said. "You know that Stefano is here for a few days. I invited him for dinner. I haven't had a chance yet to tell you, with Paolo's accident and all that. I hope you don't mind."

"No problem. I look forward to seeing him again. I may not stay up very long, I'm getting too old for these kinds of upheavals." *And for my own stupidity.*

"That's fine, Papa, you don't have to lift a finger. We'll take care of everything."

Chapter 43: Laura

Laura began to fill the dishwasher while Stefano brought in the last plates. Andreas poured three cups of espresso.

"Grappa, anybody?" Andreas asked.

Laura shook her head. "No, I'm good, just coffee."

"Sure, why not?" Stefano said.

Andreas pulled out a bottle from the liquor cabinet and poured a shot of grappa into his and Stefano's cups. They carried the cups outside. Emilia was in the living room watching a Disney movie about dogs, the Italian version of *Lady and the Tramp*.

Laura took a sip of coffee, savoring the fragrance and bold taste. Stefano put his hand on Laura's and squeezed it. He cleared his throat. "Laura and I have set a date."

Andreas kept stirring his coffee and didn't say anything. Laura and Stefano glanced at each other.

"Papa?" Laura asked.

"Hmm?" Her father looked up. "Sorry, what did you say?"

"Hello?" She waved her hand in front of his face. "Anybody home?"

"I'm sorry, I wasn't listening. A date? What date?"

Laura rolled her eyes. "What date? The date we keep talking about."

Her father still look puzzled, then smiled. "Oh, you mean . . . the wedding date?"

Laura poked Stefano. "I think he landed."

"Sorry." Her father brushed a hand through his hair. "I'm not quite here."

"What's the matter?" Laura put her hand on his arm. "Still worried about Paolo?"

"No, it was just a little much today. Anyway, so you've decided on a date. When?" He sat up straight.

"Next June," Stefano said. "My last term at school finishes end of May."

"That will give us enough time to prepare," Laura said. She hugged Stefano.

"Well, that's wonderful news." Andreas smiled.

"So you agree?" Stefano said.

"Of course. I couldn't wish for a better son-in-law." Andreas smiled more widely. "Congratulations." He got up and hugged Laura, then slapped Stefano on the back.

Stefano blushed and put his arm around Laura. "Thanks. I couldn't wish for a better father- and mother-in-law."

"As far as in-laws are concerned," Laura said, "Stefano's parents are wonderful. I'm very lucky, too."

"Have you told Mama yet?" Andreas asked.

"No, not yet. I'm going to call her. She should be home now."

"Well, why don't we celebrate tomorrow? I think I still have a bottle of Prosecco somewhere. I'm a little too worn-out for that today. I think I'm going to turn in early tonight. I hope you don't mind."

"No, that's okay," Laura said. "You do look tired. Want to wait and see if I can get ahold of Mama?"

Her father hesitated, then shook his head. "I'll call her tomorrow. Say hello." He picked up his empty espresso cup and walked toward the door. A couple of minutes later, he came back out. "Emilia is still watching the movie. I told her she could finish watching it before going to bed."

"It's okay, Papa, I'll tuck her in," Laura said.

"Thanks, honey." He gave her a quick smile and went inside.

Laura watched him, then turned to Stefano and shook her head. "Something is wrong with him. He seems so distracted and preoccupied. It couldn't just be Paolo's accident. I mean, nothing major happened to the boy. He'll be all right."

"Perhaps he's just tired," Stefano said.

"Could be." She sighed. "Anyway, let's call Mama and give her the news."

Laura got the phone and brought it outside. It was a warm evening in July. The sweet scent of the roses Karla had planted in the garden next to the patio tickled Laura's nose and reminded her that she needed to water them.

She dialed the number, and after a few rings, Rosa answered. They talked for a while and then Laura heard her mother's voice in the background. She came to the phone.

"*Ciao, cara*," Karla said. "How is everything?"

"Great," Laura said. "Guess who is here?"

"Stefano?"

"*Si*, and we set the date." Laura winked at Stefano.

"You did? Congratulations. When is it going to be? And where? Tell me all about it."

Laura was happy to have her mother's full attention, so different from her father's absentmindedness. She told her that they wanted to get married the following June in the village church, the same one where her parents had had their wedding.

"Good," her mother said. "So I guess Stefano relaxed a bit and doesn't want to rush it anymore."

"No, I think he realized that we need a little time and he's too busy with school right now to prepare it all." Laura smiled at Stefano.

"Wonderful. Did you tell Papa?"

"Yes, just tonight. We had dinner together, but he's already gone to bed. He had a difficult day." Laura told Karla about the accident with Paolo. Karla listened quietly.

"So they're still doing stuff together?" she asked.

"Once in a while," Laura said. "But Emilia found a different boyfriend in the meantime." She told Karla about Emilia's friendship with Georg and Ginger. "She wants a puppy now. She's inside, watching a Disney movie about dogs."

"Oh, God," Karla said. "Perhaps she'll lose interest once the owners of Ginger are gone." She sighed. "Too bad Andreas went to bed already. I really wanted to talk to him. I miss you guys. Can I talk to Emilia?"

"Yes, just a moment." Laura took the phone inside. In the living room, Emilia was still watching the DVD, holding her plush puppy in her arm. Laura paused the movie to the protest of her little sister.

"You can continue watching it later. Mama is on the phone, she wants to talk to you."

"All right," Emilia said with a sigh, sounding very grown-up. When she heard her mother's voice, her face lit up and she began to bombard her with comments about dogs and puppies. After they talked for a while, Emilia finished the conversation with kissing noises and informed her mother that she needed to get back to watching the movie.

Laura took the receiver from her and went outside, laughing. "See, Mama, Emilia is quite content."

"I can tell," Karla said with a chuckle. "Dogs are now more important than her mother."

"Don't worry about Emilia, Mama. She misses you, but we keep her pretty busy. But you and Papa need to be together."

"Has he said anything more about coming here? Is he still that busy?" Karla asked.

"He's pretty busy with his sculptures for the exhibition, but he got quite a bit done. I'll encourage him again to book a flight. I think he and Emilia would really enjoy it. And it would be great if you could all celebrate Grandpa's birthday."

"I know," Karla said and sighed. "Well, I'm going to book my return flight. I still have to make preparations to ship the canvases I painted."

"Oh, I'm looking forward to seeing those," Laura said. "And Mama, I'll try my best with Papa, okay?"

"Thanks, honey. Enjoy your time with Stefano and tell him I'm looking forward to having him as a son-in-law."

"You can tell him yourself. He's right here." Laura handed the phone to Stefano and he and Karla talked for a while.

After saying goodbye and putting down the phone, Laura shook her head. "We need to get my father to go to Peru and take Emilia along. You'll have to help me," she said to Stefano.

"I'll think of something." Stefano got up and sat next to Laura. "In the meantime, what about some loving? I've been starved for months." He pulled Laura close and they kissed.

Laura closed her eyes; desire surged through her body. "Me, too," she moaned. "I'm starved, too."

"Your place or mine?" Stefano asked and smiled.

"Right here," Laura said. She got up and pulled Stefano toward the cottage where her bedroom was. "Oh, wait," she said. "I have to put Emilia to bed."

"Oh no." Stefano sighed. "More waiting."

"Only a few minutes. Go into my room. I'll be right there." Laura went inside. The movie was over. Emilia was already in her pajamas. Tired out from the day, she was ready to go to bed without a lot of delays and dawdling. After kissing her good-night, Laura went back to her cottage, remembering on the way that she hadn't even checked if Emilia had brushed her teeth. "Oh well, they won't fall out just because they didn't get cleaned once."

Chapter 44: Andreas

Andreas grabbed one of his finest chisels and added a few delicate marks to a marble sculpture he had been working on. It was an abstract sculpture of two intertwined figures that suggested a mother holding a child. He gently brushed away a few particles of dust, sat back, and took a deep breath. He was satisfied with what he saw and felt it was one of the best he had done in a while. He loved the mixture of sensual and spiritual qualities and the fact that the stylized nature of the figures encouraged the viewer's own imagination.

The rough work had been done and he was ready for the small areas, which he would polish with hand tools. He grabbed one of the polishing blocks and began to carefully rub an area.

"Papa?" a familiar voice said. Emilia stood at the door of the studio. Andreas got up and pulled his mask off. "Can I come in?"

Andreas nodded. Emilia knew that she wasn't supposed to just barge into his studio. He had told her many times that it was dangerous and she could get hurt by the tools or the dust.

"What's that?" she asked, pointing at the sculpture he was working on.

"That's one of the figures I'm making for the exhibition next spring," he said. "It's called *Mother and Child*."

Emilia looked at the sculpture, then shook her head. "That's not a mother."

Andreas laughed and pulled her close. "It's abstract. You can't tell just with your eyes. You have to feel it here." He put his finger to her chest and gently poked her. "See how nice and round the stone is?" He brushed over one of the rounded areas of the sculpture. "Just like when Mama holds you, it feels nice and round and soft, doesn't it?"

Emilia looked at him, then at the sculpture. She smiled and shrugged. "Hmm."

"Not sure?"

But Emilia was already onto a topic that was of more interest to her. "Papa, can we go see Ginger?"

"No, sweetie, not again. We were down there earlier. You know that they're leaving tonight."

"But . . . I just wanted to say goodbye once more," Emilia begged him.

"It's too late, honey." He glanced at his watch, which was lying on the desk in the workshop. "They probably already left. Besides, it's time for you to think of bed."

"Please, Papa."

"Enough, Emilia, no more whining. I still have some work to do. I want you to go inside and put on your pajamas. Laura will soon be here and you can watch a movie with her before going to sleep, or I'll tell you a story later."

Emilia pushed her lower lip out and shook her head.

"Emilia," Andreas said more forcefully. "That's enough." He gave her a stern look.

Emilia turned around and left, her head hanging, obviously trying to make him feel guilty. Andreas gave a quick grin and turned back. He picked up his chisel, put his facial mask back on, and continued to work.

He felt more energized and creative than he had in quite a while. Having an exhibition to prepare for was an additional incentive and spurred him on. He added a fine groove to the part of the sculpture that suggested the face of the mother, then began to polish everything carefully. He was so absorbed in his work that he lost track of time, and when he heard a car park outside, he glanced at his watch and realized over an hour had gone by. He got up, stretched, and massaged his lower back, which was aching a little from bending over.

"Hey, Papa," Laura said as she came into the studio. "Still at it?" She looked at the sculpture. "This is absolutely beautiful. I love it." She lightly touched the stone. Andreas had used statuary marble, a type of Carrara marble of Italian origin. It was white with grey, black, and yellow veins. The parts he had already polished gleamed and sparkled in the light of the studio.

"Thanks," Andreas said. "Yeah, it turned out pretty good." He studied his almost-finished work, then turned to Laura. "How are you? Was it busy?"

Laura had spent the day at Andreas's workshop in Lugano, taking care of the tombstone business for the day. "Not too busy. In fact, I got quite a bit of paperwork done. Stefano came by. That's actually why I'm late. We went out for a drink after work. He's staying at his parents' tonight."

Andreas looked outside, where dusk began to settle. "Jesus, it *is* late. I totally forgot about the time. And it's way past Emilia's bedtime."

"Where is she?" Laura asked.

"Inside. I told her to put on her pajamas, which she probably hasn't done, little rascal." He glanced at his watch again. "But that was an hour ago. Well, she doesn't have preschool tomorrow, so she can sleep in."

"I'll check on her," Laura said. "I bet she's happy we forgot about her. More time for her to play."

While Andreas was putting some stuff away and covering the sculpture with a cloth, Laura went inside. He was surprised when he heard Laura call Emilia's name. Closing the studio, he went over to the house, when Laura stepped outside.

"She isn't in the house."

"You're kidding me. She must be inside." Andreas opened the door that led from the patio into the kitchen. The house was empty.

They searched for her inside and around the house, but Emilia wasn't there.

"Damn it," Andreas said, dropping his fist into the palm of the other hand. "I wonder . . . No, she wouldn't do that. But then . . ."

"What, Papa?" Laura asked.

Andreas sighed. "She was hounding me about taking her down to the camping place to see Ginger. I told her no and she was upset."

"Do you think she went by herself? She doesn't usually just take off and go down to the Maggia."

"No, normally not. But she was so obsessed with that darn dog, no telling what she did. Well, let's go and check. I don't understand, though. The people left tonight, so she would've come back." Andreas felt a trickle of fear run through him. "Well, we better find out."

The two of them hurried down the narrow road toward the camping ground, which was only about five minutes away, below the village and alongside the river.

"Nothing," Andreas said when they got there. The place where the camper had stood was empty. They looked at each other, stunned. "Where is she?" Terror began to rise from the pit of his stomach and press on his chest.

"Let's look in the village," Laura said, her voice constricted. "She may have walked back when she saw they weren't there and stopped somewhere . . . perhaps at the grocery store with the candy."

It was a wild guess, but it gave them something to do. They walked back across the street and up the short path to the village. The grocery store was closed, but the owner was still inside, cleaning up. She shook her head when they asked her if Emilia had been by.

"No, I haven't seen her at all today," Gabriela said. "What happened?"

Andreas sighed and brushed through his hair. "I was working in the studio and kind of lost track of time. I thought she was inside, but she was gone." He told Gabriela about Emilia's infatuation with the dog. "We thought that perhaps she had gone down again, but she's nowhere."

"Well, don't worry too much yet," Gabriela said. "Perhaps she came back and met one of her playmates and . . . did you check with the Donettas?" One of the girls of the family was a friend of Emilia's.

"No, I'm just starting to look for her," Andreas said. "I'll go by and check. Well, thanks. If you hear or see something, let me know."

"Of course, and Andreas, if you don't find her soon, come back. I'll be in the store for a while. My brother-in-law is with the local police. He may be able to help you."

Andreas exhaled deeply. "Thanks, Gabriela, I hope it doesn't come to that. She must be around here somewhere."

"Let's check with the Donettas," Laura said. "Even if she isn't there, they may have seen her."

Andreas and Laura looked at each other, then hurried up the street. They were clutching at straws, but Andreas couldn't face the fact that something may have happened to Emilia. He cursed himself for getting too involved in his work and not realizing that the wish to see Ginger again may have been too strong to resist. But then, why wasn't she down there?

"I just hope . . . God, I hope nothing happened to her. The Maggia . . ." His throat felt tight.

"Papa, Emilia wouldn't go down to the river. She's never done that," Laura said.

"She has never walked off like that before, either," Andreas said. "I should've checked on her earlier, but she was in the same house, playing or getting ready for bed . . . still." He took a deep breath, trying to squelch the fear which kept flooding him. "If something happened to her, it's my fault."

"Papa, nothing happened to her and, no, it's not your fault. You can't watch Emilia every single second. She's over four years old and she can play by herself for a little while."

In the meantime, they had arrived at the Donettas. Their little daughter, Gina, was at home, but her mother and father hadn't seen Emilia. They offered to help look for her, but Andreas said to wait in case she came by.

"She can't be very far," he said, trying more to convince himself than his friends.

Their next stop was Lena's, their close friend who had helped take care of Karla when she was little. No result there, either. Luigi, Lena's husband, insisted on helping them search for Emilia.

"Let's start at the beginning," he suggested. "Let's go back to your place. Who knows, she may have come back in the meantime. We need someone to stay home and the others to go to all the familiar places to check. Think of where she could've gone—the playground for instance." He gently patted Andreas on the back. "We'll find her, don't worry."

Andreas was grateful for the additional help and support. His mind, however, was reeling. Emilia wasn't at home, either, but Tonio, who had come by, was waiting for them. "What's going on here?" he asked. "The doors are wide-open and nobody is here."

Laura explained what had happened while Andreas again searched the whole house and the yard. He asked the neighbors, but nobody had seen Emilia. Defeated, he came back.

"Gee, Papa," Tonio said. "What are we going to do?"

"We need to get the police involved. Oh, God." He sat at the living-room table, propped up his elbows, and leaned his head into his hands. "And I used to blame Karla for not watching her properly when she snuck out of the gallery. I can't believe this is happening."

"Don't blame yourself now," Tonio said. "Let's do something."

"Okay." Andreas got up. "We need to act. Laura, why don't you stay here, in case she shows up, and Tonio, please go with Luigi to all the places you think she could've gone. No, wait." He lifted his hand and scratched his head. "Laura, why don't *you* go with Luigi? You know Emilia's where-abouts better than Tonio." He turned to his son. "Tonio, why don't you stay here, please?"

"Okay, no problem. What are you going to do?" Tonio asked.

"I'm going to see Gabriela at the store. A relative of hers is with the police. We may get faster action with her help." He got up and walked toward the door, then turned around. "You all have cell phones. Let's stay in touch. And . . . say a prayer that she's okay." His voice broke and he rushed outside.

"We'll find her, don't worry," Andreas heard Luigi call after him.

Half an hour later, Gabriela's brother-in-law, Pepe, arrived at Gabriela's with his dog, a German shepherd by the name of Alfonso. Pepe asked Andreas to get a toy or a piece of clothing of Emilia's and let Alfonso sniff it.

"If she's around here somewhere, he'll find her. Alfonso is the best search-and-rescue dog I know of," Pepe said proudly. "Alfonso means 'ready for battle.'" He winked at Andreas, who gave a quick smile, although he couldn't have cared less about the meaning of dog names.

Alfonso picked up Emilia's scent right away, walked around the patio for a while, sniffing, and then took off down the path toward the Maggia.

"That's where we usually went the last few days," Andreas said as they followed Alfonso, who stopped once in a while, sniffing, and then went on. He led them straight to the campground where the RV had been parked. He circled the area, sniffing and snorting. At one point, he began to walk toward the river and Andreas's heart skipped a beat. What if Emilia had gone down to the water after all? Halfway down the path, however, the dog stopped and then turned back, his nose always close to the ground. Again, he began to circle the parking area, then stopped and barked.

"Obviously, she was here," Pepe said. "But you said she had been down here with you several times?"

Andreas nodded. "Yes. In fact, we were both down here earlier today."

"Hmm." Pepe scratched himself behind the ear. "What kind of people were they?"

"A nice family with a young boy a little older than Emilia and that dog. They're from Germany and are probably on the way back right now. Vacationers."

"Well, it looks to me that she came down here, but that's where the trail stops," Pepe said. "Now, that could mean that she left . . . or was taken in a car or other vehicle, or went back up to the house. However, we know that the latter didn't happen."

"What are you saying?" Andreas felt the fear he had held at bay overwhelm him again.

"I really don't know at this point," Pepe said. "But we need to start an official search. If she was abducted, it is important that we find her as soon as possible."

"Abducted?" An icy cold spread through Andreas's body and he was barely able to breathe.

Pepe held up his hand. "Don't panic. There may be another explanation, but we just have to consider every possibility." He petted Alfonso and put a leash on him. "Good dog," he said and gave him a treat.

Andreas followed him back up the path as if in trance, trying to wrap his mind around what he had just heard. *Emilia abducted?* "But not by these people," he said out loud. "That wouldn't make sense. They have their own son. They wouldn't just take a child."

"I don't think so, either," Pepe said. "But perhaps someone else. She may have come down here after the camper had already left and perhaps there was someone else." He turned around and faced Andreas. "Look, I am not saying that this is what happened, but we can't leave anything out. So try to calm down and think of every detail. What kind of vehicle did they have? Color? License plate? We need to have their names, what they look like. If we can contact them via radio, we may find out more. Perhaps they had seen her before they left."

"Okay, I'm trying to remember." Andreas's head throbbed.

The following couple of hours were pure hell for Andreas and the family. It had been three hours since Emilia had disappeared. Andreas had gone to the police in Locarno and filed an official missing person report. Pepe had been kind enough to come along and help him with the formalities. He was advised to stay home and wait, in case someone with new information called. A call to police cars along the road to Germany had gone out with the few details Andreas remembered about the RV and the family.

When he got home, Laura, Tonio, and Luigi waited for him. Laura and Luigi hadn't found any traces of the child at the places they had checked. Lena, Luigi's wife, was there, as was Gabriela. A few other people from the village who had heard about the disappearance came by to express their support and asked if they could do anything. After a while, most visitors with the exception of Gabriela and Lena left. Laura made a pot of soothing herbal tea. Gabriela brought sandwiches from the store. But nobody ate much.

"Do you think we should call Mama?" Laura asked, her voice trembling.

Tonio and Andreas looked at each other, then Andreas shook his head. "No, let's wait. She would be worried sick, and it wouldn't help. She can't do anything."

"They'll find Emilia, I'm sure," Gabriela said.

Emilia

They all sat around, waiting. Andreas, however, couldn't sit still. He paced the living room, went outside, and tried to hold back the tears of terror that filled his eyes. Far away, he heard thunderclaps. Clouds had been gathering in the north for quite a while. *Please don't let it rain.* He had hardly finished the thought when the first drops hit his head and arms. It was dark outside and it was getting wet and cold. His little girl was somewhere alone, perhaps hurt, perhaps . . . He couldn't finish the thought. All the horror stories of abducted and killed children circled through his mind.

He prayed and promised himself and God never to blame Karla again for not watching Emilia properly. He thought of Susanna and his behavior with her and begged God to forgive him and not punish him so severely by taking away his child.

It was close to midnight when the phone rang. Everybody stared at it, then Tonio, who was closest to the phone, picked it up. "Hello?" he said, almost whispering.

"Yes? What? Oh my God. Hold on." He covered the receiver with his hand and grinned. "They found her. She's okay." He continued to listen to the other party. "Where? Göschenen? What in heaven . . ." The rest of the conversation he had was barely audible among the hoots and cheers from the guests. Tonio held out the receiver to Andreas, who ripped it out of his hand. He motioned to the others to be quiet.

"Hello," he said.

A little voice piped at the other end. "Papa?"

"Emilia." Andreas's voice was trembling. "Oh, honey. Where are you?"

He heard a dog bark in the background, then a male voice. "Hi there, this is Heinz. I'm so awfully sorry. We're at the police station in Göschenen. Emilia snuck into the back part of the RV while we were packing and getting ready to leave. We went to get something to eat before leaving and probably locked her in with Ginger without knowing. She must have been there for a while before we left and fallen asleep. It's a long story, but she's okay. We'll bring her home right away . . ."

The rest of Heinz's explanation drowned in Andreas's sobs and tears of relief. Laura took the phone away from him and gave it back to Tonio. She put her arms around Andreas and started to cry as well. After putting down the phone, Tonio came over and hugged them both. Gabriela and Lena hugged each other. The dread and fear of the past few hours gave way to joy.

"We'll have to celebrate Emilia's return tomorrow. Come down to the store and we'll have a glass of wine," Gabriela said. "Now, I'm beat. I have to get up early tomorrow."

"Same here," Lena said. "I'll see you guys tomorrow. If you need anything, let me know."

Andreas, who had recovered from his crying spell, got up and blew his nose. "Thanks, you guys, for all the support. It really means a lot to us." He hugged the two women, then turned to Gabriela. "And tell Pepe I'll thank him personally and I'll bring him a huge bone for Alfonso."

After the women had left, Andreas, Tonio, and Laura sat down and looked, in silence, at one another for a while. Now that the terror was over, lack of sleep and fatigue overwhelmed Andreas. He put his head against the backrest of the chair and closed his eyes. "I still can't believe this," he whispered, then sat up straight again.

"You must be exhausted, why don't you go to bed? I'll stay up." Andreas looked at his watch. "It'll take them at least two hours to drive all the way through the Gotthard Tunnel and down here again. It will be past midnight before they get here." He rubbed his eyes and yawned.

"Oh no, I want to experience the return of the lost princess firsthand," Tonio said.

"So do I," Laura said. "I'll make us some strong coffee." She got up and went into the kitchen.

Andreas sighed. "I feel bad for them having to drive all the way back. I still don't understand how this all happened. How could they not notice that Emilia was in the back? How did she get in there?"

"Well, we'll all find out once they get here," Tonio said.

The following couple of hours they sat around talking and drinking coffee. Once in a while they nodded a little.

"So it was all Ginger's fault," Tonio said at one point. "Are you going to get her a puppy now?"

Andreas glared at him. "Get her a puppy after this? She disobeys me, walks down to the Maggia on her own. Almost makes me lose my mind. If anything, she's going to get a spanking."

Both Tonio and Laura burst out laughing. "Spank her? Ha. You'd never touch a hair on your kid's head," Laura said and put a fresh cup of coffee in front of Andreas. "Well, except that one time when I almost killed Tonio." She winked at her brother.

"It happened so fast," Andreas moaned and shook his head. "One minute she was here, and the next she was gone."

"Thank God Mama didn't know about this. She would have gone crazy," Laura said.

"Oh, I don't even want to think about it. Thank God, indeed. I'm glad she didn't call today. Don't tell her what happened over the phone, please. I'll tell her in person."

He jumped up, having heard the heavy engine of a large vehicle on the driveway. They all rushed outside. The door of the RV opened and Heinz stepped down, carrying Emilia in his arms. She was sound asleep. Seeing her peaceful rosy face, Andreas felt tears gather in his eyes again.

"We're so sorry," Heinz whispered. He was followed by Verena and Ginger, who ferociously wagged her tail.

"It's not your fault," Andreas said as he gathered Emilia in his arms. Ginger gave a little bark and the little girl stirred, opened her eyes, and yawned. "Papa?"

"Hi, sweetie, I'm so happy you're back home."

Emilia closed her eyes again and continued to sleep. "Why don't you come in," Andreas said, "and have some coffee. Where is Georg?"

"He's asleep," Verena said.

While Heinz and Verena followed Laura and Tonio into the living room, Andreas carried Emilia upstairs. In front of her bedroom he stopped, then brought her to his bedroom. "You're going to stay with me tonight," he whispered. He carefully pulled off her jeans and top. Not wanting to wake her up all the way again for pajamas, he slid her under the cover in her underwear. Kneeling next to the bed, he gently kissed her forehead. "Thank you, God," he whispered.

He wasn't particularly religious and certainly not a frequent churchgoer, but he felt deeply touched and grateful. Love flooded him, for Emilia, for Laura and Tonio, for Karla, and for something larger than even his family. After a while, he got up and joined the others in the living room.

Heinz and Verena were seated on the sofa. They both looked tired and Andreas began to feel guilty. "I'm so sorry about this," he said.

"Don't feel bad. It's our fault as much as it is yours," Heinz said. "I should've checked the back again, but we were eager to leave. Anyway, here is what happened." He took another sip of coffee.

"We were just cleaning up and getting ready to leave when we saw Emilia come down. I was a little surprised since she had never come by herself. She said she just wanted to say goodbye to Ginger. The dog was still outside and she played with her a little while we were packing up. Georg and Emilia took Ginger a little ways down toward the river so she could do her business before we left."

Andreas remembered Alfonso running down halfway to the Maggia and then turn back. He must have followed Emilia's trail.

"Anyway, the sun was going down and I said to Verena that I didn't like the fact that the little girl was going to walk back by herself. One of us should take her back." He glanced at Andreas. "I know this is a pretty safe environment, but still."

Andreas shook his head. "I was in my studio working while I thought Emilia was inside. I was totally unaware she was gone. I should've been more observant. This is my fault."

"It could've happened to anybody," Verena said. "You can't watch them one hundred percent of the time."

"So we put the last things into the camper and were just going for a quick bite to eat before leaving," Heinz continued. "Ginger had already jumped inside. She usually knows when it's time. We were going to walk to the restaurant, which was only a few minutes away. I looked around for Emilia but didn't see her anywhere. I asked Georg, who had been helping move stuff inside, but he hadn't seen her, either. I just assumed she had gone back. I mean, we didn't watch her very closely, being busy and getting ready."

Heinz shook his head. "The only thing I can imagine is that Emilia climbed into the back to be with Ginger when we were busy outside. She may have curled up next to her the way she did the other day when I took a photo of her. Remember?"

Andreas nodded.

"Anyway, I closed the door from the outside, telling Ginger we'd be back soon. I could kick myself for not looking inside more closely, but it was kind of an automatic thing. I knew Ginger was in there, so I just locked the door."

"And probably locked our little princess inside," Tonio said with a chuckle.

"I know, how stupid," Heinz said. "Just goes to show, never assume anything."

"She didn't call when you locked the door?" Laura asked.

Verena shook her head. "No, we still can't figure it out. Perhaps she was busy petting the dog and only noticed she was locked in when we were away. Our area was pretty secluded and there weren't any other campers nearby. If she had called, nobody may have heard her. I hate to think that she cried and called for help while we were gone. Breaks my heart."

"I know she was tired," Andreas said. "It was late, way past her bedtime. Perhaps she kept petting the dog and then fell asleep. Perhaps she was so busy with Ginger that she didn't even realize she was locked in."

"Whatever it was, we came back, got in, and called Ginger through the door," Heinz said. "She gave her usual little bark, but we didn't hear anything of Emilia. So we drove away." Heinz rubbed his forehead. "What gets me is how long it took Emilia to wake up and call."

Verena continued. "We were just driving through the Gotthard Tunnel when I heard a voice in the back, calling 'Papa.' We stared at each other. Georg, who was half asleep, got up and went into the back. I almost fainted when he called that Emilia was back there."

"And there we were, in the middle of that long tunnel, and as you know, you can't turn around, so we had to drive all the way through. In the meantime, Emilia was sitting up front, at first quite confused, but then she calmed down," Heinz said. "We tried to find out your last name and telephone number. I realized I only knew your first name and the name of the town but no phone number or anything. Emilia did remember your last name. She said 'O'Reilly,' but of course she couldn't remember the phone number. Anyway, we thought the best thing to do was go to the police. We figured you may have reported her missing. So as soon as we drove out of the tunnel in Göschenen, we went to the police station." Heinz chortled.

"And I'm glad we did. They were already looking for us, and at first, they were very suspicious. They thought we had kidnapped the child."

"Oh God, I feel really awful to put you through all this," Andreas said. "Believe it or not, this is the first time Emilia took off like this. It may not seem that way, but we usually take very good care of her. Her mother is abroad with her family for the time being, and I try my best to be a good guardian for her."

"Please don't feel bad," Verena said. "We really should've checked on Ginger once more."

"Well, I'm just so grateful it turned out all right," Andreas said. "But what are you going to do now? It's almost four o'clock in the morning. You're very welcome to stay here and spend the night. We'd love to have you. You can sleep inside and use the bathroom and everything."

"Thanks, that's kind of you. But we'd rather leave now and make it through the mountain while it's still night. That way, we can avoid the hour-long waits in front of the tunnel. We'll stop on the German-Swiss side, and may spend a day there to relax. But thanks for the kind offer."

After packing a fresh thermos of coffee, Verena and Heinz walked outside. Ginger jumped inside and lay down in her basket in the back of the camper, this time without Emilia. Heinz pulled out a business card and gave it to Andreas. "Let's stay in touch. If you ever want to come to the Black Forest, give us a call. And, by the way, just in case you're thinking about getting a puppy. Ginger's mother is pregnant again."

Andreas smiled. "I'll think about it. I still feel she is too young. Perhaps in a year or so. I hope to see you again, too—at the latest, on your next camping trip to the Vallemaggia."

After saying goodbye and waving, Andreas, Tonio, and Laura watched as the camper took off, then went inside.

"I feel I'm about a hundred years old," Andreas said, "I'm totally beat."

"So am I," Laura said. "I'm going to get a few hours of sleep. I hope you don't expect me to be at work early in the morning."

"Please, take the day off," Andreas said, yawning.

"That's what I'm going to do," Tonio said. "I'm calling in sick, family emergency. I'll tell Mario the princess had been abducted."

Andreas waved his hand. "You have my permission." He slowly climbed the stairs, holding on to the railing. In the bedroom, he pulled off his shirt and pants, crawled under the cover, and looked once more at Emilia, who slept peacefully. He leaned over and kissed her gently on her rosy cheek, then slumped back onto his pillow. "Thank you," he whispered to the night and fell asleep.

The next thing he became conscious of was the warm sun on his face, the bright light, and the voice of Emilia.

He sat up and hugged her, as the memory of the former evening and night overwhelmed him again, then pushed her back a little. "You smell of puppy dog. You need a bath, honey. Are you hungry?"

Emilia nodded and grinned. "I slept with Ginger," she said.

"Yes, I know, and we'll have to have a serious talk about this." Andreas wanted nothing more than to hug her all day, but he needed to imprint on her that she had caused a lot of heartache and put herself in grave danger by disobeying him.

"Well, let's take that bath and then have some breakfast."

The "serious talk" after breakfast ended with Emilia in tears and banned to her bedroom for a while. "And no playing, I want you to sit quietly and think about what I told you," Andreas said as he left the room.

Back in the kitchen, Andreas poured another cup of coffee and went outside. Sitting under the chestnut tree at the granite table, he had his own inner serious talk. For the first time in his married life, he felt like a complete failure, not just as a father but as a husband. He had blamed Karla for hobnobbing with her male customers at the gallery and neglecting her duties as a mother and wife. And what had *he* done? He had lusted after a much younger woman, the age of his own daughter, and he had almost lost Emilia. What right did *he* have to blame Karla for the couple of times she had lost sight of the child?

"You're a real jerk, you know that?" he muttered to himself, sucked down the last sip of coffee, and picked up the phone. He hadn't talked to or seen Susanna since that unfortunate day when Paolo had been hurt and he had brought her home. He had been too ashamed to call and inquire after Paolo's health.

He took a few deep breaths and dialed her number. At first, he didn't know what to say when he heard her voice. He asked about Paolo's health and was relieved to hear that Susanna sounded upbeat. Paolo was all recovered and in a summer camp.

Andreas cleared his throat. "I just wanted to see how you guys are . . . and I want to apologize once more for the way I behaved. I had no right to kiss you and to create the impression that we should be more than friends."

"Andreas, this wasn't just your fault," Susanna said. "I was more than happy to kiss you, too, and yes, we shouldn't have done it. But nothing serious happened and I never had any wrong expectations. It was just a moment of weakness. Let's forget about it, okay?"

"Okay, I'm glad you feel this way. It's just I'm much older than you and I should've known better."

"I'm not a kid anymore, either." Susanna chuckled. "One good thing came out of this for me, though," she continued. "When I kissed you and you were so kind to me and Paolo, I realized what was missing in my life. After what happened with Paolo's father, I didn't want to get involved with anybody anymore. But now, I started dating someone again. He's really great and he and Paolo get along very well."

Andreas smiled. "That's wonderful news. I'm so happy for you. So, still friends?"

"Of course." There was a pause. "Has your wife come back yet?"

"No, not yet, but Emilia and I are going to Peru to be with her and her father. He'll be celebrating his seventy-fifth birthday in a couple of weeks."

The following phone call after saying goodbye to Susanna went to Peru. Andreas hoped to get a hold of Arturo or Rosa. He wanted to tell them to make sure Karla didn't book a flight back because he was planning to come over, but he wanted to surprise her.

"You called just in time," Arturo said. "She just made a reservation for the following weekend. Fortunately, she made it at my travel agency and I'm sure Antonio will be able to cancel it. When are you coming? We'll need to make up an excuse why her reservation got canceled." Arturo laughed. "You two are something else. Why did it take you so long to make up your mind?"

"I know," Andreas admitted. "Things have been kind of hectic around here. But I'll try to book the flight before next weekend." They talked a little while, then said goodbye, and Andreas pushed the disconnect button.

"Did I hear this correctly?"

Andreas flinched as he felt a hand on his back. "Oh, it's you. I didn't even hear you. What are you doing here? No work?"

"Hey, I took the day off. Remember? Had to get my beauty sleep after last night. I just got up." Tonio sat at the table across from Andreas. Dressed in navy-blue shorts and a colorful short-sleeve shirt, his hair still wet from the shower, he looked rested and didn't show any signs of fatigue.

"You're right, I forgot you stayed here overnight. I'm still a little confused after yesterday's turmoil. Want some coffee?" Andreas asked.

"Sure, I'll get some. So you're going to Peru. Finally. Great."

While Tonio went inside, Andreas picked up the phone again and called the airline. He was lucky to be able to secure a reservation for two for the following Friday. After hanging up, Tonio came outside. "What's the matter with Emilia?"

"She's in her room for a while. I gave her a talking-to. Why?"

"How long has she been there?" Tonio asked.

Andreas looked at his watch. "Ten or fifteen minutes or so. I need to get her."

"I went into the bedroom and asked her what she was doing. She told me she was thinking and that she wasn't allowed to play. Come on, you have to see this," Tonio said.

They tiptoed upstairs toward Emilia's bedroom. Tonio motioned Andreas to be quiet. As they turned the corner and peeked into the room, Emilia was sitting quietly on her low child's chair, elbows propped on her knees and her hands locked together under her chin.

Andreas and Tonio looked at each other, amused. "An almost perfect reproduction of Rodin's *The Thinker*," Tonio said.

Emilia looked up, surprised. She faced Andreas with a worried expression in her large blue eyes. "I'm not playing."

Andreas, feeling sorry for her, picked her up and hugged her. "I think you did enough thinking for today. Let's go downstairs. I have a surprise for you." He turned to Tonio. "I didn't realize I was that intimidating."

Tonio laughed out loud. "Well, you can be a little intimidating at times." He patted Andreas on the back. "But all in all, you're a good dad. So what's the surprise?"

Andreas opened the freezer and took out one of Emilia's favorite ice-cream cones. "That's one surprise." Emilia's face lit up. "And . . ." Andreas picked her up, went outside, and swung her around. "We're going to Peru to see Mama and Grandpa and your cousins. We're going on the plane, just the two of us."

Chapter 45: Andreas

Andreas felt light-headed as he walked the short distance from the plane to the main building of the small airport in Cusco, the former Inca citadel of Peru high up in the Andes. Cusco was over 3,400 meters above sea level.

"Are you feeling okay, honey?" he asked Emilia, whom he carried on one arm while holding his travel bag with the other hand. She nodded and didn't seem bothered by the high altitude. Andreas, on the other hand, had to put her down before climbing the short staircase that led to the arrival hall.

"Papa has to catch his breath." His heart was beating fast. Emilia climbed the stairs without any effort, but when she arrived at the top, she took a deep breath.

"My heart is going *tap, tap, tap.*" She touched her chest.

"Let me see." Andreas put his ear against her chest. "Uh-oh, you're right. You're okay?"

"Yeah," Emilia said. "Look!" She pointed at a group of musicians who greeted the new arrivals with traditional Andean songs.

"Let's sit down and wait for a while," Andreas said. They sat next to the luggage carousel and waited for it to begin to turn. Andreas observed Emilia for any signs of altitude sickness, but the little girl seemed to adjust well enough. She sat there, smiling happily with her small pink backpack on her back.

After the long flight from Switzerland to Peru, they had spent a day in Lima and another one in Arequipa at half the height of Cusco, so they could get acclimated to the altitude. They had visited some of the same places Andreas and Karla had stayed at during their very first trip to Peru many years before. It had been a trip down memory lane for Andreas, whereas Emilia had looked at all the new and colorful things with big eyes.

After grabbing their suitcase, Andreas wanted to carry Emilia again, but she insisted on walking. He made her put on a warm jacket, since the temperature that high up was a lot lower than they were used to from the hot summer days in the south of Switzerland. It was winter south of the equator. They left the terminal and were greeted by a breezy and cool but sunny afternoon. A few white and dark clouds hovered over the green and purplish hills surrounding the city. It smelled fresher up here in the Andes than down in the smog-filled, fog-covered city of Lima.

Andreas saw Rosa waving and she and Arturo came walking toward them. Rosa looked healthy and cheerful, and Arturo didn't show many signs of having been sick. He looked older and had lost weight, but he smiled and greeted them joyfully.

Emilia was a little taken aback at first by the enthusiastic hugging and kissing by people she had never met before. She held on tightly to her father's hand but soon warmed up to her grandparents, and after her earnest statement "Grandpa, I'm so glad you didn't die," the ice was broken and they all laughed out loud.

"You're lucky," Arturo said and patted Andreas on the back. "Your wife is outside, drawing. It was quite a challenge to hide your arrival from her."

Rosa laughed. "Yes, she almost got into a fight with Antonio when he told her that they had to postpone her departure because there was a problem with the reservation he made."

"I know." Andreas grinned. "She called me and told me that somehow Antonio had messed up her departure flight and she would come back a little later than planned. I had a hard time not laughing and instead pretending that I was disappointed."

After loading their luggage into Arturo's car, they drove up the hill toward San Blas. Andreas was again flooded by memories as the car made its way up the steep, narrow road with the uneven steps on both sides. He remembered how Karla had to close her eyes because she couldn't watch as Arturo steered his car, making sure that the tires didn't hit the stairs.

At home, Rosa brought out some *mate de coca*—a tea made of coca leaves—which was supposed to prevent or alleviate the symptoms of altitude illness. Emilia didn't like the taste and grimaced, so Rosa brought her some lemonade. Afterward, they wanted to surprise Karla, who was painting in a meadow not far from the house. Arturo showed them the way and Andreas told Emilia to be very quiet because they wanted to surprise Mama.

As they turned the corner and stepped onto the meadow, which overlooked part of the ancient city, they saw her. Karla was sitting on a stone slab with her back to them and a large drawing pad on her knees. The highlights in her hair glistened as it fluttered in the wind. Andreas's breath caught as he looked at her. He was pulled back to a time twenty-five years before when he watched the same woman as a young girl sit on a boulder and admire the sunset over the mountains, the lengthening of the shadows along the hills, and the different colors of red, purple, and blue of the stones and the horizon. It was so long ago, yet it felt like yesterday. Tears blurred his vision slightly and he brushed them away.

"Now, you can call," he said to Emilia, who had been waiting impatiently, pressing her hand over her mouth so as not to make any noise. Andreas stepped behind a tree and watched.

"Mama," Emilia called.

Karla flinched and turned abruptly. She stared at the little girl as if she saw a ghost. Then she jumped up and dropped her drawing pad. "Oh my God."

Emilia

Emilia rushed toward her and they hugged and kissed. "Oh, honey, how wonderful. How did you get here? Where is Papa?" Karla asked, scanning the landscape behind her.

Emilia looked back and grinned as Andreas stepped from behind the tree. "Surprise."

They walked toward each other and hugged for a long time. "I can't believe you came." Karla had tears in her eyes. "But how . . . oh, Antonio and they all tricked me," she said, laughing.

"Yes, they did, and they had a hard time keeping it a secret," Andreas said. "I'm so happy to be with you." He embraced Karla again and they held each other close. Kissing her, his heart swelled with love and gratitude. He felt a small hand tug at his pants. Emilia pushed herself between them.

"I missed you, Mama." Emilia held up her arms.

"And I missed my little girl." Karla hugged Emilia again. She put her arm around Andreas. "You can't imagine how happy I am. I hope we can stay until my father's birthday."

"Yes, of course, it's all arranged. Laura is taking care of the business—she is wonderful, such a help. And Tonio is helping. We have great kids, you know that?"

"Sure, I know," Karla said. "But let's go back." She packed up her drawing utensils and put them in her bag. Andreas carried the bag and the three of them walked across the meadow toward the house.

In the meantime, Antonio had come home from the office. It had been quite a while since Andreas had seen him last. He couldn't quite associate the carefree young guy he remembered from his last visit with the elegant serious-looking man in a business suit who stood before him.

"Well, look at you. All grown up," Andreas said jokingly.

"Yes, we're all getting older." Antonio smiled and pulled at one of Andreas's grey hairs.

"How are things?" Andreas asked. Karla had told him that Antonio had had a rough time. He had been married, but the relationship had failed and he had gone through an ugly divorce, which had cost him a lot of heartache as well as nearly ruined him financially. It was one of the reasons he lived at home again, at least temporarily.

"Better," Antonio said. "The new girlfriend helps."

The family spent a pleasant evening together. After a delicious dinner of alpaca stew, vegetables, and different types of potatoes, they sat in the living room in front of the fireplace. As was normally the case, the temperature dropped to freezing in the July evenings in the Andes. Fortunately, the Delgados had installed a more modern heating system in their house. Now, the bedrooms could be heated as well. During their last visits Andreas and Karla had slept under a pile of thick blankets against the freezing cold.

After dinner, Emilia got tired and complained of a headache. The altitude had finally caught up with her. Andreas gave her some medicine he had brought with him and Rosa made her a cup of *mate de coca*, which she disliked so much that she claimed her headache was gone and she didn't need it.

"You're just tired, honey, you'll feel better tomorrow," Karla said. "What are we going to do about sleeping arrangements?" she asked. "Andreas and I can stay in my room, the double bed is big enough. Do you have a mattress or something Emilia can sleep on?"

"Well, we thought that you and Andreas would like some privacy at night." Arturo winked at Andreas.

"I'm just not sure Emilia will sleep by herself," Karla said.

"What about if she slept in my room?" Antonio volunteered. "It's right next door to yours, and I have an extra bed." He turned to Emilia. "Would you like to stay with me? I think I even have some toys stacked away somewhere."

Emilia, who was usually quite shy with people at first, had warmed up to Antonio surprisingly fast. However, spending the night in his room didn't appeal to her right away.

"I want to stay with Mama and Papa."

"Well, what if I told you a good-night story?" Antonio hugged her. "Did you know that your papa used to tell me stories at night when I was a little boy?"

Emilia looked at him, surprised, then glanced at Andreas, who nodded. "That's true, I remember. Gee, that was ages ago."

"Yes, when your mama and papa were very young and came to visit, your papa slept in my room and always told me stories. When your mama and papa left, I was very sad and cried. So your papa sent me a tape with the stories. It is still here somewhere. I'll find it."

"Are you kidding me?" Andreas exclaimed. "You still have that?"

Antonio left the room and came back, smiling and holding up a tape. "Let's listen to this." He pushed it into the tape recorder in the living room, and after a small pause, Andreas's voice sounded out of the stereo. Everybody laughed out loud. Antonio held up his hand. "Quiet, let's listen."

"It's Papa," Emilia said after a while, excited.

"It is, I told you." Antonio pressed the stop button. "If you stay in my room, you can listen to it before going to sleep. What do you think?" He winked at Andreas and Karla. "And Mama and Papa are right next door, so if you get lonely, you can visit."

Emilia hesitated a little, but the temptation of hearing her father telling a story out of that little device won out. "Okay," she said.

After everybody had gone to bed, Andreas and Karla sat in the living room, each drinking a beer. Although it was late, Andreas was too wound up to go to sleep. Sitting in this house in Cusco, where he had spent important moments together with Karla and her family, brought back many memories. It was here he had felt deep in his heart that he wanted to spend his life with Karla. He had bought her an engagement ring and had proposed to her in Lima, next to the sculpture of the two lovers at the Parque del Amor. It had been the beginning of an exciting, sometimes turbulent but also satisfying and deeply meaningful time in their lives. He wondered if being here brought back similar memories for Karla.

They were quiet now that they were alone and they both seemed to feel a little awkward.

"How is the painting coming along?" Andreas asked, mainly to get the conversation started. "You were out quite a bit, painting in plain air from what I heard."

Karla took another sip of her beer. "I'm really happy with some of the paintings I did here. I feel I've reached a new level in my art. Being able to fully concentrate on it really helped."

"I can hardly wait to see the paintings," Andreas said. "Where do you have them?"

"I was able to keep them in the storage room next to Arturo and Rosa's bedroom. Let's look at them tomorrow when the light is better."

"Sounds good," Andreas said.

"What about the sculpting? You got a real break, too, with the exhibition coming up. Laura told me that she was going to put some of her sculptures up as well."

Andreas took a deep breath. "Yes, that's going to be exciting for both of us. She made a lot of progress with her sculpting. And I feel more creative again as well, thank God." He paused, thinking of the time he got so involved that he almost lost Emilia.

"So," Karla said, taking another sip, "how is Susanna?"

Andreas flinched inwardly. He felt her scrutinizing eyes on him. "What did Tonio, that nincompoop, tell you?"

"Just that you went out with a beautiful young woman. You seemed to have seen a lot of her. Funny that you never told me."

Andreas turned his glass in his hands, then put it on the table. "There never seemed to be the right time. I told you about Emilia and Paolo, didn't I?"

"Well, actually, Emilia told me about Paolo. But you never once mentioned the mother."

Andreas lifted his hands. "I don't know. Somehow the topic never came up. Besides, isn't that the pot calling the kettle black? You seemed to be out all the time with your handsome male cousin. In fact, I had a hard time getting ahold of you. Every time I called, Rosa or Arturo mentioned you were out with Julio."

Karla smiled and shook her head. "We weren't 'out' as in going out with each other. He accompanied me so I would be able to paint outside. He helped me a lot. I couldn't have gone to many of the places he took me by myself. It would have been too dangerous. Besides, he is my cousin, not my boyfriend, and you knew about it. Whereas I—"

"Okay," Andreas interrupted her. "I probably should have mentioned it. And yes, Susanna is a very nice and kind young woman, a single mother who is very devoted to her son. And it was great to have someone to share babysitting with. Emilia and Paolo got along really well. So we went and did a few things together. That's all." *Except for one moment of stupidity and I don't need to mention this.* "Besides, she has a boyfriend."

"Okay, fine."

He was relieved that Karla didn't pursue the matter, but he felt guilty. Part of him wanted to tell her about the kiss just to get it off his chest. But what would that do? It would just drive another wedge between them. He didn't love Susanna. He liked her and wanted the best for her. But what he felt during the kiss was lust, not love. And the reason he was able to pull back from the point of no return was the thought of Emilia, his family, and Karla. He wanted nothing more than to feel close to her again.

Karla exhaled deeply and smiled. "I still can't believe you're here. You were so vague about it, I gave up hope. I didn't know if you didn't want to come or if you were really that busy."

"I *was* busy," Andreas said. "I thought I couldn't take the time off now that my sculpting picked up again."

"What made you change your mind?"

"I just had to come." Andreas picked up his glass of beer, then put it down again and clasped his hands together. "A few things happened and then the work didn't seem that important anymore. It made me realize how much my family means to me . . . how much *you* mean to me." He glanced at her.

"What happened?" Karla asked.

He sighed and looked down at his large hands. "I lost Emilia."

Karla looked at him, puzzled. "You did what?"

"Yeah, I didn't pay attention for a while and she disappeared." He told Karla the whole story of that awful evening and night. "You can't imagine how I felt. I thought of all the horrible things that could've happened to her."

"Oh God, I can't believe this went on while I was away. Why didn't you tell me?"

"There's no way I would've told you over the phone. That's why I'm here." He put his hand on her arm. "I felt like a complete failure as a father . . . and a husband. I realized how fast something like this can happen, and I feel sorry for having made you feel bad about the few times Emilia got away from you."

"It's okay," Karla said in a low voice.

"No, it's not okay. I was a real bastard. I was jealous . . . of your work, of the fact that you made more money than I did at times . . . of the elegant rich guys you went out with." Saying it out loud made Andreas realize how true it was and that up to that moment he hadn't been able to fully admit it to himself.

"I always saw myself as a progressive, open-minded person. I guess I'm more of a male chauvinist than I ever thought I was."

"I always knew that," Karla said.

Andreas looked at her, surprised.

"Just kidding." She chuckled, then became serious. "Don't be so hard on yourself. I made mistakes, too. I sometimes felt that Emilia was an obstacle to my career as an artist. I didn't think it out loud, you know. I would've never admitted it to myself." She sighed and took Andreas's hand. "I often felt so selfish and alone. I couldn't understand my own feelings and I didn't dare to confide in you . . . because I felt guilty. And you and the children were so helpful, so why was I unhappy? I think my work at the gallery was to a certain degree a way to escape the pressure I put on myself at home. There, I felt in charge and successful."

Andreas shook his head. "Well, I think the pressure came mainly from me. I expected you to be the perfect mother and the perfect lover, ignoring the fact that you were twenty years older, that perhaps the pregnancy and mothering and all that hormone stuff was taking a toll. . . . I'm sorry."

Karla sighed. "We should've had this talk a long time ago."

Andreas nodded. He put his arm around her. "Well, better late than never, I guess."

Karla leaned her head on his shoulder. "I'm so happy you're here."

They kissed, first tenderly, then with abandon and passion. Coming up for air, Andreas pulled her up. "It's time for bed. Now, I'm glad Emilia is sleeping in Antonio's room."

Karla laughed. "Just remember, the walls are thin here."

Making love that night, Andreas felt deeply grateful, the kind of gratitude he had felt kneeling next to Emilia's bed after he had found her again. The scent of Karla's body, her warm, smooth skin, and the abandon with which she gave herself to him again felt like a gift, one he may not deserve but one he accepted with all his heart and all his senses.

Chapter 46: Karla

The sky was a clear blue as Karla walked out onto the courtyard, her hands around a mug of hot coffee. The morning air still carried remnants of the freezing cold of the night and her eyes watered a little as she scanned the hills in the distance. She sat on a wooden bench next to the wall, wrapping the warm woolen jacket around her and turning her face toward the sun. It would warm up fast and the afternoon would be pleasant. Andreas and Antonio had gone to morning mass together with Arturo. Emilia had insisted on going with them and had promised to be very quiet in the cathedral. Karla suspected the real reason for her daughter's sudden interest in church had more to do with her new outfit she wanted to wear for the occasion than with any deep spiritual leanings. Rosa and Arturo had bought her a colorful traditional dress made of beautiful woven fabric. It reminded Karla of the dresses her father had sent her as gifts when she was little.

It was still quiet, early in the morning. There was an occasional revving of a motorcycle or the noise of a car from the street nearby. A dog next door gave a brief bark when the owner let it out. Sipping her coffee, Karla thought of the day ahead. Unlike the other times she had been here during a celebration, the family had decided to go out for dinner and have coffee and cake at home afterward. The *padrino*, or godfather, of one of Karla's half sisters owned a restaurant in town and they had made all the arrangements for the birthday party. At first, Karla had been a little disappointed. She had always enjoyed the noisy, boisterous family gatherings at home, when all the relatives had brought their children.

The clatter of dishes sounded from the kitchen. Karla got up and went inside. Rosa was getting ready to prepare a large birthday brunch for the family. Manuela, the older of Karla's two sisters who lived nearby, would be coming with her husband and their three nearly grown children in the afternoon. Maria, the younger one, lived in Lima with her family and would be arriving sometime in the late afternoon. Karla set the table and helped Rosa in the kitchen. They peeled and washed different types of fruit for a fruit salad. Cusco was rich in many types of fresh fruit all year round because of the closeness of the jungle areas. Soon, the sweet scent of mango, papaya, watermelon, peaches, as well as some other exotic varieties such as tunas, a cactus fruit, filled the kitchen. Karla arranged the fruit in a large glass bowl and added a few leaves of mint. It was a colorful display and a feast for both the eyes and the nose. They put the bowl on the dining-room table and got ready to cut the bread. There would be scrambled eggs, different kinds of rolls, fruit salad, and yogurt.

After making the last preparations, Rosa and Karla sat in the living room and drank another cup of coffee. They were relaxing before the men came back and the guests arrived. All of a sudden, they heard someone cry.

"Emilia?" Karla got up. She went to the door and Rosa followed her. The gate opened and Arturo, Antonio, and Andreas walked in. Andreas was carrying Emilia, who cried, tears streaming down her face.

"What happened?" Karla asked. "Is she hurt?"

Andreas shook his head. "No, we just had a little incident with a dog." He put Emilia down and the little girl rushed to her mother, who took her into her arms.

"What's the matter, sweetie?" Karla asked.

"Papa scared the puppy and it ran away. He wanted to hit it with a stick," Emilia said, sobbing. She turned around and gave

Andreas an accusing look, then buried her face in her mother's chest.

"I didn't hit it, I just chased it away." Andreas said with a resigned sigh. "And it wasn't a puppy, either, it was a fully grown, dirty-looking dog, one of these street curs, and of course, Emilia, with her dog infatuation wanted to hug it," Andreas said. "The dog growled and I was afraid it was going to attack her, so I grabbed a stick and chased it away. That didn't go over well with our little animal-rescue person."

"They can be dangerous and you never know if they have rabies," Arturo said.

"It was a good dog, it didn't have a home, it was all alone." Emilia started to cry again.

"Oh, sweetie, I'm so sorry. Perhaps it was just outside for a walk." Karla tried to appease Emilia. "But you can't just pet or hug a dog in the street. You don't know if they are good dogs. Some dogs can bite if they get scared or angry."

"It was a good dog," Emilia insisted and glared at her father.

"Then why did it growl at you?" Andreas said. He tried to hug her, but she held on to Karla. "You never pet a dog in the street, especially when it is alone. You only pet it when the owner is there and says that it's okay. Do you understand?"

Emilia nodded reluctantly but kept giving him accusing looks. Andreas gave a little snicker. "I guess I'm in the doghouse now."

Antonio patted the child on the head. "She needs a pet," he whispered to Karla.

"I know," she said. "Come on, honey, let's clean you up a little and then have breakfast." Karla took Emilia by the hand. "Don't be mad at Papa," she said to her in the bathroom as she washed her face and brushed her hair. "He just wanted to protect you."

"It was a poor dog," Emilia said with a last little sob.

"Yes, I know, and it's sad. I still hope that the dog has someone who takes care of it."

Back in the living room, as they all sat down to breakfast, Karla sighed. "I think Emilia just had her first culture shock. She's not used to seeing stray animals."

"I know, it's a real problem here," Rosa said. "It's gotten a little better, though."

"I know how to cheer her up again," Antonio said. "We'll ask Manuela to bring Pierro along."

"Good idea," Arturo said. "That's a nice, clean dog. You'll like him."

Emilia, somewhat recovered from her encounter with Cusco's abandoned animals, looked at Antonio with big eyes. "Is it a puppy?"

"It's not exactly a puppy anymore, but a young dog and he likes to play," Antonio explained. "If you eat all your breakfast, I'll tell you the story of Pierro. That's the dog's name. They found him one day."

"Tell me," Emilia said eagerly.

"Breakfast first," Antonio said. He served Emilia a bowl of fruit salad and a sweet roll. "Eat up, it's good."

Emilia picked up her spoon and began to eat. Andreas laughed. "Antonio, I think we'll leave her with you. You'd make a good father."

Antonio shrugged. "Perhaps one day."

As soon as everybody was finished with breakfast, Emilia went up to Antonio and patted him on the thigh. "Tell me about Pierro," she said with an eager expression on her face.

Antonio picked her up and put her on his lap. "One day, in the early morning, there was this scraggly-looking young dog without a collar in front of the door. He was all wet because it had rained at night. Manuela came outside and at first wanted to chase him away. But something in the dog's eyes, she told me later, made her stop. She felt sorry for him and put a bowl of water and some scraps of food in front of the door. Then she left for work. When she came back in the evening, the dog was waiting for her. He wagged his tail and rubbed against her legs. 'What am I going to do now?' Manuela asked herself. The neighbor came over and laughed, telling her that the dog had defended the house. He would bark and growl at anybody who came close. 'That's a great watchdog,' the neighbor said. Since there had been quite a few robberies in the neighborhood and Manuela's husband was out of town, she decided to keep the dog for a while. Well, of course, once you take a dog in, feed it, and treat it nicely, that dog is yours. Pierro was the most loveable creature you could imagine and so grateful for any attention. So Manuela kept him and now he's part of the family." Antonio smiled at Emilia and patted her on the head.

"Now, I'm not going to tell you what her husband said when he came back from his business trip and found a dog inside the house growling and barking at him. Anyway, after a while, he accepted the situation."

"I want a puppy," Emilia said, then put her hand on her mouth and gave her father a guilty look.

Andreas chortled. "I told her I didn't want to hear that sentence anymore after her escape with Ginger."

"Well, you know, one thing is for sure," Antonio said. "You won't find the kind of unconditional love from human beings as you get from a pet. At least, not from most humans. Even between people who love each other or are supposed to love each other, there is always a string attached. I'll love you *if* you do this for me, *if* you behave a certain way, *if* you are the kind of person I want you to be, there is always some kind of condition. A dog or a cat, however, accepts you the way you are. And they come back to you, even if you hurt them."

Karla looked at his somber face and wondered if the bad luck he had had in his marriage was the reason for his negative view of human love. "You don't think there is selfless love between humans?" she asked. "What about between parents and children? I mean, you love your child, no matter what they do or how they behave. You may get angry at them, but you still love them."

Antonio nodded. "Perhaps."

"You can love a pet and that's a very rewarding thing. However, is what a dog feels for you really love?" Arturo said. "Isn't it, rather, dependency? A dog absolutely depends on you, he's attached to you."

"I think *papá* makes an important point. Love between humans is flawed. We're more complex than pets. I don't really think we can compare the two. As much as I love animals, I wouldn't want to exchange that kind of love for the messy one between humans." Karla felt Andreas's eyes on her. When she faced him, he smiled.

"I love Ginger," Emilia said in low voice, as if talking to herself.

"There you have it, she proves my point." Antonio laughed out loud and hugged Emilia. "You and I think alike."

Arturo got up and patted Antonio on the shoulder. "Well, *mi hijo*, I hope you'll have the opportunity to change your mind about love between a man and a woman. I wish that for you."

"All right, enough of that serious talk. It's time to celebrate," Rosa said. She brought a bottle of champagne from the kitchen. "Andreas, would you do us the honor of opening this thing? I can never do it. Last time, I sprayed the whole living room."

After the cork popped and the champagne began to flow, the mood became festive. Everybody cheered and wished Arturo a happy birthday.

"This is indeed a happy day for me," Arturo said. "To have all my family here, even the ones as far away as Switzerland. That makes me very glad. And to be able to finally meet my youngest grandchild." He toasted Andreas and Karla and gave Emilia a hug.

"We're very happy to be here," Karla said. "And I'm so glad you're feeling better again. You scared me." Her voice broke and tears gathered in her eyes.

"Happy birthday, and many more to come," Andreas said.

The rest of the morning was cheerful. Arturo opened some of his presents. Andreas had brought the usual Swiss chocolate for everyone, a bottle of grappa he knew Arturo liked. Karla, Andreas, and Rosa had bought him an espresso machine, so he could enjoy European-style coffee at home.

"Didn't your doctor say something about not drinking coffee?" Antonio teased him.

Arturo waved dismissively. "Oh, doctors, what do they know? Besides, they didn't say to avoid it altogether, just be moderate. And I want a cup right now." He slapped the tabletop with his hand.

"Still the *pater familias*," Andreas said.

"Absolutely," Arturo said.

Once the rest of the family and all the relatives arrived, the peaceful morning turned into the usual boisterous affair. Emilia, completely taken by Pierro, a black-and-white part-Labrador mix, played with him all afternoon. Karla had to use all her authority to get her to take a nap. The men went out to get some stuff for the cake ceremony in the evening, and Karla, Manuela, and her two daughters cleaned up the kitchen while Rosa sat down and yawned.

"I'm getting old," she said. "I'm so glad we're going out for dinner. I just can't deal with these huge parties anymore."

"We're all getting older," Karla said. "And I can feel the champagne. I may have to take a nap with Emilia."

"Oh, honey, we're so happy you're here." Rosa hugged her. "I know that was a big expense and a lot of trouble, but Arturo really appreciates it. We all do."

"Tell me about it," Manuela said. "It's so much fun having you."

"Thanks, guys." Karla smiled. "I'm happy to be here as well. And I have to say, it's mainly thanks to Andreas. If he hadn't come, I would've gone back. My only regret is that Tonio and Laura couldn't come as well."

"Yes, that's true. I hope they'll be able to visit soon as well," Rosa said.

"We'll make sure of that. You know Laura and Stefano are planning to get married next June. We're thinking of giving them a trip to Peru as a wedding gift."

"That would be great. What about Tonio?" Manuela said.

"Well, you know that he's in a relationship with Mario." Karla still felt a little awkward talking about Tonio's homosexuality with her Peruvian relatives. Being gay may not be as acceptable here as it was in Europe. Arturo and Rosa had seemingly accepted the news, but Karla didn't know if they were just being polite.

"We would love to have them as well." Rosa sounded sincere. "I haven't seen that boy in a long time."

"Thanks, Rosa." Karla was relieved. "I'm sure both Laura and Tonio are going to call tonight to wish Arturo a happy birthday."

Chapter 47: Tonio

Tonio glanced at Mario, who was paging through the Sunday paper on the table in front of him. They were sitting on the balcony in their apartment in Lugano. It was a sunny, somewhat humid day in early August. From their place they could see a snippet of Lake Lugano. The horizon above the lake had a yellowish tint created by the air pollution from the city itself as well as from the large cities in northern Italy. It was more visible during muggy days.

Tonio got up, grabbed the watering can, and began to water the potted plants and flowers on the balcony. It was a colorful assortment of irises, different types of lilies, and a large clay pot full of roses. Tonio and Mario both loved flowers and plants, and

Stefano always brought them left-overs from the garden center he worked at. Their apartment resembled a nursery now.

"Want another cup of coffee?" Tonio asked as he put down the watering can.

"Sure, thanks." Mario looked up, then studied the paper again.

"Espresso or lungo?" Tonio asked.

Mario turned the page of the paper. "Lungo is fine."

Tonio went into the kitchen and pressed the button on the espresso machine. He took a deep breath, trying to find a good moment to have a talk with Mario about a difficult subject. They had been living together for about a year. Since Tonio graduated from the fashion school, he had been working at the boutique in Lugano, which belonged to Mario's father. Tonio enjoyed his work, but nevertheless felt he needed a change.

"Anything interesting in the paper?" he asked Mario as he put the coffee cups down.

"Nothing much," Mario said. "I thought they might mention something about the initiative."

Tonio took a deep breath. He knew Mario meant the initiative about same-sex couples being able to adopt children. "I guess this is a good time to talk about it."

"Talk about what?" Mario asked and put the paper down.

Tonio put his hands together and began to crack his knuckles, which he sometimes did when he was nervous. It was a habit he had inherited from his father.

"Stop that." Mario glared at him. "I hate that sound. So what is it?"

Mario's testy mood didn't make the talk any easier.

"Well, I've been thinking," Tonio began. "You know I like the work at the boutique, but I really feel I should branch out a little, do something else for my education. I mean, my original goal was to become a fashion designer. I know it's a very competitive field, but I'd like to give it a shot." He stopped and glanced at Mario.

"Okay," Mario said in a cautious voice.

"I'd love to spend some time in Italy or France, perhaps take some more classes or work in a real fashion center." Tonio got excited at the mere thought of it. "In fact, you should do something like this as well. Perhaps we could do it together."

"Well, I can't just up and leave. My father needs me at the stores. Besides, I don't have the drive to become a fashion designer. I enjoy running the store, choosing and buying fashion and all that."

There was a moment of silence. Tonio let his eyes travel over the trees in the backyard, then glanced at his partner. "Mario, I'm too young to settle down completely. I have ambitions, dreams. I mean, I'm only twenty-two. I'd love to travel a little, perhaps live abroad for a while—"

"In other words, you want to break up," Mario said in an icy voice. "Why don't you just admit it?"

Tonio stared at him. "No, of course not. That's why I want to talk about it. I'm sure we can find a solution that works for both of us."

"How? You want to go and live abroad? That would mean one of those long-distance relationships. It doesn't work, Tonio."

"Jesus, other people do it. Look at Laura and Stefano. He lives in England for a whole year. They visit each other and it seems to work."

"Well, we'll see how long that's going to last," Mario muttered. "Anyway, it may work for them, I don't think it would work for us. I'm not the long-distance-relationship type. I thought we were planning to get married or whatever they call it for us, have a business together . . . perhaps children, who knows?"

"Mario, we are in a relationship. Does that mean we have to act like old people? Just always stay home and have children? Where is your sense of adventure?"

"Oh, I see where this is leading." Mario got up and stepped to the edge of the balcony. He looked into the distance, then turned around and stared at Tonio. "I've noticed your discontent lately. I should've known. You're too young for a steady relationship. I understand you want to sow your wild oats. Well, go ahead, if that's what you want." He threw up his hands.

"That's not true. I care for you, Mario. I want us to be together, but I have my own life, too."

"Then lead your own life. Go move back home with Mom and Dad. Live abroad, fuck a bunch of other men, or perhaps you want to try some women, too. But if you think I'm going to wait around for you to come to your senses, forget it."

"God, Mario, you're being so unfair and childish."

"Look who is childish," Mario shouted. "I've seen you stare at some of the young guys at the coffee shop—at Fred, for instance."

"Now you're really getting absurd." Tonio got up as well. "Mario, please, let's talk about it like adults."

"Well, I'm not in the mood, I'm going out. You can move out anytime you want. In fact, you should do it right away, so I have time to find a new roommate." Mario grabbed his cup of coffee, tossed the rest into the flowerpot, and went into the kitchen.

A few minutes later, Tonio heard the door slam. He sat down and shook his head. He had never expected such a reaction from the man he felt he knew and loved. How could a talk about their common future turn into a fight and a breakup?

Tonio took a deep breath as sadness swept over him. He loved Mario and he felt betrayed. He got up, took the coffee dishes into the kitchen, and sat on the balcony again. He hoped that Mario would come back and perhaps apologize. After half an hour, he put on a pair of jeans and a T-shirt, brushed his hands through his hair, and left. He was too upset to even care about his appearance or the kind of clothes he was wearing, something he was usually careful about. He needed to talk someone. He thought Laura might be in her workspace in Lugano. She sometimes worked there on the weekend.

Chapter 48: Laura

Laura was in the back room of the workshop, cleaning some of the carving tools, when she heard the door open. A pale, sickly-looking man was waiting in the entrance area. When she looked at him more closely, she recognized him and her breath caught. A few days ago, she had heard that her former schoolmate and best friend, Celia, had been killed in a car accident. The man was her father. Laura, still reeling from the shocking news, stood speechless for a moment in front of the broken man. She remembered her own father telling her that the most difficult part of his work was being confronted with a friend ordering a gravestone for a wife or a husband, or, what was worse, for a child. She sent a silent cry for help to her father. But her father wasn't here. She was now in charge of the business and she needed to do the right thing.

"Signor Pati, I'm so sorry," she said and burst into tears. She wanted to be supportive and desperately tried to get hold of herself. The man came up to her and they embraced. "I'm so sorry for your loss," Laura said. "Celia was such a good friend. I . . ."

"I know," he said, his eyes tearing up.

She asked him to sit down. "Would you like some coffee?"

He nodded. "That would be nice."

Drinking coffee, they talked for a while. He asked about the family. "I actually thought your father was here."

She told him that he was out of the country for a few weeks.

"Well, it would be wonderful if you could make a gravestone for Celia. I think she would have liked that, to have it made by a friend of hers."

Laura nodded. "I'd love to do that." She showed him the different types of stones. They talked about the inscription and a motif. He wanted something simple.

"She loved flowers," he said. "Poppies and irises were her favorites." Tears gathered in his eyes again and he gave a sob. "I'm sorry."

"Don't be," Laura said. "I could make a brief sketch of what the inscription and the decoration on the stone would look like and you tell me if you like it."

"Sounds good, thank you very much."

They talked about the details and she told him she'd be at the funeral. After he left, Laura felt exhausted. It was the first time she had talked to a mourner herself. So far, her father had always handled those cases. She knew it was part of the business, but having to do it for someone she had been close to was a difficult task.

Laura and Celia had been friends since kindergarten. They had supported each other through the difficult times of adolescence. Like Laura, Celia had not been one of the popular "hot" girls, the ones the boys were after. She had struggled with weight problems. But unlike Laura, who had often suffered from feelings of inadequacy, Celia had been more self-confident. She had brushed off the taunting of her schoolmates more easily. Cheerful by nature, she had always managed to lift Laura's spirits. They had planned to attend the upcoming school reunion together. And now, Celia was gone.

Studying the stone she had chosen together with Celia's father, Laura took a deep breath. The rough work on the gravestone would be no problem. She had carved a few tombstones before. But she wanted the design on it to be perfect. She grabbed a drawing pad and began to do a sketch, which she later tried out on a piece of stone. Somehow, her emotional attachment to the work got in the way and seemed to paralyze rather than inspire her. Every time she picked up the chisel, doubts about her ability to do her dead friend justice overcame her and she put the tool down and sighed.

She worked at it all Sunday morning, but around noontime she was thoroughly discouraged and decided to call her father. Just as she picked up the phone, the door opened and Tonio walked in. She saw right away that something was bothering him. Instead of his usual cheerful demeanor, he just nodded to her and gave a quick smile, then sat down. "Are you busy?" he asked and looked at the piece of stone in front of her.

"I'm trying to create a design for Celia's gravestone, but I'm having a hell of a time. I was going to call Papa and get some advice."

Tonio nodded. "While you're at it, could you ask him if I could move back home again?"

Laura looked at him, bewildered. "Uh-oh, that doesn't sound good. What happened?"

Tonio told her of his fight with Mario. "I don't know what got into him, but he more or less told me to move out."

"What strange behavior. That doesn't sound like Mario at all," Laura said.

"I know, that's why I have the feeling there is something else going on. Perhaps he is the one who is tired of the relationship and I just gave him the perfect reason to end it. And now, he can blame it on me. All I want to do is work at my career and explore the world a little before settling down like an old couple with cats and dogs and a bunch of kids. How could he resent that so much?"

"Doesn't make sense," Laura said.

"The guy is only twenty-eight and he acts like a sixty-year-old." Tonio shook his head.

"Well, you can definitely move back home. You know Mama and Papa wouldn't mind at all. On the contrary, they'd love it. But I hope for your own sake that you and Mario make up again." Laura paused. "I wonder if he wants to settle and have a family because his own family is so unsettled. His parents have broken up several times and gotten back together again. That's tough."

"I'm sure it has something to do with it. But he can't let his parents' screwed-up relationship mess up his own life—and mine as well."

Laura hadn't seen him as unhappy as this in a long time, not since he got beaten up by a bunch of bullies. She hugged him. "Come on, little brother, let's call Papa."

Chapter 49: Andreas

Andreas listened quietly to Laura's description of her troubles with the gravestone for her friend. He could relate very well to her plight. Memories of the first time he had to carve a tombstone for the little boy of a friend of his flashed through his mind. But that had been nothing compared to the inner struggle and turmoil he felt when he carved the tombstone for his father.

His father had been an alcoholic and booze had made him violent and abusive to both his wife and his son. Andreas's mother, a kindhearted but weak woman, had been unable to protect him from the cruel outbursts of his father. Finally, Andreas's uncle and aunt had taken him in and given him a loving home. After the divorce from his mother, his father, an American citizen, had moved back to the United States and Andreas had lost touch with him. Many years later, after Andreas and Karla had gotten married and Laura and Tonio were little, Robert O'Reilly appeared one day and wanted to make amends. Andreas had rejected him at first, but later they became closer again. The real breakthrough in his feelings for the man he had hated so much came when Robert died of a heart attack and Andreas decided to carve a tombstone for him. It had been an intensely painful but liberating experience.

This story of redemption and forgiveness he now related to Laura. "This isn't about perfection, honey," he said when she told him that she wanted to do a perfect image. "It's about the feeling you have when you carve the stone. Think of your friend when you work. Would she really fault you if the iris wasn't perfect? Remember how easygoing she used to be?"

Andreas heard Laura sigh. "I guess it was an ego thing," she said. "I wanted to do a perfect job."

"Knowing you, it will be a perfect design," Andreas said. "Leave your ego out of it. You're doing a service to her and, above all, to her family. They have to like it, not you. I sometimes have to carve a gravestone I would do differently if I had the choice. But if the family picks a crappy design and insists on me using it, I can try to do my best to improve on it, but I have to fulfill their order. That's why our sculpting is so liberating for us, because there, we can let go and just be ourselves."

"I guess you're right," Laura said. "Thanks, Papa, you helped me so much."

"You're welcome, and if you want my help with some of it, we'll be home in a couple of weeks. How is everything else?" Andreas heard a voice in the background. "Is Tonio there?"

"Yes." A slight pause, then muffled talk. "He wants to know if he can move back home again, for the time being. I said I was sure you don't mind."

Andreas glanced at Karla, who was sitting next to him, waiting for her turn to talk. "Tonio wants to move back home? What happened?"

"Well, I'll let you talk to him. Here he is," Laura said.

"Ahem." Tonio cleared his throat. "Hi, Papa, I'm not sure yet, but . . . well, Mario and I had a fight and he practically told me to move out." He gave his father a brief summary of their argument.

"I'm sorry to hear that," Andreas said. "I hope you guys work things out. But of course you can come home. You can come home anytime." He looked at Karla, who nodded vigorously and pointed at the phone. "Anyway, Tonio, you know we love you and you can always talk to us about any problems you have, okay?"

"Thanks, Papa." Tonio's voice trembled a little.

"Mama wants to talk to you. Hold on." He gave the receiver to Karla and got up. He stepped next to the window, gazing at the landscape. It was still early in Cusco. The sun was rising, pouring its golden light over the hills and mountains. He felt sorry for Tonio, who now experienced his first struggles with love and relationships, something he and Karla had lived through more than once. After Karla hung up the phone, she came over and stood next to him.

"Poor Tonio," she said. "Poor Mario," she added. "Oh, love," she said with a sigh.

"Tell me about it," Andreas said and snickered. He put his arm around her. "You still think it's worth it? Love, I mean."

Karla looked at him. "Do you doubt it?" she asked, surprised.

"No." Andreas shook his head. "I don't. You know, back home Laura once asked me if I ever regretted having married. I said, no, never. In spite of all our misunderstandings, I still think we are the best thing that ever happened. And we better keep it that way, not just for our own sake but for the sake of our children."

Karla put her arms around him. "And that's the best thing you've ever said about us and about love, and I agree."

"You do?" Andreas hugged her back. "Would you marry me again?"

Karla smiled. "Are you proposing to me again?"

"Why not? Lots of couples renew their vows. We could do the same," Andreas said. He looked into her eyes, which sparkled with a mixture of mirth and kindness. "Mrs. O'Reilly? How about it?"

Karla grinned. "That's not the most romantic marriage proposal."

"I know," Andreas said. "It's just that . . ." He bent his knee and put it on the floor, almost tumbling over. "I'm not as limber as I used to be back in El Parque del Amor, next to El Beso."

Karla, who tried to hold him and almost fell down, laughed out loud. The door opened and Rosa stepped into the living room. "Oh, excuse me." She looked at them, puzzled. "Am I interrupting something?"

Andreas waved his hand. "No, just our clumsy attempt of trying to renew our vows."

"Ah, how wonderful." Rosa clapped her hands. "They're getting married again," she said to Arturo, who came inside.

"Congratulations," he said. "Is this a Swiss custom, to get married more than once to the same woman or man?" He winked at them. "Do we have any champagne left?" he asked Rosa. "We need to celebrate."

Chapter 50: Tonio

When Tonio opened the door to the apartment, he almost stumbled over Mario's workout shoes. He shook his head and smiled, then became serious again. Mario's habit of dropping his things right at the door when coming in usually provoked good-natured bantering. Remembering their fight earlier, he knew there wouldn't be any teasing. He heard the shower running. Mario had been out jogging. On a normal day, Tonio might have joined him in the shower, which often led to passionate lovemaking. Today, however, Tonio went into the bedroom and changed into a pair of shorts and a tank top. The late afternoon had gotten quite hot and muggy. He grabbed a glass of mineral water, stepped out on the balcony, and sat under the small canopy in the shade.

He waited for Mario, feeling anxious and hoping for a more amiable discussion, but he had decided not to let his partner make him feel guilty. A while later, he heard him walk into the kitchen and open the refrigerator. Mario joined him on the balcony and sat down. Tonio glanced at him but didn't say anything.

"I'm sorry about this morning," Mario said.

Tonio let his eyes wander over the garden in front of the house, then faced him. "I still don't understand what it was I said or did that triggered such a reaction."

Mario sighed. "I've had some doubts about our relationship for a while."

Tonio stared at him. "Why? Why didn't you say something?"

"It's just . . . I really care for you, Tonio, but you're quite a bit younger than I am."

Tonio raised his eyebrows and shook his head. "You're only six years older, for heaven's sake."

"Yes, but I mean emotionally. I'm more settled than you are. I would like a steady relationship, a family, or something like it. I like my work, I feel fulfilled in my father's business. You, on the other hand, are still in the exploring phase. You want adventures, you want to live abroad and all that, and I feel I'm stifling you . . ."

Tonio glanced at Mario, then looked down at his hands. "This is a bunch of hogwash."

"No, it isn't," Mario said.

"You're looking for a reason to break up. So who is the guy?"

Mario gave him an exasperated look. "There is no guy and I'm not looking for a reason. I just feel that we're not on the same page."

Tonio's mind felt like a beehive. He pressed his hands against his head. "I just don't get it. I thought we were in a great relationship. We filed for registered partnership. You talked about adopting kids, and now . . . what happened? Why all the doubts all of a sudden?"

"It's not 'all of a sudden.' Every time we talk about those things, you become evasive. It's because you're not sure you want to do it."

Tonio got up and walked to the end of the balcony. He took a deep breath and shook his head. Was Mario right? He began to doubt himself. "Yes, it's true, I'm not that gung ho about settling down and kids and all that. I just think you're too much in a hurry and you act like an old married man."

"That's the way I am, don't you see?" Mario got up as well and stood next to Tonio. He put his hand on Tonio's shoulder. "I care for you, you know that. But I don't want to end up in a relationship where you one day feel you missed out on life. That's what happened to my mother."

"Ah, so I knew it had to do with your family," Tonio said. "But don't you see you're letting their messed-up relationship impact your life? You can't let them do this to you. I mean, my parents have had their problems, but that doesn't prevent me from trying to have a relationship."

Mario shook his head. "Your parents are nothing like my parents. And perhaps you're right. Perhaps I'm having a problem with relationships and I'm looking for something stable. But I can't help it."

"So you want to end it?" Tonio's voice faltered.

"I just want us to take a break, to step back and evaluate what we really want, both of us. This is going to be hard for me because I really care for you."

Tonio glared at him. "Well, you used to call it love."

"It's still love, and that's why I don't want to hurt you by forcing you into something you're not ready for."

"Oh, how generous of you." Tonio scoffed at him.

"Please, Tonio." Mario's voice trembled.

"Well, okay, I already told my parents I would move back in again."

"I didn't mean to throw you out. And I didn't mean the thing about a roommate, either. I won't have anybody else live here. And we can still be friends."

Tonio brushed through his hair. "We'll see. I don't know how I feel about all this. And what about work? This is going to feel really odd. I'll probably have to find another job."

"No, you don't. My father wants me to work in the main shop. He's seriously thinking about retiring. You and Ernesto could run the boutique."

"I'll think about it. Right now, my mind isn't working right. I got up this morning and everything was wonderful, and now, I've lost the man I love."

"You haven't lost me. I just need some distance."

"Yeah, right. Well, I'm going to spend the night at home. I'll just pack a few things." Tonio went into the bedroom and pulled out his travel bag, threw in some clothes, underwear, and his toiletries.

Mario was waiting for him in the hallway. "Please, try to understand. I'm not rejecting you. I love you." He tried to hug him, but Tonio pushed him away.

"Well, you sure are showing it in a funny way. I'll be back for more stuff tomorrow." Tonio opened the door.

Mario called after him. "I can give you a ride, you don't have your car—"

Tonio slammed the door closed and left. He walked briskly up the street. A woman who passed by him stared at him and Tonio realized he was crying. He took deep breaths and wiped his face, then put down his bag, feeling completely drained. His car was in the Maggia Valley. Since parking in Lugano was difficult, Tonio and Mario had shared Mario's car. Taking the train to get home seemed to require an inordinate amount of energy right then. He pulled out his cell phone and called Laura, who, fortunately, was still at the workshop in Lugano.

When she picked him up, he let himself fall into the car and exhaled deeply. "I'm totally exhausted."

"Oh, Tonio, I'm so sorry." Feeling her arms around him, he felt like a kid again, being hugged by his older sister. He let himself go and sobbed.

At home, after eating some soup and drinking the cups of soothing tea Laura made for both of them, they talked for a long time. Eventually, Tonio began to feel a little better again. In spite of the pain he felt, he was also somewhat relieved.

"Perhaps Mario has a point. We may need some time away from each other. I only realize now how much pressure I felt from him." He sighed. "I just wonder how I'll feel living at home again after all this time. Do you think Papa will still insist on a curfew?" He chortled.

"Give me a break," Laura said, laughing. "They'll be happy to have you back. Besides, you can always look for your own place."

"Yeah, eventually, but I'm happy to be able to save some money, in case I decide to go abroad for a while."

"See, you're already making plans. That's exactly what you're supposed to do," Laura said. "You've been talking a lot lately about making changes, about doing something different. Now, here is your chance."

Tonio managed a smile. "You're always so levelheaded, my dear big sister."

"That's how big sisters are supposed to be," she said.

Chapter 51: Laura

"Got your passport and ticket?" Her father put Laura's travel bag into the trunk of the car.

"I got my ID and ticket. I don't need a passport for Paris," Laura said.

"And the chocolate for Stefano?" her mother asked.

"Yes, everything is packed," Laura said. "But where's Emilia?"

"She said she forgot something. Well, here she is." Karla motioned at the door.

Emilia came rushing out of the house, her little purse in one hand, and in the other she carried one of her small plush animals. She handed it to Laura. "For you, so you're not alone."

"Oh, that's sweet of you, Emilia." Laura kissed her. "But won't you miss Snoopy?"

Emilia shook her head. "No, Snoopy wants to travel, too."

"Thank you, sweetie, I'll take good care of him, and he'll have a lot to tell you when he gets back."

"Snoopy doesn't talk," Emilia said.

"No?" Laura said, surprised. "I thought he always talked to you."

Emilia shook her head. "He just barks."

"Oh boy, Emilia is growing up. What a pity," Laura said and kissed her little sister.

"Come on, guys, no dawdling, or Laura will miss her train." Andreas opened the doors and waved them toward the car.

Laura was on her way to Paris to meet Stefano for a few days of vacation. She had been to England a few weeks before, and this time they decided to meet halfway.

Emilia

The drive to Lugano took about an hour. The traffic was unusually light and they arrived in plenty of time.

"There's Tonio," Emilia called and waved.

Tonio was on his lunch hour and came to send Laura off. He picked Emilia up and swung her around. "Hello, princess." He hugged Laura. "Ready for the journey?"

Laura smiled. "Yeah, I'm a little nervous," she admitted. "But I'm really looking forward to this trip. I've never been to Paris, so this is a totally new experience for me."

"Let's go into the station restaurant," her father said. "We have time for a quick lunch."

Inside, they sat next to the window. It was a sunny day in early September. Since the train station was situated on a hill above Lugano, they had a beautiful view of the city and Lake Lugano.

"This lunch is on me," Tonio said. He held up his hand as Karla and Andreas began to protest. "No back talk."

"You're in a good mood today," Laura said. "How's work?"

"It's still a little awkward. As long as Ernesto and I are alone at the boutique, we're fine. When Mario comes by, which fortunately doesn't happen too often, it's still, well, difficult." Tonio put down the menu he had been studying. "But I got some good news today."

"What's that?" Karla asked and put her hand on Tonio's shoulder.

"Well, as you know, I was looking for a way to get a job in one of the fashion cities in Italy or attend one of the programs for continuing education. My former design teacher at the fashion school, who promised to help me, put me in touch with a few design studios. The owner of one of them called me this morning and offered me an internship for three months, or longer if I want to."

"Oh, how wonderful," Karla said.

"Where in Italy?" Andreas asked.

"Milano," Tonio said. "I kind of toyed with the idea of going to Florence, since it's such a gorgeous city. But Milano is one of *the* fashion centers in Europe. So I'm really excited. And it's only an hour away from here and close to Florence." His face broke into a big smile.

"What a great opportunity," Andreas said. "I'm so happy for you. When?"

"He wants me to come as soon as possible, so I can help prepare the spring fashion. He's looking for accommodations for me."

The waiter served the pizzas as well as a plate of pasta for Emilia. The little girl had been unusually quiet during the conversation and looked forlorn and a little sad.

Karla seemed to pick up on her mood and hugged her. "Our house will feel very empty soon," she said. "With Laura getting married next spring and you going abroad."

"Yeah, but I'll probably be back long before Laura gets married and Milano is only one hour away. So I'll be home a lot." He patted Emilia's hair. "You'll come and visit and I'll take you shopping for nice clothes."

Emilia gave a little smile and poked at the food with her fork.

"And great toys," Tonio added and wiggled his eyebrows.

The smile on Emilia's face got a little brighter.

"And I'll be back in a week, perhaps with a present from Paris," Laura said.

"There you go," her father said and patted Emilia on the back. "Now, eat up, so Laura won't miss her train."

A little later, Laura boarded the train to Zurich, where she had to change to the TGV, or *Train à Grande Vitesse*, which would take her straight to Paris in four hours. The train ride to Zurich took about two and a half hours. It was a trip she was familiar with from the days when she made her apprenticeship in the German part of the country. She always enjoyed the journey through the varied landscape, which led from the Mediterranean-looking south, with its light-green meadows, palm trees, chestnut forests, and Italian-style houses, to the higher altitudes of the Gotthard mountain range, where waterfalls tumbled over steep granite walls and the softer greens of palm trees, ashes, and chestnut trees were replaced by pine and fir forests.

It was a bright, sunny day on the southern side of the Saint Gotthard as the train entered the tunnel in Airolo. As was often the case, the warm and sunny weather in the south gave way to cooler temperatures on the north side of the mountain. When the train exited the tunnel in Göschenen, it was raining. On the way to Zurich, they came into a thunderstorm and heavy rain. Rays of white light hit the surface of Lake Vierwaldstättersee, creating a fascinating and somewhat scary display of the forces of nature. A couple of times Laura held her breath, praying the lightning wouldn't strike the train. Near Zurich, the weather calmed down again.

At the main train station in Zurich, she changed trains and found her reserved window seat in a nice comfortable carriage of the high-speed train. She leaned back and relaxed after the turbulent journey from the south to the north of Switzerland.

The train crossed the border in Basel and drove through the French countryside, with its mix of rural and urban areas, past windmills, French farmhouses, small cities, and towns. Contrary to Switzerland, the landscape wasn't as mountainous. After a while, the gentle hills and flat green stretches that took turns with wooded areas relaxed Laura so much that she kept nodding off. At one point, she went to the bistro area of the train and got a cup of coffee, which she took to her seat. The closer to Paris they got, the friendlier the weather became.

They arrived at the Paris Gare-de-Lyon train station in the evening. Grabbing her travel bag, purse, and jacket, Laura stepped down from the train and walked toward the end of the tracks where

Stefano said he'd meet her. When she didn't see him there, she waited for a while. The main hall of the station was modern and clean and very busy with passengers coming and going after work. It looked like an indoor shopping center, with stores and boutiques.

After waiting for about ten minutes, Laura became a little concerned. She knew that his train had arrived earlier, so he should be there by now. She tried to reach him on her cell phone, but could only leave a voice mail.

Just as she slid her phone back into her purse, somebody pushed against her. She looked around, and the next thing she knew, her purse was gone. In a state of shock, she stared after what looked like a young kid dodging people and disappearing in the crowd. She screamed "Hold him" and tried to run after him, but he was already gone.

"No, this can't be happening," Laura said out loud, tears flooding her eyes. A woman who had witnessed the theft came over and waved at a policeman nearby. Laura called to him and pointed in the direction of the disappearing youth, but the policemen didn't seem to be in any hurry, as if he didn't care. Laura was desperate; she had lost part of her money and her cell phone. Fortunately, she carried most of her money and other valuables in a cloth stash around her neck—a suggestion from her father.

At that moment, there seemed to be a scuffle near the exit and people were crowding around something or someone.

"Stefano," Laura called as she recognized him. He was holding a young kid who was kicking and struggling to get free. A man next to him tried to help and, finally, the policeman seemed to wake up and blow a whistle. Stefano got hold of Laura's purse, and the thief let go and disappeared once again in the crowd.

Laura ran toward Stefano and hugged him. She was so relieved she broke down and cried. He held her. "I'm so sorry I'm late," he said. "I tried to call you, but I couldn't get through on my cell. I don't know why. My train got canceled. I just got here with the next one."

"Oh, honey," Laura cried. "You got here at the perfect time. How did you catch him?"

"I heard someone scream and I saw this kid running toward me, clutching a purse, which looked exactly like yours." Stefano pointed at the colorful tassel on Laura's purse. "I just reacted, almost instinctively, and grabbed him."

"Well, thank God." Laura hugged him again.

"Madame?"

Laura looked around. The policeman stood there with a notepad in his hand.

"What do you want?" Laura glared at him. "You didn't do a thing to help me. The kid disappeared and you just stood there."

"Psst," Stefano whispered to her. "Don't get the French police angry."

"*C'est vrai*," said the lady who had tried to help Laura. "It's true, she's right."

The policeman glowered at the French lady, then turned to Laura. "Would you like to press charges?"

"What good would that do? He's gone," Laura said.

The policeman shut his notebook. "Be more careful next time. There are pickpockets around."

"That's right," the French lady said. "They give Paris a bad name, and the authorities"—she pointed her finger at the cop—"do nothing about it."

"We can't be everywhere all the time. People have to watch their belongings and be careful."

"Oh, forget it. Come on, *mademoiselle et monsieur*." She took Laura by the arm and motioned Stefano to come with her. "Ineffective police," she murmured as she led them away. "I'm sorry you had such a bad introduction to Paris. But he did have a point. Paris is a magnificent city, but it is a metropolis and there is crime. So be extra careful when you're in crowded places. We have pickpockets from all over the world."

In the meantime, they had arrived at the exit of the main station. "You're here on vacation, I assume?" the lady said.

"Yes, for a few days," Laura said.

"If you have some time one of the next few days, I'd love to give you a tour of some of the sites. I feel I owe you a more pleasant experience after your rough introduction to Paris," the woman said.

"Oh, it's not your fault, and thanks for your help," Stefano said. "We'd love to take you up on your offer, though, if it's not too much trouble. It's our first time in Paris."

"My name is Marie," the woman said. "Where are you staying?"

Laura and Stefano introduced themselves. "I booked a hotel in the center," Stefano said. He pulled out a piece of paper. "It's called Migny Opéra Montmartre. Should be close to Montmartre and Sacré Coeur and Moulin Rouge—you know, all the famous places."

"I've only seen the hotel from the outside, but it should be okay. You'll have to take a taxi, but it's not very far. Let me help you find a reliable cab driver." They walked out of the station and Marie waved at one of the taxi drivers. She spoke to him in rapid French and all Laura was able to understand was the name of the hotel and something about the price. Marie told them the amount of the taxi fare, which was reasonable. Laura suspected they got a good price by having a Parisian negotiate for them.

The taxi driver loaded their bags into the trunk and Marie told them she would pick them up the following morning around ten o'clock. "This will give you enough time to relax and have breakfast."

They checked in to the hotel, a very Parisian-looking place, built in the 1930s. Their small but clean and nicely furnished room was located on the third floor and looked out on the *rue* Victor Masse.

Laura dropped her travel bag and checked out the bathroom. "Very nice," she said. "I need to take a shower before doing anything else," she said. Feeling grubby from the long trip, she stepped into the shower. After fiddling with the unfamiliar faucets for a while, she managed to get them to work. She washed her hair and let the hot water soothe her aching muscles.

Stefano stepped into the shower as well, wrapped his arms around her, cupping her breasts. He kissed her neck and moaned. "It's been too long."

Hungry for intimacy after their long separation, they made love on the clean, starched sheets. Lying next to each other afterward, they listened to the muffled noise of the traffic outside. A cool evening breeze brushed gently over Laura's body. "This is the life," she sighed.

"Tell me about it," Stefano said. He put his arm around her and pulled her close, nuzzling her earlobe.

"More later," she said and kissed him. "Let's go out for a quick dinner." She smiled. "Making love always makes me hungry."

"Okay, I guess I can wait for round two." Stefano grinned and gently slapped her behind. "I would like to see the Sacré-Cœur cathedral. It's close by and it's supposed to be really beautiful at night."

They went out to a nearby bistro for a quick dinner. It must have rained during the day; the streets were still wet and the air smelled of moist leaves. Laura was a little tired from the long day, but the many lights and the lively atmosphere of Paris by night revived her spirits. Sacré-Cœur or Sacred Heart Basilica was a twenty-minute walk up a hill. When they arrived on top, they gazed at the beautifully lit church and enjoyed the view of Paris by night.

"Marvelous," Laura said. "I'm so happy we're here together." She hugged Stefano.

"I know, I really missed you." He returned her hug. Just as they began to kiss, the rain started up again, and they made their way back to the hotel, looking for shelter underneath the eaves of buildings. "That's just like in the movie *Midnight in Paris*," Stefano said.

"That's right, and we're in the middle of it. How exciting." Laura opened her arms and bent her head back and let the rain fall on her face. "Oh no, my hair is going to look all frizzy now," she said, laughing.

"Who cares?" Stefano took off his jacket and handed it to Laura, who put it over her head. They arrived at the hotel, giggling and waving at the receptionist, who looked at them, amused.

Back in their room, they stripped off their wet clothes and made love again. A while later, Stefano rummaged through the well-stocked refrigerator and pulled out a tiny bottle of Cognac. They shared it, sitting in bed.

Laura made a face after taking a sip. "A little too strong for me," she said and got up, grabbing a bottle of mineral water from the refrigerator. "Oh, darn," she said as she discovered the price list. "You know how much we just spent on this tiny bottle? I think that's probably the last drink we'll have in the hotel room. They cost a fortune."

"Well, we're on vacation," Stefano said. He looked at the list Laura handed him. "Jesus, I think you're right."

The following morning they decided not to have breakfast in the hotel but rather go back to a cute small coffee shop they had seen the night before. They passed a bakery on the way and Laura sniffed the air. "Ah, fresh bread." She watched the men and women inside buying famous French baguettes.

"Let's get some," Stefano suggested.

They went inside and feasted their eyes on the different loaves of bread and the assortment of delicious-looking pastries. They bought a baguette to share. Outside, they tore off pieces of the crusty bread, which was soft inside and smelled of yeast and butter. By the time they reached the coffee shop, they had finished eating it.

"I forgot how wonderful simple fresh bread can taste," Stefano said. "In England, I got used to eggs and bacon in the morning—not bad, but this is heavenly." He put the last piece in his mouth.

The coffee shop they went to was small and quaint. The red-and-white-checkered tablecloths and the paintings and posters on the walls reminded Laura of some of the old French movies she had seen. They ordered café au lait and croissants.

"Wonderful," Laura said as she bit into her *pain au chocolat*. "Did you notice all the smells of food outside? I love all these small grocery stores. But at this rate, I'm going to gain weight on our vacation."

"I don't think you need to worry about that, we'll do a lot of walking." He gave her a quick look-over. "By the way, have you lost weight? You look like it."

Laura shrugged. "Just a little. I tried to slim down some."

"Why?" Stefano took a sip of coffee. "You're not over-weight."

"Just felt like it," Laura said and gave him a quick embarrassed glance.

Stefano chuckled and shook his head. "Still worried about your figure?" He touched her face, then brushed through her hair. "I told you before, you're beautiful. Stop worrying about your looks."

"Just go on saying it; perhaps it'll sink in one day." Laura smiled. "Well, we better get back. Marie should be showing up anytime."

As they came back to the hotel, Marie was waiting in the lobby. She waved at them, then checked out their shoes. "Ready for some serious walking?"

"Absolutely," Stefano said.

"I picked a few things that I think you'd enjoy, but you have to tell me what you're most interested in."

"Anything you show us will be fine," Laura said. "I'd love to see the sculptures by Rodin, since I'm a sculptor and stonemason myself. And Stefano loves gardens. So do I, actually."

"Well, you've come to the right place." Marie took Laura by the arm. "We have beautiful parks and gardens and lots of sculptures as well as other art. *On s'en va.* Let's go."

They began to walk up the street toward the Sacré Coeur cathedral. It was only then that Laura looked at Marie more closely. The day before, she had been too preoccupied to pay much attention to their new friend. Marie was an energetic woman, probably in her late forties or early fifties, medium height, slim, with short, curly dark hair. She walked up the fairly steep road toward the cathedral fast, and Laura and Stefano had to make an effort to keep up with her. After a while, they slowed down and told each other a little bit about themselves. Marie was married and had lived in Paris most of her life. She worked as a language teacher and her husband was a professor at one of the universities. They had two half-grown children, a boy and a girl. Marie painted in her free time and was very interested in Laura's artist parents and in her and Stefano's work.

In the meantime, they had arrived at the cathedral. "Wow, it's so white," Stefano said. "We were here last night and it looked beautiful, all lit up. But I didn't realize it was shiny white like this."

"Yes, it's famous for its color. Every time it rains, it becomes clean again," Marie said. "It also has the largest bell tower in France."

They went inside and stood underneath the huge tower. After a while, Laura's neck began to hurt from bending her head back to look at the ceiling. They walked around, looking at the inside of the church, then went on to Place du Tetre with its colorful display of street artists and restaurants. Past the Musée de Montmartre, they reached a vineyard in the middle of the city, and on top of the hill was a red windmill, a remnant of the many windmills on

Montmartre in earlier times. "They used to grind the flour for making bread," Marie explained. They continued on down rue Lepic to No. 54, where the painter Vincent Van Gogh had lived during his time in Paris.

"Oh, my mother and father would enjoy this," Laura said.

"Now, something special for you two," Marie said. On their way down to the Place des Abbesses, they passed lots of small boutiques and food shops, from which all kinds of exotic smells wafted into the street. In the small garden on the square itself, a street musician played the accordion, and in the middle of the Place des Abbesses, there was a large wall where the words *I love you* were inscribed in 311 languages.

Laura snapped a picture of the wall, then Marie took a picture with Stefano's camera and his cell phone of Laura and Stefano standing next to the wall, pointing at the Italian words. Afterward, Laura sent the picture with an email to her mother. Marie laughed out loud. "Miracles of modern technology."

They saw the famous cabaret Moulin Rouge. Marie told them that Toulouse-Lautrec used to make posters for the shows and Edith Piaf also performed there.

After having lunch at a cute restaurant that served wine and simple meals, they walked down to the Seine and the bridges. They crossed Pont Neuf, or New Bridge, which was a misnomer according to Marie because it was actually the oldest bridge in Paris. They walked past the Concierge, which used to be the royal palace before the Louvre was built. Here, Marie Antoinette was imprisoned before being guillotined. Laura made a face. "Ouch."

They strolled along rue de Lutece, where they saw a colorful flower market, which Stefano and Laura wanted to look at more closely. They delighted in the sight of the wide assortment of flowers and the many different colors. "You'll see a lot more beautiful gardens in Paris," Marie said. "Wait until we get to the Tuilleries gardens."

Next, they admired the façade of the beautiful Notre Dame church. They went inside, where Laura studied the carved screen, which depicted stories from the Bible. After spending some time in the quiet, peaceful atmosphere of the church, they left and walked the short distance to the Quai aux Fleurs flower garden. "Look at this," Stefano said. "What a view." Before them was the river Seine. Marie pointed to the spire and the flying buttresses of the Notre Dame cathedral. "*The Hunchback of Notre Dame* by Victor Hugo," she said.

Afterward, they walked back along the Seine toward Musée d'Orsay, since Laura wanted to see the famous sculpture *The Gates of Hell* by Rodin. She stood in awe before the magnificent work of art. Marie told them she would show them the Rodin museum, so they could spend a leisurely few hours the following day. "There is also a wonderful walk along the Seine and across the many bridges," she said. "Seeing the sights when the sun sets is quite an experience."

They crossed another bridge, which brought them to the Quai des Tuilleries and the fabulous Tuilleries Gardens, where they rested from their long walk. They relaxed in the garden tearoom before walking through the gardens, which were a feast for the eyes of both Laura and Stefano. Aside from all kinds of plants, trees, and flowers, the garden was an open-air museum of modern sculptures.

In the meantime, it was late afternoon and Marie suggested she take them back to their hotel. She invited them for dinner at her home the following day. "It's going to be a simple home-cooked French meal, nothing fancy," she said.

Stefano protested. "That's so kind of you, but we wanted to invite you out for dinner, you and your husband, as a thank-you for all you did for us."

Marie waved his protest away. "You can invite us another time. It's more relaxing at home, and I don't live far from here. Besides, you might get tired of restaurant food after a few days." She gave them her address and drew a small map. "*Salut. A demain.* See you tomorrow."

"What a nice lady," Laura said, as they watched Marie walk away. "She certainly doesn't fit the stereotype of rude Parisians."

"Yeah, so much for stereotypes," Stefano said.

"Well, so far I've encountered a young thief and pick-pocket, a lazy and rude policeman, and a kind and generous woman. And I've only been here a day. Not bad."

"You forgot your loving fiancé," Stefano said.

"Oh no, how could I forget you, gorgeous?" Laura put his arm around him.

"Let's go to our room and engage in a little relaxing." Stefano winked at her. "At sunset, we can take a walk along the Seine, as Marie suggested."

As the sun began to set, Laura and Stefano walked along the famous Avenue des Champs Élysées and through the park with the same name. Champs Élysées meant "Fields of Paradise" and the gardens with their beautiful plants and flowers did the name justice. Aside from the flowers, they admired the view of the Élysée Palace, the residence of the presidents of France. They strolled across the Place de la Concorde down to the Seine, crossed the bridge, and walked along the river to Pont des Arts, the Bridge of the Arts. They arrived at the bridge just as the sun was setting, and began to cross it.

"Look at this," Laura whispered. The view from the bridge was breathtaking. On one end of the bridge, the French Institute stood tall and impressive. On the other bank of the river, they saw the Louvre and, farther down, the towers of Notre Dame. The setting sun spread a golden shine over the buildings and the river. As the darkness slowly descended, the glow of the sun was replaced by a plethora of lights. The buildings, cathedrals, churches, and towers were wrapped in light, and the Eiffel Tower beamed through the dark. The surface of the Seine shimmered as it reflected the lights of the streetlamps.

Stefano put his arm around Laura. "No wonder they call this the City of Lights."

Laura nodded. She was overwhelmed, not just by the beauty of this city but by an upsurge of her own emotions. Watching the play of lights on the water, feeling the cool breeze from the river across her face, smelling the water and the city, feeling the man she loved next to her—it was almost too much. Happiness and sadness stirred in her in equal measures. Tears gathered in her eyes and she quickly brushed them away.

"Are you okay?" she heard Stefano's concerned voice. He put his hand under her chin and turned her head toward him.

Laura smiled through her tears, just as a soft sob rose from her chest. "I'm fine, I don't know what's come over me. I'm happy, really."

Stefano hugged her. "Hmm, tears of happiness? You're sure?"

Laura nodded. "I've just been under a lot of pressure. But let's go and eat. We can talk about it there."

"Sounds good," Stefano said and hugged her. "Let's go to the place we saw back there. Le Basilique, I think it's called."

Having regained her composure, Laura took Stefano's hand and they walked back toward the restaurant they had seen near the Palais du Bourbon.

It was a small family-type place that served traditional French cuisine. They ordered roasted chicken, pommes frites, vegetables, and the red house wine. The food was simple but tasty.

Laura sat back and sighed. "This is great, being here with you, just enjoying myself. I haven't had this for a while." She took a sip of wine.

"What brought on the tears?" Stefano asked, putting his hand on hers. "The situation with your family, by any chance?"

"Yes, worrying about my parents, about Emilia, not knowing what was going to happen. My mother took off for Peru, my father went out with this young woman. I still don't know what that was all about. Tonio breaking up with Mario." Laura felt tears rising again. She brushed them away. "I'm sorry, I don't know why I'm suddenly so emotional."

Stefano squeezed her hand. "Because you've been holding it in for too long. It's okay to have a little breakdown. It's okay to cry."

The waiter came over and asked if everything was okay. Laura wiped her eyes and smiled. "Yes, everything is fine. The food is excellent."

Stefano ordered coffee and asked for the dessert menu. "Sugar will cure anything," he said to the waiter, who smiled and nodded.

"You know, Laura, you have to start thinking more about yourself," Stefano said with a serious face. "You've been trying to hold the family together. You worry about everybody else's problems. You are a very kind person, but you can take it too far. Your parents are old enough to deal with their own lives, for heaven's sake. So is Tonio. One way or the other, Emilia will be taken care of. You have to be a little more selfish." Stefano sighed. "I wish we weren't so far apart, I could keep an eye on things."

"I can just see it, you're going to scold my parents and get them back in line." Laura laughed. "Well, fortunately, things have really improved. Ever since they came back from Peru, they get along much better. I think they're even in love again. Tonio has new opportunities and he is more cheerful again. But you're right, I need to focus more on my own life again, my sculpting. I'm really looking forward to that exhibition my father and I are going to be in."

The waiter came back and served them the pastries they ordered, raspberry tarts topped with whipped cream, and coffee. "The pastry is on the house," he said and smiled at Laura.

"Amazing," Stefano said after the waiter left. "Everybody is so generous here. I think it's you, Laura. The French love you."

Laura chuckled. "Well, except for the little pickpocket. But that's nothing personal, he's probably just poor."

After dinner, they took a leisurely stroll back to the hotel, enjoying once again the lights and hustle and bustle of the exciting city.

The following day they spent exploring different art museums, among others the Musée Rodin, which Laura had been looking forward to since she knew she was going to Paris. Rodin was considered the most famous sculptor of the nineteenth century. Both Laura and her father had been fascinated by his art. He had been a controversial artist during his time. Many of his sculptures seemed unfinished, which was intentional and a trademark of his work. He gave the viewers enough room to use their own imaginations. His mastery was most visible in his bronze and marble sculptures, which had become an inspiration for Laura since she took the marble workshop in Peccia.

"His works are so sensual, so full of life," she kept saying to Stefano as they slowly walked through the garden and the inside of the museum. "He was able to transform this hard material into something smooth and erotic." She stood in front of *The Kiss*, one of Rodin's many sculptures. "What?" she said as she looked at Stefano, who chuckled.

"I agree," Stefano said and hugged her. "It just made me think of last night."

Laura slapped his arm lightly and laughed. "You're incorrigible. Men."

Stefano gave her a look of mock despair. "We just can't help ourselves." He pointed at a bronze sculpture of a man leaning back and extending his arms. "Look at this. It's something like raw emotion."

"Exactly," Laura exclaimed. "It inspires me to let go more with my own work, not to be so . . . how shall I put it . . . controlled. Oh, look at this." She grabbed Stefano by the arm. They stood in front of the sculpture called *The Hand of God*, which showed the creative process itself: God holding a lump of clay in his hand, from which He created the world, just as the sculptor, holding a lump of stone, created his work with chisel and hammer.

Laura took a deep breath. "How wonderful. I feel like going home and sculpting right now."

Stefano hugged her. "You're feeling better, aren't you?"

Laura nodded. "I'm so glad I came here."

They continued to look at the rest of the sculptures, then went on to a few other museums, enjoying the many impressionist and expressionist paintings. Laura's mind, however, kept coming back to the sculptures of Rodin. When they relaxed once again in the Tuilleries gardens, she pulled out her drawing pad and began to sketch, while Stefano walked around, studying the plants, bushes, and flowers. She stood up and stretched her body, feeling more alive than she had in a long time.

The remaining days of their visit to Paris went by too fast. In the evening, they had dinner with Marie's family, which they greatly enjoyed. The following days they spent visiting the Eiffel Tower, the Pantheon, the Louvre, the Arc de Triomphe, and many more sights. But the day when they had to say goodbye again for a few weeks approached all too soon. After a lot of hugging and kissing, Laura once again sat in the train on her way to Switzerland. She was sad leaving her fiancé behind, but also felt a new kind of creative energy and looked forward to working with one of her favorite materials, the crystalline marble from the quarries in Peccia.

Tonio picked her up at the train station in Lugano. They talked animatedly on the way home to the Vallemaggia. Laura told him about her trip and Tonio had news as well. He would be leaving for a three-month stay in Milano in two weeks. At home, another surprise awaited Laura. After dinner, her mother and father gave her an envelope. In it was a schedule of classes at the sculpture school in Peccia as well as workshops in Carrara, Italy.

"We decided you needed a break from your regular work," her mother said, as Laura looked at her stunned.

"Tonio is furthering his career in Milano, Stefano in England, and you, of all people, who helped me so much when Mama was gone, really deserve to branch out a little as well," her father said.

"Well, I had my workshop in Peccia a few years ago," Laura said.

"That was too short, you need to be able to work on a project uninterrupted for a longer period of time." Her father pointed at the pamphlets. "You can choose to either take classes in Peccia with Enrico or some other teachers. Or, if you want to go to Carrara, they, of course, are famous for their marble and there are some real master sculptors there."

"Oh, Papa, I don't know what to say, this is so wonderful. I got so inspired in Paris with all the Rodin stuff. You really mean this?"

"Of course we do, sweetie," her mother said.

"Well, I'll think about it . . . actually, I'd much rather stay here and take classes in Peccia. I love working with Enrico, and that way I can still see Stefano when he comes home. I don't want to be apart from him even more, and that would be the case if I went to Italy," Laura said.

"Well, think about it. You really need to do what's best for you," her mother said.

"I think that's what's best for me. You can't imagine how happy this makes me." Laura rushed over to her parents and hugged them. "But what about my work in Lugano?"

"Don't worry about it," her father said. "I can find someone else to fill in for you. My partner's nephew would like to make some extra money for Christmas. I may have him do some of the office paperwork."

"Does that mean I may not have a job with you anymore when the classes are over?" Laura looked at him thoughtfully.

"Honey, you can always come back. There will always be a job for you with me, if that's what you want. But I want you to consider other options as well. Mama and I talked about this."

Her mother nodded. "Yes, Laura, you need to spread your wings, even if it's only for a few months, before you buckle down and get married."

Laura stood up and spread out her arms. "Thank you, you're wonderful. And yes, I'll spread my wings."

PART FOUR: TENDING THE FIRE

Chapter 52: The Wedding

"Hold still, sweetie," Karla said as she watched the hair-dresser fiddle with Laura's hair.

"God, I hate it when my hair curls like this." Laura shook her head and glared at herself in the mirror.

Karla, Laura, and Emilia were at the beauty shop, getting ready for Laura's wedding.

"Don't worry, we'll take care of your curls," said Sonia, the hairdresser and a friend of Laura's from school. She grabbed the curling iron and straightened Laura's hair, then added a few waves in the appropriate places and sprayed on some shine. "There, better?"

Laura turned her head left and right. "Actually, it looks really nice." She had a modern bob with a few wavy strands that gave her a soft, feminine look. Her hair sparkled from the shine and her face shimmered lightly from the makeup. As a final touch, the hairdresser fastened the bridal hairband.

Laura already wore her wedding outfit, so she wouldn't have to mess up her hair putting it on. Tonio had designed it for her and everybody agreed that he had outdone himself. It was a simple long white dress. The puffy sleeves and the top were decorated with a lace flower pattern, and the feather-light fabric flowed elegantly down her body, giving her strong figure a nice shape. Instead of a veil, she wore a headband made of the same lace, which held her dark thick hair in place. A simple emerald-like stone on the headband picked up the color of her eyes.

"You look like an angel," Emilia said and gently brushed her hand over Laura's dress.

"Oh, you look so cute yourself." Laura kissed five-year-old Emilia. She was wearing a pink-and-white fluffy dress and two strands of her light brown hair were braided into French braids and decorated with pink ribbons. She was going to be the flower girl.

"You do look beautiful, honey," Karla said to Laura, her eyes misting over. "Oh no, I can't cry now, my makeup," she said and carefully dabbed her eyes.

Sonia laughed. "Don't worry, I put water- and smear-proof makeup on both of you. I wouldn't let you go to a wedding with runny mascara."

"I'm still too nervous to cry," Laura said. "It'll probably happen at the altar or, perhaps, when I see Stefano in his tux. I've never seen him in anything more elegant than slacks and a shirt with a poorly knotted tie."

Karla laughed. "He and Andreas are one of a kind, although I think Andreas is worse. Fortunately, Tonio offered to help them get dressed."

"When did Papa come back last night from Stefano's bachelor party?" Laura asked.

"Around midnight," Karla said. "He said he was too old to stay out late, but I think Tonio and Stefano and their friends stayed on."

"Oh no, I hope they didn't do anything stupid, like getting Stefano drunk."

"Don't worry. Stefano seems like a pretty sensible guy. He wouldn't get drunk the day before his wedding," Karla said.

Laura wrinkled her forehead. "Fortunately he isn't into alcohol, though he did acquire a taste for English ale when he was at Kew Gardens. But you never know. He may have been nervous and—"

A knock on the door interrupted their talk. "Are you ladies presentable?" It was Andreas's throaty voice. They heard more male voices in the background.

"Oh, don't let them come in," Laura said. "Stefano isn't allowed to see me, it's bad luck." She scooted behind a floor-length screen as fast as her long dress allowed her.

Karla opened the door and pushed Andreas back, then closed the door behind her. "Don't you dare peek." She glanced at three elegantly dressed men. Tonio had done a good job helping Stefano and Andreas get ready.

"You guys look stunning," Karla said. Stefano was wearing a dark-green tux, white shirt, white-and-green-striped tie, and a white rose on his lapel. His face was a little pale, probably from the night out or nervousness. Karla touched his arm. "You look great. Relax."

He gave a little smile. "How's Laura doing?"

"She's fine, looking very beautiful."

"I can hardly wait to see her." He glanced at the closed door. "You don't think—"

"Oh no, you just have to wait." Karla then turned to Andreas and Tonio.

"Thanks, Tonio, for helping these two fashion-challenged men look so gorgeous."

"I present my creations to you, lovely lady." Tonio bowed and made a sweeping flourish with his hand at Andreas and Stefano.

"Oh, stop it," they both said. Andreas tried to loosen his tie.

Tonio grabbed his arm. "Don't you dare."

"You look very good yourself," Karla said to Tonio. He was wearing an elegant but conventional black suit, a dusky-pink shirt, and a matching tie in a darker shade than the shirt. The only sign of his more outlandish taste in fashion were the heart-shaped dark-dusky-pink cufflinks. Tonio was going to be one of the groomsmen.

Karla went up to Andreas and hugged him. "You do look smashing." Andreas was wearing a dark suit, a linden-green shirt, and a dark-green tie. The tie and shirt emphasized his lively green eyes.

Andreas gave a quick chortle. "Well, for this occasion, I sacrificed myself. Besides, I can't look too shabby next to you and my beautiful family. You look lovely, as always." He hugged and kissed her.

Karla was wearing a long one-shoulder dress, another design of Tonio's, made of green silk that flattered her slender figure. "Thanks. My shoes are killing me," she whispered. She wasn't used to wearing high heels anymore.

Andreas put his arm around her. "You can take them off when you sit down in church."

At that moment, the bells of the small village church next door began to toll and friends and family gathered in front of it. "You better get Laura and Emilia," Andreas said. "And where is our ring bearer?"

"Don't worry, I'll get them. Meet us at the presbytery," Karla said. Andreas was going to give Laura away. One of Stefano's little nephews, Sebastian, was the ring bearer. Karla waved at Stefano's family and motioned the little boy to come with her. He looked darling in his suit and tie and freshly brushed hair. *He and Emilia will look cute together,* Karla thought.

Inside the small building next to the chapel, Karla helped Laura make the last few preparations. She handed her the flower bouquet and gave the flower basket to Emilia.

"I'm so nervous," Laura said.

"I know. Take some deep breaths." Karla gently patted her back. "I remember my own wedding as if it were yesterday."

Andreas walked into the presbytery and gasped as he saw Laura in her stunning dress. Memories of her as a baby, an unruly little tomboy, an insecure young girl, and a lovely daughter rushed through his mind and tears flooded his eyes. The person who stood in front of him was a grown, independent woman. And for the first time it really hit him that today was the day he would lose her.

They always said when your child gets married you gain a son or a daughter. That was only partly true. He would walk her down the aisle in church and hand her over to another man, and his role as protector and provider would be over. Andreas shook his head, trying to chase away these thoughts. It was her wedding day; he didn't want to spoil it by being an emotional wreck.

"My God, you look beautiful," he said. He walked toward her and wrapped his arms around her.

"Careful, Papa, my dress." Laura held him off a little bit.

"Sorry," he whispered. He couldn't even hug her properly. Instead, he kissed her gently on the cheek. He cleared his throat and looked at Karla. As their eyes met, a silent understanding passed between them. For them it would be a day of having to let go.

Karla smiled and walked up to him. "Time to go," she said. "Stefano and his father and the best man are probably already at the altar."

"Papa, let's go," Emilia called from the door. Andreas looked at the lovely flower girl next to the young boy and said a silent "thank you." He still had a child at home.

"Coming, honey. Lead the way." He handed the young boy the small ring pillow. "Okay, now, remember, wait until the bridesmaids and groomsmen are at the altar. And then the two of you walk right in front of Laura and me. Go nice and slow up to the altar, okay?"

The two nodded and Emilia began to toss flowers. Andreas snickered. "Wait until we are inside the church." Feeling that his emotions were under control again, he took Laura by the arm and led her to the church entrance. The music began to play "Ode to Joy" by Beethoven as the wedding procession made its way slowly down the middle aisle of the church.

The small cathedral was filled to the last seat with villagers, friends, and family. Andreas felt all eyes on him and his daughter as they followed the flower girl and ring bearer along the middle aisle to the front of the church. Emilia scattered the flowers and waved to her friends, to the amusement of the guests. Stefano, his father, and the best man were waiting next to a young priest. At the altar, Andreas squeezed Laura's hand, then placed it in Stefano's hand and stepped back. He glanced at Stefano's father, who smiled and gave a quick nod. The two men sat next to their families.

Andreas put his arm around Karla's shoulder. She smiled briefly while dabbing her eyes. A quick glance at Stefano's mother showed him that she was tearing up was well. As he watched and listened to the ceremony, the words of the priest, the exchange of rings, and the kiss the now married couple exchanged, he saw himself and Karla twenty-five years before, exchanging vows at the same place. He had been a little clumsier than Stefano was; he had dropped the ring and had to run after it, to the amusement of the priest and everybody around him. The memory made him smile. In spite of all the turmoil, their flaws, and weaknesses, he and Karla had survived and were able to celebrate the union of their daughter with a wonderful young man.

Laura stood next to Stefano, trying to listen to the words of the priest. Her heart was beating fast. Stefano's hand felt a little sweaty and he was pale. This was the moment that decided their future life together. Had they made the right decision? The thought shocked Laura; did she have doubts? It was a little late for that, wasn't it?

She listened to the priest as he addressed Stefano, her soon-to-be husband. "Stefano, do you take Laura to be your wife? Do you promise to be true to her in good times and in bad, in sickness and in health, to love her and honor her all the days of your life?"

Stefano squeezed her hand. "I do."

The young priest faced Laura and repeated the question to her. Laura took a deep breath and said with conviction: "I do." At that moment all her doubts fell away.

Emilia

The priest looked around for the ring bearer. Emilia and Sebastian seemed to have lost interest in the ceremony. They were looking around the church, not paying attention. Stefano's father came up and gently pushed the inattentive ring bearer toward priest. People snickered in the background and the priest smiled. He blessed the wedding rings and Stefano took Laura's ring and placed it on her finger. "Laura, take this ring as a sign of my love and fidelity. In the name of the Father, and of the Son, and of the Holy Spirit."

Laura repeated the words and placed Stefano's ring on his finger. The priest uttered the traditional "Now, you may kiss the bride" to Stefano. They embraced and kissed. A few prayers and blessings followed, and Laura and Stefano left the church as man and wife. While they passed by their family, Laura glanced at her parents. Her mother smiled through her tears, her father put his handkerchief away, and Tonio winked at her. Emilia and Sebastian, relieved of their wedding duties, skipped toward the exit. Emilia tossed her last flowers at Lena, Luigi, and their family, and Sebastian threw the now-empty ring pillow unceremoniously into the air and caught it again.

"Stop that." Stefano's father walked after him, grabbed him by the shoulder, and gave him a punishing look. The little boy ducked and left the church without any further upset. Laura and Stefano looked at each other and grinned, grateful for a little comic relief after the intense ceremony.

Outside, they were greeted by friends and villagers and a picture-perfect sunny day. Church bells were ringing. Laura took a deep breath. A limousine, decorated with flowers and ribbons, was waiting for them. It would take them and their families to the reception at Casa Berno, above Ascona, where Laura's parents had booked the newlyweds a room for a few days, so they could relax and pamper themselves before their trip to Cusco to visit Laura's maternal Peruvian grandparents.

Tonio followed his parents as they left the church. Although he hadn't let on, the ceremony and what it entailed had made him wistful, even a little sad. Laura and he had been very close, even more so since his breakup with Mario. Although they were still brother and sister after the wedding, something had changed. Laura was now Mrs. Bertani-O'Reilly; she would have her own family and a full life away from him. It was okay, he told himself; they would visit and he was certainly happy for her. After all, he had his own life, too.

For the past few months, Tonio had lived in Milano and worked as a junior fashion designer with the company where he had made his internship. He enjoyed his work and the life in the interesting metropolitan city. He was able to experience the world of fashion firsthand. He had helped organize some fashion shows and had begun designing his own line of fashion for young people, which had received positive reviews. His boss was very supportive, and he had a good relationship with the other employees. Being the youngest of the designers, the older and more experienced staff didn't see him as a threat to their own positions yet. The field of fashion was highly competitive and drew people who loved being in the limelight, which led to some ugly intrigues and back-biting not just between models but among designers as well. So far, Tonio had been able to keep out of it.

The company hired interns on a regular basis. Knowing from his own experience that a start in a huge city like Milano could be lonely and difficult, Tonio tried to help the newcomers get familiar and showed them around the city. On many of the weekends, though, he took the train home and spent time with Laura, his friends, and the family, and Laura had visited him a few times as well.

That was the extent of his social life and he was okay with it. In the world of fashion there was no shortage of gay men, and Tonio had made a few friends. However, he hadn't felt like getting involved intimately with anybody. He wanted to concentrate on his work and education. That was one of the reasons, the other one being that he still had feelings for Mario.

Thinking about these things as he walked out of the church with his father and mother into the June sunlight, he got a jolt when he heard his mother ask, "Isn't that Mario over there?"

"What? Where?" Tonio looked in the direction she motioned at. Sure enough, Mario, a small package in his hand, stood at the other end of the village plaza, looking lost.

"Can you wait for a minute?" Tonio asked his parents as they were getting ready to climb into the limo.

"Sure, go talk to him," his mother said. "We should've invited him, but I didn't know how you'd feel about it."

"Yeah, I know. I thought about it, too. He's a friend of Laura's as well, but I thought it would be awkward for everybody," Tonio said.

"Well, he's still a friend of the family," his father said. "It's up to you, Tonio, but as far as we're concerned, he's welcome at the reception. But only if it doesn't make you feel uncomfortable."

"Yeah, ask him to come," Laura said. She leaned out of the limousine and waved to Mario.

Mario acknowledged her with a smile and came up to the car. "Hi there," he said, looking embarrassed. He turned to Laura, who had stepped out of the car. "I'm sorry to just show up, but I wanted to give you this and wish you the best of luck." He handed her a small package. "You look absolutely gorgeous," he added and hugged her.

"Hey, man," Tonio said.

"Hi." Mario hesitated, then walked up to Tonio, and the two embraced.

"I thought about inviting you, but I didn't know how you'd feel about it," Tonio said, "or how I'd feel about it. But I'm really happy you're here and we all would love it if you joined us at the reception."

"I can't do this," Mario said.

"Why not?" Tonio asked.

"Because . . . well, for one thing, I'm not dressed for the occasion."

Laura laughed. "You're dressed just fine. Come on, it would make me really happy."

"You're wearing a nice suit and tie. So what's wrong with that?" Tonio said.

"Well, I didn't want to show up in my jeans, but, I mean, it's a wedding reception." Mario looked down at his pants and shoes. He was wearing a grey suit, light-blue shirt, matching tie, and shiny black shoes.

"You look perfect," Tonio said. "Come on into the limo."

"I have my car here," Mario said.

"Well, okay, why don't I drive in the car with you? That way, you can't back out, because you have to take me to the reception."

"Are you sure?" Mario looked at Andreas and Karla.

"Absolutely," Andreas said. "Let's go and I'll see you guys at the reception. Don't be late." He climbed into the limo and waved at them.

Mario and Tonio watched as the decorated car slowly drove along the narrow road through town, onto the highway.

"Good to see you," Tonio said. "Let's go."

They got into Mario's car, which was parked nearby, and followed the limousine.

"So, how are things—" they both asked at the same time, then laughed.

"How is Milano?" Mario asked.

"Great, lots to learn, but it's exciting. I've started to develop my own fashion line."

"I know, I've seen pictures." Mario glanced at him, then looked back at the road.

"You saw pictures?" Tonio asked, surprised.

"Yes, believe it or not, I'm following your career. You were favorably mentioned in one of the fashion magazines as *the* innovative fashion designer of the year."

Tonio chortled. "Don't exaggerate. It said 'promising and innovative.'"

"Hey, that's great. You should be proud." Mario tapped Tonio's shoulder as he drove around one of the narrow curves on the road along the river.

"I'm happy about it, but would you mind keeping the car on the road? I'd love to attend my sister's wedding reception."

"Hey, relax, I'm in total control." Mario put his hand back on the steering wheel.

It was quiet in the car while Mario concentrated on the curvy road. "I miss you," he said in a quiet, serious voice a while later.

"Yeah?" Tonio said.

"Yes." Mario glanced at him, then slowed the car down and stopped at one of the turnouts along the side of the road. "Let's talk for a moment. We probably won't have a chance at the reception. Okay?"

"Okay, I guess we have time," Tonio said.

They rolled down the windows a little and listened to the roaring of the mountain river Maggia down below the road. Tonio leaned his head back and closed his eyes, enjoying the light breeze brushing across his face and the clean smell of cold mountain water.

"I shouldn't have let you go," Mario said.

Tonio faced him but didn't say anything.

"What I mean is, I shouldn't have pushed you away. I'm glad you chose to work at your career as fashion designer. It was the right thing to do." Mario lowered his gaze and looked down at his hands.

Tonio nodded but kept quiet.

"I have been thinking a lot these past months, about you and me, my own career, my own life. You were right when you said I was acting like an old man. I guess I was just afraid. I was always looking for stability, some kind of a cozy home I never had. You were right about that, too." Mario brushed through his hair.

"Anyway," he continued, "after you left, I was relieved at first. I didn't have to deal with your constant plans and new ideas anymore. I could retreat into the shell of my supposedly stable life. I went to my accustomed job, lived my regimented existence, but you know what?" He faced Tonio, who shook his head.

"I was totally bored, with my life, my work, everything. And I missed your youthful enthusiasm, your ideas, your plans—you. I missed *you*."

Tonio gave a little smile. "I missed you, too, believe me. I was devastated after we broke up, but I knew I had done the right thing when I decided to focus on my career. Designing fashion is my passion."

Mario nodded. "You're right and you're very good at it. See, I love fashion designing, too, but what I really like is buying and selling fashion, stocking my stores with great stuff. I love that aspect of the fashion world. It's just that I went the wrong way about it. I took over my father's ideas of what men's fashion is supposed to look like—you know, the elegant, tasteful, typical conservative Italian men's fashion, the ones you see in elegant stores in Italy and Lugano. And that's okay, I'm not belittling this kind of fashion. But I want something more, some new hip stuff for young people, the kind of fashion you began to design."

Tonio stared at him. Mario's skin was flush and his eyes shone. "Boy, you sure look and sound different," Tonio said. "You seem twenty years younger."

Mario gave a quick grin. "Thanks, I take that as a compliment. But anyway, new ideas, that's where you come in."

"Me?" Tonio wrinkled his forehead.

"Yeah." Mario took a deep breath. "I don't mean to push you into anything, but I have a suggestion. You don't have to give me an answer now, but just think about it."

"Oh? So what is it?"

"I don't know for how long you plan to stay in Milano or what your plans are in general. But I want to change the second store into a boutique for young fashion and I'd love to have you develop your line of fashion and display and sell it there." Mario lifted his hand as Tonio tried to say something. "You wouldn't need to be there all the time. I'd encourage you to travel to all the important fashion shows or take other classes or whatever. I'd have someone else manage the store, so you could concentrate only on the design aspect."

Tonio's head was spinning as he tried to figure out what an offer like this meant. "Mario, this sounds . . . well, very tempting. It's just a little unexpected. I . . . don't know what to say. I mean, I don't intend to live in Milano permanently. I'd love to find a way to work in Lugano. It's just I have a job and I still have a lot to learn. I can't just up and quit right away."

"I understand," Mario said. "It doesn't have to be today or tomorrow. And as I said, you don't have to be here all the time. Besides, I'll be gone for a while. I registered for a three-month fashion course, combined with a language class, in France. It's mainly about the business aspect of the fashion industry."

Tonio stared at him. "What? I can't believe it. The home-body ventures out into the wide, wild world? That's great. I'm proud of you." He gave Mario a gentle push, then squeezed his arm. Their eyes met, and Mario removed his seat belt, bent over, and kissed Tonio gently on the mouth. Tonio pulled him close and they kissed until they heard a car horn next to them. A bunch of young kids in a pickup truck hooted and one of them made an obscene gesture, and the car drove off.

"Jerks," Mario grumbled.

"We better leave," Tonio said. "We have a wedding reception to attend. They'll probably wonder where we are."

"So you'll think about it?" Mario said as he grabbed the key in the ignition. "And about us?"

"About us?" Tonio raised his eyebrows. "I thought you were with Ernesto?"

Mario removed his hand from the key and shook his head. "That was a fling, it lasted about two weeks, it's over. I guess I was looking for some comfort after you left. How did you know about this, anyway?"

"Hmm. Word gets around." Tonio grinned. "I was keeping tabs on you, too, you know."

"Well, I haven't been with anyone else. And you?" Mario asked.

"Nothing," Tonio said.

"So you'll think about it?"

Tonio rolled his eyes. "Yes, I'll think about it. Now, would you please start the car and get us to the reception. I'm getting really hungry." He winked at Mario.

Karla inhaled the scent of lilacs the breeze brought from the gardens of Casa Berno. She stood on the terrace facing Lake Maggiore at the bottom of the hill and the mountains behind the lake. Taking a break from the festivities, she looked toward Italy. The surface of the lake shimmered in the early-June sun. It was pleasantly warm, but the northern wind brought an occasional chill. It was responsible for the clear view of the mountains to the south, which were often shrouded in haze from the air pollution the southern wind brought from cities like Lugano or even as far south as Milano.

The floor-length windows to the private dining room were open. The wedding guests were finishing up their pieces of wedding cake, coffee, and liquors. At one end an area was reserved for dancing. Behind it, the DJ tested the loud-speakers. Karla suppressed a yawn. She had been up early and was getting sleepy from the activities and the lavish supper. Guests got up from the tables to stretch their legs. Karla was joined by Andreas, who stood next to her and put his arm around her shoulders. She leaned her head against him.

"Tired?" he asked.

"A little sleepy."

"We're getting a little old for such festivities," Andreas said, then chuckled. "We have to keep in shape. In another twenty years, we may be here again, celebrating Emilia's wedding."

"Oh my God." Karla groaned. "What a thought. We might be walking with the help of a cane by then. What made you think of that?"

"Well, Emilia told me that she wanted a pink dress for her wedding, not a white one." Andreas chortled. "That made me realize we'll be in our seventies by then."

Karla sighed. "Having children that late brings up a whole bunch of questions and issues, doesn't it?"

"Do you regret it? Having had her that late?" Andreas asked.

"No, of course not. Just sometimes I think it was a little irresponsible. If we're lucky, we'll be around to see her grow up and get married and all that. But you never know," Karla said.

"A lot of younger people die unexpectedly and older folks hang on for a long time," Andreas said. "And to be honest, when I gave Laura away today, I was so grateful to still have a little one at home."

"I agree, I feel the same way," Karla said.

Laura and Stefano stepped outside and joined them, followed by Emilia and Sebastian. From the inside, they heard the DJ turn on the music.

"Papa, we want to dance." Emilia held a slightly reluctant Sebastian by the hand and pulled him toward the reception room.

"Okay, sweetie, but you'll have to wait. First, Laura and Stefano are going to dance, and then Papa and Laura and Stefano and his mom. I'll let you know when it's your turn."

Recently Emilia had developed a taste for singing and dancing. She had participated in some school functions and her teacher felt she had talent. Karla suspected, however, that her eagerness was not just her love of music but the desire to show off her pretty dress.

They all went inside and sat at the table. The man in charge of the entertainment, a friend of Tonio's, called the bride and the groom to the dance floor. Emilia, pulling Sebastian behind her, followed them, obviously unconcerned about the traditional order of things.

"What the . . . I told her to wait." Andreas scrunched his forehead and stood up. Karla was just about to call Emilia back when Andreas put two fingers into his mouth and gave a quick high-pitched wolf whistle. The DJ looked up, surprised. The guests stopped talking, and there was complete silence in the room as everybody stared at Andreas. The two children turned around and looked at him, shocked. He motioned them to come back and they obeyed immediately.

"I told you to wait," he said to Emilia with a stern face. She gave him a guilty look, then snuggled up to Karla. Tonio and Mario, who were sitting next to each other at the family table, snickered.

One of Stefano's aunts glanced at Andreas. "You can tell who is in charge in that family," she said.

"Exactly," Andreas murmured.

"My husband, the emperor," Karla remarked with a smile.

"Proceed, and I'm sorry," Andreas called to Laura and Stefano.

The music began again and the couple danced to the Elvis Presley song "Can't Help Falling in Love." Seeing her daughter and her son-in-law dance to the romantic music brought tears to Karla's eyes. "Don't they look beautiful together?" she said to Andreas, and he nodded.

He gave Emilia, who made a sad face, a hug. "You'll get to dance, don't worry."

After the dance was over, Stefano brought Laura to Andreas, and father and daughter went to the dance floor. "A Song for My Daughter" began to play. Karla put her arm around Emilia. "Next, Stefano's mom and Stefano are going to dance, and then Papa and Mama, and then you and Sebastian can dance all you want, *bene*?"

Emilia nodded. "Does Papa know how to dance?" she asked.

"Well, he's quite good at it," Karla said. "See?"

"What a great father-daughter picture." Stefano's stepmother sat next to Karla. Karla nodded as she watched Andreas and Laura dance slowly to the beautiful song. She thought back to the time she and Andreas danced at their own wedding. It had been in a smaller, less elaborate restaurant. Arturo, her father, had danced with her and that dance had been one of the high points of the wedding. Having her father, who had traveled all the way from Peru, give her away had made her very happy.

"Mom, lovely lady, may I have this dance with you?" Stefano asked and bowed in front of his mother. Mother and son joined Andreas and Laura at the dance floor. As Karla watched, she saw Tonio walk up to the DJ and talk with him. He came back with a smile on his face and winked at Karla.

After the piece of music was over, the DJ called the parents of the bride. "And as a special tribute to the mother of the bride's Latin American heritage, the parents will dance to a Latin tango."

"What? He can't be serious," Andreas said.

"Come on." Karla laughed. "You used to be very good at it."

"Used to be, yes, but that was twenty-five years ago, or even longer."

Karla, however, didn't give Andreas a chance to back out, and after a somewhat hesitant start, they put on a slow but almost-perfect performance, including Karla's backward bend over Andreas's knee at the end. There was a lot of hooting and clapping, which marked the end of the formal part of the evening. The parents of the groom and the other family members joined the dancers. Emilia, finally able to let loose, pulled the still-hesitant Sebastian to the dance floor.

Andreas and Karla took a break, with Andreas wiping the sweat from his forehead and giving Tonio a stern look. "This was your doing, wasn't it?"

Tonio burst out laughing. Andreas shook his head and smiled. He turned to Laura and Stefano. "We didn't mean to steal the show."

"Papa, that was just perfect," Laura said. "Besides, I was getting tired of that traditional stuff. Come on, Stefano, now the fun part starts." She pulled him back to the dance floor.

The remaining part of the celebration was upbeat and relaxed. Everybody danced with everybody. Emilia's partner, however, soon got tired of dancing and left her standing alone while he escaped onto the terrace. Andreas lifted her up and danced with her, then handed her over to Tonio. He and Mario took turns dancing with her, and Emilia soon forgot her first partner's ungentlemanly behavior.

The festivities lasted into the night. At one point, Karla, Andreas, and Tonio took a break out on the terrace. Mario had left a little earlier, since he had to work in the store on Sunday.

"So, Tonio, how are you and Mario getting along? Any new developments?" Karla had noticed that the two had spent some time by themselves, talking.

"Well, he made me a tempting offer." Tonio told his parents about their talk in the car and of Mario's suggestion that he develop his fashion line and sell it in his boutique.

"That sounds like a great plan," Andreas said. "What do you think?"

"I'm seriously considering it, at least for next year. Right now, I want to stay on with my current job. I can still learn a lot, but having the opportunity to work as a fashion designer in Lugano sounds very tempting."

"That would be wonderful," Karla said. "Do you think you'll get back together again? You seem to still care for each other."

Tonio nodded. "Yes, we do. He changed a lot. He's become much more adventurous with regard to his work and in general. But I'll take it a day at a time. I want to be sure and not rush into something and then get hurt again."

"Wise decision," Andreas said.

Tonio gave him a playful push. "You probably hoped I'd fall in love with a sexy Italian woman, didn't you?"

Andreas shook his head and gave a quick smile. "No, I'm not that naïve. But if it has to be a man, then I think Mario wouldn't be your worst choice," he countered Tonio's teasing.

Tonio and Karla laughed. "You've come a long way," Karla said.

"I guess." Andreas shrugged. "But don't you think it's about time we old folks retired and let the young people celebrate undisturbed?"

"'Old folks'? Speak for yourself," Karla said, suppressing a yawn. "But you're right. Besides, Emilia needs to catch a few hours of sleep. She'll be a wreck tomorrow."

"I'm ready to go, too," Tonio said. "I'm catching the train back to Milano tomorrow. How are we getting home?"

"We booked the limousine," Karla said. "Laura and Stefano are spending a few nights here, before leaving for Peru."

"Lucky devils," Tonio said.

After getting Emilia and saying goodbye to everyone, Karla, Andreas, Tonio, and Emilia were driven in style to their home in the Vallemaggia.

Chapter 53: Andreas

Andreas rubbed his forehead and grimaced. He had a slight headache from lack of sleep and a little too much wine the evening before. Yawning, he went outside and sat at the granite table. After a few sips of the strong, slightly bitter coffee, he felt revived. It was another sunny but breezy day. A dry gusty wind, the *tivano*, was blowing from the north. It whisked away any clouds and created a clear, sharp view of the hills and mountains and of the stretch of the river Maggia Andreas was able to see from his home. He took a deep breath and smiled as he inhaled a sweet scent the wind brought, something like honeysuckle or jasmine.

Feeling something stir behind him, he looked around. Emilia was standing at the door. She was still in her pajamas, her eyes full of sleep and her hair disheveled. She held an old plush bunny in her arms and made a gloomy face.

"Hey, sweetie," Andreas said. "You're up early."

Emilia gave no answer; she crossed the patio barefoot and sat next to him on the bench, hugging her plush animal.

Andreas put his arm around her. She climbed up on his lap and leaned her head against his chest. He hugged her. "You're still sleepy. You should go back to bed."

Emilia shook her head. "Where's Laura?"

"She's still at Casa Berno with Stefano. They're staying there for a few days before going to Peru. You know that."

Another shaking of the head. "I don't want her to go."

"She'll be back soon. You're just in a gloomy mood because you're tired."

"No," Emilia protested. She sat up. "Where's Tonio?"

Andreas sighed, sensing where this was heading. "He's in his room, probably still asleep."

"Is he going to stay?"

"No, Emilia, he's leaving for Milano today. You know that, too. But he'll be back soon for a weekend. And we'll be able to visit him."

"I don't want him to go." Emilia's voice broke.

"I know, Emilia."

"They're all leaving and I'm all alone." The first sob erupted and Emilia's small shoulders began to tremble.

Andreas hugged her tight. "Mama and I are still here, and your friends from school and all your friends from the village. And Laura and Stefano will come back soon and they're going to live really close by. And you'll see Tonio on weekends."

There was no answer, just sobbing. The door to the patio opened and Karla stepped outside. She was wearing a yellow top and jeans, and crossed her arms in front of her chest against the breeze. "Gee, it's nippy." Her hair fluttered in a gust of wind. She raised her eyebrow when she saw Emilia crying. "What's the matter?"

"Heartbreak and lack of sleep," Andreas whispered and continued to cradle Emilia in his arms.

Karla patted Emilia's head. "Sweetheart, it's going to be okay." Emilia looked up; tears were streaming down her face. She moved over to Karla, buried her face on her chest, and continued to cry. Andreas noticed Karla's eyes tearing up and he was getting sad himself. Emilia expressed what they all felt. Loved ones were leaving and the family was getting smaller and they hadn't gotten used to the changes yet.

"Well, what's going on here?" Tonio, carrying his travel bag, came over from the guest house next door. "Why is the princess crying?"

Emilia lifted her head and, seeing Tonio's luggage, began to cry harder. She slipped down from Karla's lap and ran into the house.

"Oh God, now I'm starting too," Karla said with a sob.

"What's wrong?" Tonio asked and put down his travel bag, staring at his parents, perplexed.

"Sad about you leaving," Andreas said.

"Jesus," Tonio said. "I'm only going to Milano, it's only a little over an hour by train, I'm not going to Siberia. I mean, I'm touched that you miss me so much." He sat next to Karla, putting his arm around her.

"It's not just about you. Emilia feels she's losing Laura and you at the same time. I understand how she feels," Karla said. "Think about it. You two are her best and closest friends."

"I understand, poor thing. Well, let me see if I can cheer her up a little." Tonio got up and walked into the house.

Karla wiped a tear away. "I'll take her to Lena's later on. Her grandchildren are here, that may make her feel better."

Andreas smiled and brushed his hand over her smooth hair. "She'll get used to it, but now life seems bleak to her. You know . . . what we were talking about the other day. I still think she's a little too young, but then again, it might help her. It'll keep her busy and teach her some responsibility."

Karla nodded. "Yeah, I was actually thinking about it, too."

"We just have to be aware what it would mean," Andreas continued. "She's still too little to be that committed. In other words, we would be stuck with the work and the responsibility. It also means walking every day."

"Yes, I know," Karla said. "I wouldn't mind, and I need the exercise anyway."

Tonio came back, carrying Emilia, who had stopped crying. "I'll be coming home next weekend and I'll take the princess to the zoo. We're going to see the baby monkeys, the new baby elephant, and the penguins. They said they missed Emilia."

Emilia gave a little smile. "They did not, they can't talk."

"Sure they can, they talk Penguinese and I speak the language, too." Tonio winked at her.

"No, you don't." Emilia laughed.

"How are you getting to the train station?" Andreas asked Tonio. "I can give you a ride."

"Actually, Mario is coming to pick me up. He wants to talk some more about our project," Tonio said.

"Ah, good, it sounds serious. So we may have you back next year. That would make us all happy," Karla said. "Wouldn't it, Emilia?"

Emilia nodded. "Is Mario coming to the zoo, too?"

"Perhaps. I'll ask him," Tonio said. "Oh, here he is."

Mario parked his Lancia in the driveway and got out. He picked up Emilia and swung her around. "I missed you, princess."

The farewell went fast and Emilia seemed to be okay with the promise she'd see Tonio again the following weekend, along with a trip to the zoo.

Chapter 54: Karla

"Emilia, get dressed," Karla called. It was Saturday morning. Karla and Andreas were sitting on the patio, sipping their first coffee of the day.

"Don't want to," a bored voice came from inside. Emilia was still in her pajamas, moping around. During the week she had been in preschool and hadn't missed her older siblings. The past weekend, Tonio and Mario had taken her to the zoo; but now, being alone at home with her parents, she walked around aimlessly, picking up a toy here and there and putting it down again.

Andreas grabbed his cup of coffee and went into the living room. Karla began to set the table on the patio. It was sunny and warm and they planned to have breakfast outside.

"Did you hear what Mama said?" Karla heard Andreas say. "I want you dressed in five minutes."

He shook his head when he came back out. "I guess we won't have to worry about having another artist in the family. At her age, Laura and Tonio would be scribbling and painting and pounding on stones. Emilia doesn't seem to have that creative urge. She gets bored easily."

"She's different," Karla admitted. "She's smart, though. She may become a veterinarian or something else to do with animals."

Andreas chuckled. "I can just see her with a house full of dogs and cats."

"Would you mind finish setting the table? I'll check to make sure she gets dressed."

When Karla walked into Emilia's bedroom, she found her daughter still in her pajamas, in front of the closet. "Let me help you," Karla said. She pulled out a pair of jeans and a top.

"I want to wear a dress," Emilia said.

"Not today, we're going to a place where you'll be more comfortable in pants or shorts."

"Where?" Emilia asked.

"It's a surprise. Now, get ready. You took a shower last night, but I want you to wash your face. Pants or shorts? That's your choice."

Emilia decided on her new pair of shorts. Karla helped her get ready and they went outside to have breakfast on the patio.

"Where are we going?" Emilia asked again.

"You'll find out," Andreas said. "It's a surprise."

"But where?" the girl insisted.

"If we tell you, it's not a surprise anymore," Andreas said. "Eat your breakfast. The faster you finish, the faster you'll find out."

Emilia

Emilia stuck her spoon into her bowl of cereal and drank a sip of her hot chocolate. "But . . ." she tried again.

"No buts." Andreas grinned. "You just have to wait."

He tickled her nose and she pushed his hand away. "Don't do that, Papa. It makes me sneeze."

Andreas smiled and gave her a quick hug, then grabbed another roll and slathered it with butter and marmalade. Karla cut up a papaya and gave each of them a piece. Emilia picked one of the slippery slices up and dropped it onto her shorts.

"Oh no," she said, with a guilty expression on her face. "My new shorts. I'll have to change."

"No, you don't," Karla said. She got up, got a wet rag, and rubbed the stain off Emilia's shorts. "It's fine. Finish your breakfast."

"You better get used to stains and dirty clothes," Andreas said. "I'm afraid your time of girly stuff is over."

"Why?" Emilia looked at him with her large blue eyes.

"You'll see," he said and got up. "One more sip of coffee and then we'll leave."

Ten minutes later, Andreas lifted Emilia into the back seat of their new station wagon and they all took off.

"Where are we going now?" Emilia asked.

"To visit a nice man I just met the other day," Andreas said.

"You said it was going to be something fun," Emilia grumbled.

Karla turned around and looked at her. "How do you know it's not going to be fun?"

Emilia stared out the window. She hugged her plush dog and made a long face. Andreas and Karla looked at each other and snickered.

They drove to Ponte Brolla, the beginning of the Maggia Valley, and took the road to Ascona. When they arrived at Lake Maggiore, Karla put on her sunglasses. The surface of the lake glimmered in the sunshine and made her eyes water. They took a narrow road up the hill toward the mountains.

"That's it," Andreas said and motioned at one of the elegant homes tucked away behind some eucalyptus trees. He parked on the driveway next to the house. "We're here," he said. He opened the door and lifted Emilia out. As soon as they stood outside, a dog began to bark and a young man with curly blond hair and blue eyes, dressed in shorts and a T-shirt, came walking toward the fence. He opened the gate and invited them in. They shook hands and he introduced himself as Marco. They walked into a beautiful, lush garden.

Karla turned to the man. "Sorry to hear about your loss."

"Thank you. Yes, it was quite unexpected. He was always in good health, so I'm still getting used to the fact that he's gone," he said sadly.

Andreas had heard about Marco through a friend of his. Marco's father had died of a heart attack. His father had had a young dog and Marco was looking for a new home for him. Andreas had visited him once before to have a look at the dog. He felt that he might make a good companion for Emilia.

When Marco shook hands with Emilia, he smiled. "So that's the young lady who loves animals."

"That's her," Andreas said.

Emilia hadn't said a word yet; she just looked at the adults with a puzzled expression on her face.

"Well, let's see where Skippy is," Marco said. "I haven't had a chance to walk him yet, so he may act a little exuberant. Don't be afraid if he tries to smother you," he said to Emilia. "I locked him inside so he doesn't scare you off right away." With that, Marco walked to the front door, behind which they heard a dog bark.

Karla squeezed Emilia's hand. "Here comes the surprise."

A puppy with a shiny golden-and-light-brown fur and floppy ears came charging at them, wagging his tail so much that his whole backside swayed left and right. He went right for Emilia, who got on her knees and gave a squeal of delight. "Oh, oh, he's so cute." She put her arms around his neck and the dog licked her face. "Mama, Papa, look how friendly he is."

"Yes, he is, isn't he?" Andreas said.

Marco laughed. "How about that for a declaration of love? You two seem to get along really well." He patted the dog. "See, Emilia, Skippy belonged to my father, who unfortunately got ill and died a short while ago. Dad and Skippy were very close, and Skippy is young and needs a lot of exercise. I have to travel a lot because of my job, and I don't want to leave Skippy with dog sitters all the time or put him in a kennel. That's not fair to him."

Emilia listened with a serious face.

"So I'm looking for a kind person to give him a home and the love and care he deserves."

"I'll take care of him," Emilia said. "Can I, Mama? Please, Papa?"

"You like Skippy, don't you?" Andreas said.

Emilia nodded vigorously and looked up at him with hopeful eyes.

"Let's talk about this for a moment," Andreas said. "If we take Skippy home with us, he is going to be your responsibility, okay?"

"Yes, yes," Emilia said and bent down to pat the dog again.

Andreas took her by the hand. "Leave Skippy alone for a moment and listen carefully. That means you'll have to feed him in the morning before going to school and you'll have to walk him every day and clean up after him. Mama and Papa will help you, of course, but we don't have time to babysit a young dog. So you'll have to take care of him. And that may not always be pleasant. You'll have to scoop up his poop and put it in the trash. He may throw up or pee in the house. You'll have to help clean it up. A dog isn't a toy that you can play with when you feel like it. If we take him with us, he's is going to be a member of the family. You understand?"

Nothing seemed to dampen Emilia's growing joy. "Yes, yes," she said, her face flush with excitement.

"He's pretty well-trained already," Marco said. "He's had all his shots, he's neutered and housebroken. So you shouldn't have a problem with that."

Karla smiled. Emilia's enthusiasm began to affect her. She remembered how happy she had been as a young child when her aunt let her have a kitty. "I think you'll do well. We'll all help. Walking a dog is good for us as well. Helps with love handles." She grinned and gently grabbed one of Andreas's small bulges around his waist.

"Ha, speak for yourself," he said and chuckled, sucking in his stomach. "All right, then. We'll take Skippy home."

"Oh, Papa, Mama, thank you, thank you." Emilia was beside herself. She embraced the dog, who wagged his tail and licked her hands and face.

"How wonderful, I'm so relieved," Marco said. "I'll miss the little guy, but I'm happy he found such a loving family. It'll probably take a while until he's used to his new home. You'll have to watch carefully at first, so he doesn't run away and get lost."

"We're aware of that," Andreas said. "My aunt and uncle used to have a dog when I was a kid, so we're not completely new at this. What breed is he? Golden retriever, right?"

"Yes, mainly golden retriever, but he's a mix. There might be some Labrador in him as well."

While Emilia was playing with her new companion, the adults sat at the table outside, sipped tea and mineral water, and admired the view of the lake, the mountains, and the town of Ascona at the bottom of the hillside. Marco handed them the registration documents and Skippy's health history. They put his basket, food bowl, leash, and toys into the car, so he would have some familiar items.

When the time came to say goodbye, there were a few tearful moments. Skippy jumped into the back seat of the car next to Emilia, but when he realized that Marco wasn't coming with them, he began to whimper, which in turn got Emilia started. She sobbed and hugged the dog, and Marco surreptitiously wiped his eyes.

"Come and visit him anytime," Andreas said to him. "You have my address. Just give us a call."

"I'll do that later. I'll wait for a while to give him a chance to settle in," Marco said. "If you ever need someone to pet-sit him, I'll do it, as long as I'm around." He waved at them as they drove away.

After a while, Skippy stopped crying and put his head on Emilia's lap, seemingly resigned to his fate. Every once in a while, he lifted his head and gave another little whimper and Emilia hugged him.

"He'll be fine," Karla said. "He's just a little homesick, but he'll get used to us soon." She patted Emilia's knee. "Happy, sweetie?"

Emilia nodded and kissed Skippy on the head.

At home, they left the dog in the house at first, so he wouldn't run away. They put down his water and food bowls in the kitchen and debated where to arrange his basket and toys. He immediately began to investigate his new home, running from one room to the other and sniffing every corner.

"Can he sleep in my room? Please?" Emilia looked at them with her begging puppy eyes.

"Well, why not?" Karla said. "Dotty always slept with me as well."

"Dotty?" Andreas asked.

"My cat when I was little," Karla said.

"All right." Andreas carried the basket into Emilia's bedroom. He put it down and added the few toys. The dog immediately jumped into the basket, sniffing his toys, then jumped out and made a thorough investigation of Emilia's bedroom. Having finished, he looked up at them and barked once.

"I think it's time for a treat," Andreas said. He went into the kitchen and came back with a dog biscuit. He gave it to Emilia. "Now, make him sit first, like Marco showed you."

Emilia gave the command, and after a few repetitions, Skippy sat down and looked at her expectantly. She gave him the biscuit, which he took gently from her hand and ate, licking up the last few crumbs on the floor.

"He has good manners," Karla said.

And so the rest of the afternoon and evening they spent trying to make their new family member welcome. Soon, Skippy followed Emilia everywhere. When Karla and Emilia took him out onto patio on a leash, he didn't seem to want to run away, but pulled Emilia around, exploring the neighborhood. Karla accompanied them and helped Emilia hold the leash. Skippy was young but strong, and if he had wanted to run away, Emilia wouldn't have been able to hold him back. Once he was comfortable with his new home, they would be able to let him run around the yard.

"Can I take Skippy to school with me?" Emilia asked when they were eating dinner and Skippy was slurping and licking his bowl in the kitchen.

"No, Emilia, that's not possible," Andreas said.

"Then who is going to watch him? He'll be lonely again," Emilia said with a sad face.

"No, he won't, we'll entertain him," Karla said. "And I'll take him for a walk when school lets out and we'll pick you up. You can introduce Skippy to your friends. How about that?"

Emilia's face lit up. "Okay," she agreed.

Emilia

At bedtime, Karla read a story to Emilia, and Skippy lay curled up in his basket, making occasional little snoring sounds. As she read the last line, Emilia, too, was asleep. Andreas came into the room, kissed Emilia gently on her forehead, and gave Skippy a little pat. "Looks like both youngsters are exhausted," he said. "It's been an exciting day."

He left the room and Karla covered Emilia with a light sheet. It was still warm outside and she left the shutters and the window open. Standing by the window, she inhaled the nightly summer fragrances—honeysuckle, jasmine, and a whiff of damp grass. Nearby an owl hooted, and a full moon was rising behind the mountains to the east. Karla smiled and took a deep breath. She left the door open on her way out, so there would be a breeze, and went to the master bedroom. Andreas was sitting in bed, reading. He yawned when Karla came in.

"I'm getting too old for all this excitement," he said. "Thank God it's Sunday tomorrow and we can sleep in." He put down the book and looked at Karla. "Oh no, we may be up at the crack of dawn when the dog wakes up and needs to go outside." He shook his head. "What did we get ourselves into here?"

"Too late to reconsider," Karla said jokingly. "We're stuck." She went into the bathroom, took a shower, and put on her nighty. When she stepped into the bedroom, Andreas motioned to her.

"You got to see this," he whispered and walked down the hall to Emilia's bedroom. Karla followed him.

They stood at the door and looked inside. Skippy was no longer in his basket. Instead, he was lying on the bed, curled up next to Emilia, his head on her tummy. Emilia's hand cradled his paw. The moon shone into the bedroom and covered the two with a golden glow. Skippy lifted his head and looked in their direction for a brief moment, then lay down again, seemingly reassured that everything was all right. Andreas put his arm around Karla's shoulder and the two watched the peaceful scene for a while.

"I guess we can dispose of Skippy's bed," Andreas said back in their bedroom.

"He'll protect her," Karla said.

Andreas chuckled. "A guardian angel, in the shape of a dog."

Karla smiled and yawned. "Yes, something like that. But we better get some sleep."

Lying in bed next to each other, Andreas turned to face Karla. "Talking about angels," he said, "in a way, Emilia is something like an angel, although she doesn't always act like one."

"How do you mean?" Karla asked.

He lifted himself on his elbow and bent over to kiss her. His green eyes had a brownish tint in the soft light of the bedside lamp. "Sometimes I think she was sent to us to test us, you know, our commitment to each other . . . to the family."

"Hmm," Karla said. "We almost flunked the test."

Andreas nodded. "But only almost." He sighed. "When you were in Peru and Emilia disappeared that one night, I realized how much this all means to me and how much I still love you."

"So, in a way, Emilia did save us," Karla said.

"Yes." Andreas pulled her close. "So we better make sure we deserve to be saved."

Chapter 55: Andreas

Andreas arranged the coal in the barbecue, then pulled off his working gloves and wiped his forehead. It was a warm Saturday in late August, with a deep-blue sky and just a touch of a breeze. It would be a perfect evening for a cookout with the family.

"Need help?" Tonio stepped out of the house, carrying two bottles of beer. He handed one to Andreas.

"Not at the moment, perhaps later. How is the apartment search going?" Andreas unscrewed the top of his beer bottle and took a sip.

"I looked at a few places and one may pan out," Tonio said. He was home on a break from his job in Milano. He had accepted Mario's offer for a position as fashion designer in his boutique in Lugano starting the end of October and he had given notice at his present job.

"Mario wants me to move in with him again, but I decided to find my own place first. He's a little miffed, but that's just too bad. I told him if we decided to live together again, we're going to find a new place, so that it belongs to both of us. That way we can build something together from scratch."

"Good idea," Andreas said and smiled. He felt that Tonio had done a lot of growing up during his stay in Milano. "Is he going to join us?" Andreas asked.

"Yeah, as soon as he is done at the boutique. He and Ernesto are clearing out the summer stuff to make room for the fall fashion. But where's Emilia?" he asked, looking around the yard.

"She's taken Skippy for a walk," Andreas said.

Tonio grinned. "So how is the princess doing with her new companion?"

"Actually, she's doing amazingly well. She and the dog are inseparable. She gets up in the morning and feeds him. She picks up after him, and she even gave him a bath the other day. And she walks him regularly. She's a very responsible little girl."

"Skippy is the talk of the town," Karla said as she stepped outside and overheard their conversation. Andreas handed her his bottle of beer and she took a sip, then handed it back to him.

"How so?" Tonio asked.

"Well, in the beginning, Skippy whimpered whenever she left for school. I used to take him for a walk and we picked Emilia up from school. He got so used to the routine that he started to bark and look at me or Andreas whenever it was time. He somehow knew when school was out. Don't ask me how." Karla grabbed hold of her hair, gathered it into a short ponytail, and fastened it with a rubber band. "It's hot," she said and shook her head.

"Anyway," she continued, "one day we were both busy and decided to skip the walk to the school. After barking for a while and impatiently running back and forth, Skippy decided to take matters into his own hands—or paws."

Andreas chuckled. "Yeah, and he scared the heck out of us."

"He just took off. He wouldn't listen to our calling him. Normally he's is pretty good about obeying, but he just raced down the street, his ears flopping up and down," Karla said. "I was afraid he'd run down to the highway, and you know there are cars."

"We both rushed after him," Andreas said. "But all he did was run straight to Emilia's school. We found him sitting outside the door, quietly waiting for her."

Tonio laughed out loud. "Smart dog."

"Yes," Karla said. "Ever since then, at exactly three o'clock Skippy looks at us, and if we don't feel like walking down there, we'll just tell him 'Go get Emilia' and he takes off. Everybody in the village knows him and knows where he's going."

At that moment, they heard a bark, and soon Emilia and Skippy came running up the hill.

"So, in other words, there goes your daily exercise," Tonio said.

"Tell me about it," Andreas said. "The only creatures who get regular exercise around here are Emilia and Skippy."

"Ah, and here come the newlyweds." Tonio motioned at the blue Honda driving up the hill.

Laura and Stefano got out of the car and were greeted by the rest of the family, including an enthusiastic, tail-wagging, hand-licking puppy. "Oh, he's so cute," Laura exclaimed and hugged Skippy, then Emilia. "You must be so happy."

Emilia nodded. "I gave him a bath and brushed him," she said, stroking Skippy's golden-brown fur.

"She wanted him to look his best for your return." Karla hugged Laura and Stefano. "I'm so happy you are back safe and sound. Did you have a good time?"

"Oh, it was wonderful," Stefano said. "I love Peru, I want to go back."

"We had so much fun with Grandpa and the family," Laura added.

They all sat on the patio underneath the chestnut tree, relaxing. Karla brought a pitcher of homemade lemonade and Andreas grabbed a few bottles of beer from the ice chest. He offered them to Stefano and Laura, but they both opted for lemonade.

"We had enough beer in Peru—too much, in fact," Stefano said. "At least, I did. That Cusqueña is really tasty. But now . . . no more booze. Doctor's orders."

"Huh?" Andreas scrunched his forehead and gave Stefano a measuring look.

"Nothing to worry about," Stefano said. His face stretched into a grin and Andreas noticed the exchange of quick glances between Stefano and Laura.

He wondered if he had misjudged his son-in-law when it came to alcohol. Andreas was sensitive about excessive drinking because of the bad experience he had had with his abusive alcoholic father. He himself enjoyed a glass of wine for dinner or an occasional beer, but he was a very moderate drinker.

The rest of the afternoon, they relaxed. Stefano and Laura talked about their trip to Peru, and Tonio told them about his upcoming new job as fashion designer in Mario's boutique. Skippy and Emilia took a little nap on a shady patch of grass underneath a wisteria vine. Every once in a while, however, Andreas scrutinized Stefano. All of them had continued to drink lemonade and water through the afternoon. It was hot and they decided to leave the wine for the barbecue in the evening. Andreas was thinking about Stefano's remark. Was he indeed trying to wean himself off alcohol? *Doctor's orders?* What did that mean? He decided to keep a close eye on him.

He got up, put on his gloves, grabbed the tongs, and turned the hot coals on the barbecue. Laura and Karla went into the kitchen to prepare the salad and vegetables, and Tonio and Stefano brought out the dishes and began to set the granite table under the chestnut tree. Skippy lifted his head and sniffed the air, probably dreaming of the scraps of leftover meat he was going to get, but Emilia was still asleep.

"The princess is tired," Tonio said.

"She got up really early this morning," Andreas said. "Skippy decided it was time for breakfast at five o'clock. Another dog was howling nearby and that got him excited.

"Should we wake her?" Tonio asked.

Before Tonio could decide, Skippy took care of it. He got up and started to bark as Mario drove his car onto the driveway. Emilia sat up and rubbed her eyes. She patted the dog, who welcomed the newcomer, wagging his tail.

Andreas put the pieces of chicken, which Karla had marinated in olive oil, herbs, and spices, on the barbecue, and soon the smell of grilled meat wafted through the air. Skippy pressed his body against Andreas's legs, trying to get as close to the goodies as possible. "You're going to burn your nose, buster," Andreas said. Emilia lured the dog away with a bone and an extra biscuit.

Soon, everybody sat around the table, enjoying a meal of grilled chicken, vegetables, and salad. Karla poured Emilia a glass of lemonade and Andreas brought a bottle of Merlot to the table. Again, Laura and Stefano shook their heads and opted for the lemonade.

"Would you rather have some Prosecco?" Karla asked.

"No, lemonade is fine," Laura said.

"We've joined Alcoholics Anonymous," Stefano said, keeping a straight face.

Andreas glared at him with narrowed eyes. "What? What's the matter with you? I didn't realize you had an alcohol problem."

Laura, taking a sip of lemonade, laughed and sputtered and began to cough. Stefano patted her back and chuckled. "I think we better tell them. I'm getting a bad reputation."

"Relax, Papa, it's only for nine months," Laura said.

There was silence for a few seconds.

"No," Karla said. Her dark eyes opened wide.

"Yes." Laura nodded.

"You're kidding me." Karla got up and hugged Laura. "How far along are you?"

"Two months," Laura said.

After a moment of confusion, Andreas finally understood. He hit his forehead with his hand. "I feel like an idiot. I thought . . . I don't know what I thought. I guess that's good news." He exhaled, relieved. "You sure didn't wait very long," he added.

"Well, Papa, as you know, we O'Reillys aren't very good at birth control," Laura said.

"Yes, I know, I was hoping the Bertani side of the family would be a little smarter." He gave Stefano an amused look.

"We actually planned having a child soon. But it is going to happen a little sooner than we expected," Stefano admitted.

"I think it's wonderful," Karla said. "Wait . . . that means in seven months I'll be a grandmother?"

"Yeah, and I'll be a grandfather. I was trying to postpone this event by becoming a father again. I guess that didn't work out," Andreas said.

Tonio hugged Emilia. "And you're going to be a six-year-old auntie."

Emilia looked at everyone, surprised. "Why?"

Karla pulled her close. "Laura is going to have a baby and you'll be his or her aunt."

Emilia scrunched her forehead. "Is it going to be in Laura's belly?"

Laura nodded. "Yes, right here." She patted her stomach. Emilia touched Laura's belly. "I can't feel anything."

"She got to touch Gina's mother, who is eight months pregnant, and she felt the baby kick," Karla said. "Laura's baby is still very tiny and can't kick yet," she explained to Emilia.

"Can I hold the baby once it's big?" Emilia said with a glint of excitement in her eyes.

"Of course you can, sweetie," Laura said. "You can help take care of it."

"The princess is going to be a nanny, how about that?" Mario said. "How wonderful."

"I'm not a princess," Emilia protested. "I'm going to be a fet . . . a fet . . . what's that called, Papa?"

"A veterinarian, or an animal doctor," Andreas said.

"What? No royalty in the family anymore?" Mario winked at Emilia.

"No." She shook her head and made a serious face. "I'm going to make sick puppies well again." She hugged Skippy. "We're going to have a baby, Skippy." The dog acknowledged the news with a vigorous wagging of his tail.

After a dessert of raspberry and chocolate ice cream, Emilia and Skippy went to play in the nearby meadow and the adults cleared away the plates. Karla and Andreas brought out cups of espresso and a cup of tea for Laura.

"I'll leave the grappa inside for the time being," Andreas said and smiled. He still couldn't wrap his mind around the fact that his daughter was pregnant and there would be a grandchild in a few months. He was both excited and a little worried. He watched Karla's reaction. A sunny smile lit her face and made her look young and beautiful. He tried to imagine her as a grandmother, with greying or white hair, her face lined with wrinkles. She didn't show her age yet at all. He looked at his family and his heart seemed to expand, as a feeling of love, gratitude, and a touch of wistfulness flooded him.

Chapter 56: Karla

Karla shot up in bed as thunder cracked. The hot day of the barbecue was followed by a night of heavy storms. Rain pounded the roof and patio. Right after the first thunderclap, both Emilia and Skippy came running into their parents' bedroom. Emilia jumped into bed and Skippy took one leap and landed on Andreas's stomach.

"Ouch, you almost killed me," he yelled. "What is this, anyway? What kind of a dog are you? You're supposed to protect us, not hide under the covers."

Emilia and the dog crawled under the blanket so they wouldn't have to listen to the frightening noise. Skippy was trembling and Emilia wrapped her arms around him.

"What a bunch of cowards." Andreas patted them both, trying to calm them down. "Nothing is going to happen."

Another thunderclap sent the two even deeper under the covers. Karla laughed, but when lightning lit up the bedroom and more thunder shook the house, she scooted close to Andreas and held on to him.

"Great," he said. "I have a brave family." He put his arm around Karla.

"Well, it's kind of scary. I just hope the lightning doesn't strike anything," Karla said.

"Nah, it might hit one of the tall trees or just bounce off the mountains," Andreas tried to reassure her.

"Bounce off the mountains? Since when does lightning bounce off mountains?"

Andreas chuckled. "I don't know, it just sounded kind of reassuring."

After about fifteen minutes of pandemonium, the thunder slowly receded and the only noise left was an occasional faraway rumbling and the sound of steady rain. Karla got up and looked outside. Once in a while flashes of silent summer lightning appeared on the horizon, but otherwise everything had calmed down.

Slowly, Emilia and Skippy stuck out their heads. Skippy yawned and Emilia rubbed her eyes. "Hi there," Karla said and stroked Emilia's hair. "It's all over, you can relax." Emilia nodded, put her head on the pillow, and closed her eyes. Skippy snuggled up to her and got ready to turn in as well.

"Excuse me, you two," Andreas said. "Would you mind going to sleep in your own bed, so Mama and I have some room? I don't want to sleep in a bed full of dog hair."

No answer and no reaction.

Karla laughed. "I'm thirsty." She got up and followed Andreas, who carried Emilia to her bedroom. She was already asleep again. Skippy settled on his accustomed spot on the bed next to her. In the kitchen, Karla opened the door and stepped outside to assess the damage to the plants. The patio was strewn with leaves and the roses in the corner had taken a beating, but they would survive. Fortunately, there hadn't been any hail. The rain had stopped and the only sounds were the water flowing through the pipes outside and the trickle of drops falling from the leaves of trees.

Karla inhaled the cool, clean air and drank small sips of water. After a while, the cool air began to feel chilly and she went inside. Standing by the window, she watched as the birches swayed in the night breeze. The dark clouds overhead parted, and an almost-full moon lit the landscape and the receding clouds tossed shadows onto the fields.

"How beautiful," Andreas whispered next to her.

"Yes," Karla said. "The storm reminded me of something. It was after a thunderstorm just like this almost six years ago when I first suspected of being pregnant again. I was so worried and upset."

"I remember," Andreas said.

"And now . . ." Karla took a deep breath.

"And now?" Andreas put his arm around her.

Karla leaned against his warm body. "Now, I feel blessed."

"So do I," Andreas said quietly.

"I'm looking forward to Laura's baby." Karla hugged Andreas. "We'll be parents and grandparents at the same time."

"Lots of work." Andreas chuckled. "And don't forget our upcoming art exhibitions. We better get some rest . . . Grandma."

"Yes, Grandpa."

The End

Acknowledgements

I would like to thank my family and friends for their ongoing support. A special thank-you to the beta readers of my work-in-progress and their helpful suggestions: authors Susan Dormady Eisenberg, Linda Cassidy Lewis, and Elizabeth Egerton Wilder. Thanks to my friend and designer-par-excellence, Diane Busch, for yet another beautiful cover. I would also like to express my deep appreciation to artist Nada Schönenberger-Petrak in Switzerland, whose sculptures became the inspiration for one of my character's art works, and to Lilian Garcia-Roig whose gorgeous paintings served as models for Karla's art. And last but not least, I want to thank my editors and proofreaders, Scott Nicholson and Neal Hock, who helped me, once again, to make my novel a better work of literature.

Christa Polkinhorn, originally from Switzerland, lives and works as writer and translator in the Los Angeles area in California. She divides her time between the United States and Switzerland and has strong ties to both countries. She is the author of six novels and a collection of poems. Her travels and her interest in foreign cultures inform her work and her novels take place in several countries. Aside from writing and traveling, she is an avid reader and a lover of the arts, dark chocolate, and red wine. She can be reached by email at cpolkinhorn@msn.com or you can visit her at her website www.christa-polkinhorn.com.